The Interpreter

The Interpreter

A Novel

BROOKE ROBINSON

HARPER

NEW YORK • LONDON • TORONTO • SYDNEY

HARPER

First published in the United Kingdom in 2023 by Harvill Secker, an imprint of Penguin Random House UK.

HarperCollins books may be purchased for educational, business, or sales promotional use. For information, please email the Special Markets Department at SPsales@harpercollins.com.

FIRST U.S. EDITION

Library of Congress Cataloging-in-Publication Data has been applied for.

ISBN 978-0-06-329988-7 (pbk.)

23 24 25 26 27 LBC 5 4 3 2 1

Prologue

One good push releases the handle, and the brass tongue withdraws into the lock.

"I'm sorry, we're actually closed." A young woman is fussing behind the counter.

Entering, I peruse the shelves closest to the door.

"Victorian fittings—it never locks properly unless I use the key. Sorry." Her words travel toward me; I swat them away.

There's a blackboard sign by my feet with the shop's opening hours announced in pink and emerald chalk. Upcoming events are listed, author talks and playgroup sessions. Stickers in the shape of lions and elephants dot the clean white walls.

"We open at nine. If you'd like to come back tomorrow?" She's speaking loudly now, all wide mouth and heavy vowels in case I am deaf or don't understand English. My fingers dance across the merchandise as my heels strike the hardwood floor.

The lights at the shop's entrance have been switched off; only after another step forward is my face fully lit. I take my time. I move past the fabric books for babies and linger over a puzzle display. The girl has emerged from behind the counter and fiddles with a string of colored flags which droop from the ceiling.

"I only get paid till six and I've already closed down the system," she says. "So I can't sell you anything."

I cannot come into a children's bookshop during business hours, not when there would be parents and children inside. A few weeks ago I ordered a gardening book online. When the delivery came I pried it open on my doorstep and saw a rectangle peeking out from behind the front cover.

It was a promotional bookmark: Give your child the gift of reading this Christmas. *Underneath the text, images of the five top-selling children's titles this year printed in a single column. It felt like the rubber band I wore on my wrist as a girl; the au pair would snap it when she caught me biting my nails. Snap. Standing outside my front door, the bookmark dropped from my fingers, into a puddle of the previous day's rain. It's still there, three weeks later. I close my eyes and step over it to leave the house each morning.* Give your child the gift of reading this Christmas. *I only took one brief look at it but that was enough.*

All day today I've been thinking about the time I read to him from James and the Giant Peach, *a favorite from my own childhood. It was summer so we lounged in the garden, a stone plate of sliced white peaches sat between us. Has anyone read to him since me? That's what I keep wondering. I think I know the answer, but the question keeps on tunneling. Christmas is coming. How am I supposed to survive until the new year?*

"I only get paid till six?" the girl says again.

It is twenty minutes past six. I extract a single note from my handbag, the new £50 with Alan Turing, and hold it out until she comes.

"Is this . . ." she says, taking it.

"Overtime."

"Wow. I guess I could turn the computer back on." She looks lovingly into Turing's flat, red eyes.

"He died of cyanide poisoning," I tell her, scanning the books filed under the letter K. "It's a profoundly slow and painful death. Your whole body convulses. Then there's a flood of blood, vomit, bile—until eventually, you run out of oxygen. But only after you beg for it to end."

She steps backward and almost crashes into a giant Where's Wally? *cut-out. I tilt my head to examine the picture books: one about a wombat, another with an alligator on the cover. My thumb presses their flimsy spines, so easily snapped.*

"Were you looking for anything in particular?" she asks, voice cracking on the final syllable.

There's a famous comic where the villain is trying to build an acoustic weapon. "The Calculus Affair," I say. "It's a Tintin book."

"Let me see if we have it." The girl scoots behind the counter. "I know we have Tintin in Tibet and one of the hardback collections."

Sound is a wave that can move through air, liquids, solid human bodies, building up pressure. It's been calculated that 240 decibels is required to make a human head explode. If I had one wish, this is how I would like to kill you.

"No, sorry," she says, disappointed, wondering, no doubt, if this means she'll have to return the money. "I can order it in for you. Can you wait a week?"

The wish would grant me an evil scientist with crazed hair who would be glad to do it. One word is all it would take. Special headphones over your ears pumping at a 240-decibel volume, not music but speech; one word, repeated over and over until you died. Just one word.

"That won't do," I say, turning for the exit. "I'll find it somewhere else." When I reach the door: "Keep the money."

One wrong word in the right place can be enough to kill.

But you already know that, don't you?

I.

I don't always jump when the phone rings, but today ELLIOT SCHOOL flashing on the screen sends my unsipped coffee to the floor. I do my best with a fistful of napkins as I answer the call.

"Elliot's all right, but you need to collect him; he's not feeling well." The barista's machine gasps and splutters and I step out of the café in order to hear. "How soon can you come?" The voice belongs to the school receptionist.

"He was happy when I left him an hour ago. I don't understand how he could feel poorly so quickly." It is Elliot's first day of year two. He doesn't love school, but he went today without too much complaint.

"I'm sorry, Revelle," the receptionist says, her tone suggesting she means it. "I know this is probably inconvenient. Are you at work?"

"I was about to walk in."

"It's the policy, in case he's infectious, you know?"

From outside I wave an apology to the waiter for the mess. "I'm coming," I say, and speed-walk down Fleet Street to flag a black cab. Inside, I give the address for Elliot's school. He has changed primaries three times already, according to the social worker, Lydia, a fresh classroom of unfamiliar faces with each new foster family. I could have asked her for permission to move him to the school local to me, but I decided to wait until the adoption is confirmed, to not be presumptuous, to not tempt fate. Once the adoption is settled I won't need to ask Lydia for permission to change schools or for anything at all.

Inside the car, I rush through my phone's contact list looking for someone who isn't in the office on a Monday morning. Other people would call their partner to see if they could work from home for the day, then they'd try the grandparents. I have no plan B.

When we arrive at Greenwich, I ask the driver to keep the meter running. Elliot and the receptionist stand waiting, my son with his sleeves rolled up and a school backpack on his back. *My son*. The words arrive of their own accord; not forced, for once not strange. I can't help but smile. "Hey, Batman, you're not feeling well?" I crouch in front of him.

"My throat's a bit sore." Elliot twists around my leg.

"Honestly, he was fine this morning," I say, remembering his summer cold last month, but he's been well since then. "Weren't you, love?"

Elliot shrugs and plucks his Draggie-the-never-washed-dragon toy from his bag—a crutch he's probably too old for. Should I insist on washing it? Is that what parents do? I don't have time to think about that as I bundle him into the car. 9:27 a.m.

Elliot loves black cabs. He wants to sit in the front seat, and I try to explain why it's unsafe without going into gory details about car accidents and what could happen, horrible accompanying images smashing through my mind. Beside me, his eyes are fixed on the window, and I do another scroll through my contacts.

"Gherkin tower. Draggie will beat the Gherkin!"

I reach L then M then all the way to T with still no idea as to who could take Elliot.

"He sure will." There is no one, absolutely no one I could call.

9:53 a.m. The car turns onto Newgate Street. Paused at traffic lights, the driver's hand finds the radio button, and three words in, it's obvious what the announcers are discussing.

"Sorry, would you mind switching off the sound?" I don't want to hear any commentary or opinion on the matter immediately before court. Not this case, it's too depressing.

The driver eyes me in the rearview mirror and presses the button with a grunt. The trial is in London's ether. Its molecules have edged out the truck fumes and usual pollution, so that this month, it's all anyone is breathing in.

"Batman." I gently pull him back from the window. "Would you like to come with me to work today?"

He's uncertain.

"Oh look over there, it's a block of firds," I say, pointing.

Elliot snorts. "Flock of birds!"

"You're too good at this." We ran out of time this morning for my pre-rehearsed game of spoonerisms over breakfast.

"Are you . . ." My jaw drops in mock disgust. "Are you nicking your pose?"

"I am *not* picking my nose," he laughs.

Three months ago, the weekend before he came to me, I bought a book of kids' jokes. I memorized as many as I could, but then, neglecting to ration, used them all up by the end of our first forty-eight hours together. Maybe it was just as well. Children can tell when you're trying too hard.

As we approach the Old Bailey, the cab crawls through puddles of people spread onto the road. "Bloody circus," the driver says. "You'll have to get out here."

Groups of press, onlookers, cameras, TV vans, and tents smother the entrance to Central Criminal Court. When the cab door opens, the roar from the crowd pushes inside.

Why did you catch a bug today of all days? I think to myself, guiding a curl behind Elliot's ear. 9:57 a.m. The defense team will be looking for me. Elliot's palm burrows in mine as we walk toward the door.

Four witness service volunteers loiter at the entrance. All hands on deck for the final days of a fraught proceeding. "I'm the interpreter," I tell one of them. "Court thirteen."

"There's a juror caught in traffic," she says. "We're on Old Bailey time, as usual, so you've about another ten minutes."

"Thank you," I say.

"Is this your son?"

"Normally at school on a Monday." Could she look after him while I'm inside the courtroom? Between soothing jittery witnesses—no, that won't work. "Don't worry, he won't be coming in with me."

"Bit young for work experience."

I summon a laugh.

Her voice changes gear. "Children can't enter the building."

"I know. I have someone coming. They'll wait outside together," I say. She nods, approving, while I feel increasingly shaky. "A friend." I gesture to my cell phone as though it is proof, as though the received calls are not all from Elliot's doctor and his school; the text messages more personal than automated alerts from my bank. What am I going to do with him?

Two minutes until the trial starts. I thought this would happen one day, but not on my first court booking since fostering Elliot, not on such a significant case. A case that, if I don't go inside, could be adjourned. This crime that has the nation gripped with its themes of class and privilege, a luxury car and a dead baby. They need the best interpreter. They need me.

I look at my phone again in case a miracle might occur, his teacher calling to apologize for the confusion, she'll be here to whisk him back to school any second now.

"I don't know what to do," I say to the volunteer.

"Your friend isn't here?"

"I should be in there already. But my son was sent home from school." My pleading tone tells her the friend was never coming.

"Good morning, stranger." I hear a familiar voice from behind.

"Arkam," I say, turning around. "Hello." He's one of the few courthouse security guards whose name I know.

"Multitasking this morning, eh?" He grins into Elliot's face.

"I'm trying but . . ."

"No children inside," he says gently.

"Exactly."

"I can watch him for a bit. Don't tell anyone." Arkam winks.

Right before Elliot, I worked here on a three-month murder trial. Interpreting almost feels, briefly, like a normal job on those lengthy cases; going to the same place each day, seeing the same people.

"Thank you. You're saving my life."

"No problem."

"I don't know what I would have done. This is Elliot. He has some things in his backpack to keep him occupied." I slip my cell phone into his pocket.

"A cupcake after this, I promise," I tell Elliot. Then, in a more serious tone: "Be good, yeah?" The parental need to set boundaries and teach manners, when all I really want is to get him to like me. "Love you."

"Love you," Elliot replies. I try to forget a previous foster parent taught him to say it by memory while I walk toward the wooden doors.

The jury looks exhausted. In the public gallery, the grief-stricken, groups of law students and the plain nosy sit staring straight ahead, at the floor or at the ceiling. This is a rare place on earth that does not allow the distraction of cell phones. In summer, even the new courts can be sweaty and oppressive, sometimes unbearably so. Now sighs and sniffles of the alleged victim's family members spread through the room before we fall into silence.

The day begins. It's a complex dangerous-driving case. Immediately, my eyes occupy themselves with the defense barrister's hands. Back straight, chin raised, he limits his hand movements to open, relaxed gestures. "How would you describe what you saw that evening?" Everything about him expresses authority, honesty.

Seated next to the smartly dressed witness, I inhale the room's stale leather and stagnant air as I wait for my turn to speak.

"Who made the call to emergency services?"

The thirty-something woman answers the barrister's questions succinctly, and it's no trouble interpreting her Italian into English. She can understand English well enough and doesn't really need me to repeat the questions into her native tongue.

"How would you describe the sound?"

As I interpret the questions and answers from Italian to English, English to Italian, I keep my eyes on the barrister's palms, his clean pink flesh without one trace of sweat.

The woman I'm interpreting for, a tourist visiting London last June, attended the opera on the night of the alleged crime. Out of sheer bad luck she saw the incident take place and is here to provide evidence, summoned by the defense.

"And what did you see when you stepped closer?"

After *Madame Butterfly*, my witness returned to her rental car in the opera house parking lot and saw the defendant reverse her £150,000 Mercedes SUV, hitting a member of the catering staff. Then the defendant drove off. The charges include dangerous driving, failing to stop at the scene of an accident, and child destruction—the victim survived, but her five-month unborn baby did not. The witness statement from the Italian tourist apparently supports the defense claim that from inside her very large car, the accused was not aware that she had hit anyone, much less someone who was pregnant. Ignorance, it seems, is the best defense when the charge is failing to stop. The press, titillated by this case and its glamorous fifty-year-old accused, heiress to an energy company and a Knightsbridge resident, is predicting an acquittal on the gravest charge of child destruction. Legally speaking, it is almost impossible to prove; rarely is anyone convicted of killing an unborn child. I let my eyes rest on the defendant. She is in a dark navy suit with tiny earrings that reflect the light when her head turns. I could not stand to listen to the radio in the cab this morning because I knew they were going to say she'll go free.

Some cases I work on, I really can't tell which way the jury or judge is likely to go. Today, my being here seems futile. The defense team appear so assured—my guess is they hardly need this witness to bolster their case. And now in the final days of the trial, the prosecution barrister is visibly struggling to hide his gloom. But you never know when things might turn around. My witness could fluff one of her answers, wobble off course and do more harm to the defense than good. Though that probably won't happen.

"At what point did you notice the woman was pregnant?" I repeat the question in Italian with complete accuracy. Then the answer into English. To me, the words must all taste the same. I will say whatever is demanded of me. In this room, I have no personal morals of my own. I am not really here. That's what I have to tell myself. Some days, during some assignments, I need reminding, until the reality of my job really sinks in. I bet the accused gets away with everything except for the dangerous driving charge. But I am not allowed to care.

It's now twenty minutes since I left Elliot.

The questions keep coming. Twenty-five minutes since I left Elliot. He has my phone, and knows how to use it, but who would he call? I recall the earlier scroll through my contacts list and mentally pause on the letter D: these days, it's blank. But there's no use dwelling on what-ifs.

Should the prosecution question the witness for even half as long as the defense, I'll be stuck in court for almost an hour. What if Arkam has to leave his post? Someone may have already called social services about the boy dumped in the Old Bailey with the world's filthiest soft toy.

Cross-examination begins and I rush my sentences, the Italian words colliding, saving a few seconds of time.

"No further questions, my Lord," the barrister says. "The witness is dismissed."

My pumps skid along the floor.

Recess. The court spills into the foyer, everyone desperate for the bathroom, a drink of water, or a surreptitious Walnut Whip. Through the crush I head for the building exit.

"Where did you learn Italian? Your accent is very good." The witness has inserted herself into my eyeline.

"Thank you." I avoid eye contact. I need to go outside. I have to find him.

"Have you been to Vomero, in Naples?" The woman beams. "My hometown."

"No."

"The pizza is the best in the country."

I crane my neck to see past the woman's middle. Through the doorway I can see a group of people right by the exit, but no sign of Elliot.

"You should visit," the woman says. "They'll think you're Italian."

"Excuse me." I dart past her, push through tight circles of on-lookers and officials until I reach the spot where I left Elliot and Arkam.

They're gone.

2.

I need to find Elliot, but a man steps in front of me and clutches my elbow. "I noticed you in there," he says. "I heard everything you said." I recognize him from the newspapers and the magazine covers in Tesco. His eyes look faded, as if drawn onto his emaciated face with pale watercolors. He probably hasn't eaten anything solid since his partner was injured and his unborn child died.

"I'm very sorry for your loss." I regret my choice of words—it's a stock phrase he probably hears ten times a day. What else can I say? Really I shouldn't be speaking to him at all.

"'It was *dark*.'" He's imitating the defendant's voice. "'Perhaps I brushed against a parked car. Certainly not a *person*.'"

His partner lost their baby, the ability to conceive again, and the permanent use of both of her legs. The life they had planned gone in an instant. I think of the Georgian word for being pregnant, which translates to "having two souls." There's a Polish phrase for pregnancy equivalent to "you are at hope" in English. Maybe they'll adopt? They might feel too broken after this. The process can be grueling and adoption doesn't guarantee a happy ending. I am queasy at the thought of Elliot's whereabouts. "It isn't true—what you said in there." He's shaking his head. "You're a *liar*."

Is he bilingual? My stomach flips. He's suggesting that I mistranslated some of the evidence.

"Sir, I assure you I interpreted with complete accuracy." What word is he talking about? There was nothing particularly challenging about the testimony; nothing that could be misconstrued. Other interpreters do a tidy up. They leave out the background "ahhs," the "hmms"; a passive phrase becomes active because it's easier—they're not a slave to the code of conduct; they don't see the point. But I never do this. I made one mistake, one solitary error earlier in my career, and it will never happen again. The price is too high.

His eyes pinball from me to the ceiling. The man in front of me is disorientated and needs help, but I must get to Elliot. I release my arm from his grip and spin on my heel. I need to find another security guard who'll know where Arkam is.

"Arkam?" I call. "ELLIOT!" The terror in my voice attracts attention. "Have you seen a six-year-old boy? Blond curly hair, wearing a school uniform?" I say to everyone within earshot. "Elliot!"

"You're a mother." The alleged victim's husband reappears. "Do you work for child killers too?"

"I work for the courts. I'm not *with* the defense today, I promise you." We terps are often mistaken for members of the defense team, but I am freelance, I don't work for anyone. My assignments come through Exia Translation and Interpreting Services, which holds the current contract with the Ministry of Justice.

"If a pedophile needs an interpreter do you help them? Say their lies for them and watch them get away with it?"

Their lies. He isn't challenging my translation, he's talking about the client. He's barely even looking at me now. He's angry and hurt and doesn't know what to do with it. I'm a good target precisely because he knows I'm not to blame, like the hedge fund manager who loses a million pounds on a bad trade and screams at the guy who makes his sandwich. But I can't deal with this while I'm trying to find Elliot.

I turn my back on him and call: "ELLIOT!" There. To the left of the exit. A staff member. I run toward another security guard.

"Found him." A low voice from behind stops me in my tracks.

"He's out there with your *friends*." Through the crowd I see past the exit a blur of Elliot's backpack and then his face, cheerfully munching through a packet of chips. I turn to thank my helper and see that it's him again: the husband of the alleged victim.

"Oh gosh, *thank you*," I say.

Elliot is standing outside with two women, one of them crouching at his height, smiling as he chews. She dabs his mouth with a tissue then straightens up in her dark navy suit. The defendant. Elliot is with the heiress, the hit-and-run driver. Now the bereaved father is watching this cozy scene, with that woman's hands on my son.

"You're not on the side of the defense today, yeah?" The man is muttering to himself, but I know he means for me to hear.

"This isn't what it looks like; they're not my friends," I tell him. "That's my son, but I don't know them. I'm impartial, sir, I assure you."

It can be difficult for people to see us as neutral. In court, we sit knee-to-knee with the person we're interpreting for. We lean close and whisper into their ear. If the client is the defendant, we sit beside them in the dock, the two of us squashed together like co-conspirators, sealed off in the Perspex box for everyone else's safety.

"You're corrupt," he's saying under his breath. "You're all corrupt." His fists pummel his forehead until a woman, a friend or relative, drapes her arm over his shoulder. I don't think this man would hurt anyone deliberately but he has the quality of little-left-to-lose and that makes him dangerous. I rush toward Elliot and, as I go, turn back to check he isn't following me.

"Elliot, where did you go? Where's Arkam?" my anger toward the security guard cuts through my voice.

"I'm sorry!" one of the women says. "I knew the second we moved, court would come out and you'd be looking for us," she sounds breathless. "Elliot needed the restroom. They won't let children in the court building so I took him to a café. I hope you weren't very worried." My hand around Elliot's is slick with sweat, my heart not yet returned to normal pace. Arkam should not have let Elliot go off with a stranger under any circumstances. What was he thinking?

"I'm sorry I had to leave you," I tell Elliot, squeezing his hand tighter. "I won't do it again."

"I'm Sandra," the woman says. "I was speaking to the guard and Elliot while I was waiting for my boss." She looks toward the defendant, who has drifted a few yards away from us, now talking to her barrister and solicitors.

A male solicitor in a blue shirt speaks rapidly to the heiress. From here, I can't make out what he's saying, but I can tell she isn't listening; her eyes roam the outdoor space, as though trapped in a tedious conversation at a party, scoping for someone better. I saw her on the telly last night, exiting the court tall and proud, not the usual bashful defendant holding a jacket over their face to hide from the cameras. She's not embarrassed, it's there in her body language. No humility about the death and destruction she's caused. I think she's looking for the cameras, that's why she's loitering by the entrance. She's confident of an acquittal and this case has made her famous.

"I'm Revelle," I say, realizing I haven't told this woman my name. "Thank you for looking after him, Sandra."

"We kept each other company, didn't we?" Sandra squats to Elliot's level and they exchange a smile.

"Yeah," Elliot agrees. I like that she hasn't commented on his appearance. So many strangers consider it appropriate to note the vast differences in our looks. "It's so light, it's practically white!" they say, fingering his hair. "Don't worry, it'll darken like yours once he gets older," or, once, comparing us: "His father must be practically albino!" Maybe he is.

"If you ever want a babysitter for real," Sandra's voice breaks through my thoughts, "I'm on Silver Balloon—do you use it? The child-minding app. Sandra Ramos. Though I'm only free Sundays because the rest of the week I work for—" She dips her head toward the heiress.

"You work seven days?" I ask.

"That's why I'm in the UK. To work. And looking after lovely children isn't work, actually."

"Thanks for the tip about the app. As you can see, I don't have my child-minding sorted out."

Elliot is holding a piece of paper up to my face. "What's this?"

"It's me," he says. "Sandra drew it when we were waiting."

It's a pencil sketch of Elliot. Sandra shrugs. "I like to draw. It gets me off Facebook." I don't know much about art, but it's very good.

"You're really talented," I tell her. "Elliot, you said thank you, yeah?"

"Yeah." She's captured his big eyes and accentuated the thick waves of his hair.

From the corner of my eye I see the heiress approach us and Sandra gestures for Elliot to tuck the picture down by his side.

"David Hockney strikes again," the heiress says, sniggering at her own joke. Hockney was primarily a painter, even I know this. If she's going to be mean, she could at least come up with a better reference. The heiress looks at me and there is a beat before she says: "You were our interpreter in there. Thank you." *Our.*

I give a half-smile and nod. Of course she thinks I work for her. Over the years, I've had many defendants strike up conversation as though I were a trusted confidante on the defense team. They've told me all about their wife's job, their brother's stocks and shares portfolio, asking my opinion on their mother's ailments. Once, a particularly chatty Spanish client loved discussing the problems with London transport—he was a town planner in a previous life—and one morning in the dock, I agreed the subway was bad that day and accidentally mentioned my stop. Then an accused double murderer knew roughly where I lived. I was relieved to see him convicted.

"Let's go!" the heiress says to Sandra, clapping her hands together. Up close, I can see her hair is in an intricate braid, like a little girl's. It's impossible to do that kind of hairstyle on yourself. Did she make Sandra do it for her this morning? What type of work does she do for her? I wonder.

"Where's the car? HELLO?" Then she stalks away and it is clear that Sandra is supposed to scurry after her.

I raise my eyebrows in a gesture of solidarity. "What a lovely boss you have there."

"I hope she loses this case," Sandra whispers, putting a finger to her lips. "I've got to go. Bye, Elliot!"

Sandra is gone, and I promise myself that I will never let Elliot out of my sight like that again.

At home, we look for a place for Sandra's drawing. Elliot wants it in prime position, stuck to the door of his closet, the first thing he sees of a morning when he wakes up. He's obviously feeling better and hopefully will be happy to go back to school tomorrow. His hand dives deep into the cookie jar and now my tablet is pressed against his nose, playing cartoons. He is calm and focused, content to entertain himself, which I know can't be said of all children his age. I wonder how much of his personality is down to inherited genes. Is his self-containment a coping mechanism from his earlier years, survival by tuning out what's happening around you? I know there were substance abuse issues in the birth family, before he was taken into care. I have a folder from our social worker, Lydia, with various forms and reports that tell the story of his background. I've read some of them, I'm aware of the major problems, but I stopped short of reading the details of every police visit, every troubling episode between his parents. I realize Elliot isn't coming to me as a blank slate, but if I know each detail of his family life and what he experienced, I'll treat him differently. I know I will. Like a tragic social services case to be fixed instead of a real child. My child. I don't want to watch him eat dinner and read trauma in his every gesture, obsess over which behaviors are manifestations of what prior experience. This is his second chance. So the folder is there in the locked bottom drawer of my desk and I guess I'll decide how old he should be before I give it to him, if he wants to read it for himself.

Did Elliot mention to Sandra today that I wasn't his real mother? He told a woman on the bus the other day who leaned across the aisle to compliment his NASA T-shirt. He does call me Mum. The first day he came to me, Lydia told me to expect it. Some adopted children take years to call their new parents Mum and Dad, and some never do at all. Elliot was famously quick to offer it up with all of his previous foster parents. It's an attachment thing. Of course I like hearing him say it. I wish the social worker hadn't told me he uses it with everyone.

"How are you going there, do you need anything?" I ruffle Elliot's hair. He shakes his head "no" without raising his eyes from the screen.

While Elliot is busy I should do something useful like laundry, I decide. The adoption agency provides advice about the practical side of taking a child from the care system, but no one tells you how to do the very basics of parenting. Suddenly in charge of a six-year-old, I am scrambling to catch up, without experience or help. I look at the overflowing laundry basket and sort through Elliot's clothes. The first T-shirt has a band of grass stains down the bottom, his black trousers caked with splotches of mud. Normal mothers would know what to do with this, with baby and toddler years to draw upon. Hot water for these types of stains, cold for those. On my laptop I search "grass

stain removal" and open tab after tab. As I read, my eyes keep dropping down to my forearm, the red finger-marks of the bereaved father in court long faded but I can still feel them, or imagine that I can.
There is one visible scratch in the skin but I think my own nails did
that, in the panic to find Elliot.

I follow the advice of a mummy blogger from outside Toronto
who claims to be an authority on mixing mimosas and all types of
laundry. One part distilled white vinegar to one part water. Soak
for thirty minutes, then rub and rinse. Repeat. Do I have any vinegar? How do I know if it's distilled? I think of how it would sting
to drip some onto the scratch mark on my arm. Three months in,
and already I almost lost Elliot. If I hadn't found him within the
next couple of minutes, I would have gone to the police. They
would have issued a special alert and maybe they would have found
Elliot within a few hours, but only to return him to the adoption
agency to be given to someone else. I install the Silver Balloon app
on my phone and find Sandra Ramos. This is what I'm looking for:
her child-minder profile has dozens of glowing reviews. I'm somewhat reassured that my recklessness today in leaving him with the
security guard wasn't as risky as it could have been.

I place all of Elliot's clothes into the front loader and select the
longest, hottest wash cycle.

What must that bereaved man at court think of me? His unborn baby is tragically killed while here's me, an unfit mother with
a healthy child I clearly don't deserve; it's unfair. He's convinced the
whole thing is unfair—the trial, that I was working for the callous
heiress, but in that respect, I did nothing wrong. He is right about
one thing—I *would* interpret for a child killer, an accused pedophile, if required. Interpreters turn up to each booking often with
no idea as to the content of the case. We might not even know who
we're speaking for—victim or accused or witness or a member of
the victim's shattered family. We can't walk out in the middle of a

police interview or court case because we decide we don't want to help our guilty client. We must swallow every reservation and keep going. If you find yourself disturbed, take your revulsion home and sort it out on your own time. I know that's how it needs to be. If I was ever on the other side of the justice system I would expect pure professionalism from all involved.

When the washing machine stops, one of Elliot's shirts emerges shrunk to half its original size. The grass stains are as vivid as before.

The next morning London churns with news that the jury from the dangerous-driving trial has retired to consider its verdict. On the walk to the hospital, I switch my phone from Radio 1 to Spotify. I want music only, and no chance of hearing about the heiress and thinking about the bereaved father.

St. Thomas': a public hospital with a five-star London view. I'm taking the stairs, gazing at Westminster Bridge and the twirling pods of the Eye. After signing in, I write REVELLE LEE on a visitor's name tag and head for Cardiology. A Russian-speaking man is being treated for heart disease and my own chest flutters as I approach the nurse's desk. Medical assignments aren't my preference. Once I had to tell a man that his wife was dying and by the time I got the words out in Hindi, she was already gone. There's a sense with police and court work that justice might happen, the wrong might somehow be corrected and the person at fault given their dues. With health there's no one to blame. Who can you punish when the villain is your own body?

In the ward, I'm presented to a man—clammy, his face leached of color. He's happy to see me, relieved to express in his first language just how rough he feels. The doctor in front of me thinks the Russian man's condition isn't serious. I repeat this for the client and he raises his hands to the heavens in relief. In conversational Russian, the same word is used for the human arm and hand—potentially dangerous in some settings. I think of the British woman living in Italy who had an unnecessary mastectomy last year after her medical notes from Wales were mistranslated. A Spanish man in Scotland had the wrong kidney removed after the interpreter made a mistake on the medical consent form.

The consultation with the cardiologist ends and I head home. I go grocery shopping on the way and after the bags are unpacked in the kitchen, I make an appointment for Elliot to have his hair cut. When I collect him from school, he is full of stories about one teacher's broken tooth and another's fractured arm and how the two must be connected in some funny way, and for the whole evening, I do not think about work. We have dinner and watch a game show and after Elliot goes to bed, the TV is still on in the background while I check my emails. I have forgotten about the result of the hit-and-run trial. I'm happy. But then the late news comes on.

3.

Not guilty.

Not guilty on the major charge of child destruction. The heiress will pay a fine and serve a community sentence for the dangerous driving and fleeing the scene, but that's all. I keep the television sound low to avoid waking Elliot. The defendant's expressionless face fills the screen; the smooth-as-silk defense barrister stands next to her, smug. A ripple in the newsreader's voice betrays the disgust she hasn't entirely left in the dressing room. To what extent did testimony from the Italian tourist affect the outcome? I wonder. When the bereaved father comes on the screen, ghostly and hollowed-out, I hit the standby button before his eyes can reach me. I try to scrub him and the case from my mind, scramble the words and flush them away.

I hope she loses this case. I'm reminded of what Sandra said just before we parted ways at the Old Bailey. Why would she say that about her employer, in such a serious trial? Sandra must think the woman is guilty of all charges. People like the heiress often reveal themselves in front of their staff; their true self pokes through the mannered facade with waiters, drivers, cleaners—anyone they think is not worth the performance. Sandra probably knows that woman, and what she's capable of, better than anyone.

I should have had a complete news blackout this week. Ordinarily with a court assignment, I pop in on the relevant day, interpret for the person who requires it, and I'm on to my next job by the time the trial concludes. Unless the client is the defendant, I'm usually not there for the verdict; the outcome of the trial is none of my business. Early on, I learned to stop being curious. I can't control the result, so I let it go. But when it's a case like this, how can I avoid hearing about it?

Sleep for me feels out of the question, and so I take the opportunity to sort my court invoices for this financial year. There isn't a great deal of information in the documents, a variation on *Southwark Crown Court, June 5, R v Fernandez*; I need to unspool my memory to recall details of each job. Here's one I remember: invoice #38575—I attended a police station in East London to interpret for a Portuguese tourist who found human remains in Walthamstow Wetlands. I vaguely remember reading news reports at the time about the foot belonging to a missing Bethnal Green woman. I never heard whether or not anyone was arrested. I can't even remember reading the woman's name.

Into Google I type various combinations of "foot-found-Walthamstow-Wetlands" to locate the case. An article in *The Telegraph* says an East London man was being held for the murder of a twenty-eight-year-old woman. My eyes scroll to the end of the story: charges dropped, suspect released, the case seemingly cold. I spent six hours that day speaking for the Portuguese tourist, describing his discovery, his shock, his fear, the sickness that rushed to his throat when he realized what was in front of him (a human foot, female-looking) and what that meant, and it never occurred to me afterward to learn whether or not they found the killer. It can't occur to me. I do my job, I say the words, and I go home. I need to remember that. I know the cruel details of court cases will stay with me if I'm not careful. They will gather inside, slow poison accumulating, like sucking lead from the end of a pencil. So I am careful: I am Teflon. The words I interpret travel straight from my ear to mouth, said and gone without leaving a trace. I repeat the words without metabolizing them, swallow sentences whole and try to make sure they never touch the sides. Even though I speak in first-person, recounting every story, every action, event, fear and feeling of the client as "I, I, I," said as though we are one and the same.

Another memory drops into view. A rape-murder case from a few years ago, a teenage girl killed in her own home. The accused, the girl's neighbor, nominated his Polish-speaking boss as a character witness and I was hired by the defense to interpret. The man spoke convincingly of his employee's good character, but even so, the evidence seemed considerable and surely the accused is in prison now. My computer flashes "low battery" and I scramble to connect the cord. "Old-bailey-teenage-girl-rape-murder." Page one, two of Google. So many rape-murders but not the one I'm looking for. Page three, four. An image by the court artist; I recognize the defendant's smirk.

Acquitted.

Step away from the laptop, I tell myself. This is not helping anything. I know it's only a matter of statistics, a coincidence these particular cases were not-guilty verdicts. Sometimes justice wins, sometimes it doesn't. They could have been innocent. I need to find *one* case that resulted in a conviction, and then I'll stop.

A motorbike roars past the building, the engine an explosion against the stillness of the night. Last year I was summoned after midnight to interpret for a Russian-speaking Estonian woman chased through the residential streets of Muswell Hill by a man on a moped. In the North London police station, she spoke English extremely well but the terror of the incident caused her mind to withdraw, to take refuge in her primary language. "Muswell-Hill-Moped-Sex-attacker." I find it.

Guilty.

There.

I did that. I didn't work for the victim. I was neutral, but I helped to create a detailed statement, a specific and clear witness account, and I was part of the group of people who convicted this man and got justice done. But this follow-up, this interest in the verdict, cannot become my habit.

The television is off now. I make a diary entry about the hit-and-run case so that later I can check I've been paid correctly. Then my hands close the book shut.

On the Exia app I scroll through the available interpreting jobs for the rest of the week. There are a number of hearings taking place outside London—the city's courts are still drowning in back-log from the pandemic and subsequent barrister strikes—but I don't want to travel too far and risk being home late for Elliot. On Sunday they need someone for a business conference in Watford. That could be good, something easy and bland; just what I need after today and, crucially, a much higher hourly rate than court work. It would mean giving up a weekend day with Elliot, the first since he's been with me. But it would be worth it if the higher rate allowed me to then be more choosy about my weekday assignments, and helped to ensure I always get to Elliot's school in time for pick-up. I switch to the Silver Balloon app and check that Sandra Ramos is available for this Sunday. She is, and I book her in. I need to work, and that means leaving my son with people, and she has already proven herself with Elliot. I'll do the business conference. Maybe I'll get to translate some bad scripted jokes from the MC. It might even be fun.

As it nears one o'clock in the morning, I'm still too restless to sleep. I have sedatives in a drawer somewhere but I don't want to be too knocked out and not hear Elliot if he calls me during the night. I load a Russian film on my laptop and set the subtitles to Italian; two language practice sessions for the price of one, and it'll force me to concentrate and stop thinking about today. Back on the app, I accept an assignment tomorrow morning at a legal chambers in central London—it's simpler than going in to court—and settle in to watch the film.

There. I can't help but feel a burst of satisfaction that it didn't get past me. On the screen I spy a mistake in the Russian to Italian translation. Whoever did these subtitles doesn't know the difference between the Russian word for "light blue" and the one for "dark blue." An embarrassingly basic error. I fast forward to the end of the film and write down the name of the company who provided the captions. After finding a contact, I begin writing an email informing them of their mistake before I change my mind and delete the draft.

They're better off not knowing.

I'm not overly familiar with this part of London, but I'll concede that this appears to be a relatively good street. It is inside the UNESCO World Heritage buffer zone and the houses are all Georgian, decently if not immaculately restored. I am in neat trousers, boots, and a simple tailored shirt. I would be underdressed for my square of London, but here in Greenwich I believe I blend in. My nose is against the glass and my hands cup my eyes. In the space between the curtains I see parquet floors and a great deal of timber. There seems to be a courtyard at the rear, cramped and dreary. The bedrooms must be upstairs. I lean back and get another look at the totality of the house.

The brickwork and wood of the door have been painted over in a weak yellow. There are flower boxes, leaves diminished by the weather. I move to the second ground-floor window and put my eye to the gap between the curtains. I drink in the room and visualize him playing here. My right hand scuttles to the flower box, and of its own accord, wrenches a plant from the soil, roots and all. The act releases something inside of me. I toss the dead plant into the gutter, I don't think anyone saw, and continue peering through the window. There is a For Sale sign three houses down which works in my favor. To any observers, I must be on a real-estate mission. I am sure this is how passersby see me: they imagine my husband at work, picture my two children, one of each, at school, while I scope the market for our forever house, doing my due diligence on our future neighbors. Nothing suspicious. This front room has bare white walls and is devoid of any real personality or life. I do not see any children's books. Still, I'd rather him here than with you.

I step away. You and he are on the other side of town and there is no purpose to my being here. I turn out of his former street and walk up the hill toward the Observatory. It is more physical activity than I would typically do and my heart muscle makes known its displeasure. Halfway up, I need to stop. I rest my hands on my knees and breathe heavily through my mouth. I am overtaken by tourists who excitedly point out to one another St. Paul's, The Shard, the O2 Arena. I reach the top and keep my back turned on the view. I didn't come to Greenwich to admire the city, but what am I here for? If I had one wish.

Over there is the prime meridian line and as expected, someone is posing for a photograph, standing with one foot on either side. People come here just to stand simultaneously on both sides of the marking. They like to split themselves into the two time worlds, too obtuse to know that it doesn't work. Because you cannot escape this world, nobody can; on either side of time, I know that everything will feel the same. I'm still me, you're still you, he's not mine.

I hear them before I see them. It's a weekday during term and there is bound to be a school group on excursion. This is something I studiously avoid—children's bookshops, museums, anything educational—but this morning I felt the irresistible urge to press on the bruise. A mass of children in school uniforms come into view and I realize that I'm fine, I can withstand this, because they are the same, they are nothing to me, anonymous little bodies indistinguishable from one another, boiled sweets melted down and stuck together. If my son was among them he would stand out as if lit by a single spotlight on a dark stage.

Two teachers in fluorescent vests attempt to herd the children but their skills are limited. A child, any of these children, could readily be whisked away. Then a small girl bumps into my leg, takes one look up at my face, shrieks in terror, and runs to a teacher. I do not carry a mirror these days but I can guess the state of me, and anticipate how she'll later describe my face to her friends. I am not fine near these children. Coming here was a foolish thing to do. I turn away from the Observatory and head down the hill as quickly as I can, boots skidding along the wet grass; at any moment, almost falling, almost unleashing an uncontrollable scream.

My phone starts to ring.

The number is blocked. "Hello?" *I am breathless.*

"Do you accept a call from HMP Bronzefield?" It's a woman's voice. I don't immediately respond. A cramp has formed in my abdomen; it twists and ties into a knot. "I have a prisoner here who's trying to get in contact with you."

"My sister," I say. I knew this day would come. If I had one wish. If wishes are being distributed, could I have one more, please? With two I would kill the both of you. "Yes," I say into the phone. "Put her through."

4.

On Sunday, Sandra arrives at half past eight in the morning. Elliot is thrilled to see her again, and pulls her into his room to point to where we hung her drawing.

"Did you find the flat okay?" I ask.

"I know this street actually," she says. "Sometimes I go to the Catholic church around the corner. A friend lives not far."

Isn't church usually Sunday morning? I hope she isn't missing it because of me. "Oh, would you otherwise be there?"

"It's okay. I can't take communion now, anyway. I haven't been to confession for too long. Too many sins I haven't told the priest about." She laughs.

What would demand repenting in Sandra's mind? Perhaps she stepped on an ant on her way here. Her list of wrongdoings would be very different from mine.

"You could take Elliot," I say. "If you can get him to sit still for that long."

Sandra smiles and waves the idea away. "What work are you doing today?"

"Some kind of trade conference in Watford." I think of the un-usually high hourly pay rate they promised me, and how much I need it. "For the 'flexible plastics industry,' whatever that is. One of the speakers is Spanish." I want to ask her about the trial, and what she thinks of the verdict, but I don't know how to raise it delicately. "How's your week been?" I say instead. Before she has a chance to answer, Elliot is yanking Sandra toward the tablet, in-sisting she watch him play a game.

"My daughter's the same. Can't survive for long away from the screen."

"You have a daughter?"

"Tala. She's nine. She's in the Philippines." She must be the reason Sandra is doing domestic work in the UK. As though she reads my face: "I've been in London for five years. I hope to go home in a year or two. Once I've saved enough money to send Tala to a good secondary school."

So Sandra left the Philippines when her daughter was three or four. How often does she get to see her—once a year? Would the heiress even let her go home for Christmas? She must miss her fiercely. I would worry that my child wouldn't even remember me, much less love me. I don't suppose you can ever make up for those lost years. And then what would that reunion be like? Your child grown shy and detached from you, the air between you thin and fragile, and you wonder if it's going to be like that forever. Five years taken from Sandra and Tala. Over six missing for Elliot and me.

"Have you been to the Philippines?" she asks.

"No." As the word falls out, I remember that my mother went when she was almost six months pregnant with me. She started carting me around even before I was born.

The first time we moved abroad we went to Porto, where my mother taught a human geography seminar series over the summer. She had finished her PhD in London and come to the end of a two-year research position. It was typical, she explained to me, then seven years old, for new academics to need to go overseas for at least a few years until they had enough experience to be offered a full-time job at a university in London. I didn't understand the nuance of what she was saying; I thought after Portugal we'd come back to England in September.

She accepted a one-year maternity-leave cover at a university in Madrid, then there was another one-year contract in Warsaw and a two-year lectureship in Berlin. I went to international schools with the children of diplomats and multinational executives and learned the local language by watching children's television and reading the packets of supermarket cookies while my mother worked late. I kept asking her about this permanent job at a university in London. She said her struggle for a long-term appointment was because she was a woman, and academia, especially geography, a masculine field, was run by dinosaurs who were loath to give up their positions. A pink vintage Chanel blazer became her uniform and was carefully folded at the top of her carry-on luggage each time we moved.

"I lived in twelve different countries as a child," I tell Sandra. "So I'm not big on traveling nowadays."

"I understand."

"Well, help yourself to anything in the fridge and the pantry. Glasses and mugs are in the cupboard above the fridge. Plates and bowls to your left there," I say, gesturing. "I'll see you this afternoon."

"Have a good day."

"Thanks, Sandra. Love you, Elliot."

"Love you," he says. I analyze his tone and wonder if it was different this time. I decide that it was, and I am convinced today he really meant it, but by the time the door closes behind me, I change my mind.

The trade conference finishes at four o'clock and I head straight home. Flexible plastics sounded benevolent enough but I had to interpret for a business figure whose presentation was about ways to dismantle government regulation around recycling. Add "contributing to the death of the planet" to my list of misdeeds. One of the subway lines is suspended, adding an extra twenty minutes to my journey.

"Thanks again," I say to Sandra when I arrive, tossing my bag onto the dining table. "I'm so sorry I'm later than planned." I notice she's even given the place a tidy while I've been gone.

33

"No problem at all," she says. "It was fun." I make a mental note to increase my tip on the app's payment settings.

"And of course I'll pay you for the extra time. Say bye to Sandra, Elliot." I reach for his shoulder but he shrugs me off.

Sandra lifts her bag and cardigan from the sofa. "It's been my pleasure." Elliot takes hold of one of her sleeves and grips it with both hands.

"Stay!" he says to her. "The match isn't finished. We have another quarter, still."

"He was playing a football game on the tablet," she explains. "I was the cheer squad." Sandra squats to meet Elliot's eyeline. "Your mum will finish this game off with you. I'll play again next time."

"No!" he shouts, his voice rising to a level I haven't heard before. Elliot pulls again on Sandra's cardigan.

"I promise." She tries to gently unpeel his fingers. "Next time."

"Stay!"

"*Elliot*," I say. "You've had a nice day together. Now Sandra needs to go home."

"No!" He stamps both feet on the carpet and lets out a wail of frustration. Sandra manages to pry his palm from around her sleeve.

"I'm so sorry," I say to her. "I don't know why he's doing this."

"He was such a good boy all day," she says.

Elliot's cheeks are flushed an angry pink. "I want Sandra to stay!" Then he picks up the device and flings it at the wall.

"Oh my goodness, *Elliot*!" I retrieve it. "I'm sorry, Sandra—this is so embarrassing. He's never done this."

"I suppose I should be flattered," she chuckles, and sneaks out while Elliot is facing the back of the sofa, hitting it with the flat of his hand. The door shuts behind her and now Elliot realizes that Sandra is gone.

"I want to play more with *Sandra*!" Spittle gathers in the corner of his furious mouth. He wants Sandra. I'm not nice enough. I'm not fun.

"She'll come back another time. I'm glad you had a great day with her, but she had to go home. Let's sit down." I drop to the floor cross-legged, hoping he'll copy. "I'll play with you."

Elliot picks up the tablet and hurls it to the wall again, missing my head by an inch. The screen is now covered in spider cracks. I think of what it will cost to have it replaced and shut my eyes.

"Elliot! You could have hurt me."

"Good!" His shout morphs into a prolonged scream. It carries on for the next ten minutes, Elliot moving through the living room like a hurricane, me trying to protect him and the furniture. The neighbors must be hearing this. If one of them calls the police, social services will be contacted, and there's no way Lydia will proceed with the adoption.

"Elliot, please." I must not lose control and let him see my panic. "Sit down. Tell me what you want to do. Are you hungry? We can play something—anything."

"I want Sandra to come back!" He writhes away when I reach for his hand.

"Please just don't yell—you don't need to shout. I can hear you, I'm listening." The kitchen window is open an inch—I rush over and close it tight to try and keep the sound inside. My blood pressure escalates but I know I must stay relaxed and allow Elliot to get this emotion out of his system. Elliot wanted Sandra to stay. He wanted me not to come home today and for Sandra to look after him instead.

"Shall we order pizza?" I say, my voice now high and bright, but perilously close to the edge. Maybe he needs to burn off some energy. "Or we could go for a walk?" No, going outside is not a good idea. If this tantrum continues in public then someone could eventually call child protection.

The broken tablet is back in his hand and the roar of the computer-simulated football crowd blasts from the speakers. "No!

This isn't *right*," he's shouting at the device, or at himself, I can't tell. It makes me flinch.

"We could play another sort of game? With your Lego or something else?" I take a step closer to him.

"*No*."

I retreat into the kitchen. His cranky snorts get further and further apart, and eventually stop. He's better with me out of the room. Perhaps it's a good thing that he feels safe enough to explode in front of me. I never would have dared to perform like this in front of my mother.

What does Sandra think of me as a mother? She was gracious, but must have noticed me deer-in-headlights in the face of Elliot's meltdown, not a single parental skill apparent. I don't have a plan for what to do if this happens again. I tried to bribe him with pizza, for goodness' sake, when he almost knocked me out with the tablet. What if he does something like this the next time Lydia visits?

I know what's going to happen now. Instead of being a proper parent I'm going to be extra nice to him, let him do or say anything to keep him happy. I want our relationship to work. I need it to.

At his age I was desperate to impress my mother, which continued on until I was about sixteen. I made sure to excel in every school subject I possibly could, studying by flashlight into the early hours of the morning, wrecking my eyes and requiring glasses for distance by the time I was twelve. He'll never have to do that for me.

Peering around the kitchen wall, I see Elliot engrossed in his computer game, despite the cracked screen, allowing me to creep past to my bedroom. Pushed against the window is my desk with its locked bottom drawer, and inside, the social worker's folder. My thumb runs down the length of the key. I do not open it. I know Elliot is kind and sensitive, but he will have his bad days, and I will deal with them.

5.

The repair shop by the train station is not much larger than a phone box. I guide Elliot inside, the two of us in single file, and put the broken tablet on the counter.

"You're only looking to replace the screen?" the young man says, holding the device up to the yellow light, squinting.

"Yes, please." I couldn't find the time to get here during the week. Elliot is mostly interested in the tablet for cartoons and his football game but it is useful for some of his homework activities and so we need to get it fixed.

"Forty-five pounds and ninety-nine pence," the man says. It's even more than I feared. He offers a slight smile and keeps his eyes on the ceiling light.

"Although it's only cosmetic damage to the screen?" I hold Elliot in place as he struggles to reach up to a phone display cabinet. If a screen costs this much to repair, I can't afford for him to break anything in there, although I know he wouldn't mean to. Since last weekend's tantrum, he's been his usual cheerful self.

"It is, yeah."

"Okay, thank you." I take back the device. "I'll try somewhere else then."

"I'm afraid that's what they all cost around here. I just work here. I don't set the prices. Sorry," he says.

It is nine thirty and we are due at Elliot's school at ten. By the time we finish for the day, most repair places will likely be closed and I don't want to spend all of Saturday carting Elliot from shop to shop only to save ten pounds.

"Forty-five pounds and ninety-nine pence?" I say.

There's a pause, then: "I can probably put it through the system as forty pounds."

"Thank you. That's very kind."

Elliot waves goodbye to the tablet and we head to school.

Elliot's school is, as the latest e-newsletter proclaimed, *striving to be a Royal Horticultural Society Five Star Gardening Primary School!* This involves hosting plant sales and compost donation points, cooking school-grown rhubarb during breakfast club, classes on cultivating Pea Head People and Mr. and Mrs. Cress plants, and visits from celebrity hedgehogs and earnest recycling experts. Most of all, it means coercing parents into performing unpaid labor at the *Get Your Grown-Ups Gardening!* days. I do not know my wildflowers from my weeds, but I want Elliot to be interested in gardening, in everything. I want him to have friends. So here we both are, at school on a Saturday. Next term, after the adoption, I'll enroll him in a school closer to home, but if he really settles in here and wants to stay, we could move house and find a rental in this school district.

Passing through the school gates on a Saturday has the feel of a secret backstage tour. Apart from the brief teacher meeting when Elliot first came to live with me, I haven't been on a school property since my own childhood. Hand-painted stones line the pathway, decorated by children, and blue play equipment dominates the space. Stray tennis balls rest in the dirt and a set of swings stands in the far corner, everything miniature. A quote comes to mind about the world of little girls being small only to adults; to each other, of course, everything is full-sized.

"Okay, parents!" says a perky woman, chair of the school PTA. "I'm going to split you in two. These mums and dads here . . ." She points at a group huddled by the birch tree. "Can I have you doing

38

the beds and borders, please. We need the seeds sown and for the raised beds to be dug and ready for planting." Parents collect trowels and disappear to the back of the school grounds. "Everyone else," the chair says, "we need our spring-flowering bulbs planted in the prepared ground to our left. These should have been done so we really need to get them in today. Let's go! Go!"

I carry a bag of fertilizer and follow my group. The weather feels about to turn and I wonder if this will be our last sunny weekend for the year. When one of the dads rhapsodizes about his love for crocuses and hyacinths, I nod as if I know exactly what he means. Elliot joins the children to play by the pond area, supervised by two Instagram-ready PTA mums whose clothes say they have no plans to come into contact with a plant today. At least they're here—that's what their children will remember. I had to get caught tipping sulfuric acid into the chemistry class fish tank to coax my mother down to my school via a threat of suspension. A tiny splash got under my nailbed and I bit my tongue while I raced to the faucet, tasting iron. I glance down at the finger in question—fifteen years later the scar is still visible if you know to look for it.

"My son's Matthew, in the Man U shirt," a woman says to me. I'm supposed to remember her name from introductions but today is my day off and I let my listening skills slide into the background.

"Elliot's mine," I say. "With the curls."

"Where are you from? I can't place your accent."

"I'm British—technically. My accent is mongrel. I went to school in a lot of different countries. International schools."

"Ah. I'm a teacher. At a Catholic secondary school in Shepherd's Bush. That's why I go off-leash at the weekends." She flicks her hair and a green spray-paint streak flies up.

"You could get detention for that," I say.

"I'm already doing it, aren't I? Isn't that what this is?" Above her head she makes a circle with her shovel and laughs. Once I figure out her name I'll invite Matthew to our flat for a playdate. "What do you do for work?"

"I'm an interpreter."

"What do you interpret . . . ?"

"Languages. For the courts, police, hospitals. Sometimes business conferences."

"You're bilingual?"

"A polyglot." I cover a daffodil bulb in fertilizer.

"What a shame, I thought you were going to say polygamist," she winks. "So how many languages do you speak then?"

I take an extra split second to get the number right. "Ten."

"Bloody hell, you should be off at the UN or something, not picking soil from your fingernails." She rubs wads of dirt from her hands. "Which ten?"

"Spanish, Portuguese, Italian, Polish, Russian, Dari, Hindi, Hungarian, French."

"And your English isn't bad." She laughs. "What's the most interesting thing you've interpreted?"

I'm sure her eyes would light up if I told her I worked on the heiress case. Instead, my mind goes to a suspect charged with murdering a man he met on a dating app. At the police station he confessed, his limbs sly and feline, like a cat who brings its owner the gift of roadkill. Police had found the murdered man's clothing but were unable to locate his remains. Despite pleading from the bereaved parents, even the suggestion of a reduced jail sentence, the killer refused to reveal the location of the body. Eight hours in total I spoke for him in that low-ceilinged interview room, repeating his confession, the details of how he tortured his victim. I forgot myself, as you do during a lengthy session speaking as someone else, the muscle aches and joint pains of my own body melting away. I was his voice, his mirror, his clone. I became him. I knew that I was supposed to be sickened by the client—even the detectives were visibly affected by the crime. But the truth is, I enjoyed that assignment. All those things in real life I'd never say, never do, never allow myself to think, that day uttered in my voice. Forbidden words vibrated from my tonsils, down my body. Actors like playing villains in films, don't they? Aren't those supposed to be the very best parts?

This woman might be thrilled if I tell her about that case, but she could equally be disgusted and that would be the end of any potential friendship. Not a friendship for me, I remind myself; for Elliot.

"Well, this was more of a translation than an interpreting job," I say. "But recently I checked over the court transcript for an asylum-seeker case, an Afghan man trying to stay in the UK. If I hadn't picked up his interpreter's mistake, the judge would have sent him back to Afghanistan and he probably would have been killed by the Taliban."

"Jesus. I *said* you should be at the UN."

The interpreter confused the term for *marriage partner* with *business partner*. There was no one bilingual in the courtroom that day and so the error went unnoticed. The interpreter must have been nervous. Mixing up words can be a stress response for some people, along with raised blood pressure, muscle tension, sentences that trip on your tongue while your body shakes uncontrolla-bly. That's no excuse. Meaning can so easily be misconstrued and we are trusted to get it right. The interpreter in that case was Af-ghan Pashtun and the asylum seeker Hazara—two tribal groups in bloody conflict—so I can't help but wonder if the mistake was deliberate. The interpreter was disciplined and removed from the public service register, but that's hardly a fair punishment if he did try to have a man sent to his death. Was he really prepared to have that asylum seeker tortured by the Taliban? Maybe he didn't fully consider the consequences—that a wrong word in court can determine a person's entire fate. How a sound can kill someone, an intangible thing, just a puff of air from the back of the throat. Words are as violent as bullets: it only takes one.

I push my trowel into the dirt and feel it hit a rock. "So your son Matthew's really into football, is he?" I ask the boy's mother.

"Oh yeah, Man U, got that shirt from his uncle. Bit of a father figure." My gardening is becoming less and less productive as I keep the conversation going with Matthew's mum. I remind myself again that this is for Elliot only—I'm making a friend for him, not for me. One day, maybe, but not yet. I haven't earned the right.

"It's just Elliot and me too." Then, quickly: "Sorry, I shouldn't assume." I know I must be careful broaching the topic of single parenting. For most people, it isn't the life they had planned for themselves, but something they cope with, and have adjusted to.

"No, you're all right. Yes, single mum. My brother's a much better dad than his real father." She rolls her eyes. It feels like she's inviting me to join in, to comment on Elliot's father, my ex-partner.

"I'm adopting him," I say. "On my own." It's a choice, I haven't been left, I want it this way.

"Oh, good on you. That's properly impressive."

"Elliot's mother?" A PTA mum materializes in front of me.

"Yes," I say. Her face is taut. "Is he okay?"

"No, he—things are *not* okay."

Elliot emerges from around the corner and scoots behind my back.

"What's going on?" my new mum-friend says.

My arms wrap around my son.

"Elliot just killed Nemo," PTA mum says.

"What?"

"The school goldfish. He took him out of the water and killed him—in front of the other children."

Elliot knocks his head against my side. As a kid, about Elliot's age or slightly younger, when I got into trouble my mother would become extraordinarily calm and walk to her closet, turning her head ever so slightly to ensure I was trailing behind. She'd extend the step ladder and pull her wheelie suitcase down from the high shelf. And she'd start packing. Slowly but methodically she'd lift T-shirts, balls of gray socks, winter and summer pajamas from her drawers, and place them inside the suitcase in little piles. A pair of flat shoes would go in and whatever containers were already out on her dresser—perfume and Boots face cream and a hairbrush. The first time she did this, I asked her what she was doing and she simply said that she was leaving; she was going to live somewhere else. I watched for what item she was going to reach for next, curious. I didn't know leaving was possible. I'd heard of children running away, in books I'd read and movies on television, but never adults, particularly not in families where there was only one. She tried the packing routine three times during my childhood. I can't remember now what I did to provoke her, but she would put down the suitcase and agree to stay if I promised not to do it again. The step ladder was folded and stored against the center wall of our living room, her bridge to freedom only half concealed by the television. It was the first thing I saw when I walked into the room each day for breakfast, and the last thing at night before I went to bed.

"I don't understand," I say to PTA mum.

"The fish has been . . ." She leans in to whisper so that the children don't hear. "He poked his little head off with a stick."

"What?" I rear back from her. "The children must have been playing some kind of game or . . ." Last week, Elliot came home saying he'd told the children that day I was his "new, but real" mum. I don't know what he told them about his previous foster family, or if the children really understand what fostering is. Since then, he's been on the receiving end of teasing, a couple of

43

practical jokes in the playground. I know he wouldn't do this. He doesn't retaliate.

"They *saw* him." PTA mum points to two prim boys.

"Maybe there was an accident. The boys had a disagreement. Elliot would never deliberately pluck Nemo from the pond and kill him."

"I think it's best if you take Elliot home for the day." The perky PTA chair moves closer, waving her gardening gloves in my face. No support from Matthew's mum; she's already stepped away. "It's animal cruelty. We'll have to report this to the head teacher on Monday."

"Now wait a moment," I say. If this is reported to the head he's bound to mention it to Lydia when she next calls to check on Elliot's progress.

Elliot can't have done it. He's afraid of fish, their slimy eyes. One of our first outings together was to the aquarium and he ran screaming at the first tank.

"Elliot, what happened? Did you hurt the fish?" I ask.

His face contorts as tears stream down his cheeks. He shakes his head, finds Draggie from his backpack and pulls the dragon toy to his chest.

"He *did*!" says one of the boys. The other sucks his teeth. Their statements grow louder with each word. Increased volume is a tactic to defend a lie. I hear it in police interviews all the time.

"Why don't we all sit down and work this out," I say.

Children and parents from both gardening groups flock around the PTA chair. They busy themselves with flower pots but it's obvious their chief concern is not missing the drama. It's essentially a mob of thirty against two. I look toward Matthew's mum but she avoids my eye. Even when you do have friends, they let you down.

How can I persuade these people that Elliot wouldn't have done this? "Really. He just wouldn't." Then I repeat it, because I am outraged and they're the only words I can find.

"It is best if you leave," the chair says. I want to fight them on this, but most of all, I want to protect Elliot. My hands twitch at the thought of this having any lasting impact on him, another childhood memory of rejection.

Elliot pulls me toward the school gate and I let myself be led. My arms quake in anger, every vein and artery pumping fiery blood.

"I didn't do it, Mum," he says, once we're around the corner and out of sight of the school.

I cup his shoulders. "I know, Batman. It's all right. We don't need them. Any of them. Let's go make our own fun." My first school parental test and I failed it spectacularly.

"*They* took the fish out," his words choppy and wet. "I tried to save Nemo. Like Batman would."

I hold him tight until his face goes dry.

All I have are negative thoughts. In 2019 when the Joker *movie came out, I walked to the cinema on Curzon Street and bought a ticket for the two o'clock afternoon showing. Several years earlier there'd been a mass shooting at a screening of* The Dark Knight Rises *in America and some "credible threats" were made for follow-up massacres with this new film. The nervousness drifted across the pond and the UK took special security measures during all showings of* Joker. *At the cinema entrance I unclipped my crocodile clutch and displayed the lining to the staff: no gun.*

I sat in the front row and had finished my popcorn by the time the trailers were done. I could say that I wanted to see the film for its clever intertextual conversation with the Scorsese/De Niro film The King of Comedy, *but I won't insult you. The week before I'd caught the second half of the trailer by accident, an auto-play advert on the homepage of the* Financial Times. *My screen stalled and wouldn't allow me to scroll down, then I heard Joaquin Phoenix say into the camera:* All I have are negative thoughts. *I wouldn't have put it like that exactly but hearing it aloud, articulated so crudely, I realized: me too, Joaquin Phoenix; all I have these days are negative thoughts. And who could blame me?*

The movie is about a lonely young man who is desperate to become a comedian. He's attacked and he's given a gun to defend himself and discovers that his talent is not for comedy but for violence. He wanted to be great at one thing, at something benevolent and good, but he was denied the chance and so he was forced to become something else. It's terribly sad what they did to him. It's unforgivable.

In Mayfair's Screen 2 I felt a connection to him. You know why, don't you? I was going to be selfless, caring and utterly devoted, but you denied me that. And now I don't know what to do with myself. Although I am getting a few ideas. Simplify it and call it revenge, if you wish. Revenge is natural. Chimps do it. Elephants, wild dogs, even tigers have been known to hunt down poachers and go after cruel park rangers. If a macaque monkey is set upon and their attacker is too strong to overpower, they will even the score by going after one of the offender's weaker relatives instead.

We arrived at the now infamous subway mass-shooting scene and the only other patron in the cinema walked out. Fair enough, it was a bit much. I don't like violence either, but I didn't look away. People think this is difficult—watching graphic violence. This is not hard, I assure you. What's hard is having a child, a precious little innocent child, taken from you, and not knowing what happened to them. Imagine that, picture living with that. Mass shootings I could watch all day.

They took the Joker's hope, his purpose. Mine too. I had the room to myself then, so I said aloud: I see you.

6.

We spend the rest of the morning in the park in Greenwich, then walk along the river eating from a bag of french fries. Elliot saves a bite from each to toss to the seagulls, blowing on it first, making sure it isn't too hot for them. There is still black soil under one of my thumbnails that refuses to dislodge.

"Look," Elliot says, dropping to the ground. "Coin!" He picks up a discarded bronze coin and rolls it along his palm. "It says five."

"Five-cent euro. Do you have this one already?" I ask.

"I don't think so. This is a really, really good one." He gives it to me for safe-keeping until we get home. In his bedroom is a collection of about two dozen coins, lined up along his windowsill. It's a hobby he began with his previous foster family, and the rules seem to be that the coins must be found by chance while out and about; it doesn't count if someone gives it to him.

"People don't carry cash much anymore," I tell him. "When I was your age, you'd come across a dropped coin on the street almost every day. You have to be extremely good to be a lost-coin collector these days."

"I am good!" He runs ahead, eyes down for more.

I wonder if the events of this morning are all forgotten, and hope it won't come flooding back when he goes to school on Monday. What would my mother have done? Bulldoze the other parents, who she would have thought vapid and dim, with rhetoric about child psychology, and probably threaten to sue while she dragged me out of there. But she never would have been at my school voluntarily, so it doesn't matter. Richard might have gone. He definitely would.

Later, after Elliot goes to bed, Richard is still on my mind.

Hi Richard, I type before deleting it; too informal. *Dear Richard.* Nobody writes texts like that. I decide on *Hello,* the word on its own line, the final letter like a great big hole. My reply is a week late. It is almost midnight. I am groggy and soon ready for bed and now is when I am able to send the message as painlessly as possible: in the almost-asleep twilight, semi-anesthetized, not fully here.

Immediately, my phone begins to ring with a video call. It's Richard. He knows I'm awake. I have to answer it.

"Hi, Revelle."

"What time is it for you?"

"Coming up to seven in the morning."

"Sorry I didn't get back to you last week." Our faces next to one another, spilling out of the two squares on my phone screen, I realize we aren't too dissimilar. He also has shadowy features and straight dark hair—we could be related. He's around sixty, almost a thirty-year age gap; certainly old enough to be my father. I try to picture his height, the last time I stood next to him, but can't find a memory.

"I just wanted to update you about the probate situation," he says. "The conclusion is that she didn't have any type of will. We never discussed it, not really. I think people make wills when they have children together, don't they? When you meet at fifty, it doesn't seem to matter."

"I don't mind, Richard, I don't want anything." I've told him this before. "Money-wise, I'm all right, I don't need it," I say it confidently and smoothly, thinking of all the tells I've come to learn about liars. Nothing gives me away.

"I've passed it to a lawyer—a Kiwi guy here in Singapore. I think it's going to be a very slow process. I'll keep you posted."

"Sure, okay." Once this matter is settled, I doubt Richard and I will find a reason to speak again, and I'm surprised by how much this disappoints me.

"I got your thank-you card, and the wine." He smiles and leans closer to his camera. "That was nice of you."

"It took ages to get there," I say. "I should have used a company local to you."

"So it all worked out? The little guy's with you?"

"Yes." I have no desire to explain to Richard the complexities of the adoption situation.

"I guess he's in bed." He wants to see Elliot. I like Richard, but I was in my early twenties when he got together with my mother and we've never even lived in the same country, so I don't really know him. We've had more contact in this last thirteen months since she died than we did in the previous nine years of their relationship. Now that my mother is gone, I wasn't intending to ever introduce him to Elliot, I didn't think there would be any point. "Well. Send me a picture to tide me over until I can see him another time."

"Sure." I hope he doesn't mean right now. I don't want to show Elliot off to anyone while there's still a chance he's not going to be my son, the downloaded photo in the bowels of Richard's computer for years after Elliot is placed with someone else; the child I briefly had, now a digital ghost.

"And how's your work, you're still interpreting?"

"I am. It's always quite busy."

"Good."

He speaks slowly . . . filling the time because I am scarcely contributing to this conversation. I am tired and I don't know what shape this relationship is supposed to take. "As long as you enjoy it." Do I? *Enjoy* isn't quite the right word.

"I couldn't do anything else," I tell him.

"Nonsense." He dismisses it as modesty, but I know there are few employment opportunities for someone who speaks a large number of languages as their sole qualification. Au pair? Until recently, I had no experience with children. Foreign sales executive? I'm not a natural networker. A diplomat? I'd never pass the civil service exams because I'm not an all-rounder. I excelled at every interpreting and translation test I attempted but in me those abilities come at the expense of numeracy, spatial and visual skills. A secondary school language teacher? I'm not adept at explaining things. A flight attendant? I spent my whole childhood moving around. All I want now is to live in one place. In the jobs market, languages are considered to be complementary, a bonus seen to enhance some other primary skill. They aren't meant to be everything you have to offer to the world, to add up to an entire existence.

"Your mother always said you could have been an academic too," Richard says, grinning like a proud uncle after three Christmas gins. Of course she tried to convince me to do a PhD in linguistics and follow her into academia and *make some proper money from your talent.* There were many universities, she'd add, where the requirements for entry were lower, and where the standards of work demanded were more *achievable.* Achievable to me. I never wanted to follow that path. For me, languages are a living thing, not something to be analyzed and examined for study's sake. A skill to be acquired for use in the real world. You can read a play or a film script, take it apart and see what it's trying to say, but you'll never *know* it, and you definitely won't *feel* it, because it's designed for the mouths of human beings and can only ever leave a smudge on the page.

"I should go," I tell Richard. "It's getting late here."

"Yes, yes, go. I bet the little one wakes you up early." He smiles to himself. "You'll let me know if you need anything else?"

"They won't have to interview you again."

"I wasn't thinking about the reference—I mean . . . with anything."

"Oh." I almost didn't apply for adoption. I didn't know who to ask to be my references. Because I was independent by the time he met my mother and they lived on the other side of the world, Richard qualified as a requisite non-family member. I'm not sure what my mother told him about my childhood, and how she explained why as an adult I kept my visits and phone calls to a minimum. He wrote a generous full-page letter to the agency, exaggerating how often we saw each other during the ten years of his relationship with my mother, giving the impression he knew me much better than he actually did. He wrote that I was smart and resourceful, generous and "capable of forgiveness." I've tried to ignore that. I should just be grateful for what he did for me and not fixate on that one, minuscule thing. But those words bother me, and I want to know if it was a deliberate dig. "And about the reference letter . . ?"

"Oh yes?" His voice sounds so hopeful. He wants to keep the call going. If I've read too much into that comment, I'll offend him, I'll mess this up. Maybe I don't want to know.

"I only mean to say—thank you again. For everything you've done to help me with the adoption."

"You need anything else, you let me know." Why did he even agree to write it? Afterward, he had to be interviewed and re-affirm his claims about me, so it was no small ask. Did he feel sorry for me because my mother had recently died and I was drowning in guilt about not saying goodbye? Did his own grief make him delicate and pliable and willing to agree to anything for a distraction? He must wonder why I asked him, of all people. It looks desperate.

He would know it's because I obviously had no one else to ask. He either pities me, or sees me as a weird loner, or both. I had a friend, Doreen, who would have written me a brilliant letter, been the very best reference, but we haven't spoken now in eight years and probably never will again.

On our video call, Richard is waiting for me to say something. Before today, the last time we spoke was right before his interview all those months ago. He asked me how long I'd been thinking of adopting and I told him the truth—it had never occurred to me until she died. Next he was about to ask me why exactly I wanted to adopt, I was sure of it, but then he closed his mouth and nodded and there were no more questions.

Richard believes he knows me. He thinks that he understands why I'm doing this.

"Don't be shy," he makes his point again. "Anything you need, just ask."

Keep chatting, his face is saying. I should make more of an effort with him. He was kind when I didn't fly to Singapore for the funeral he organized. I try to recall a nice anecdote from my childhood to share with him and then I can say good night and go, but none come to mind. Instead I think of the way people teach non-English speakers the word "grief," focusing on the long "e" sound in the middle, but it's the "f" that goes on forever. I say it under my breath and taste the letter trapped behind my front teeth.

"What was that?" Richard says. He heard me.

I quickly say goodbye and end the call.

Eight months into our life in Milan, my mother informed me we were moving to Russia at the next school term.

"I'm not going," I said, matter-of-fact. "I'm staying in Italy."

"Oh, are you?" She was amused.

I hadn't had a proper friend since year two in South London. I was exhausted being the new kid every year or so, required to explain myself yet again, to work so hard to make a fresh group of children like me. So I stopped trying. I wasn't lazy, I was being practical. I knew making friends meant I would start imagining a life for myself, in that place, at that school, around those people, and I'd only have to erase it when my mother announced we were moving again. I didn't know when or where we were moving to in the years ahead. I had no control, or say in the matter. You learn how to live without connections to people or plans, so that you don't need to constantly wipe away your future. My insistence that I was staying in Italy kept the smirk on her face for the rest of the day.

Richard is a nice man, but we aren't family, or friends; we're nothing to each other, not really. We don't share a name or DNA, or now, anyone.

7.

I'm up early, woken by back pain. Sharp pangs in my lower spine appeared out of nowhere a couple of months ago; it must be the sudden increase in my physical activity, all of my running after El-liot, kicking the ball in the park after school. Bending and twist-ing while gardening yesterday at school didn't help. On YouTube I search through physiotherapy channels and videos looking for re-medial stretches I can do. On the carpet by my bed I try to follow along with a back-bend but it only seems to make things worse. The next video plays and the therapist speaks directly into the camera:

These patients didn't respond to treatment, and their pain had no struc-tural cause. I had one patient whose lower back pain started shortly after her sister's terminal cancer diagnosis. She didn't respond to medication, physical therapy, or even surgical intervention, and I eventually concluded that it was psychological—she was experiencing pain-related guilt. The connection between pain, disability, and guilt is an underexplored field of medicine but is increasingly considered by mainstream practitioners.

This sounds like alternative medicine and I've never had much time for unproven treatments, yet I keep watching until the end of the clip. The physical therapist on screen is about Doreen's age; not her age now but the age she was the last time I saw her. Her voice even sounds similar. Am I really remembering the sound of some-one's voice I haven't heard in eight years, someone who I only ever knew for twelve months? It must be a false memory. I close the laptop and take two acetaminophen.

Elliot soon stirs and we eat breakfast. It's the second Sunday in a row where I'm leaving him to go to work. He's excited to see Sandra again so it will be no hardship from his side of things, and he deserves some fun after yesterday.

I wait until nine o'clock to ring her: no answer, nor at ten minutes past or nine fifteen, and at nine thirty I call customer service for the Silver Balloon app. They try to find another babysitter in the area but I don't want to leave Elliot with just anyone, not after what happened at the Old Bailey. Now I'm late for my assignment. It isn't unusual for interpreters to cancel a booking—the job insecurity in this industry runs both ways—but I always follow through on my commitments and have never once pulled out at the last moment. This could be the first of many occasions, now that I have Elliot, where I'm left with no choice. It's embarrassing to have to phone Exia and apologize. I hang up, my posture hunched, more twinges in my lower back. Sandra must have slept in. Not now, surely; it's past ten. Something has come up and she's changed her mind. I would never simply not turn up for a commitment. She's obviously flaky. She can't have forgotten as we only made this booking yesterday and she said she was glad of the work. Flaky and capricious and too inconsiderate to even bother with a phone call.

Elliot is dressed and fed, backpack packed in case Sandra wanted to take him out. "She's not coming," I tell him, hearing some residual anger in my voice, directed at Sandra of course, not Elliot. He is probably used to this kind of thing, being let down by his birth parents, people not turning up for him or following through on promises. He needs to know it isn't because of him, and he should expect more from the adults in his life, demand better. "She wanted me to tell you that she's very sorry," I quickly add. "She was looking forward to seeing you, but she's not feeling well today." I think back to his tantrum when Sandra went to leave last time, and the shattered tablet.

"Oh," he says, finding some more Nutella on his fingers. "Oh well." Not too worried.

"So I'm going to stay home with you today."

"Okay," Elliot says, indifferent to that piece of news too.

"Do you like ships?" Surely his previous foster family took him to the maritime museum at Greenwich. "Boats?" He isn't sure but he looks interested. If I'm not working today there's no use us wasting a warm Sunday inside.

We take the subway to London Bridge and walk to HMS *Belfast*, the ship-cum-museum where we climb ladders and poke through narrow hatchways. There are wax figures so real Elliot insists they are olden-day sailors come to life. We move around the engine room and on to the galley kitchen, with 1930s recipes taped to the walls and mock tins of ancient flour. He presses every button and spins every wheel within reach but doesn't give a clear answer when I ask if he's been on a boat before, in his life before me. There is a trace of jealousy when I consider that someone may have already taken him to see a ship like this, maybe even a better one.

Elliot is running his hand over a turret as I flip through the guidebook and realize exactly what it is I've brought him to. HMS *Belfast* was a warship. It served in the Arctic, in Korea, and was the second ship to open fire during the Normandy landings. People died in here, and killed others from here. They saw unimaginable horrors; the stuff of a lifetime of torment.

What happened to Elliot before he was taken into care? He generally seems fine, but what kind of private trauma is stored inside? When the authorities first remove a child, the idea is for it to be temporary, for the birth parents or other close family members to be given a chance to sort themselves out. While the child is in foster care they often maintain connection with their birth parents through supervised contact visits in the presence of a social worker. These meetings usually take place in council buildings, little rooms that sigh with despair the moment you walk in. I know this, because I've been in one of those rooms.

When I think about my room, I can smell the stench of cigarettes smoked by construction workers on the street below and my lungs fill with the black mold that reached up the walls. My room had a stack of plastic chairs in the corner, strip lights that couldn't be arsed to glow, and carpet so filthy even the stains had stains. I was anxious to appear professional and almost vomited the breakfast I didn't eat. I sat silent in my chair, trying to do what was expected of me. My legs twitched underneath me, skin itchy in my new clothes, my first cheap business suit.

Elliot has almost certainly been in one of those rooms. So there's that experience we have in common. Maybe Elliot's memory will shelter him, wipe itself clean the way mine did sometimes during my childhood.

We disembark the ship and make a plan to head home via Pizza Express. Elliot is delighted to find a grubby penny coin on the footpath and drops it into my bag. "We'll have to clean this one before it can go on your windowsill," I say.

"A Coke bath!"

"That's right. Coca-Cola will make that coin shiny again." What did Elliot do at the weekends and school holidays before he was taken into care? Did he understand the difference of the end of the week, or was each day of his life simply more of the same? We jump on a bus and immediately stall at traffic lights, tangled in the weekend rush. I watch pedestrians pour across the road. When we're out in large crowds like this, I find myself regarding the faces of strangers, cheekbones and nose-ridges, hair and eye color, scouting for Elliot's features; the possibility of unknown cousins, aunts, and even estranged sisters or brothers.

By six o'clock in the evening there is still no apology text from

Sandra. I try calling her again even though I don't expect her to answer. She'll probably ghost me now. Her phone doesn't even ring. I give up. But then her face appears on the screen. The television screen. I drop my water glass, spilling it all over the dining table. Sandra is on the news. I let the liquid spread and drip to the floor, and slowly rise to my feet. If I can move closer to the TV, the images will look different and the newsreader's words will change. I am too far away and misunderstanding the story. Yes, that is what's happening. But now I am almost on top of the television and Sandra's face is still there.

Police are searching for the killer of overseas domestic worker Sandra Ramos, 42, found dead in the home of her Knightsbridge employer. I increase the volume as I move closer to the screen, closer still, transferring grease from the takeaway pizza to the remote control. *Murdered.* I hear it again. My ears are playing tricks, the way the human eye sees things upside down and the mind has to correct the image, spin it around. *Homicide detectives.* This can't be real. My feet are frozen in place as though I have knocked the pause button not on the TV, but on me.

"What are you doing?" A voice. Elliot.

I spring into action and press the power button before he looks up and asks me why his babysitter is on the news. "How are you going there?" I move back toward him, trying to smooth over the fracture in my voice. He is drawing Batman—he was expecting to be drawing today with Sandra. "Do you think you'll be doing that for a while longer?"

A grunt that says "yes."

"That's good. Keep going."

I've interpreted on murder trials before, and suspect interrogations where multiple people have been killed. But those victims are on some level conceptual, that's how I manage to do the work;

names on a page but not entirely real people, never someone I've actually met. Sandra came to the UK to work for a better life for her daughter and this is how things turn out.

On the laptop, I search for her. It takes three reads of the police press release until I've fully absorbed the words. Then I work my way through each of the news links on the first page of search results. Last night Sandra was found dead in the Knightsbridge house where she was employed. Her body was discovered at the bottom of the kitchen stairs. The fall killed her, but police are treating it as murder. The door leading to the back garden was found open and broken crystal glass shards in the kitchen and at the top of the stairs indicate a struggle. The crime is described as an attempted robbery gone wrong. Sandra would have been terrified.

I carry my unfinished pizza to the trash can and end up tossing in the whole plate; it all feels contaminated with horror. I mop up the spilled water and then spray disinfectant onto the dining table, scrubbing frantic circles until I feel woozy on the fumes. I was so self-righteous today, thinking to myself how *I* would never simply not turn up for a job, congratulating myself because *I* follow through on commitments, no matter what. Part of me was relieved that Sandra failed to show. I couldn't bear another display of Elliot refusing to let her leave at the end of the day, of him choosing her over me. That slice of pizza I ate is now a brick in my stomach. Sandra's nine-year-old daughter. What's going to happen to her?

I sit back down and read through the news articles again. One report says that nothing in the house was missing or stolen. Why would someone break into a mansion in Knightsbridge and not take anything? *The Times* says about the open door that there was no sign of forced entry. Why would anyone kill a domestic worker? A stranger doesn't make sense. This story says the heiress was home. I open a new tab in my web browser and read that she was upstairs at the time of the murder, listening to music with headphones. She heard nothing and discovered her maid's body some hours later. The music was so loud that she didn't hear crystal smashing, screaming, fighting? A body falling down the stairs? She's worth half a billion pounds and sits in her mansion listening to ear-piercing black metal? Screeching punk? I don't believe it. It's very convenient for someone who is already responsible for one baby's death, and the mother's life-changing injury. The police can't buy this. They're pretending to go along with it so they can gain her trust and investigate her, the way they do with husbands and male partners when the wife goes missing. Maybe Sandra said something to the heiress after the dangerous-driving trial—they got into an argument and it went too far. That woman shouldn't even be free. I think back to the trial: the not-guilty verdict felt like an inevitability. The witness statement from the Italian tourist seemed to have little to no effect, but it may have, had it been changed. Changed by me.

"Mum, I'm *thirsty*." Elliot. I close the laptop and look at the time. Half past eight. He's not in bed. I've been sitting here for three hours.

"Oh, love, I'm sorry, I lost track of the time." He has a final glass of juice and we brush his teeth and get him to sleep.

I leave the night-light on in the hall in case he wakes up. It's a frosted orange globe in the shape of a dinosaur, illuminating the path from his room to mine. I touch the light with the back of my hand to make sure it isn't overheating. Seeing it side-on in the pitch-black like this, the dinosaur, with its open mouth and bared teeth, is actually quite frightening. Not so much scaring the darkness away but emerging from it, waiting for the right moment to devour its prey. How could I ever have bought this thing? I rip it from the wall socket and throw it into the trash along with the cold pizza and the dinner plate I couldn't face washing.

A terse email from Exia warns me against canceling assignments last minute if I want to remain on their books. To make up for it, I reply, tomorrow I'll work any job they need to fill. I stay up for the late news so that I can see Sandra's face again.

"Milk?" offers the detective constable.

It is Monday morning and we are on a break in the police station kitchen.

"Yes, thank you," I say. A *Take Back Control* Brexit novelty mug floats in the sink. I've borrowed someone's hand-painted *Mummy* mug for my Earl Gray.

"We'll let him stew for another five minutes before we go back in," the DC says. The man in the interview room has been asked to come down to the station "to chat" about one of his drug-dealing associates. He is not yet under caution, and he does not have a solicitor present. "He's lying through his nasty yellow teeth, isn't he?" I steal a sip of tea to avoid answering. "*You* must be able to tell. You know the grammar, the normal speech patterns. I don't know what an honest denial is supposed to sound like in French."

"I'm interpreting as accurately as possible." Last night after Elliot went to bed, I kept searching for information on Sandra's murder. I did not get much sleep, but I know it's not affecting my performance.

"I'm not suggesting you aren't. But I can't judge his delivery when he's speaking through you." He's right: the client is lying through his poorly maintained teeth. I've been doing my job and repeating every word of it. "He's saying he has no idea why he's in here. That he's ignorant of his associate's line of work."

Oh, he *knows*. This I'm sure of, because I know the client. Though he hasn't recognized me, out of sheer coincidence, I've interpreted for him twice before. Something to do with drugs. Both times he charmed the officer into releasing him with a police caution. It's obvious this detective is unaware of the man's previous cautions—occasionally the records don't flag during Police National Computer checks, weren't entered correctly in the first place, or are not fully verified.

"I can't tell from his body language," the DC says.

"Don't they teach you how to read that in the academy?"

"There was a course. But I was ill that day. Man flu."

"Can't be helped."

"I didn't bother to re-enroll, didn't think I'd need it. I thought everyone I'd encounter in this profession would be totally honest." Police are often good at banter.

"You're suggesting they aren't?" I ask.

"I suppose we do get a good few fibbers roll through our door." He takes a big gulp of his tea. "So, as the bilingual speaker in the room"—he thinks he's disarmed me with that fun little exchange—"what do you think—is he lying?"

"I can't give my opinion. You know this." Sometimes during a job it takes all the discipline I have not to scream the roof off the place. The police, the solicitors, all that training and experience, yet unable to see what's right in front of them.

"We're just having a friendly chat during tea break."

"It would be against protocol."

"You're not on the clock right now."

"He's the client." If I was ever to play outside of the rules, it wouldn't be like this, a clear misstep with no plausible deniability.

"You're a *police* interpreter. You work for us."

I shake my head. "You use my service. As an impartial."

"If this French guy went to trial you'd be called as a witness for the prosecution."

"To testify about what was said in here today. To attest to my translation," I say. "Still an impartial."

"Your personal opinion."

"I'm sorry."

He nods and empties his mug. We're quiet as a debate between two officers breaks out in the open-plan room. "Answer me this," he says. "When you repeat them, how do his words feel in your mouth? Like something natural or bullshit?" I'll need to excuse myself for the bathroom if this conversation continues. "*Well?*"

Back inside: the cramped table, the suspect that's not officially a suspect. The DC asks another question about the exact nature of the man's work with his known drug-dealing associate. I repeat it in French and wait for the client's reply.

"Honest," the Frenchman says. "If I knew something, I would tell you. I don't even drink. Maybe a little Cognac at home."

"Right," the detective suppresses a smile. A charmer is still a charmer when speaking through an interpreter.

"Let's circle back to your business with this man," the DC says. In other words: back to where we were an hour ago.

"Officer, he's no friend of mine. If I knew something about him, I'd tell you."

I repeat the French words into English. It's clear to me the detective doesn't have enough to hold this guy. If he knew about the previous cautions things might be different; he could use them.

"Right. One last try. Is there anything you *do* want to tell us about your associate?"

"Ah," the client says, then a pause while he thinks. It's all for show. "No, I don't think so." A wide toothy grin. He's just so cocky, this guy, with the confidence of someone who knows they'll never get caught, not properly caught. Should I tell the officer this man is a serial offender? I am not supposed to know anything about the client's past, not meant to think or have an opinion. I finger a pen and consider scribbling down a message—*he has previous cautions, check the PNC*—and passing it across the table. No. I can't do it. This is how it starts—and then what? A few years ago a Vietnamese court interpreter in Lancashire was found to be in the pay of a drugs gang. A cannabis gang hired her to pass messages between its members during prison visits and she helped to forge a birth certificate and identity documents so that its leaders would avoid prosecution. She was sentenced to twelve months in prison for conspiracy to pervert the course of justice. I bet that wasn't the only time that interpreter did something she shouldn't have. Maybe she started with something as small as this. So minor that she didn't even realize until later what it was she'd done. I bury the thought, visualize pouring sand over the top of it. The idea is gone. I am not in the room as an informant. My job is to give this man the same opportunity to communicate with police as any other English speaker. If the detective doesn't know his background, then neither do I. Another lie pours out of the client's mouth. I repeat it in English.

In court the other week, it seemed certain that the heiress would avoid punishment for her crimes and I watched it happen. Sure enough, the heiress went free, and then Sandra was murdered. I don't know why the heiress would want to kill her, but then why wouldn't she stop if she accidentally hit someone in a parking lot? There were witnesses, copious CCTV, and no chance of her fleeing the scene unidentified. She had to be aware that she'd hit the pregnant woman. The heiress and this French man in front of me both think they're untouchable. To them the rules do not apply. Body heat from the client crowds the room, presses into me. At Elliot's school gardening day, I didn't defend my child, I walked away. What did I do with those two little boys? I showed Elliot that liars win. There's nothing I could have done in the heiress trial, but here all I need to do is write a message to the detective.

I open the front page of my notebook. The cardboard bends back but then my fingers change their mind and the notebook shuts. It isn't my place to get involved. I am only the interpreter. Then I think of Sandra again and start to write. I keep my eyes on the detective as my pen bores into the paper, fast and messy. He goes to speak, and his eyes meet mine. *Wait!* I try to communicate with my retinas. *I'm writing this for you!* A beat. The client looks from me, to the detective, and back again. I return my pen to the table and still my trembling hand. The notebook slides toward the DC. We both look down at it.

The ink is completely spent. I realize now that the page is blank.

"Do you need that last question repeated, interpreter?" he asks.

Here's where I can ask the DC for a bathroom break; he'll wait for me in the corridor and I can tell him what I know. I can cough and request a drink and then follow him to the water cooler and have this man arrested, or at least held overnight for further questioning. I do none of those things.

"No," I say, closing my notebook. "It's fine."

"Interview terminated." The audio recorder is switched off.

Did I will that pen to fail? Staying silent is ethical but now this man is going free because once again I sat feeble.

I'm no Batman. When action is required, I look on, prostrate. I'm not even Robin.

8.

It might be a shipping terminal at midnight if I'm working for the drugs squad, a windswept rest stop near Dover if I'm interviewing truck drivers for immigration, but this is the first time in over eight years of interpreting where I've had an excursion to a nail salon. A neighbor called the Modern Slavery Helpline with concerns about this salon's employees and the National Crime Agency prodded a detective from the local station to check it out.

We enter the shop and the police officer tells me this is an unannounced visit. When the owner appears, I can't shake the feeling that he knew we were coming. The neighbor's concerns could be real—cheap nail bars and car washes are the businesses of choice for today's slave owners. Or they could be racist, disgruntled from their recent shellac polish; that happens too.

The business owner leads the detective into a back room and I follow. Umbrellas hang on hooks with two woolly scarfs and a pair of wellies rest on the floor. On the table is the remains of bubble tea and reheated meals, noodles and pearly red rice. The owner claims this is the staff room, the space his nail technicians use for their lunch. The officer is supposed to be wondering whether or not this is actually the kitchen and these women are forced to live upstairs, trapped at a job they didn't choose. To me, the umbrellas look unused. The scarfs could have been left behind by distracted customers. Topped off by the wellies, I think the whole scene is trying a little too hard to echo the one thing these women are allegedly not allowed to do— go outside. But I'm not the one doing the investigating.

The officer is hanging back in the lunch room, asking the owner questions in English about his business security, name-checking recent burglaries in the area, trying not to spook the horse. The man insists on speaking to the detective in English and so there's really no need for me to be here. I walk into the main room of the nail shop and smile at the woman seated by the door.

"Choose your color," she says in Spanish. A blue face mask grazes her throat.

"No, I'm not here for . . ." My fingers brush against a bottle of gleaming silver nail polish as I switch to her language. "The police officer is here to speak to your boss. I'm just the interpreter." Worry flickers across her face. "But it seems he doesn't need me; your boss speaks English."

"I don't want to talk to the police." She gestures for me to lift my hand, and examines my masticated nails. "You should get acrylics. It would stop you from biting them."

"How much is a full set?" I ask.

"Fifteen pounds."

"And how long does it take?"

"One hour."

"Only fifteen pounds?"

"It's a good price." Somehow the business owner pays rent on this shopfront, electricity, taxes, other expenses, staff wages—all covered by charging only fifteen quid an hour for their services?

"How much of that do you keep?" I ask. What do I think I'm doing?

"I earn tips as well."

"That wasn't my question." I'm not the one investigating this situation, I remind myself. Besides, I want this job to be over as quickly as possible so I can go home. Elliot's social worker is coming to our flat this afternoon and I need time to prepare. That's what I should be focusing on.

"For you, shellac would be nice. Round shape, square edges."

I bite my tongue to stop myself from asking further questions. I speak for other people, not for myself. While on the job, I shouldn't ever be uttering a single word that wasn't fed to me by someone else. This woman could be like Sandra, tolerating the situation for a few years. She knows it isn't great but she's taking what work she can get, sending money back home where her family, her real life is. Or maybe she doesn't get a choice.

"What's your weekly wage?" I check to make sure her boss is still occupied in the lunch room. "How much are you paid?"

"I earn twelve pounds an hour." She turns away from me. It's never the truth when they can't look you in the eye.

Then the salon owner emerges from the kitchen with the officer close behind.

"Are you sure you're okay here?" I whisper, before the man is within earshot. As if on cue, a blond woman enters the shop and the nail technician launches into "choose your color," pointing at the shades on offer. I don't get an answer.

"We'll be off then," the detective says to me. I follow him out. We pause in front of a vape shop next door. "Sorry that was a waste of your time."

"Don't you want to speak to the woman? I can interpret for you."

He shakes his head. "She's hardly going to say anything in front of the boss. He gave me some garbage about the safe he uses out the back—claims he *prefers* customers to pay with card. Much to his annoyance, most insist on using cash. Never mind the 'cash only' sign in the window. I couldn't see any hard evidence for slavery, but it's probably happening." He scratches the tip of his nose. "What did you talk to her about?"

"I asked her what she earns per hour."

"What did she say?"

"She said . . ." If I give a figure below minimum wage, £4 or £5, he might go back inside and try to speak to her. If I tell him the

69

working conditions are illegal, the police will have to investigate further. But I don't. "She's paid twelve pounds an hour."

"Bollocks?"

"I don't know." If I get this wrong, I could be making things worse for that woman. If the police investigate, the owner would probably assume she said something to me, and if they still don't find adequate evidence to shut down the business, she wouldn't be rescued, and he'll be free to punish her for speaking out. I don't want to be responsible for someone coming to harm. Never again. "Sorry I didn't get anything useful," I say.

"You know what the NCA of 'National Crime Agency' really stands for, don't you?"

"No?"

"Never Catch Anyone." He chuckles, as though it's an open secret how ineffectual they are. If that is true, are NCA officers all right with that? Content to follow procedure, throw up their hands at the end of the day, and go home? That has to be the real skill, the rare quality needed for a long career. You can probably test for it, put it in one of the psychological entrance exams. Plenty of people can become trained investigators, but I bet fewer can block out their frustration, case after case. And they don't want officers in their ranks who are vulnerable to that feeling, because that's when you do something stupid. I won't do anything stupid, I tell myself once more.

On the bus ride home, I search the news for updates on Sandra. The murder was three days ago now and the heiress has not been arrested. A BBC story says she is not considered a suspect. The crime is still described as a robbery gone wrong. On my phone I watch a short CCTV video clip released by police. The gray-scale camera is positioned outside the Knightsbridge house; it pans across the rear garden and covers the back door, leading to the kitchen where Sandra was found. On the screen, Sandra emerges from the house and deposits three wine bottles into the recycling.

She goes back inside without closing the door. Why would she do that? Her hands were full with the three bottles—perhaps she had more garbage inside and was planning to make another trip to the trash? But a few seconds later a shadow passes in the garden and I gasp. It's a person, looming on the edge of the video frame. The picture isn't clear but it's almost certainly a man; it isn't the heiress. Then the video cuts out and we don't see the person go inside. But someone was there. I press play on the clip again. I know Sandra is already dead but I want to scream out to her to close that door, don't take a chance and leave it open, not even for a second. I want to shout for her to turn around, to see them coming; that could have made all the difference if she knew, she could have called for help or run. The heiress upstairs, music piping through her head-phones, the rest of the world blocked out, how blissful for her. I'm being unfair—the heiress might be sick with guilt. She didn't care about her victims in the parking lot but maybe this is different: a violent murder, her own staff, in her own home. If she is, her re-morse is useless. The most pointless of emotions, it helps no one; not the person wronged, or the one who's guilty. It's futile but you feel it anyway. The bus slows to turn a corner and I chew my thumb nail until it bleeds.

I quickly exhaust the news stories about Sandra that I haven't already seen. Journalists have lost interest in the case since that first day she was killed. Not the right victim: too foreign, too poor, not titillating enough. Even Elliot hasn't asked about Sandra. I'm not going to tell him the truth. If he does mention her, I'll say she's gone back to the Philippines to be with her daughter. I don't want to lie to him; I'd rather not have the conversation at all. But I can't help feeling sad that he hasn't asked.

The social worker is due in an hour. Elliot is at school and Lydia is coming around to discuss procedure for finalizing his adoption.

Elliot has been with me for over thirteen weeks now, which means enough time has lapsed for us to apply to the court for his legal adoption order. Under the tap, I wash the dried blood from my thumb. Maybe I should have lied this morning and told the detective the nail technician said she needed help. Sometimes a lie can be purer than the truth.

I've lied to Lydia. I've omitted certain facts about myself, obscured things and let her make her own assumptions, but I've never told what I would describe as an unforgivable, terrible untruth. For her first visit, I prepared every inch of the flat. I sliced celery sticks and dripped the contents of an almond butter jar onto a serving dish. Then I swirled it messily around the plate, snapped some of the celery sticks in half, bit the tops off others, before returning them to the dish. I placed a small glass of orange juice on the rug— plastic, unbreakable, half-drunk by me. After arranging two cups on the countertop with the apparent remnants of tea, I ran coral lip gloss over my mouth and kissed the rims.

Lydia rang the bell that day last year at exactly twelve o'clock. I had perused all the parenting subreddits, threads on Mumsnet, forums for fostering and children in care; I knew that social services workers are commonly referred to in Britain as the "SS." And yet, I made a rookie error: a joke about Lydia's German punctuality.

"Sorry," I said. "I have all things German on the brain. I'm supposed to be making gingerbread this afternoon but I've run out of brown sugar. Practicing for Christmas." Too much? I would have thought so, as it was only October, but she smiled and sank into my sofa.

"Sorry about the toys." I pretended to fuss over a train and plush seal lying on the rug. Had I remembered to peel the price tag from the wheels? "My colleague and her son were visiting earlier." A harmless lie. "I haven't had a chance to clean up."

"Don't apologize," she said. "This isn't a house inspection." I had smeared a finger of strawberry jam across the front of the seal to mute the appearance of its just-bought white fur. "How old is your friend's son?"

"He's three and a half." The median age of children adopted in England. "His name is Harley."

"Nice name, I like that," she said. "Do you see them often?" A neat segue, probing my experience with children. I couldn't fake the existence of nieces or nephews, but evidence of entertaining a colleague's child was easy enough to create.

"As often as we can get together." A chunk of hair went over my shoulder in a carefree toss. "Every couple of months. I like to think of myself as his unofficial godmother." I'm not sure if godparents are declared only at baptisms and at the time of birth, or if older children can have one appointed too. Not that I have anyone for Elliot. Doreen would have been his godmother, even though she's not religious, either. It would have been a nice gesture for them both since it was she who first gave me the idea to adopt, although I only realized this fairly recently, after my mother died.

"Are you religious?" Lydia asked. Topic successfully moved on from the fictional child. That Harley godmother line: deflect follow-up questions. Tell the truth in a way that leaves a false impression. So many little lies to get Elliot to be mine. I only did exactly what needed to be done.

"Well, I suppose I'm agnostic. I wouldn't push a particular religion onto a child. I hope they'd be open to exploring what's out there, in their own time." Lydia nodded and made a note in her folder.

"The next preparation group is on religion and culture," she said. "Would you consider adopting a child from a different religious or cultural group?"

"I would. Absolutely." That was the truth.

"Have you ever lived with a partner, Revelle?"

"Only at university. My boyfriend at the time moved into my house-share when we needed someone else to help with the bills."

I had been "accepted to be assessed" by my local authority as a potential parent for a child in care. She was here for the first of numerous home visits to determine my suitability as a mother. It was okay to be single. The agency didn't rule you out if you rented instead of owned your own home. But they were notoriously choosy and I was aware that on paper I wasn't the most stellar candidate who'd ever filled out their form.

"Your flat is lovely," Lydia said.

It would want to be—I was paying £2500 a month for it, which was more than I was earning. I'd moved in just before applying to be assessed, traded in my Catford studio for a two-bedroom on Finchley Road.

"Good schools in this area," I said.

"I'm sure."

"Can I give you the tour?"

"Yes, please."

I guided her through the flat, lingering on the bright feature wall I'd asked the landlord for permission to paint. The second bedroom was essentially bare. I'd hung soft curtains and placed a row of cacti in the windowsill of the otherwise empty room, crafting an impression of space in my life, both literal and metaphorical.

"Good-sized bedrooms for London. How much time is left on your lease?" This was something I knew she would check.

"Nine months, though there's no reason the landlord wouldn't renew. I plan to live here long term." I was already in the hole £3000 for the rent. Diverted to a credit card registered to my mother's address in Singapore so it wouldn't flag in the credit checks I assumed Lydia would do.

She consulted her folder again. "Your mother lives abroad?" She was fishing for information about my support network.

"That's right." I neglected to tell her that my mother had just died.

"And you're an only child?" I told Lydia before that I didn't know who my biological father was, which was true. What I left out was that my mother always refused to discuss his identity. I assume he was a colleague or fellow PhD student, but I'm only guessing. I do know I was a mistake.

"Yes. Only child. Because my mother had used a sperm bank overseas, to have me, after years of uncomfortable, heartbreaking fertility treatments. She wasn't going to go through that more than once." I hoped it didn't sound too rehearsed.

Lydia nodded in sympathy. "She really wanted you." My adopted child was going to feel wanted, I'd make sure of that. I vowed to one day tell them about all of this—we'd laugh at this story of the crazy lengths I went to in order to be approved.

"Mum always said having plenty of friends is better anyway; good friends are the family you've chosen," I said. Tell the truth in a way that's misleading—I had no real friends now, but I didn't claim to.

Lydia made another note, then picked a ball of lint from her trousers. "Would you like to see the communal garden downstairs? Last week I planted broad beans." I visualized the boxes and ticked them: nurturing, resourceful, practical. I led her to the ground floor, taking the route that would have us walk past my organic vegetables, freshly delivered. "Mind the step," I said, to make sure she clocked the well-labeled box. She saw it. Social workers are trained to notice everything.

Now I have ten more minutes until Lydia will arrive and when she does, I'm worried she'll see the filthy state of Elliot's dragon toy. I could hide it in a cupboard but she might ask about it, seeing as it has been a real crutch for him. For the first time this week Elliot has started leaving it at home while he's at school. He has been teased about it, and is now embarrassed to be seen with it in front of the other children. The moment he gets home from school he rushes to it, and makes me promise not to touch it while he's out.

He'd notice if I washed it and would be upset with me, but this feels like a weak explanation if Lydia sees it.

I decide on a compromise—I'll spot-clean the worst of the stains so it won't look like such a health hazard and hope Elliot doesn't notice. Another parenting first—I've never cleaned a toy before. I go back to my Toronto mummy blog but she does not offer any suggestions. I can't tell what the fabric is and if I spray a stain remover and bleach the color then Elliot will really be angry. On the base of the dragon is a black label—no laundry instructions but it says the name Kyoshi and an eight-digit number. I type "Kyoshi" into my laptop and land on a website in Japanese. Google Translate claims it's a toy company in Kyoto. I scroll down the homepage but don't see any toys that resemble Elliot's. I search again for Kyoshi with the eight-digit number. It isn't a barcode; it's a serial number. Up pops suggestions for eBay and Alibaba. There it is: Elliot's Draggie is some kind of collectible, designer toy. It's worth £600. That can't be right. Japanese is a language I know relatively little about, so it's possible Kyoshi is a common word with multiple meanings. I keep searching. I scan through other Japanese websites, and instead of using Google Translate, plug the key words into a Japanese–English dictionary. I'm running out of time before Lydia's arrival but I can't tear myself away. I check over every inch of the toy. Then I zoom in on the image on the screen, looking for differences between the two. There are none. This is definitely the same toy. I've been assuming his birth parents gave it to him, explaining why he clings to it so fiercely. So someone wealthy donated this dragon to a charity shop and Elliot's birth mother or father paid a pound for it, having no idea as to its provenance, the shop's staff clueless as to its worth? It happens—you hear of people paying a tiny sum for an artwork or teapot at a garage sale and it turns out to be a valuable original or genuine antique. That's most likely what happened.

Otherwise, who would have given him such an expensive toy?

9.

I leave the toy for now and do a final quick tidy of Elliot's room. Still pride-of-place on the closet door is the cartoon Sandra drew for him. She really captured his lopsided smile, the slight to-the-left head tilt he does when he's being cheeky. Elliot loves it and he's been practicing his drawing every day since they met at the Old Bailey. There must be a class I can take him to during the half-term break, a kids' program at the Tate or one of the other galleries. Who taught Sandra to draw so well? Maybe she had plans for art school in the Philippines, a different career. She may have had hopes to teach her own daughter how to draw when she returned. I can't stop thinking about her now. And why haven't the police contacted me as part of the investigation? They would have access to her phone and the Silver Balloon app—presumably they can see that she watched Elliot for me. I suppose if it's a robbery gone wrong, they must have decided there is no connection to her casual acquaintances. I think about contacting the police until I remind myself that would be stupid and merely waste their valuable time. I have nothing to offer them—the reality is, I hardly knew her.

Back in the living room I do another sweep of the flat. The outside buzzer sounds—it's bound to be Lydia. I'm light-headed and place a hand on the wall for balance. Lydia says Elliot's adoption is as good as certain, but I don't share her optimism. Things can still go wrong; things can always go wrong. And if I don't get to keep him? My calendar now is color-coded with events and reminders for Elliot's school: green for his medical appointments and social worker visits, blue for football training sessions, purple for school holidays blocked out, days bookmarked for museum visits and trips to pick-your-own fruit farms in Surrey. Police and court interpreting work is mostly last moment, twenty-four hours' notice if you're lucky. Before Elliot, I lived one day at a time, the future week after week of empty white space.

I open the door and let Lydia inside. "Have you eaten?" I ask, as she drops onto my dining chair.

"I have a lunch meeting after this. But some water would be lovely."

I fill two glasses from the tap—my best glasses—add ice and lemon, all the trimmings.

"So, how are things, Revelle?"

I want to ask her if there's a chance Elliot is from money. I would have guessed most children taken into care come from relative poverty. A background of financial struggle coupled with factors such as severe mental illness, addiction, abuse. That's my own bias, I suppose; wealth doesn't preclude you from any of those things. I don't expect social services remove many children from privileged homes but it must occasionally happen, and I'd hope the rich aren't exempt from scrutiny.

"Good. Yes, it's been wonderful really."

Lydia places her water glass on the table and casts her eyes around the room. Her gaze lingers on the entrance to Elliot's bedroom. She's waiting for an invitation.

"Would you like to see how his room is looking?"

"Great," she says, already on her feet. The window is the first thing you see when you enter Elliot's room. "Ah, his coin collection." Lydia gestures toward the money lined up along the windowsill. "I remember them from his room in Greenwich."

"He's had a few new additions lately."

"It's cute. A very quaint, old-fashioned hobby." She turns slowly, taking in the details of my son's bedroom. The dragon toy is perched on the edge of the bed. Her eyes move over it but she doesn't say anything. It's so much more filthy since the last time she saw it, it's possible at first glance she hasn't even recognized it.

"He's still taking that dragon toy with him everywhere he goes. Except to school now, to avoid teasing from the other children," I say.

"The one from his birth parents?"

"I guess that's where it's from." Unless Lydia volunteers the information about the family's wealth, I can't come right out and ask her. The last thing I want as we settle the adoption is for her to think I'm after Elliot's inheritance. "It looks as though it hasn't been washed in years. He won't let me take it even for a couple of hours. I have to promise not to touch it while he's at school." I laugh.

"He'll grow out of it." She heads back to the living room and I follow.

"Has Elliot always had it with him—since you've known him?" I ask.

"I think so, yes, as far as I remember. I wouldn't let it worry you."

"I'm not worried." I give her another second to offer up something more. Nothing. I need to change the subject so she doesn't think I'm oddly preoccupied with a simple toy.

"So, he's been well? You're getting along?" I should tell her about Elliot's tantrum the other week when Sandra went to leave. Up and down behavior is to be expected in all children of his age, regardless of whether or not their background has been stable.

"He had one little, quite weird meltdown recently. But nothing of note and nothing I wasn't prepared for." I won't mention the tablet, shattering against the wall inches from my head.

"Good. Good," Lydia says, nose in her folder. "And school?"

The gardening-day fish incident blew over and she clearly wasn't informed by the school or else she would have mentioned it before today. Technically I should probably tell her. But Elliot didn't do anything, so why should I report a false accusation? I don't want Lydia thinking I can't handle even minor challenging situations.

"Fine, he's happy to go each day. He does his homework," I say.

"You said there was some teasing?"

"I'm keeping an eye on it. I think it's under control." She nods. "He's four foot two now. I measured him yesterday."

"Tall for his age!"

"He'll tower over me by fourteen, fifteen at this rate." Elliot a teenager. *My* teenager. I've been taking each stage of this process as it comes, not allowing myself to fully picture him as grown. As fully grown-up with me.

"And you're okay, yourself?" For a moment she seems to look right through me and I feel myself shrivel from the attention.

"Completely. I'm good."

"Is that another new language or are you doing a refresher course?" Lydia is looking at my Mandarin language book splayed on the dining table. I've been attempting to learn Chinese Mandarin for over a year, still stuck on introductory pinyin.

"Just leafing through that book for interest. I don't speak Mandarin. Maybe I'll take it up when I retire." Perhaps I've reached my capacity for languages. They can be difficult to acquire, but equally hard to forget. If only Chinese characters could override the German language in my memory, draw straight over the top, transforming it with a scribble, the way a short curve of ink can change a 6 into an 8.

"Well, this is only a brief visit to see how you're getting on," Lydia says. "Is there anything else you'd like to discuss?"

"I don't think so, no." I pack up the Mandarin textbook. Then I take a seat across from her.

"You seem nervous today."

"I admit, I am wondering where things are at with the legal process." A mouthful of the water makes me shiver. "I haven't had an update in a while."

"Don't worry. Remember, this stage of the process is really about the birth parents and social services presenting their case in court. It's between us and them. All you need to do is concentrate on looking after Elliot."

"You're expecting the birth parents to contest the adoption?"

"Based on my past interactions with the birth parents, it's not a good idea for you and Elliot to be there at the first court hearing." She's being diplomatic.

"Is there any chance the judge will . . ." I can't finish the sentence, the words unendurable.

"No," Lydia says quickly. "I shouldn't say that. Theoretically, there's always a chance. The parents would have to show that there has been a significant change in their circumstances since Elliot was removed from their care. I'm confident everything will go smoothly."

"Okay," I exhale. "Thank you." I'm reassured by this. There's nothing Pollyannaish about Lydia.

"In fact you probably won't need to attend any of the court hearings. The legal process will carry on in the background, the solicitors will do their thing. The family court will notify you of hearings in the mail and I'll update you as often as I can."

"Thank you."

"In the event the judge decides you do need to attend court—your identity is protected and there are procedures to make sure you don't cross paths with the birth family on the day."

"That's a relief."

"Well," her eyes lift to mine, "that's all." It's over, I passed, I'm almost there. "Do you have any questions?" I want to walk her out of here before she changes her mind. I go to speak when there's a knock at my front door.

"Ignore that. I'm not expecting anyone. It must be a courier with a package for one of my neighbors," I say, even though I know a courier couldn't get past the building's external security door.

"You have the information I gave you before about the timeline for getting Elliot's new birth certificate? Passport if he needs one?"

"Yes," I say, though Lydia doesn't hear me over the pounding at my door.

"You better get that."

I move quickly. Whoever this is, I'll get rid of them and focus on wrapping this up with the social worker.

On the other side of my door is a man in his early twenties, all bug-eyes and shaven head. "Can I help you?" I say.

"Revelle? Revelle Lee?"

"Yes?" I try to sound bright and polite in front of Lydia but already have a bad feeling about this.

"Your man sent me with your white key."

"I'm sorry?"

He pulls a bag from his pocket. "Your delivery," he says. He holds a clear bag of white powder up to my face.

"What... what is that?"

"Your white chalk. From your man." His voice is exasperated.

"I don't know what you're talking about." Behind me, I hear the sofa groan; Lydia has stood up. "You have the wrong flat."

"You said you were Revelle Lee?"

Lydia approaches from behind.

"Yes, but... whatever you have there is *not* mine." My trembling hand finds the handle and I slam the door.

"Oh my God," I say to Lydia, my words running together. "Who *was* that? How did he get my name?"

"Are you sure you don't know him?" She walks back to her seat.

"No, *I*, my God, Lydia. I don't do drugs, of any kind. I don't even smoke! I've never smoked! No one ever comes to the door here; it's a very safe area. I've never seen him before, I'm sure of it."

She listens and manipulates a gold dome earring in her lobe. I stay standing, and grip the back of the chair, my boy's jumper draped over a cushion. I hope he's still my boy after this. The arms of the clothing twist in my hands. Think. What I say next is crucial; it feels as though everything is riding on this moment. I need to be very careful with how I choose my words now. Everything I've done, all of the planning to get Elliot, could unravel in this moment.

"Should I call the police?" Yes. "I think I'm going to call the police."

"Revelle, wait. I need to ask you again: Do you know that man? Do you use the . . . the services of a drug dealer?"

"*No*, NO! I have security clearances with the Metropolitan Police, you know this." Her eyebrows rise. "I'm cleared to interpret on terrorism trials, on drug smuggling cases! I've been *thoroughly* vetted by police and other government agencies. I have no idea who that man was or why he had my name."

"You do recall that there are issues of substance abuse in Elliot's background?"

"His birth parents!" I blurt. "Could this have been them? That man sent by them?"

"Why would they do that?"

"I don't know. You said they want to contest the adoption."

A sound from Lydia that's almost a scoff. "First of all, his birth parents do not know either your identity *or* your whereabouts. Second, if you say this has never happened before, what would be the chances of that man coming to your door when I'd be here to witness it?" She's right. The odds are astronomical. I am being

83

paranoid. I sound unhinged. For the shortest second I consider laughing, attempting to backtrack and pretend that comment was a joke. I decide that could backfire and make it seem as though I'm not taking this seriously. It wasn't Elliot's parents—that's impossible.

There is a silence between us, stiff and agonizing. "I need some more water. Can I fill you up?" I clap my hands together, hoping the sound will scare the awkwardness away. Don't lose your composure, I tell myself. She's watching me. It's Lydia's job to assess my behavior, watch my every move. As I walk to the kitchen, I know I'm trying too hard to do so normally, now conscious of every muscle movement which should be natural. I must look like a robot without knee joints.

"I'm fine, thanks, Revelle." Is she going to cancel the first directions hearing? Can she do that? She's probably obliged to submit a report and this is obviously a major red flag. Elliot will be placed with another foster family who'll also want to adopt him and he'll be gone, as though he was never mine.

Stop. I must stay cool and not make this any worse.

"I'd say he got your name from some mail sticking out from under your door," Lydia says finally. "There is a scam going around where people knock on your door and ask if you need any gardening work done; they hand you a business card for their landscaping business, that kind of thing. It's an excuse to assess the contents of your house. Scoping you out for a future robbery. You're in a flat here and don't have your own garden—so maybe they pretend it's drugs instead?" She shrugs.

Yes. Maybe that's what happened with Sandra. Someone watched the Knightsbridge house—as a domestic worker, she probably has a predictable schedule where she cooks, takes the garbage out, does the same tasks at the same time each day. Her killer could have been watching and noticed a glitch in her routine, her habit of leaving the door open between trips to the garbage, and they made a plan to pounce. The shadow person on the CCTV. In those extremely wealthy areas you wouldn't knock on the front door pretending to canvass for gardening work and certainly not drugs—you'd go around the back and target the staff.

I release a steady stream of breath. That man was checking my suitability for robbery and Lydia believes me. "You think so? That makes sense, that must be it," I say. Although it doesn't entirely make sense. A robber posing as a gardener, yes. But not a drug dealer. If you were a burglar, you wouldn't want to put your future victim on alert. You wouldn't risk them calling the police and reporting an interaction with a local criminal *before* you had a chance to rob them. But if Lydia believes it, I'm not going to contradict her.

"Keep your door and windows locked. Maybe have a word with your neighbors?" she says.

"I'll do that."

Lydia's eyes study me for another long second before she leaves. Don't even blink, I instruct myself, don't give anything away. When the door seals behind her I slump against it, her empty water glass digging into my palm. It hurts. Sensation is returning to my limbs. The air in here is not quite what it was before.

You could walk around here with a gun and nobody would notice. I know it seems like a normal, high-density part of London but Mayfair is actually very quiet. Houses appear as though they're flush up against each other, my living room and yours sharing a well-lacquered wall, but we all have our privacy, I assure you. Many of the owners live abroad, running multinational companies and countries, and so their properties are empty for most of the year. It's estimated that during the cooler months, some residential Mayfair streets are up to 80 percent vacant, the only warm bodies a security guard or domestic worker dispatched to sweep the leaves. At night I like to oversee the row of houses opposite, behind each window a frozen scene of empty chairs and tables; a world fled. I zoom in on the children's bedrooms, the scene evacuated, tiny playthings abandoned. Did they leave for their summer house, or did they run in the middle of the night in fear? Could someone, another observer, have plucked this family from their perfect life? With my eyes I move the furniture from room to room as I imagine their fate. My private dollhouse world where I'm the only toy. Of course, your house is my real target, but these neighbors make for good practice.

My sister hasn't even asked. She just assumes I'll allow her to live with me. I suppose it's in my interests because I want her where I can see her too. I'm putting her in the bedroom with the smallest window, the view marred by next door's new extension. There is visible dust on the windowsill and the mirrored closet doors need attending to but I am a maid short this week and I do not clean.

Rita has worked for me for almost two years and so I suggested she bring her daughter to the house to say hello. I had to insist several times before she eventually brought the girl round one day after school. "You finish cleaning upstairs," I told Rita. "And I'll take her to the park to feed the ducks." After the park, we went to Harrods. I had the girl's hair cut, then a personal shopper selected a new dress and shoes for her to wear, disposing of the tired outfit she had on when we came in. On our return, I found Rita coiled, waiting for us by the front door. Silently she gripped the girl's arm and left and I haven't seen or heard from her since. Not even a letter of resignation.

I suppose I overstepped. I get things wrong sometimes, I know that. I gave her daughter a peek into a world she previously didn't know existed but which was right there the whole time, like Narnia behind the closet. I made Rita feel inferior as a parent, and I made her jealous. That wasn't my intention. I tried to apologize but she hasn't replied to my messages. I'm sure she is a very fine mother. But who would know? There's no test you need to pass; no license is required. Even though you cannot possess a firearm without one, or ship an antique to Italy. You must apply to keep a funnel-web spider as a pet; to sell tobacco, alcohol, or any kind of gambling product. If you are planning to run a competition or a lottery, drive a vehicle or even watch TV, you will need one. You will need a license if you work in a salon in one of dozens of American states and wish to, in the course of your profession, shampoo someone else's hair. And yet, no country has ever demanded a license to create a child. China's birth permits were only ever in place to enforce the one-child policy. In North Korea the state must approve your hairstyle but you can feel free to procreate no matter who you are.

And so, we arrive at this situation where children are trapped with unfit, dangerous parents and there is very little we can do about it until it is too late. How can people be expected to know that and drift off to sleep and get up in the morning and live in this world?

I can't save them all. I would have been happy with only the one. I've no real interest in Rita's child and I was not trying to replace her as a mother. I don't want just any child; only he who belongs to me. When they're rightfully yours, a mother will do anything to have them back.

IO.

I collect my mail from downstairs and ensure there's nothing remaining with my or Elliot's name on it. Then I shake our windows and check the locks are secure. I hope Lydia is right—that the faux drug dealer is actually a serial burglar and that bag in his hand nothing more than a scoop of washing powder. If that's the case, he would have seen there's little of value and moved on to robbing someone more worthwhile in Hampstead or Swiss Cottage. This flat was never meant to be our forever home. Even if I wanted it to be, I can't afford it. Once it did its job of impressing the adoption agency and Elliot is made legally mine, I had always planned for us to move. Our next flat, our proper home, will be safe. As for today, Lydia will forget. She understands that it's just one of those weird things that happen when you live in London. It won't count against me. But nothing like this has ever happened to me before, and the timing, during such an important visit from Lydia—am I really that unlucky? Or was it not a coincidence? In which case, who else would it be but Elliot's birth family?

I find the key to my desk drawer and pore through Elliot's folder, right here on the floor. I work through the top half a dozen documents that appear to be brief memos about when and why he was removed from his family. One mentions a police altercation, and the next notes his parents' substance abuse issues. I knew Elliot's parents were addicts and assumed there would have been police involvement at some point. There is also a doctor's report that notes nutritional deficiencies—Lydia mentioned this when he first came to me; it was all addressed with his previous foster family, his iron and calcium levels now in the normal range. I flip past and work my way through the rest of the pile. I'm reading the same thing twice, I realize. The stack of papers half an inch thick is now out of order and I've lost track of which sides I have and haven't read. I spread everything out around me in an arc and move across one by one. They're duplicated. The phrasing is exactly the same. Most of these reports are photocopies, and now I've reached the end. Elliot was put into care because his parents were drug users and several times neighbors called the police citing violent disturbances. I had imagined there was something more substantial in here but apparently this is all we know. There's nothing to indicate his parents would be capable of any sort of sophisticated plan to get Elliot back. I wonder if this is a normal amount of information to have received about a child's background? He might remember more disturbing things about his parents than is in these reports. Elliot could need some kind of therapy. Now, or when he's a little older? I wish I had Doreen to ask.

After I return Elliot's folder to my desk, I log in to Facebook and find Doreen's profile. It would be so easy to type her a message. I start composing one in my head, ordering my thoughts, listing everything I want to say. I do this all the time, I've come to realize. During a pause in court, or a quiet moment in the middle of a police interview, in my head I'll be drafting a letter to her. I'm not aware I'm doing it until the talking resumes and I am back to being the interpreter in the room. In the split second that I imagine sending her a letter explaining everything, I can taste something new on my tongue: relief.

On my phone, I scroll through all of the recent photos I've taken of Elliot. There, that's the one. Two weeks ago, Elliot playing in Hyde Park; I managed to press the button at precisely the right second, capturing him mid-flight, both feet off the ground, running straight at the camera, his arms out as though reaching for it, for me. That's the first photo I would send to Doreen. But I know that I can't. I put the phone down and close out of Facebook.

Soon enough it sounds and I fumble for it, bracing myself for a message from Lydia. *I'm sorry, we've decided to give Elliot to someone else.*

It's a call from Exia.

"This one's not on the app—it's urgent." I didn't catch his name, this man calling from the agency's main office. "Thorpe Park, in Surrey. There's been an incident. Need a French terp, ASAP."

"I'm in North London. It will take me two hours to get there by the time I get to Waterloo and change trains."

"In a car you'll be there in an hour."

"I don't have a car. And it's half past one; my son finishes school at—"

He interrupts me. "We're sending a taxi."

"You haven't even said what kind of incident it is?"

"Thanks, Revelle, I'll text you details for the cab."

"Wait, I—"

He's gone. I ring Elliot's school and arrange for him to attend after-school club. Two minutes later, my taxi is here.

The driver takes the A40. Chicken shops give way to sleepy golf courses and the palest of green trees. I spend the car journey exploring Thorpe Park's list of attractions on my phone, calculating how many Elliot is old enough to ride. In a couple of years I'll take him here, and he'll bring a friend. I'll still have him then, won't I? I check my phone again for Lydia. Nothing.

After being approved by the adoption panel, I received a formal letter in the mail informing me the decision had been ratified. Then, not quite four months later, a phone call telling me I'd been matched with a child called Elliot. He was six years old. On the call it felt like I'd won; triumphed over something I couldn't articulate. But by the time we'd hung up, the kitchen where I stood came into sharp focus, as though for the very first time. The hotplates and the knives and the mandoline slicer. Objects that are incredibly dangerous to children but none of them as dangerous as me. Because I had no idea what I was doing. Who on earth would give a child to me? Elliot was being fostered with a family in Greenwich, experienced parents with three biological children of their own and a rescue Maltese terrier. For our first introduction, I went to their house and sat on a sofa in the front room while one of the older children led Elliot in from the garden. My stomach felt like I was on a turbulent long-haul flight. The plane hit by a high-altitude storm, scooping and dropping without warning; your body jolts to the roof while your soul, exposed, clings to the seat. The following day I returned as planned. The foster father encouraged me to take Elliot out, alone, to the local park. I brought a handful of Freddo Frogs and produced them from my handbag when we reached the swings. Elliot ate them, of course he did. But I immediately felt like a fool, trying to bribe a boy into liking me, like a dog. He didn't meet my eye those first two visits. It took the fourth meeting—a trip to a nearby ice cream parlor, I was bribing him with food again—when he looked me square in the face and smiled and I melted faster than my caramel gelato, into a puddle of sticky sweetness.

The big day came and Elliot moved into the flat on Finchley Road. I spent the week cooking and freezing containers of his favorite meals—macaroni cheese, spaghetti Bolognese, chicken nuggets—the oven filling the house with smells he found comforting and familiar. His foster family gave me their bamboo cup and dinner set he'd latched on to while in their care, so there would be continuity and security in his first meal with me.

Lydia presented me with a book on "intense therapeutic parenting." The idea is that you can make up for lost time, for the life your child lived before you, without you, by cocooning for one week for every missing year. For six weeks, apart from school, we stayed at home together where we chatted, we laughed, we played, we watched cartoons and finished huge puzzles, baked cupcakes and made up games. Because I couldn't afford to not work at all, I told Exia and the police I was unavailable for in-person jobs, instead logging in to the telephone service, LanguageLine, whenever Elliot fell asleep, interpreting for any and every voice that called through. Each time there was a break in the calls, I'd curl my neck around Elliot's half-closed bedroom door and get a dose of him. Enough arrests and crises happened in the early hours to keep most of my bills paid.

By day, we followed the routine Elliot had been in at Greenwich as closely as possible, leaving some space to develop our own. We kept things in the order he was used to: evening pajamas, teeth brushing, then book reading, lights out, snuggles and good-night kisses. We ventured to the O2 shopping center down the road where he chose items in the housewares store to decorate his room. Fairy lights helped to create a reading nook along with a beanbag, while a giant poster of catalogued bugs and spiders animated the wall. I wanted those six weeks to never end, and for us to somehow carry on indefinitely in that private world. When the school holidays came, I even spent an afternoon researching homeschooling options for the new year before I came to my senses.

Now the taxi stops and the driver tells me we're here. Thorpe Park is enormous and it takes three bubbly teens in golf buggies, two radio calls to more senior staff, and another car ride to deliver me to where I'm supposed to be. At the sight of Met Police uniforms, my knees give way. I hope this isn't some horrific accident, a French tourist flung from a thrill ride, one of those cheery gap-years who directed me here tasked with finding the body parts. We are entering the section of the park called The Jungle. The area has been cleared, or else punters themselves could sense trouble and voluntarily moved their groups along. Carriages in the shape of bananas swing empty; a circular coaster is idle on its track.

I see the clients: half a dozen people bunched on a grassy strip, their mouths silenced by the sealed car windows around me. The park employee behind the wheel stalls the engine and indicates for me to get out. "Good luck," my driver says.

I count six police cars in total, and maybe a dozen officers. One of them side-steps the group and meets me on the approach.

"All we've managed to get from them in English is that a three-year-old and a seventy-something grandmother are missing," he says. "And the grandmother has some sort of Alzheimer's."

"They're lost somewhere in the park?" I ask.

"They couldn't have gotten much further, but you never know. There's nothing to suggest it's an abduction. We're treating it as misadventure at this stage, but every minute counts." He looks tired. He's trying to seem bright and alert but his efforts are only making it worse. He's probably just come off a night shift, this emergency pulling him back from the home-time brink. There are so many police here, not counting the officers in the helicopter circling overhead. A child going missing is very different to an adult murder investigation, but I can't help wondering if Sandra's case is getting quite this much attention given how quickly the news stories fell away.

"The family's French?" I ask.

"They said they live in Kaiser something or other, close to the France-Germany border."

He leads me to the family. A woman stands alone, grinds a knuckle into her temple: she must be the child's mother. I'm told the rest of the group is an extension of aunts, uncles, cousins. A young boy pesters his mother to go on the Derren Brown Ghost Train while there's no line. An uncle rages at the on-hold Muzak from a call to his embassy.

The problem is, they're not speaking French.

I pull the detective aside. "Exia told me this assignment was French."

He glares at me as though he cannot understand what I'm telling him. "I'm sorry, but I don't speak any German," I say. "Someone's made an error."

"I've been waiting for you for *ninety minutes.* You are *not* telling me they've sent the wrong interpreter." He grabs at the flesh on his chin, tips his head back, and growls. "I need you to get a full description of what grandmother and child are wearing, what they were doing this morning, everything that was said between the various family members, what their plans were for the rest of the day. Okay?" A pause. "Great, thank you." On answering his own question, his voice brightens, as though he has already forgotten the inconvenient facts I just explained.

"I'll call the agency, they'll find you someone." I stop speaking because a scuffle has broken out between two family members. One man shoves another, who staggers back and lands in the dirt. He's unhurt but his forehead ripples, composure no longer possible. Sprays of German, arguing over who is to blame, whose turn it is to house the aging grandmother once she's found.

"Do you know what they're saying?" the detective asks.

"No."

We stand in silence for a moment as the officer watches the family. At some point his eyes walk back and he is staring at me.

"I thought you said you didn't speak German?" He's stepping closer, invading my concentration. My lips must have been moving. It's been so long since they've been allowed to speak German they couldn't resist the opportunity to catch this conversation and play along. "You do know what they're saying, don't you?"

Understanding writ all over my face. "I only speak a few stray words."

"What did you catch from all that?" He turns away from the family.

"They were arguing."

"That much I got."

"You should wait for a German interpreter."

"I told you, I've been waiting for almost two hours!" He massages his eyebrows, hard, trying to push them off his face. One of my favorite German words is *Torschlusspanik*, literally translated into

English as "gate-shut panic," the bloom of anxiety that time is running out for you to act. I want the gate to close. Faster. Now. Don't do something you will regret, I tell myself. Shouts erupt in German as the family members still stood on the grass divide into two teams. A nearby police officer jogs over and positions himself in between.

"Something's going on. I need to know what they're saying," my officer says. It seems as though there was an agreement that after this vacation, the grandmother would go and live with her son in Berlin, but the son had always planned to renege on the deal. Is it relevant information to the search for the missing child? The police should know in case the grandmother was misdirected today out of spite, deliberately left on the spinning teacups rather than accidentally lost.

But I can't help them. Acknowledge the desire, I think to myself, but do not give in to it. It's that same feeling some people get when they walk close to a cliff drop or the rim of a harbor; the urge to fling their phone, their valuables, or even themselves, over the edge. Apparently it's fear, but it feels like temptation.

The men continue to argue. My mind knows what's best for me. It scrambles the words into an unintelligible soup. "You should ask them about their care arrangements for the grandmother," I say. "It sounds as though some members of the family consider her a burden."

"What else?" His fingers around my elbow, steering me away from the family.

"That's all I got." No more.

"You need to help me question them."

"I'm not qualified to interpret in German."

"Have a go, *come on*, you can obviously speak more than you're letting on."

My shoes dig into the ground. "I'm not registered for that language. I would be reprimanded for working outside of my official languages—probably removed from the register."

"We're talking about people's lives here. A three-year-old is *missing*."

"I'm not fluent enough, I'm sorry." I can't go there, even if a child is missing. Especially when it's a child.

I rub my eyes. Behind my lids, the grandmother is there, trying to cross the main road but collected by a truck. I watch the child wander into the sweaty arms of a kidnapper, little him or her coaxed into a stolen car filled with dead-eyed teenage boys. Another favorite word: *Kopfkino* is German for "head cinema," a word describing the phenomenon when your mind turns auteur filmmaker, directs a short movie about how things might go and forces you to watch.

"You're okay with a three-year-old being in potential danger?" he says, real loathing in his voice now. "You're happy to stand there and not help?" Then, under his breath: "Don't have children of your own, I suppose."

"I do, well, sort of, it's complicated." He shakes his head. His hand is indicating I should shut up unless I'm going to help. Of course I'm concerned about this three-year-old. I glance toward the woman who I'm assuming is the mother. My son's not in danger, but I might be in the process of losing him too. I know how she feels. No, I don't. What am I talking about? Elliot might be taken from me and given to another family but the chances are they'll be better than me, with siblings, two parents, aunts, uncles, more money, a better house. I'm just being selfish. I'm not worried for Elliot's sake, only for my own.

"If you're just covering your arse—" Then the police officer turns to look at the two men talking furiously in German. "I won't write this up. I won't record you as the German interpreter but if you understand *any* of what they're saying, you need to let me know," he spits. "*Now.*"

"I would like to help you." More than he could guess. But my words come out deadpan because I am trying so hard to hold everything back. With his eyes, the officer grabs my shoulders and shakes. You don't want my help with this, I want to tell him, anyone but me.

Then a message lights up my phone:

You were assigned to Thorpe Park job by mistake. Language is German. Terp on their way. You'll be paid for one hour plus travel time.

I see the car approaching—3D, not a mirage—and start to wave. I move toward it as though it is me they are here to help instead of the child's family.

"I think that's the German interpreter," I say.

"Thank Christ for that." The police officer is already jogging and runs past me. I feel so much lighter, I might just lift off from the ground and float away. Thank Christ indeed. I need to rest for a moment. I squat down on the grass and breathe.

They've all but closed the park, the place now swarming with police and search teams in high-vis. I walk by a ride called Rush, a giant swing which goes seventy-five feet into the air. No one will notify me to say the grandmother and child have been found, or to update me on the situation. It doesn't occur to them that the interpreter would be anxiously waiting for a happy resolution. But I'll be watching the news and hoping it's okay and that there's no ongoing search. Even if I was the German interpreter today, and worked with the family for many hours, still no one would think to call and tell me the end result. If the grandmother and the child are found safe and well, I bet the police officers will gather for a pint after work; debrief after an intense day, toast to a happy ending. I'm just the translation service. Not supposed to be emotionally invested, barely human, not worth a phone call to reassure or console.

I climb onto the ride, and hope the jolt will scare today out of me, the way uppers are prescribed for mania; because like treats like. The safety bar comes down and locks into position. *You're not tall enough for the rides*, my mother would say, *there's no point us going*, even when the shortest kids at school all went to the theme park during vacations. I take a big breath, ready to scream.

II.

Now over a week since her death, Sandra is back in the news as police fail to arrest anyone in connection with her murder. En route to Elliot's school, I read through the most recent articles on my phone and watch another clip of CCTV released by police. This new video shows a stocky man walking down Sandra's street in Knightsbridge, carrying a very large bag which he drops periodically and drags, as though his arms can no longer bear the weight. Police are calling on the public to help identify this person whom they would like to speak to about the crime. An eyewitness, a neighbor of the heiress, is quoted in a BBC story. She saw this man, on the Saturday of Sandra's murder, loitering in the area. The woman says that she has seen him on numerous other occasions hanging around the street, being aggressive toward passersby. He's a local homeless person. He could be the shadow on the CCTV taken from the heiress's back garden; that must be what police are suspecting, and why they're looking for him. The man on the screen has little to identify him: his face is unclear, his hair a generic brown, his build average. There is nothing distinctive about the bag. If he has nowhere to live, presumably he has no colleagues or neighbors of his own, and few family and friends. It will take some luck for anybody to see this video and know his name.

From school, Elliot and I collect the tablet from the repair shop. The young man passes it across the counter for me to inspect—it looks brand new.

"Perfect, thank you." I reach over with my card. The machine says £45.99. "I thought this was going to be forty pounds?"

"Screen repair for this model of iPad is forty-five pounds and ninety-nine pence."

"I know that's the official price, but you offered it to me as forty." His eyes on mine, blank. "You don't remember?"

"I don't set the prices, sorry, I just work here."

I release a slow sigh. "That's what you said last time." He stares as though waiting for me to make a decision. Six pounds here and there—it all adds up. But what am I going to do—refuse to pay, abandon our device to this shop?

"Fine." After paying, I steer Elliot outside and he turns and calls "Bye!" to the man in a very cheery voice, and today I wish my boy wasn't so friendly with strangers.

When we get home: "I'm sorry I hurt the computer," Elliot says.

"We all get upset sometimes." I squeeze his hand. His voice is so brittle it occurs to me that he's been carrying guilt about that tantrum. "It's completely, very fine. The computer wanted me to tell you that he has forgiven you and in fact he enjoyed the little vacation to the repair shop." Elliot giggles and the brittleness is gone. "It is homework time. But you better test the iPad out first, don't you think? See if it's working okay?"

"Yes!" He takes it and hugs it to his chest.

"Ten minutes, okay, then homework."

Of course ten minutes turns into twenty and it is then a rush to get through Elliot's schoolwork while trying to make dinner.

A text message shows on my phone. *Are you home? I'll be there in ten minutes.* Before I have a chance to reply, Lydia is at my front door. A voice inside says: This is it. Our social worker spent the day lining up an alternative foster family for Elliot and now she's here to take him away. I open the door, my face holding a mock smile. My body is blocking the doorway, stopping her from coming in. Play nicely, I tell myself, and don't let her see your panic. I move aside with a flourish and wave her through.

"I was in the area and realized I forgot to get your signature on this," she says, coming inside. "It's just signing to say I was here last week." She is holding a loose sheet of paper. Lydia's finger points to where I am to scribble as her eyes sift the room. I don't believe her. I've never had to sign something like this for her before. This is a deliberately impromptu visit to check up on us after the drug dealer incident. There is mess spread all over the kitchen worktop. A timer goes off on the oven as the fridge begins to beep because I have left the door open. I am disorganized and spent. "It's all happening in here, isn't it?" Lydia says. Under the saucepan, the gas ring needs igniting again and if it doesn't light on the first go, I just might cry. She wanted to catch me off-guard and she has succeeded.

"How are you, Elliot?" Lydia is traveling through the living room and at the dining table, crouches to peer over his shoulder. Elliot gives a quiet "hi" with his chin pressed against his chest.

It is ten minutes to five o'clock and we've been doing homework for the past half hour. A resources pack came home from school and it is apparent that Elliot is considerably behind the other children, in almost every area. Six years old and his class is already taking regular tests. I don't want Elliot to feel like a failure. One night I changed the "sound of the week" question on his quiz sheet to one which I was sure he could answer.

"He's doing his homework," I tell her. Today it's a dot-to-dot puzzle and a single A4 page of math questions. It takes so long for him to settle and properly concentrate, I try to supervise while cooking dinner, but each time I leave him to check on the stove, I return to find his math cast aside and a colored pencil in his hand. He just wants to draw.

"I like that," she says to Elliot. "It's very good. Is that your mum?"

"No, it's Sandra." There is a second where I think I must have misheard. Sandra. That's what he said. Behind the kitchen worktop, the serrated knife escapes my hand and catches my bare leg on its way to the floor. Lydia can't have seen it from where she's standing. I don't react.

"Who's Sandra?" Lydia asks. During this early stage of the adoption process, new people should be introduced to the child very carefully. I don't want to have to tell her that I left Elliot in the care of someone else. I can't. Not with this drug dealer strike against me. Don't mention that day at court when she took you to the restroom, I tell Elliot silently, please have forgotten about that.

"She drew a picture of me," Elliot says. I sprint to the dining table to see what Lydia is looking at. Play it cool, I tell myself, don't overreact and make her suspicious. The social worker is quiet as she observes Elliot's drawing and I am imagining it is a composite police sketch and Lydia will recognize Sandra Ramos from the news and know I left my son with someone who was brutally murdered. Between the killing and the drug dealer, she will think I have criminal connections and am in no way fit to raise this boy. I reach the dining table, and the picture, in purple and yellow pencil, does not resemble the real Sandra. He's six, of course it doesn't. It's an uninhibited series of squiggles, nothing more. Sandra is a common name. It's crazy to think Lydia would jump to that conclusion even if she is aware of the case. My shoulders relax. I pick onion skin from my fingers.

"That's nice of her," Lydia says as I move back to the stove.

"But she's gone now," Elliot says. I kick the fridge door shut a little too hard and the appliance wobbles. Please, Elliot, I want to say, please stop talking. Earlier today he did ask me what Sandra was up to and, as planned, I said she went home to the Philippines which is why, sadly, we won't be seeing her again. What else could I have said? The first person I introduced to him in his new life has been murdered.

"That's lovely, Elliot." I walk back to the table. "Should we put it on the fridge?" I whisk the paper away before I get an answer. "Now finish your puzzle homework, yeah. Then you can watch some TV before your bath."

Lydia follows me into the kitchen. Yes, good, I need to get her away from Elliot. "I thought of you today," she says. "I needed an interpreter for something at work."

"Oh?" I take my time pinning the picture to the fridge to avoid her eyes.

"You're a hyperpolyglot, right?"

"Generally, the accepted cutoff for being a hyperpolyglot is eleven languages. I speak ten."

"You're one short." Actually I'm not. "Anyway, have you ever done work with child protection? My boss says we're often struggling for interpreters in various languages." I reposition the magnets, pretend I'm taking my time to place the drawing in precisely the right spot.

"I only do court and police stuff really," I say in the flattest tone I can summon, as though it is dull and I actually have no interest in my work. "You know, legal and criminal type things." I hold my breath and wait for her response. All of the previous work-related conversations I've had with Lydia—did I ever mention an assignment with children? No, there's no way I would have let that happen. When I went through the adoption application process, she spoke to an account manager at Exia and confirmed I was who I claimed to be, my average income and qualifications. Privacy rules mean the agency wouldn't have gone into specifics on any of my previous assignments, even if it did come up in conversation. Don't make a mistake by overreacting, I tell myself again. She won't know unless I betray myself.

"We sometimes have to use an interpreter for a child removal, family supervision, interviews, that sort of thing," she says, watching me press down the paper corners.

Where's that disengaged tone of voice? I need it again. "If you're ever in a bind," I say, noncommittal, "give me a call. If it's one of my languages, maybe I can help." That's what Lydia would be expecting to hear; what a normal person would offer in this situation. Exia would not have told her that I now insist on no child protection or social services assignments. She would not be aware of the note in my file.

As far as Lydia knows, my first and only contact with social services was last year when I applied to adopt. How would she know otherwise? The only way would be through Doreen. Even if Doreen had stayed in social work, she'd have retired before now, and it's unlikely she would have overlapped with Lydia. I don't have to worry about them knowing one another and talking. But what about Doreen and I talking again? I think back to Doreen's Facebook account, her profile image a wide shot of her on a creamy beach. Naturally we aren't "friends" and most of her photos and posts are locked down, but the five photos set to "public" appear to have been snapped through the window of a helicopter during a joyride. The city below could very well be in Australia, which is where she said she was going. Doreen is on the other side of the world. I can get back in touch with her later, once Elliot is legally, irrevocably mine. But right now, I can't risk her becoming involved.

"Well, I got what I came for," Lydia says, waving her form. "I'll let you get on with your evening."

I thank her and show her to the door.

During his bath, I ask Elliot why he wanted to draw a picture of Sandra.

"Where's the Philippines?" He pronounces the country so that it sounds like Philip-pines.

"It's in Southeast Asia. A long way from here."

"Can we go there?"

I shake my head. "It's too far."

"What about on vacation? Sanjay at school is going to Thailand for Christmas." I don't know who Sanjay is, but his family clearly have a lot more money than I do.

"Plane tickets are very expensive. One day. But I'm afraid I don't have the money for that right now."

While Elliot brushes his teeth I think of the one vacation I had with my mother. She was still working in England—this was before all the moving, the country-hopping. We went to Suffolk for a week, nothing exotic, in the chilly off-season when the hotel would have been cheap. The town, Aldeburgh, had very poor phone reception and so there were no demands on my mother's attention for the full seven days. The beach was covered in huge stones, some practically boulders. We scrambled along the shore each morning rather than strolled. It rained quite a lot, and the locals stayed inside. It felt for that week we were the only two people in the whole world.

"We'll go on holiday," I tell Elliot. "You and me, sometime. I promise."

Once Elliot is in bed I make myself a cup of herbal tea to unclench. I think I passed Lydia's assessment. I really hope this was the last one. I won't leave the flat so messy again, in case she makes another spontaneous visit.

After packing Elliot's school bag, I finish the washing-up. When I lift my purse to put it away, it feels unusually heavy. I don't carry cash anymore, so I don't know what the weight could be. I open the zip and see the coin compartment, usually empty, is now stuffed full of coins of every color and currency. Oh no.

On tiptoes I walk into Elliot's room, nudging the door open slowly to avoid waking him. The windowsill is bare. My haggling with the computer repair guy, the talk about expensive vacations—Elliot has noticed money is a bit of a problem for me, of course he has; children pick up on these things. But I shouldn't have allowed it to be visible to him. Not with his background, and everything he's been through. It's my responsibility to shelter him from concerns like money. I empty my purse onto the carpet and spread out the coins. Tomorrow I'll return them when he's at school. I'll say the bank deposited the money into my account but said he could still keep the coins as they are part of his special collection. I turn over each one and read the markings. Apart from the dragon toy, his coin collection is the only real possession he had when he came to me. I know how much it means to him. A deep ache expands in my chest. I know I don't deserve him, and Lydia likely agrees. One of the euros is shiny enough for me to see my reflection.

12.

My new morning routine is to check the news on my phone the moment I wake, looking for updates on Sandra's case. There's nothing again today. If anyone has gone to the police this week identifying the homeless man with the bag on the CCTV, they haven't released it to the media. I go back to the BBC article where a Knightsbridge resident, a neighbor of the heiress, is quoted as having seen the man with the bag on numerous occasions. The article doesn't give the neighbor's name so I can't look them up. Instead I search through Twitter and Facebook to see if there are any comments which seem credible. On Facebook I find a closed community group called *SW3/SW1X*, the postal codes of Knightsbridge and nearby Chelsea. I update my profile image, set my location as the heiress's street, and ask to join. An hour later my request is accepted and I see the group has been discussing Sandra's murder. One of the members has linked to the two CCTV clips released by police. The first is from the heiress's security camera in her back garden showing Sandra going out to the trash and leaving the door open before someone in shadow approaches. The second is the footage taken somewhere out the front of the house, down the heiress's street. It shows the stocky man carrying a very large bag along the footpath, periodically dropping it and readjusting his grip.

That's him, someone in the group has commented. *I've seen him before. He's a homeless man known to the area. He's aggressive, always spitting, muttering to himself. I couldn't give the police a better description. To be honest I try to avoid him and stay away. That's him. In both clips of CCTV.*

Other group members chime in, mostly to say they agree.

They've also seen the man in the area; he frightens their children. No one has had a good look at his face, not enough to be able to help police flesh out their identity sketch. No one has seen him in this past week. They wonder if he's aware of the news and knows that the police are after him.

My phone beeps. I close out of Facebook. I'll come back later and see if these neighbors have written anything else about Sandra. On my phone is a message from Lydia instructing me to check my mail. She writes that there has been a change to the first court hearing for Elliot's adoption and I've been sent some paperwork outlining what's now going to happen. *I don't want to cause undue worry. We need to let the system do its thing.* That sounds ominous. I scramble out of bed to check my mailbox, my long pajama legs trailing on the dirty ground. The box is empty.

Then hours later, after I drop Elliot at school, I return to see a postwoman on a red bike, pedaling away from my street. The mail has been delivered. I tear through the envelope and speed-read a letter from the court.

The mother was granted leave under s 47(5) of the Adoption and Children Act 2002 to oppose the adoption application.

I read the sentence again. Elliot's birth mother is trying to get him back. She was a drug addict, according to the papers in Elliot's folder. Could she have cleaned herself up so quickly, enough to impress the courts and convince the judge that he belongs with her? My knees give way and I collapse in the gutter. I read through the remainder of the letter. Elliot's birth mother has been granted leave to oppose the adoption on appeal, and so now, for the first hearing, his previous Greenwich foster parents and I have been called as witnesses. I will have to attend court. The concrete is damp and I can feel moisture seeping into my trousers. I have to get up and go. I accepted a booking for this morning, at a police station in East London. There is nothing I can do to change this situation and I can't sit here rereading the letter all day. I will go to court and say whatever I have to in order to keep him.

"I don't want interpreter," the Hungarian woman says when I arrive at the police station. "Tell her—go," she says to the two detectives on the opposite side of the table. I'm seated next to the client, her back twisted away from me as she tries to shoulder me out of the conversation. People often take offense when a police officer suggests they need an interpreter for their interview. They become indignant and time is wasted getting them to concede that letting me help is a good idea.

"We need the interpreter to make sure we get everything right," one of the detectives says.

"I speak English. English!" the client shouts, leaning across the table.

"I can see that," the detective continues. "But you are under caution and we need to ensure you understand exactly what's happening." When it's clear someone isn't perfectly fluent in English, police insist on the use of an interpreter so that a defense team can't later claim language misunderstanding as a reason to dismiss evidence.

"Tell her—go," she says again. I sit in silence while the detectives try to convince their suspect to let me help.

I think about Elliot's court letter folded in my handbag. I won't sleep tonight. I'll have that nightmare again where I go to the bathroom in the middle of the night and the architecture of the flat has inexplicably changed. In the few hours I've been asleep, not only is Elliot gone but his whole bedroom has disappeared, the wall sealed over as though it was never even there. A bitter thought enters: I was right to not send Richard a photo of Elliot because he *is* going to be taken from me.

How am I going to explain all of this to Elliot? On some level, he understands where we are in the adoption process and what it means when it is finally confirmed. Yesterday, over breakfast, he asked me if I was adopted too. I should have expected him to ask about my parents, his grandparents, soon enough, but I didn't have anything prepared and said my mother lived far away and I floundered under his follow-up questions. My answers surely stood out to even a six-year-old as lies.

"She not Hungarian," the woman is saying in the police interview room, still ignoring me. Then, she unleashes a volley of Hungarian swear words—undisputedly the language with the richest variety of curses. She switches back to English and for the first time, looks at me. "See?" she says to the detectives. "She not understand."

"I understand," I say in Hungarian and then in English. I get her shoulder again.

There might be a few of the most extreme Hungarian swear words I'm not familiar with, but I know most of them. When you're fifteen and learning a new language, rude words are what you memorize first.

Gabriella, a classmate at my Moscow international school, would draw Hungarian profanities in pink bubble letters onto my science folder. I think of the day I went to the library to return a book after the bell rang and saw my mother. She never came to school. Not once had she picked me up. Something had to be wrong. So I followed her and when she went inside the principal's office, I took the vacant seat in the corridor next to Gabriella, waiting for her detention to start. My mother spoke loudly—a lecturer used to shouting to disinterested undergraduates, her voice easily traveled through Mrs. Eades's closed door.

"I was hoping you could facilitate it—I understand you have a sister-school arrangement in Marseille?" This was how I learned that I was moving to France after only one school term in Russia. I could not hear Mrs. Eades's reply. "There's an important international symposium next week," my mother continued. "It's very prestigious. I have a paper included—it's been chosen to feature as part of the main presentation, actually. And there's an opportunity for me to be a visiting professor afterward." My mother's voice went quiet for the next couple of minutes. "I *know* she has exams, but I can't afford boarding school."

Gabriella's pink pen stopped moving across my folder as she listened to my mother's increasingly shrill voice filling the corridor. "What do you suggest I do with her then?" She sounded exasperated. I looked down and fiddled with the chunky black bracelets around my wrists—I'd fully embraced the Russian love of all things gothic—embarrassed that Gabriella was hearing this, and that Mrs. Eades had more concern for me than my own mother. For the next few minutes the teacher lowered her voice and I could only decipher every third or fourth word. But it was clear my mother was getting a telling-off.

The door opened abruptly. My mother glared at me, her cheeks as red as Lenin's Mausoleum building I'd visited the week before. I stood and followed her out of the school grounds. Whatever Mrs. Eades said to her had worked. We stayed in Moscow until the end of the school year, by which time I was reasonably fluent in both Russian and Hungarian. That was the year I fully committed to learning as many languages as possible, spending every spare moment outside of school studying, and practicing speaking. I wanted to impress my mother with my linguistic repertoire but she didn't find it remarkable, even when my teachers gushed at the compulsory parent-teacher interviews. In these foreign countries, I liked that my mother sometimes relied upon me. She gave lectures in English and never had much time or inclination to learn the local language, so whatever country we were in, it was always me who was the stronger communicator. Occasionally, I'd watch her struggle with a government form, looking up words in a Collins two-way dictionary, before she'd relent and ask me to do it. She didn't want me, but occasionally she needed me.

Just like this Hungarian woman needs me now. The detective sat across from me asks his first question and it is obvious the client requires me to repeat it in her language. The client is a care nurse who police believe, when she discovered one of her elderly patients had died at home alone, continued to invoice his family for the upkeep of their father, until four weeks later, they finally investigated why he wasn't answering the phone. By then she'd apparently helped herself to his cash and valuables.

"Okay," the client says, nodding toward me. "She can talk." The next question comes and the woman is already flustered. I translate the question into Hungarian for her, twice. Without me, this interview would be terminated. If she did what she is accused of, this woman exploited the absolute trust placed in her. I know a home care nurse for the elderly is not a sought-after career, but who else has that much power? The final years of someone's life in your hands, them no match for you physically, nor often mentally, with no witnesses to see what you choose to do with the upper hand.

She denies stealing from the old man. No doubt she was poorly paid; we don't value support workers and nurses nearly enough. Perhaps she thought she was entitled to a little something extra after he died. But to leave his body rotting, putrid and alone in his recliner for weeks on end? You have to wonder how much respect and care she had for him when he was alive. And I can tell she's lying, I can always tell when they're lying. Interpreters say the words and mimic the client's emotions too and I can feel whether or not they're sincere. I listen to the Hungarian client again. There's no strength to what she's saying; her words are weak and flavorless. Fear and guilt push through human faces easily. It takes a skilled liar to keep them back.

"The invoicing was a mistake," she says. "It was automated. It shouldn't have happened. They should have been turned off in the system. There was confusion with my boss." I repeat it into English. She claims to have not known that the elderly man was dead. He had stopped being her patient months ago. She assumed his family had hired another nurse through an alternative agency. She doesn't say any of this with conviction, and it's clear to me the detectives don't believe her, either.

In Hungarian the word for "friend" and "boyfriend" are the same; you need the context of the sentence to tell you which the speaker means. She explains to the detectives that her "friend" runs the private care business where she works and she lives with her "boyfriend" in the house where some of the stolen goods were found. It's my turn to say it in English. All that's needed is to switch them up a couple of times. First I repeat the facts correctly, tell the detectives that her friend runs the business and she lives with her boyfriend. Now I could flip it around. It would appear as though she is changing her story; she'd grow frustrated and angry, which would only make her situation worse. I bet she'd start saying "no comment." It would be all too predictable and she may as well confess.

Could I get away with it? It would be just. The woman would deserve it, for what she did to that poor man and his family. If she isn't punished, who is to say that she won't do something like this again? I think through what I know of the procedure. When a suspect interview concludes, the tape is sent straight to the police clerk who listens and types up a transcription. The clerk records the interpreter's English translation, this transcription becomes the exhibit in court and no one should have reason to listen to the tape again. Even if they did, my deliberate mistake would be easy to miss as, technically in Hungarian, I didn't misinterpret so much as a single word. But I might be asked to appear in court and confirm the accuracy of my translation. That would mean committing contempt of court. If I was discovered, a possible jail sentence. I would almost certainly lose Elliot.

I don't switch the "boyfriend" and "friend." I don't change any of her words. When there is confusion, I explain the cultural difference to the police officers and ensure they understand exactly what this woman is trying to tell them. From the corner of my eye I look at the client and realize she's older than I first thought, the delicate skin around her eyes vulnerable to wrinkles. Now I can see real fear behind her bravado. In this room, I'm her home care nurse. I think she did what the police are alleging, but that's for them to work out. My job is to help her defend herself if that's what she wants to do. This woman understands exactly the imbalance between us—that's why she didn't want to use an interpreter in the first place. I will not abuse my power. I'm better than her, I tell myself, although I'm not sure I entirely believe it. I probably would have gotten away with changing her statement, but that isn't who I want to be.

After the interview concludes: "A bit colorful was it?" the police officer asks as he signs my timesheet. "Those swear words she was saying to you in there?"

"I'll live." I like to think all the swearing was because that woman is angry with herself, an expression of her inner guilt. In Russian there's no single word that describes guilt as a feeling. In English and other languages "guilt" is a verdict in court, a legal fact, but it's also a sensation, a human emotion. There's an Inuit tribe whose language has no specific word for "forgiveness." When some religious missionaries arrived they insisted the tribe needed a way to point to forgiveness so they worked with the Inuit people to invent a word in their language. What they came up with roughly translates as: *not being able to think about it anymore.* I think that's just brilliant. A word that tells you to turn off the tap of endless thoughts before it's too late. Before the nagging drip wears you down like a river gradually carving away at a stone.

I leave the East London police station and head back home. I carry my handbag close to my body. Inside: Elliot's court letter. On the train, I take it out and read the words again, returning it to my bag when I suspect another passenger is following along over my shoulder.

A text from Richard reminds me to send him a photo of Elliot. Immediately I write back, asking him to first send me one of my mother. The last picture he took, but before all the illness and weight loss, so I can show my son where I came from.

"Well, this is the first time I've seen inside one of these houses, that's for sure," says the woman entering my hall. I carry my sister's bag into the reception room and release it to the floor—it is not fit to come into contact with any of my furniture. "Nice," the probation officer says, running a finger over the wallpaper. "Very nice."

"Thank you, officer. I'll get her settled in and will ensure she reports to you the day after tomorrow," I say, my rehearsed line.

"You don't have to talk about me as though I'm not here!" my sister says, reacquainting herself with the fruit bowl. Again I think of cyanide. Alan Turing's painful death after taking a bite of his poison apple.

"Call me any time," the officer says, taking one last peer around my front room before she leaves.

My sister drops a half-eaten plum to the coffee table and I can feel her sticky fingers contaminate the back of my shirt.

"Are you happy I'm home?" she asks.

"I'm going to have a meal delivered. From an Italian restaurant around the corner. Tell me if you would like something and I'll add it to my order." Italian food which should be enjoyed with wine but now that my sister is here, alcohol is forbidden. My eyes drift upstairs toward my en suite bathroom where my pills, even the acetaminophen, are now under lock and key. Downstairs, the wine cellar is secured and I even had the maid remove her alcohol-based cleaning products.

"I just wanna crash," my sister says, and spills onto an antique chair. Her sweat is staining it already.

"You're tired?" I try to summon concern. "Then I'll show you to your room. I had the maid clean it this morning."

"Even though I was getting out, the wardens made me work right up until yesterday. Painting the new wing of the prison. Up and down, up and down." She demonstrates flicking a paintbrush in vertical strokes. "I can hardly lift my arm now."

"Come on." I head up the stairs and indicate for her to follow. "Get your bag. I'll come back up later and bring you some provisions on a tray." She trudges behind me, not bothering to remove her shoes, or even wipe them on the mat. I swallow a ball of hot loathing.

As we take the last of the stairs, I silently count to ten. I'll give her ten more seconds to mention him, to make reference to his existence. Nine. Nine and a half. Ten. She says nothing. She can't say I never gave her a chance.

I lead her down the hall, slowing my pace as we approach his bedroom. The door is wide open. One tilt of her head to the left and she will see inside, observe that it is untouched. Still she says nothing. Inside her bedroom I pause, and wait for her thoughts to gather. Now she will say something; she must. "Actually I am a bit hungry, hey," she laughs. I turn away from her as my face splinters.

I prepare a tray with three kinds of fruit juice, coffee, crackers, two types of cheese, and her favorite chips. I rest it on the kitchen worktop for a moment while I go into the ground-floor bathroom. "She is my sister and I love her," I say, eyeing myself in the mirror. I prick my finger against the tip of the nail scissors until a red dot forms on the skin. I say it again.

13.

Everything good for today?

I reply to Lydia's text as the kettle boils: *Yes, I'm feeling positive, I'll see you there.* Green tea warms my throat. "Elliot, school," I say from the kitchen. "We have to leave in ten minutes!" I've convinced myself that Elliot's birth mother opposing the adoption order is a good thing. Without the appeal, I would never have been called as a witness and wouldn't have the opportunity to make my case to the judge, to tell him or her in my own words how much Elliot means to me. Today's the day.

I drop Elliot at Breakfast Club and make my way to the station. I'm wearing my usual attire of black trousers and a plain collared shirt but as I board the train, I chastise myself for not selecting something else this morning, something which I would otherwise not wear to court. Today is the first time I'm appearing inside a courtroom not as an interpreter, but as me. Lydia is still confident things will go our way. We will wait a few weeks for notice of the final hearing, essentially a formality where the judge should sign the adoption order and Elliot will be legally, permanently mine.

Once I get to Paddington, the train to Swindon takes an hour. I purposefully have not prepared my answers for the judge. At every stage of this process I presented as exactly what the adoption agency was looking for. I molded my responses to the shape of what it was the social workers wanted to hear. Benevolent deceit. I was who they wanted me to be. But no more—today I'm going to court as the real me.

At Swindon I'm glad to depart the stifling train where the crisp

October air hits me and corrects my temperature. The family court is a ten-minute walk from the station and now I start to feel my nerves switch on. What if I say something wrong that cannot be reeled back in? I'm assuming that by not pre-preparing my answers, I'll show the judge my genuine feelings toward keeping Elliot, unpolished but compelling. But what if I instead come across as nonchalant? His previous foster parents might say something that supports the case of him returning to his birth parents. The judge could simply be that way inclined and maybe he or she will be right, that the best thing *is* for Elliot to return to his real family, and not be with me.

I reach the court building and look for the coffee shop where I'm due to meet Lydia. I pass a Primark and a medical center but can't see any café. I check my phone to see if she mentioned further details and see there are four missed calls, all from Lydia. She's left voicemails too, the first over half an hour ago. I must have lost reception on the train.

She picks up on the second ring. "Revelle. Finally. Where have you been?"

"I'm here. Am I looking for a Costa or a Starbucks—I can't see where you mean?"

"You're an hour late," she says. A statement of fact with anger underneath. "I'm standing right out front of the court—where are you?"

"I'm *late*?" I'm early, if anything. "I thought we said—"

She cuts me off. "Where are you?"

"I'm here. I'm standing by the sign, 'Gordon Gardens'—you can't miss me."

"*Gordon Gardens*?"

"The white street sign, yes."

"I don't know where you are, Revelle, but you were supposed to be here an hour ago. Use your phone's GPS, for heaven's sake.

Regent's Park Road, it's right by Finchley Central, I don't see how you can miss it."

Regent's Park Road.

"Revelle? Hello? Are you there? HELLO?" I can't answer because now there is an alarm going off in my head, drowning everything out. Regent's Park Road is in London. Finchley Central is in London.

"I don't understand." I must have misheard her. It's going to be all right. "I'm at Swindon family court. That's where the second letter said to go."

Lydia has moved the phone away from her mouth. I can hear her talking to someone else, her voice a puny squeak.

The road seems to shimmer in front of me and I know what to do. I'm not going to panic. I start running and get back to the station in four minutes.

"There's a train to Paddington every fifteen minutes," I tell Lydia as I climb the platform stairs, two at a time. "It will take me ninety minutes to get to Finchley, at the most."

"Revelle, it will—"

"The next train is in two minutes!" I'm breathing hard. "An hour to Paddington then I'll change to the subway and—"

"It'll be too late. They're wrapping up. Court is booked back-to-back, they can't just wait for you. Why are you in Swindon?"

"The first notice from the court said Barnet was the location but the second said—"

"There was no second court notice!"

"I received it last week—a couple of days after the letter about the appeal. It said our case had been moved to Swindon because of the backlog. I read it in the news—some courts still have a two-year backlog from the pandemic, so they're moving a lot of cases out of London and—"

"I don't know what you're talking about, Revelle, there was no second letter from the court."

"I received it. Someone must have made an error. They mixed up our case with another."

"Look. I need to be on my way to visit a family. I'll call you on Monday."

"Wait, Lydia, please. Ask the judge to—"

"The judge was furious enough when he thought you were running late, I'm not going to tell him you went to the wrong court and you're still ninety minutes away." She cuts me off again. "On Monday, we'll have a frank discussion."

"What happens now? I can't wait until then."

"I'm flagging a cab, I need to go."

She hangs up and I slump to the concrete. How could this happen? I didn't bring the court letters with me because there was no need, but I can picture them both and they are almost identical. The first was about the appeal with details of Barnet family court and the second noting the change of venue and the revised start time. Lydia is confused, something has gone wrong; she needs to clarify with the judge so that they know this isn't my fault. I try ringing again but she doesn't pick up. Is this another black mark against me? What judge is going to remove a child from his family and place him with a woman who cannot even manage to turn up to court? On the platform I stagger to a bench. The train to Paddington arrives and I drag myself on.

I lose reception. I change carriages, running up and down the aisle, my eyes on the phone screen, searching for a bar of signal. I write Lydia three lengthy text messages and eventually they send before the signal cuts out again. As we approach London, normal service resumes and I try calling her but now there's not even a ring—she's immediately rejecting the call.

At home, I race inside to my desk, heading straight for my court documents folder. The second notice, the most recent one I received; I left it on top. I know I did. I'm not imagining it. The letter about Swindon family court arrived and I left it with all of the other paperwork I've accumulated since I applied to adopt. And now the whole folder is empty.

For the next hour I scour my flat and I am certain that nothing else has been taken; there is not so much as a missing teaspoon. Someone was in here. The drug dealer came back. Not for drugs—he's a relative, he has to be, from Elliot's birth family. His mother appealed. She was granted leave to oppose. She's cleverer than Lydia thinks she is. She wants Elliot back and is going to sabotage me.

It's only half past one—far too early for me to collect Elliot from school. Should I call the police? Apart from the missing paperwork, there's nothing to report; the windows aren't broken and the door locks are intact—I don't even know how someone could have possibly got inside. They won't take me seriously, and if I file a police report, it will only get back to Lydia and make the situation worse.

I retrace my steps that day. Checking the mail, opening the envelope. The font was the same, the layout—everything about the court notice seemed genuine. Did his birth mother or another relative fabricate the letter, have me sent to Swindon and then arrange for the contents of my folder to be stolen to remove the evidence? How else could this have happened?

Once more I check our windows and examine the two locks on our front door. They haven't been tampered with. It's possible copies of my keys exist—but the estate agent isn't going to hand them out to anyone who asks. If someone has access to our flat—are we even safe here? Is Elliot in danger being with me?

They say mother birds and squirrels abandon their young if they can smell that they've been handled and cared for by a human, but it's a myth. The mother animal happily takes her baby back to her nest. And that's what worries me the most. My thumbs grind into my eyes. If Elliot is returned to his birth family, what kind of situation is he going back to?

I pick up my phone to call Lydia. No. I stop myself, drop the phone on the coffee table and step away. I need to be very careful about what I say to her. I cannot appear unstable; I need her on my side. The sofa suddenly looks very inviting. I sit down and observe the room, the hall, the open kitchen—everything is completely normal—and I seem to snap out of it. I *am* unstable. My behavior is completely irrational. No one broke into our flat, magically, without leaving a trace, stealing nothing except for that one stack of papers. I read the wrong court address. I probably saw Swindon court attached to an interpreting job and got the two confused. I haven't been sleeping well. The stress and anticipation about the adoption has gotten to me. I've done other absent-minded things this past week, like finding the washing powder in the fridge after spending an hour looking for it, and accidentally returning Elliot's tub of ice cream to the cupboard instead of the freezer, only noticing when the chocolate liquid started to drip down the wall. We're safe here. I need Lydia to lobby that family court judge, and she won't do that if I keep pestering her. I put a cushion over my phone and vow not to touch it.

It is a long wait until I can collect Elliot from school. I am desperate to see him. He knows today I was doing something related to his adoption and I can only hope that in the excitement of after school, he forgets to ask me how it went. I cannot contact Lydia, but I want to know what happens now. What are the odds of the judge ruling in my favor? Surely this kind of thing has happened before—people make mistakes and arrive late at court for all sorts of reasons. Some people would have a car accident on their way and not turn up at all. I need to know that I still have a chance.

Doreen would know. She'd be able to advise me. But she could also shut down the whole thing. I remind myself that I cannot contact her now.

When I met Doreen, I'd been working as an interpreter for

about three months. Exia Translation and Interpreting Services called me very early in the morning with an address in West London, the location for a supervised contact session with the local authority. According to my online search:

Gives the opportunity for birth parents to interact with their child where the child is in the care system. Social workers observe and write a contact report for the local authority, the family court and solicitors (where applicable).

The job was to sit next to the social worker and repeat all of the interactions that passed between the German-speaking mother and child. The little boy was currently in the care of foster parents; the local authority was considering returning him to his mother pending this contact report. I felt comfortable by then doing police and court work, but this was the first time I had an assignment involving a child. I had the jitters as my feet climbed the stairs. At the top was a squalid little room. Soiled carpet, broken ceiling lights. Mold clung to the air. A glamorous introduction to the world of interpreting for a local authority.

"You must be the interpreter." A fifty-something woman appeared in the door frame, hand outstretched for me to shake. "I'm Doreen. I'm sorry I haven't had a chance to call you—the session's been delayed by an hour. Can you still do it?"

"Sure. This is my only job today," I said.

"Good, great. We're always short of interpreters. I don't know who I'd get to replace you. No one in the office speaks German. Come on, let's go across the road and kill time in the café. The least I can do is buy you coffee."

I followed Doreen out of the building and into the café where she chose the table closest to the window. "I'm sorry again, for wasting your time. Add this hour onto your timesheet, won't you. So you get paid for it," she said. I was still nervous about the job and let Doreen do most of the talking. "It's just so *fascinating*—interpreting. It's one of those professions that I think is extremely difficult but made to look easy. Like professional athletes. You watch the Olympics and think that anyone can throw a javelin. But that's the magic of it. That's when you know someone is really good." She used her teaspoon to carve a poppyseed muffin in two. "I never had any contact with social workers myself growing up, but my parents both had alcohol problems. I wasn't abused or anything but their money went on booze and there was often not much food in the house, and I went to school in the wrong uniform. You know, the usual stuff." Doreen chewed her way through the smaller of the muffin halves and gestured for me to eat the other.

"When I was about twenty, I was working at a hairdresser's and thinking about retraining to get into social work. One of the shop's clients was a lady who was a retired social worker, so one day I asked her to tell me about the job. She told me that what stuck most with her—by then she'd been retired for over ten years; when she reflected on her career she didn't remember the poverty she'd witnessed or the child neglect—what she thought of most was this inescapable human thing, that no matter what a parent does to a child, even if their mum is Rosemary West, their kids will always love them, and want to be with them. Her last ever case before she retired summed this up perfectly. She went to this woman's house to remove her little girl and literally had to peel this bruise-covered child from the mother. Even as the woman was dropping her cigarette ash on her head, screaming for the kid to get off her, that she was happy to be rid of her, that she never wanted her in the first place—the child clung on," Doreen said, sipping the last dregs of her coffee. "I don't know what it was about that story, but I signed up for the social work course the very next day. I thought *I'd* had a rough childhood, but this job has shown me some perspective. How'd you get into interpreting? Where'd you grow up?"

Doreen was genuinely interested in hearing the answers. She kept asking me more and more questions about my life. I had hardly touched the pot of tea in front of me, afraid of scalding my mouth right before this important interpreting job.

"I was born here in London. But grew up everywhere. My mother is an academic who used to work mostly one- or two-year contracts. So we moved countries almost annually."

"That's how you got into interpreting—you knew all the languages. Children pick them up so quickly, don't they? That's why it's too late for me and Japanese." She laughed. "What language did you speak at home?"

"English. My mother doesn't speak any other language, not really. She was never interested." My lips pursed as I thought about her in Singapore and tried to remember how many weeks it had been since our last phone call. Then my mouth opened and said the words I'd never said aloud before: "She was never interested in learning a second language, or in me. I was a career impediment."

Doreen nodded, and brushed the muffin crumbs into a neat pile.

"Most people I encounter in this job think about children as babies, toddlers, maybe teenagers at the most. And when people say they want, or don't want, a child, those are usually the years they're thinking about. When they're crawling around under your feet, when you're watching their under-eights football team, taking them to ballet lessons. But the truth is, your child is only *a child* for a relatively short time. They're still your kid when they're thirty, when they're forty-five. And those are the years people should think about when they decide whether or not they want a child. Forget the nappy stuff, the school years—sure, that's when they need you in a practical sense. But think about all of the long decades when you're both adults and you're equals. Those can be the really good years. Because when it's good, your child is the best friend you've ever had."

I poured a splash of tea into my cup and spilled most of it. Doreen sopped it up with a wad of napkins without missing a beat.

"Your mother might have struggled when you were younger, especially if she was single, but there's still time is what I'm saying. How old is she?"

"She's fifty-three."

"See. Same age as me. You've got probably thirty more years together! Now are the best mother-daughter years. This is the time when you'll appreciate each other," she said. "You may not have felt wanted when you were nine, but you're wanted now, let me tell you. Even if your mum can't put that into words."

. I've replayed this conversation in my mind so many times in the intervening years. After everything that happened and I decided to do something positive with my life, as a kind of penance, I remembered Doreen's words about parenting. I wouldn't only adopt a child to atone. I'd also be doing it for me. Because when I pictured my life in the coming decades, unless I took action, I realized it was going to be more of the same. What would have the greatest impact would not be a close work colleague who'd eventually fade away, or a partner who'd one day leave me, or be pushed; but a best friend. That's what would change my life. Why couldn't that be a good reason for wanting a child?

"Holy cow, it's ten fifty-nine!" Doreen said. She threw a tenner onto the table and we ran from the café, back across the road to the council building, laughing as her shoe caught the edge of a pothole and she had to limp the final stretch. We made it in time. That part went to plan. But I can't think about what happened next.

14.

Elliot and I finish his homework by five o'clock so that it's off our minds for the weekend. Then he starts on a puzzle, a one-hundred-piece jigsaw with pictures of shark species. Would he like me to sit next to him and help? Nope. Please get out of my way. He is slightly cold toward me this evening, and I have this crazy thought that he somehow knows what happened this morning. I messed up the court appearance and potentially the course of his entire life. No wonder he is angry with me.

Elliot is more quiet than normal over dinner and I am conscious of trying too hard to engage him.

"Did anything good happen at school today?" I ask, moving the chicken around my plate.

"I learned a joke."

"Oh yeah? I'd like to hear it."

"Why did the restroom paper roll down the hill?"

"I have no idea."

"To get to the bottom."

We both erupt with laughter. I laugh so much that a single tear snakes its way down my cheek. I've laughed more in these last months with Elliot than in the rest of my life put together. Having him has been like trying a sport for the first time or a new gym class and your muscles come alive; they were there all along, you just weren't using them.

"Fancy some ice cream?" I ask. "I remembered to put it in the freezer this time."

"Yes, please." Now he's giggling at the memory of his chocolate ice cream melting in the cupboard.

After dinner, the phone buzzes and I pounce on the first ring.

"Lydia?" I say hopefully, even though her name did not display on the screen.

"Revelle Lee?"

"Yes?"

"I'm calling from Exia. Met Police need a Polish terp in central London. Now."

"I'll pass," the words like bitter medicine. I don't want to speak to anyone but Lydia. "Thank you anyway."

Half an hour later, he calls back.

"It's a quick job but we need someone reliable with a good reputation for this one."

"I can't tonight. I'm looking after a child." Who is not necessarily mine. "I won't be able to find a babysitter this late." I'd better get used to thinking of Elliot as someone else's son.

"Bring them with you. This time of day, the police station will be pretty empty. Leave the kid in the office. It's an alibi interview. Quick statement and you're out of there."

"You said Polish? Then you must have someone else who can do it."

"You're the fifth interpreter I've called," his voice firm. "They only have eight hours left to hold the suspect. We need someone there *now*."

"I'm sorry. I can't do it."

"We'll pay two hours minimum even if you're done in half an hour. Plus travel time, okay?"

"Tempting. But I can't."

He sighs. "Have you seen the news? Do you remember that woman killed in the posh Knightsbridge house three weeks ago? The maid?"

Sandra. I swallow hard. "I think I heard something about that."

"Do I have to beg? Take the damn job."

Could he really be calling me about Sandra? What other murdered Knightsbridge maid would it be? Police have someone in custody. Finally, a person who they believe responsible. A member of the public identified the homeless man on the CCTV I suppose, and they found him. I should declare that I knew her. Ethics dictates that I tell this man I knew the victim and he'll find another interpreter. I realize it's urgent and he just wants to find someone, but he needs to know; I should not be assigned to this job. I look across to Elliot on the other side of the dining table, dinner plate pushed away, his drawing paper and pencils spread out on the placemat. One day, when he's older, if I do get to keep him, I'll tell him the truth about what happened to Sandra. I'd like to tell him that I did everything I could to help catch her killer.

"I'll do it."

At the police station I apologize for bringing Elliot and set him up in the open-plan office with his drawing, supervised by a constable typing with two index fingers. Elliot unwinds the scarf from around his neck and pulls off his red jumper. "I'm too hot!" he says dramatically, making the constable smile. I overloaded him with clothes because there's a mild chill in the air and I often find police stations to be drafty.

"Put it back on if it gets cold, okay?" I say. I think back to the day at the Old Bailey when we met Sandra. Here I am, once again leaving Elliot in order to complete a job. This can't become the norm. If I do get to keep him, I refuse to have his childhood memories consist of strange locations and unfamiliar people, entertaining himself while he waits around for me, feeling like a problem to be solved. I know that feeling, and I don't want it for him.

I walk down the corridor toward the police interview rooms. A thought grows that it isn't too late for me to refuse to do this job. I can change my mind and take Elliot home. The best excuse would be to tell one of the detectives that I knew the victim. Ethically, that's exactly what I should do. But alibi interviews need to be conducted without delay and the agency had trouble sourcing another Polish interpreter at this time of day. If I walk out now, it could affect the police investigation. I have to stay. I'll be fine, I reassure myself. I want to help Sandra and I'll do it by getting the words exactly right. I'm neutral. It doesn't matter that I knew her. I'm the best interpreter for the job and that's what Sandra deserves.

"You're the interpreter?" A man appears at my side.

"Yes."

"I'm one of the detectives. Let's go." He walks me the rest of the way to the interview room. "Bloke arrived in the UK a few months ago. Very limited English. He's been named as an alibi for someone in custody."

"He's Polish?"

"That much we got." He stops dead in the corridor and I pause alongside him, leaning against the wall.

"Oh and he's homeless. They both are." Homeless. It's him. I try not to react. Someone did identify the person on the CCTV, the man with the bag who the Knightsbridge neighbors saw, the shadow who crept past Sandra's open door. "I suppose you know procedure—interpret the interview, take notes. We'll do a written statement and send you both on your way."

"Only a written statement?"

"Yes, in Polish then in English. He's not a significant witness so there's no video or audio recording."

"Okay."

"The bloke came of his own volition so don't worry, he won't be aggressive or anything."

"Right."

"No solicitor, only the three of us," the detective says. "I'll keep it short." He resumes walking to the interview room and I follow.

Inside, the detective wants to place me beside him. Less common, but not unusual. The default position is for the interpreter to sit next to the client, close enough to whisper deep into their ear. The detective gestures again for me to take my seat. I sit, and look to the client on the other side of the table: two against one. Once, an investigating officer made me sit directly behind the client as if I was an audio-only service, a full-color shadow of the suspect, best tucked away out of sight. I've also been placed in front of the suspect like a mute puppet, supposed to hang open my wooden mouth and wait for speech from my master. I've heard of some interpreters being told to stand flat against the side wall during a police interview, part of the scaffolding of the room, not a person inside of it. They think we're so dispensable, sometimes treated like the work experience student, tolerated as a favor.

"Thank you for attending," the detective says to the man being interviewed. I say it in Polish for the client. "Can you tell me your name please?"

"Mariusz Dorobek," he says. And now this feels real and oddly unfamiliar, intimidating, as though I've never interpreted an alibi interview before and don't know what I'm doing. The client knows the person in custody for Sandra's murder. The stocky man with brown hair, the one dragging the bag? There are no pictures in front of the detective—apparently this isn't going to be one of those interviews where police slide photographic evidence across the table. "I told the police before, Adam didn't kill that woman. He's never seen her. I've never seen her." The client's words come out in a rush. I translate them into English.

"Okay, okay, hold up," the detective says. "Mariusz, can you tell me where you were on the evening of Saturday, September sixteenth?"

"Where I always am, in Knightsbridge."

"Where exactly?"

"Where exactly? The tunnel. The covered walkway on Brompton Road. That's our spot."

"Alone?"

"Alone? No. With Adam, I told you. He speaks Polish, his mother is Polish." I repeat the response into English for the detective.

"'Your spot,'" the detective says. "Do you mean that you live there?"

"Do I live there? Yes, I do. Adam too."

The client is repeating the detective's questions before answering them. Liars do this in order to stall, to give themselves extra time to formulate their story.

"For how long have you both lived there?"

"How long? Nearly three months for me, Adam joined about two months ago," the client says. "I came to the UK. To Luton first. A friend arranged a job for me on a construction site in West London. I was injured during my first week, bad luck. My employer says there's no insurance, doesn't pay me anything, so I lose my accommodation in Acton, West Acton, and there's no money for a plane ticket home, prices have gone up." I repeat his words into English. "I met Adam. He was in a similar position. And he speaks my language."

Now he's overexplaining, giving extraneous details, much more than what's required to answer the question. It's another symptom of lying.

"You're saying Adam Birch was with you on the evening of Saturday sixteenth of September?" the detective says. Adam Birch. The name rolls, silently, over my tongue. Adam Birch yet to be charged, but the man presently in custody for Sandra's murder. He could be an innocent homeless person who happened to be in the area. But his friend here is plainly lying about his alibi.

"Saturday sixteenth of September? Yes," replies the client. "From five o'clock."

The detective writes on his form. "Until what time were you with Adam Birch that night?" I repeat the question in Polish.

"Time? All night."

"Could he have left for a short time, half an hour?"

"Left? He didn't."

"Did you fall asleep at any point?"

"No, I didn't sleep."

"How can you be certain of that?"

"We sleep during the day. It's safer."

"To confirm: you were by Adam Birch's side from five o'clock that evening until when?"

"With Adam from five o'clock, yes, until the sun came up. About six o'clock," the client says. "Could be twelve, no, thirteen hours altogether, yes."

He's still overthinking and overexplaining: lying.

"Okay," the detective says, jotting on his form. Is that it? Will the detective conclude the interview now and accept this alibi, meaning the man in custody goes free? The Polish client is lying; he's clearly covering for his friend. I've seen it happen before. It mostly occurs between gang members—attempting to cover for each other, afraid of what will happen to them if they don't. But other communities too. Loyalty's free I suppose; even the homeless can afford it.

The detective drops his pen. He's going to send this man on his way and release his friend—Sandra's potential killer. I can't let him do that without probing the client further. He can ask more questions. He can push him, try to break the alibi. I don't think he's that skilled as a liar. If the detective challenges him, I imagine he could crack. But the detective is rubbing the stubble on his chin and he seems as though he's about to call this to an end. This time I won't sit here and do nothing.

I produce a scratching noise from my throat and force a cough. I cough again, making the sound more rough, now louder. The detective looks at me and I hold my hand to my throat as though I cannot speak. I stand up and leave the room, making a show of gasping for air as I do. The door shuts behind me. In the corridor, I carry on coughing loud enough for him to hear. It's not working. I'm about to give up when he flings open the door.

"Kitchen. This way," he says and I follow.

He hands me a glass of water. "Thank you." I take a few sips and begin to taper off my fake cough. "Sorry about that. I'll be okay to go back and continue in a moment."

He nods and refills my glass from the tap. "We're almost done in there, anyway."

No we aren't. "Do you think he's being honest?" I do my best to make it sound like a throwaway comment, something said to merely fill the silence.

The detective is startled by my question. He looks at me with curiosity. There is a long pause and I wonder if he is not going to answer, or if he'll reprimand me for even asking.

"You obviously have an opinion," he says. It's a statement, not a question. But here's my chance. I'll tell him what I think. I'm not meant to have any kind of influence, but he's the detective, it's his responsibility to ethically and professionally carry out this investigation. If I step over the line, it's his job to push me back.

"I've been doing this for eight years. It's a little like acting, right? Speaking for, becoming someone else, wearing their skin. A police interview's a performance. I inhabit them and I might only be in a room with them for an hour or two but when you're their interpreter, you can't help but feel that you really know them—you take apart their words, their thoughts, and you can see through them. And yes, I think my client today has been dishonest with you."

There is another pause and I brace against the kitchen sink for a telling-off.

"We have to go back inside," he says. He's going to do it, isn't he? Release the Polish-speaking client, let the other homeless man go. Sandra's killer is probably going free. And this officer might report me. Oh no. I've spoken out of turn and he would be within his rights to make a complaint about me. Metropolitan Police work makes up fifty percent of my income most weeks. A black mark against my name with Exia could affect me getting other bookings as well. I can't change his mind about the Polish witness, but I need to apologize and protect my livelihood. What was it the man from Exia said on the phone? *We need someone reliable with a good reputation for this one.* A reputation which for years I've done my best to earn, but still don't really deserve because what's already happened cannot be undone. No matter how good I am now.

"I shouldn't have spoken," I tell him. One complaint from a senior officer is all it would take for Exia to no longer regard me as the best they have. "I'm sorry. I've never done that before, I assure you. It's been a stressful day. I want you to know that I interpreted today accurately, to the best of my ability. It's unethical for me to have given you my opinion on the client and for that I'm sorry."

"Look." He's taking a step closer to me, lowering his voice. "I shouldn't tell you this but yes, I agree, the guy is probably lying. Or confused, mixed up, and accidentally covering for his friend. Because that friend—we have his DNA on the body of the deceased. All over it. He did it."

All of the air in my lungs escapes.

The detective stalks down the corridor to the interview room and I jog to catch up. Police finally have Sandra's killer in custody.

They have evidence and they know he's the one. I knew the client was lying. I replay his words:

Adam didn't kill that woman. He's never seen her. I've never seen her.

If they never met, how would his DNA be on her body at the time of her death?

My heart spins in my chest. I need to relax. This detective is just happy that he's got his man, so I don't think he'll submit a complaint about what I said. He agrees with me, and he doesn't seem worried that I overstepped.

When I sit back down at the interview table, I try to forget that I knew Sandra. I'm impartial. My job is to say the words; the context is not my concern. Focus on getting the words right, I tell myself, that's all I have to do. That's how I help Sandra. But then I think of the heiress's hit-and-run trial at the Old Bailey: acquitted. So many acquittals. Having this man arrested and in custody is not enough. The police knowing that he's guilty is not enough.

But I can't think about the trial. The outcome of that is not my business. All I need to do is translate the client's statement and then I can take Elliot home. Translate his lies about being with Adam Birch at the time of Sandra's murder.

We have his DNA on the body.

I will get the words right. I always do what's expected of me. I've said lies before, I'm certain of it. In court, in British citizenship interviews, medical consultations, in other police interviews—I've repeated my client's mistruths because that was my role. My job is to translate correctly, not to tell the truth. But maybe it should be. All of those cases I interpreted on where the suspect, the defendant, went free. How many of those could have had a different outcome if I had changed the client's statement from their lies to the truth? The liar isn't always the person I'm interpreting for—very often they're the innocent one. What's that woman doing right now in the nail bar? She couldn't tell me the truth about her situation because she was afraid; the real liar was her boss, her probable captor. Then there's the French drug dealer—is he out there on the streets at it again, because I didn't tell the officer about his previous cautions?

I don't make mistakes. I said it would never happen again and it hasn't. *Someone reliable with a good reputation.* I keep my promises because I am reliable. I have a reputation for being the best because that's what I am. But Sandra is not an abstract victim, another name on a legal document, or an anonymous face on the news. I knew her and she knew Elliot. She cared about him, and he liked her. If Elliot is going to be my son, how can I look him in the eye one day and say that Sandra was murdered without telling him the rest of the story? Will I explain that police caught the right man, they were certain of it, but I facilitated a false alibi and even though I knew this person was lying, I did nothing to stop him? I let it happen, Elliot, and Sandra's killer went free. A one-time babysitter from his past, he'll scarcely remember her, but he'll remember what I did. That she was an innocent person briefly in our lives and I stood back and watched.

"Sorry about that," the detective says to the client, meaning our delay in the kitchen. "I just have a couple more questions." I translate it into Polish. "So, all this time—from five o'clock in the evening until the sun came up, you're saying six o'clock in the morning, you were with Adam Birch in the place where you both currently live. And you didn't sleep during this time?"

"Did we sleep? No, I told you, it's safer to sleep during the day," the client says.

"So then what were you doing? During this approximately thirteen-hour window—what did you both do exactly?"

The detective will have asked Adam Birch this same question. He wants to hear it from the client before Birch is released and they have a chance to talk and get their stories straight.

"Adam was reading for a long time," the client says. I repeat it in English.

"What was he reading?"

"A book from the street, you know, one of those street libraries where people donate used books."

"Adam was reading but you weren't?"

"Those books are all in English and I don't read English good enough."

"So which book was Adam reading?"

"I don't know the English title."

"He didn't talk about it? Say what it was about?"

"Did he talk about it? No. I don't really know what it was about."

"You must have got a look at the cover?"

"It was big, a very thick book. Fantasy, I think. A dark cover with dragons. Something like that," the client says. Here are details the detective will be looking to match with Adam Birch's statement. If there are any discrepancies between the two accounts, when it goes to trial, Mariusz Dorobek will be seen as an unreliable witness.

"It was a small, thin book," I say in English. I look to the client for comprehension: he hasn't noticed what I've just said. "A thriller, I think. A man was on the cover." The detective takes notes. I brace myself for an outburst from the client. He could sense that something isn't right even if he doesn't fully understand my words. He's leaning on his elbows and cupping his head with both hands. He's stressed and worried; he's not paying attention to my English.

"What else did you do from five o'clock that evening until six o'clock in the morning?" the detective asks. I say it in Polish for the client.

"We ate some food from earlier in the day."

"What food did you eat?"

"Both of us had a sandwich. I had a banana sometime too."

"Both of us had a sausage," I say in English. If Adam Birch told police he ate a sandwich, in court the prosecution can use this to discredit the witness in the eyes of the jury. In preparation for the trial, the defense team will notice the discrepancies between the men's statements and will probably drop the alibi defense, and not even bother to call this witness. The Polish word for "banana" sounds too similar to the English. There's no way I can change that term without the client noticing. "I had a banana," I tell the detective.

"Okay, so I'm going to read out the notes I've made," the detective says. He pauses for me to translate into Polish for the client. "The interpreter is then going to write a statement for you in your language. You'll read it, sign it and she will then write up an English version and submit it to me."

I cough again, then pretend to struggle with the cap on the pen to buy myself a few extra seconds of thinking time. What else can I do to help ensure Adam Birch is convicted? I could change the times on the client's alibi statement. Though if I change the time when I write up the English version of the client's statement, someone bilingual could compare it to the true window of time on the Polish statement and clearly see that I got it wrong. The same with the details about Adam's book and what they ate. There'd be no reason for them to think the mistake was deliberate. Though, if police started interviewing some of Sandra's babysitting clients and my name came up, then I'd have serious questions to answer. I can't risk it. I'll have to make the errors in the Polish version of the statement. That way it's the fault of the witness: it appears as though *he* gave the wrong details and I merely translated *his* error. The client could try to correct them later, but it would be too late. As a witness, if you sign something that's incorrect, you're useless to the defense team, immediately unreliable in the eyes of the jury.

But how am I going to get the client to sign the statement with all of this wrong information? The skin on my right palm is twitching. I stretch out the fingers to disguise the beginnings of a tremble. Messy handwriting: that's how I'll do it. I'll make sure the first couple of sentences of the statement are difficult for him to read and hope he gives up.

I complete the statement in Polish as quickly as I can—I want to get this over with. When I reach the place to write the time, my hand is squeezing the pen too tight and it skids across the page. I write that he was with Adam Birch from six o'clock in the evening until four o'clock the next morning. It's only a small change but it's another discrepancy to cast doubt on the witness. It contradicts the time window he gave to the detective during the interview, and hopefully the time stated by Adam Birch. I spell out the numbers as words and pray the client doesn't notice.

I've done it. The air in here is heavy, moisture spreads at the back of my neck. After all these years, I've made a mistake again.

I pass the sheet of paper to the client and swallow the rock in my throat. They can't catch me, I tell myself, they won't take Elliot. I let the client try to read the first couple of lines. I need to get the paper out of his hands before he sees the time and details about the book and food. "I could read it back to you?" I say in Polish. "I know my handwriting is terrible. If that would make it easier?"

He looks at me from across the table. I need to swallow again but I'm too afraid to make even the slightest of movements.

"Please." He hands the paper back to me.

I begin to read. I hold the page up, tilted toward me, to make it more difficult for him to see. I'm speaking rapidly, *too* quickly, but I'm trying to outrun my panic and it's the only way to keep my voice steady. I read that he was with Adam Birch from five o'clock until approximately six o'clock the next morning. Mariusz Dorobek listens to my words and nods along. If he catches me now, sees what I've written, I'll feign embarrassment that I mixed up something as simple as the time. An entirely innocent mistake; all I'd have to do is laugh it off. Nothing criminal. I will deny, and I will not disintegrate. I reach the sentences about Adam's book and what the men ate and I say "fantasy" and "dragon" and "sandwich" in Polish—everything the client is expecting to hear.

I read the last line of the statement and place the page on the table. The detective pushes it closer to Mariusz Dorobek and passes him a pen. The second it takes him to uncap the pen feels like an hour. After he signs, the detective will let him go. I'll stay behind, study the Polish statement and write up the English version.

The client curls his hand around the pen.

I should not have told the detective that I think this man is a liar. I regret showing that bias because if they do catch my mistakes, I've freely given him my motive.

The hovering pen lowers.

He signs.

Outside the interview room, I float down the corridor. My neck straight, limbs effortless and light. Elliot is there, still seated beside the same two-fingered typist, his nose practically level with his drawing. "Sorry, Batman," I say. "I'm done now. Let's go home."

I rub his shoulder, smooth his hair. He says goodbye to the police officer and we exit the building.

"What did you do in there?" he asks.

"Batman stuff."

His eyes go wide. "*You* caught the criminals?"

"That's right. I did."

15.

On Monday morning I do not check the Exia app for available assignments. Today, I can't bear to do any in-person jobs. After last Friday, I don't want to go near a police station for a while; it feels like returning to the scene of the crime. I helped Sandra. It was the moral thing to do, the just course of action, but I said I'd never change a word again and eight years later, here I am. It's good that I feel guilty. It means my promise to myself was sincere, and I really did believe that I would go the rest of my career without another error. I made the right choice last week, but I still have to live with the consequences.

Elliot and I kept to ourselves all weekend. Yesterday we went to the cinema during a quiet session and on Saturday checked out an exhibition at the British Library first thing in the morning. I avoided the headlines. I did not look at any news websites. I don't want to think about Sandra's murder and Adam Birch while I'm waiting to hear from the family court. Today I can't afford to not work at all so instead of in-person interpreting, I connect to the telephone interpreting service and work from home. Lydia could call at any moment regarding the judge's decision. I don't want to be in the middle of interpreting a court hearing when the phone vibrates with news that Elliot will be taken from me.

The first client on LanguageLine is a Spanish-speaking man trying to book an NHS appointment for his father in palliative care, then a Portuguese woman calls to negotiate with her insurance company about her house which has just burnt down. Comic relief comes from a Hindi-speaking tourist who has wandered into a York police station for, as it turns out, directions to the cathedral, not to report a crime. As I translate for these clients, I keep my eyes on my cell phone on the coffee table. Between jobs, I unlock the screen to double check that I've not somehow missed Lydia's call even though the volume is set to ear-piercing maximum.

There is a five-minute break between calls and this has become completely intolerable—how can Lydia expect me to carry on with life without an answer? I've been waiting all weekend. But the phone ringing is not necessarily what I want today, I realize. It could be Lydia or it could be the police questioning me after last week. By now one of the detectives may have compared the witness's statement with that of Adam Birch, and noticed the discrepancies. The interview went smoothly, I interpreted at speed, not once did I ask the client to repeat himself and nor did I stumble. He agreed that the client was probably lying so logically he'll assume the errors are simply the witness tripping himself up. Won't he? Don't they say all liars eventually lose track of their story? But detectives might re-interview the witness. If Mariusz Dorobek sits down with a new interpreter and the alibi statement I recorded, he'll see the errors, remember that I offered to read it to him so that he wouldn't need to check it before signing, and he might put two and two together. I perverted the course of justice. And if I am caught, technically that charge carries a maximum sentence of life in prison. I'm afraid to check the news. I don't want to know what happened after the alibi interview.

When the phone sounds, I flinch so violently it feels as though the top of my head might hit the roof. I answer. It isn't my cell, it's LanguageLine. Someone else needs my help.

It is time to collect Elliot from school and Lydia hasn't called. There remain a couple of hours left of the workday; hope she'll be in touch this afternoon. I never imagined I'd receive the adoption decision in front of Elliot. What if I answer the phone and he's standing right there and it is bad news? I won't let him see me react. He's the one

143

with the emotional needs and I'm the steady parent, even if they are taking him away. We should go out this afternoon and keep busy. Online, I find an after-school art class for children aged four to six and we go there straight from school.

In the Tate Modern's Turbine Hall you will always find people lying on the sloped floor, bodies starfished as if relaxing on a concrete beach. The current exhibition is by a Danish artist, titled Truth Serum. Is it self-centered to wonder if this exhibition is here today specifically to hit my exposed nerve? An oversized hosepipe and garden sprinkler reach up to the roof. As their metal parts spin, a fine mist is dispensed, falling over a group of teenagers dancing on the artificial grass. On our way to the stairs, Elliot crouches to brush his fingers across the wet green plastic. In the gallery's education space, he leans over the paint-splattered table and copies the facilitator as she demonstrates to the children how to fold origami fish. Parents line the room, all eyes on their cell phones. I look at each mum or dad and imagine what it is they're doing on their phones. Instagram. Work emails for her. This one's playing a game but pretending he's reading something very serious. None of them are waiting to hear if their child is about to be taken away, or bracing for a phone call to say they could be off to prison.

Ten minutes before the end of the art class, my phone rings. I leap outside into the corridor and watch Elliot through the glass.

"Revelle. Afternoon." It's Lydia. "So, look. The judge was quite furious with you on Friday. I don't know what happened. You say you received some kind of a second court notice about a change of location."

"Yes, *yes*, I told you, I . . ." I stop speaking when I remember that I am no longer in possession of the letter. If I labor the point again, Lydia may ask to see it, and then where will I be?

"Given that usually the adoptive parents *aren't* required to attend the hearing, the judge decided to proceed with the adoption order."

"Proceed. To what?"

"That's it, Revelle, it's done. He's yours."

Invisible fists pummel against my chest. "But they appealed?"

"They failed," Lydia says. "Birth families hardly ever win. It's cruel to give them the hope, I suppose. Adoption is a last resort, so for a case to have got that far, there's almost always more than enough evidence to show the child should not be with the birth family."

"So . . ."

"That's it. Look out for paperwork in the mail. Contact the family court if you're having trouble with that. You're done. No more visits from me."

We speak for another five minutes but I am in a dreamlike state, not really taking her in. It's done. Elliot is irrevocably my son. Lydia and social services and the family court are out of our life forever.

I hang up and walk slowly back into the art room and place my hand on Elliot's shoulder, hesitant, as though this might not be real and if I touch too firmly, he might break. Elliot is mine.

The class ends and we head to McDonald's—Elliot's choice. It is bursting with teenagers and young families. Men with concrete on their boots eat swiftly on stools by the window. Elliot's purple origami fish sits on our table between cheeseburgers and two strawberry thickshakes.

"So remember I told you that the court, the family court, was going to make a decision about where is best for you to live?" I ask.

"Yeah." He senses this is serious and has stopped shoving fries into his mouth.

"Well, the judge did decide that it's best if you stay with me, and you and I can be a family now, forever."

"What about Lydia?"

"Lydia agrees with the judge. She thinks you and I should be together too. She's finished helping us now, so that's it, we won't see her again."

"Okay." His cheeks hollow as he sucks on his straw.

"Does that sound good to you?"

"I think so." He wipes his mouth.

"Nothing is going to change, not really. You know I was your foster mum already, so it just means now I'm your forever mum. No more speaking with Lydia or any of those other adults. And you won't have to move schools all the time. That's it really, it's just you and me."

"Okay, that's good."

I study him for signs of longing for his birth parents, wishing it was one of them in this greasy booth instead of me. Don't do that, I tell myself, enjoy this moment—we made it! Elliot is playing with his origami fish and everything feels incredibly anticlimactic after all this time. But what did I expect? He's six. He's been in care, passed around between adults since he was four years old. Of course this doesn't mean to him what it does to me. I think he's happy. He'll be happy from now on, I'll make sure of it.

I ask a man in the next booth to take a photo of us. McDonald's isn't my ideal venue for this moment but the important thing is we're together.

"Thank you," I tell the stranger as he passes back my phone. I show Elliot the photo. "What do you think—should we get this printed and put it on our fridge?"

"I'll see it and want McDonald's all the time."

"I might have to photoshop out the fries. Swap them for apples or something—what do you think? Maybe broccoli?"

He makes a face and laughs. When he finishes eating, Elliot's attention goes to the street outside, to the man sitting on the ground by the entrance, his empty coffee cup asking for coins. Through the window I see the man's hair and coat are wet—he must have been caught in the storm earlier this afternoon.

"Doesn't that man have a home?" Elliot asks.

"No. I don't think he does right now."

"Why?"

"It could be lots of reasons. Something's gone wrong in his life recently and he may not have enough friends or family in London who can help him."

"Like me?"

"No, not like you. Why would you say that?"

Now he is shy and his chin is skimming the table. "I don't know," he says.

"Do you understand what I was saying before? That I've adopted you. I'm your mum. We're family. Nothing can change that now."

"Okay."

I lunge across the table and pull him into a hug. "You're never going to be homeless, okay? You don't have to worry." My face is hot and I can feel the back of my eyes sting with tears. I've got to keep it together. I look through my purse, crossing my fingers for something, anything.

"Ah, I have a fiver!" I hand it to Elliot. "Why don't you go outside and give this to the homeless man? Put it in his cup and come straight back."

Elliot jumps down from the booth and pushes his way to the exit. Through the window I watch him squash the note into the cup before he turns and runs away.

"Good job," I say, as he sits back down across from me. "What do you want to do now? Do you have room for apple pie or something else?"

"Yeah."

I thought so. Elliot wants to buy it himself so I give him my card and watch him stand in the line and approach the counter. As he gives our order, the girl behind the register looks over and I wave to say it's okay. Two policewomen stroll into the shop, chatting, and join the line. It feels like a slap; a warning not to relax. I could still be caught. I scramble for my phone—no new calls or messages. It's now outside of business hours, but the police could contact me at any time with questions. I told Elliot we'll always be each other's family, but if they catch me, it's possible I'd get a custodial sentence. And then what will happen to Elliot? Through the McDonald's window, my eyes stray to the homeless man and I think about the statistics I've read concerning children in the care system finding themselves in the justice system, how an unstable childhood so easily leads to a lifetime of chaos and uncertainty. I'm a single parent. Elliot only has me. I can't take any more risks. He comes back to the table with our desserts and we eat.

"You did very well there," I say. I am calculating how long it will take me to get his adoption certificate and then his passport, when we can flee to a country without UK extradition where, if they catch me, it doesn't matter because they cannot split us up. Is this the guilt showing itself? Yes, that's all it is. I made one mistake, now two. I was never caught for the first one, eight years ago. Why would I assume that I'd be found out this time? It will be okay, I tell myself. I can't let the remorse from all those years ago gnaw at me now.

Elliot is playing with his origami fish when I summon the nerve to search for "Adam Birch" on my phone.

Police have arrested a man for the murder of domestic worker Sandra Ramos. Adam Birch, of no fixed abode.

Arrested. The news story was published on Saturday. Not in for questioning, not held on suspicion. They got him.

"What?" Elliot says. I look up from the screen and see he is grinning close to my face.

"Nothing."

"You're smiling."

"I'm just happy. You're smiling too." I poke a finger into his ice cream and lick.

"Hey!"

I read through to the end of the news article. Police are alleging Adam Birch broke into the Knightsbridge home intending to rob the heiress when he encountered Sandra. They struggled and he pushed her down the stairs, killing her. This isn't the first time he's committed robbery and breaking and entering—he has a previous conviction recorded from over twenty years ago. A crime which also took place in the Knightsbridge area. I rest my phone on the table and let the news settle. I *knew* that Polish witness was lying. I wedge both hands under my knees to keep them under control; I suddenly have too much energy. When it goes to trial, Sandra's killer won't have an alibi, and unlike the heiress and countless other cases I've worked on, he will not be acquitted. No one will know that it is thanks to me.

Later at home, when Elliot has gone to bed, I watch the BBC News, and Channel 4, and ITV and Sky and every channel I can find because it isn't enough to see that Adam Birch was arrested on one news program, I want to see it on them all. His mug shot shows a man with brown hair, stocky and disheveled, just as he appeared on the CCTV. I am glad I found the courage in the police station. But I must not become smug and feel too pleased with myself because there is still Doreen.

Now that Elliot is mine, a thought plays that it's safe for me to contact her. She can't react badly and try to stop his adoption, and so really I have no excuse. I open my laptop and navigate to Facebook. The text is not in English. I refresh the page and it reloads as the same. It's in German. What is going on? I move the cursor to settings and change the language. I press enter and it's fixed. What was that? Why of all languages would it suddenly revert to German? I close the screen, and push the laptop away from me. The muscles in my neck have tensed and welded together. There must be an explanation. I rarely use Facebook, I remind myself. The algorithm would have little to go on and this has happened before; once everything displayed in Arabic and another time Bahasa Indonesia. It's just a bad coincidence, it means nothing. I find Doreen's profile and click on message. I begin to type.

Up close you weren't what I was expecting. Don't worry, you didn't disappoint me, it's simply impossible not to form a mental image of someone you've never met and this image never marries with the actual, does it? I knew the local authority was incompetent but a drug dealer comes to your home during a social worker visit? You miss a court appearance and they still let you adopt? I shouldn't be surprised. But I can't bear to see him with you. The sight of that beautiful boy in your home, in your company, makes my flesh ignite and feel as though I am about to combust.

Yesterday evening, through the window, I watched him play computer games. I was there when he ate dinner with you. And for those two hours, that was enough, just to be near him and breathe against the glass and know that he was okay. Of course I wanted to knock on the window. I was tempted to let him see me. Do you know how easy it would have been to have rung the bell and pushed my way inside and just taken him? I don't want to do it that way because I am not that sort of mother. But I'll step in if I need to. If I see you fail him in some way, I won't hesitate to do what's required to protect him.

Now here you are feeding him McDonald's. Sodium and trans-fats and carcinogenic preservatives. What these chemicals are doing to his growing body is unforgivable. I've been in this "restaurant" so long without ordering or eating that I'm starting to draw attention from the staff.

I step forward. "I'll have a Big Mac," I say at the counter. The young man asks a series of questions about meal deals and drinks, and I say "fine" to everything. Nothing is fine and soon you will be very far from fine. After paying, I steal one last look at you and him in the booth and take my leave. Outside, I dump the paper bag of food on the ground next to a beggar.

"Thank you!" the man croaks into my back.

I take a taxi to Kilburn Library. I'm doubtful social services are savvy enough to map IP addresses, but just in case, I will use one of the library's computers. Lydia, the social worker, lives a few streets from here. I open a web browser on the ancient council PC and navigate to the child protection website. I type a message as a concerned neighbor, ever so worried about the violence and neglect I've witnessed between the woman in number eleven and her two children. I reread my message and insert a few spelling and grammar errors before I press "send." Let's see how the social worker enjoys being investigated by her own colleagues.

But I won't waste too much time on Lydia. I have squandered more than enough time. There will be no more wishing and watching and fantasizing and imagining. The observation phase, this mild interference in your life, is over with, and now it is time for me to act.

16.

At Southwark Crown Court, the security guard drops my handbag into the tray. It's Arkam.

"Good morning," he says. "How have you been? How's your son?"

The last time I saw Arkam was that day at the Old Bailey when he let Elliot go off with Sandra, a stranger, to the bathroom. He's always so lovely, there's no use in being angry with him now.

"He's good, thank you. He's retired from attending court, though."

He laughs. "Glad to hear it."

"Have a nice day." Past the metal detector, I wait for my belongings to reach me. Arkam waves and ushers through the next person. Southwark Crown is all severe yellow brickwork with random narrow windows, inserted by the sunlight-hating architect only as a reluctant afterthought. After a day of remote telephone interpreting, I am itching to get into court.

Inside I locate the client and together we wait for him to be called. In the dock today is an obnoxious-looking English lad, on trial for sexual assault. His facial expression: ice-cool confidence. The client is a witness for the defense, new to the UK, an Uber driver who had the misfortune of driving the victim and the accused home on the night in question. He's a defense witness because he saw the pair kissing in his rearview mirror, which, as any misogynist knows, means anything that subsequently took place between the two must have been consensual.

The alleged victim gave pre-recorded evidence, as is now the prerogative of complainants in these types of cases. During cross-examination, the counsel addresses her as "madam" three times. A solicitor once told me that defense teams do this in rape and sexual assault cases to give the jury the impression the victim is worldly, strong, confident, womanly. Not a victim, not a girl, and never innocent. She is only nineteen.

"I swear by Almighty God that I will well and faithfully interpret and make true explanation of all such matters and things as shall be required of me according to the best of my skill and understanding," I say to the courtroom.

Today I'm speaking Hindi. I learned it in India as a teenager when my mother was a visiting scholar at a university in Mumbai. Richard. I need to tell him about Elliot. I wince at the thought of how slack I've been toward him. I vow to make time to speak to him properly and let him meet Elliot, even briefly on a video call.

"Please sit down, Madam Interpreter," the judge says.

Why did I have to be assigned to a sexual assault today? You'd think the universe could throw me a bone after Sandra's case, give me a reprieve from particularly awful cases for a while. A nice bit of money laundering would be okay, some harmless insider trading, or I'd happily take a government fraud situation; Southwark is a designated serious fraud center, after all. Anything but a nasty trial like this.

I watch the pre-recorded evidence with the victim and I cannot deny the overwhelming feeling that I believe her. Across the room I glance over at the prosecution team, and then at her. *Victim*: I hate that combination of letters, such a full stop of a word. I think the English lad is guilty. Now a day discussing insurance clauses and NHS bureaucracy on LanguageLine isn't looking so bad. Hopefully the counselors keep their questions brief. I can interpret for the Hindi witness efficiently and have enough time to go home before I collect Elliot from school.

The gravity of the situation has got to him and the client speaks fast. We speed through examination-in-chief. There is a lot of discussion about the backseat kissing.

Cross-examination. If a witness is going to crumble, this is where they usually do—under the mounting pressure of a skilled advocate poking holes in their story. The witness gives his first answer, speaking into the court microphone in his language. Does anyone here understand Hindi? I scan the faces of both legal teams and the public gallery for comprehension. It's a common language in London; someone here is bound to. But this is not typically something I think about when interpreting during a hearing or trial. Why does it matter to me today whether or not anyone else here knows what my client is saying? Dread pools in my gut. I know the reason. But I'm not going to acknowledge it because it is foolish; a fleeting, unreasonable idea that I dismiss and it passes right through me. The lad should go to jail. I know the odds are in his favor, I'm aware of the low conviction rate for sexual assault trials, but there's nothing I can do.

"The victim looked uncomfortable with the accused, didn't she?" the prosecution asks. I whisper my interpretation into the client's ear. I drop the equivalent of the English "un" to make the question, "The victim looked *comfortable*, didn't she?" There is a lag between my speech and my ears registering what it was I said. What did I just do? Without turning my head too far, I check the client's face for any signs of confusion. If he understood the barrister's question he would wonder why I contradicted him.

"Yes, I thought so," the client agrees and I repeat it into English for the room. I breathe out steadily through my mouth. He didn't understand what the counselor said. I see the defense barrister fidget—that wasn't the answer he was expecting, the answer the witness previously provided on his written statement. Why did I change that word? I wasn't immediately conscious that I was doing it. This cannot happen again. Sandra's case was different—that alibi statement was a one-off and that was calculated. I thought through the procedure and identified a way I could make some small changes without being detected. But now, that word has slipped out, as though I am not in control. And that's the part worrying me the most, because it means that it is not like the alibi statement, but closer to the other error, that first time. I adjust my posture, picture a rod in my back. I will concentrate. I stare at a brown smudge on the floor and block everything out except for the words, like a ballerina focusing on a spot on the wall as she spins and turns. I will not get dizzy. Words in, words out, all I have to do is repeat them. No mistakes will occur.

"Do you wear eyeglasses for driving? Spectacles?" The next question from the prosecution. I whisper it into the client's ear in Hindi.

"Yes." I repeat it into English for the room. My eyes dart from juror to juror. In a jury trial, the twelve members of the public listen to witnesses and defendants, analyze the contents of their statements, and, usually subconsciously, assess the speaker's body language. They're supposed to be looking at the witness, but when the witness is not speaking English, I become the object of their scrutiny. I need to present as professional and reliable, otherwise the jury will think poorly of my client. But I am appearing nervous right now, shifting in my seat, and my gaze is bouncing from one juror to the next. I must stop this. I'm potentially undermining the credibility of this witness and I realize that is exactly what I want. I had to help Sandra. I needed to change that alibi statement because I met her and she knew my son. What about this victim here today? She's a stranger, so therefore she's nothing to me? I'll accept my place in the justice machine and do nothing for her? I am Elliot's legal guardian and there's nothing Lydia or anyone can do about it now. If I change the witness's words and I'm discovered—what's likely to happen? Contempt of court would be difficult for anyone to prove as who is to say that my mistakes weren't genuine? What's the evidence for anything other than my incompetence? Other interpreters make translation errors all the time. They don't go to jail. I'd lose my work, but not Elliot. They could catch me but he'd still be mine.

The next question comes: "You didn't have your spectacles on that night, did you?" I whisper this into my witness's ear as, "You *did* have your spectacles on that night, didn't you?" No one else in the room can hear my Hindi. They will not know how I chose to interpret the question.

"That is correct," the client says. I check his face again for signs of having understood the English. His expression is neutral—he doesn't know what I'm doing, and he has no idea what he's confessed to.

"It was dark so you couldn't see properly what was going on in the back seat, could you?" I let this question go, say it correctly. Maybe I've done enough. Stop now, I tell myself, minimize the chance of getting caught; accuracy from now on.

"I could see well from the streetlights," the witness says. I rest my gaze on a woman on the jury: fifty-something, henna tattoos and chunky rings, a pen taking notes with her left hand. Which way is she planning to vote in the jury room? I sense that cross-examination is almost finished. I'll give a perfect translation for whatever comes next and everything will be fine. My teeth start to grind, signaling they won't obey, and when the next question comes, my vision blurs as I listen. The woman's henna tattoos seem to come to life and launch from her arm. I blink to regain my focus, and remind myself not to push this too far.

"What color was the victim's dress?"

I translate it for the witness as, "What color was *the accused's shirt*?"

"Blue," the client says. I say it in English.

"The victim's dress was pink," returns the barrister.

Someone's breath catches in the public gallery. That did it. I tell the client that the barrister just said the accused's shirt was pink. He looks confused but doesn't speak.

Even if the witness clarifies his answers during re-examination, the damage has been done. He was called by the defense to attest to the alleged victim and accused kissing in his car and he has contradicted his supplied written statement on various details. Thanks to me, the prosecution has successfully challenged his memory. In the eyes of the jury he cannot be trusted. "No further questions."

Outside, the witness asks me if I'm familiar with the Southwark area and where he should go for lunch. He clearly did not enjoy the court experience but he is pleasant and courteous toward me and I am confident his English is limited enough that he does not suspect me. We say goodbye and instead of heading for the subway, I start to walk, and cleanse myself in the autumn breeze.

Three days later, by a majority verdict of 11-1, the jury finds The Lad guilty. I read the news on my phone while queuing in the post office, and almost give a fist pump into the air. Would the prosecution have got there without me? Was it my words which pulled the jury over to our side? Well, eleven of them anyway. Whom couldn't we persuade? Hopefully not one of the women.

I played my part. I ensured The Lad was put away and that's the right result.

The just outcome.

I know this, because on Sunday morning, the media reports that three other victims have come forward.

17.

Four victims that we know about. And how many others? The ground beneath me warps as I read the news. If I hadn't changed the questions put to the Uber driver, those women may never have come forward. I came *this* close to not misinterpreting that day. If the accused had been found not-guilty, they might have gone their whole lives thinking they wouldn't be believed but now they have a real chance of seeing The Lad convicted for these crimes, too. I won't be caught. The defense team is unlikely to ask for the trial's audio for review. I doubt they'll even appeal; surely they are consumed with defending these new charges that the Crown Prosecution Service says it is aggressively pursuing.

I made the right decision again, but misinterpreting cannot become a habit. I am not reckless. Unless there are compelling circumstances, I won't do it again. If someone noticed and Exia scratched me from their books, it wouldn't be easy for me to change jobs. A period of unemployment is something when it's only me, but quite another when it affects Elliot.

It is four o'clock now, making it late night in Singapore. I message Richard asking if he's awake. A few minutes later, a video call comes through my laptop.

"I know it's late," I say. "Sorry I haven't been in touch earlier. It's been busy here."

"Hi. I'm happy we can connect. How's it all going?" Richard is sitting in his study, a large window right behind his desk. There is tropical rain coming down in great sheets. I can almost taste the humidity through the computer screen.

"That's what I wanted to tell you. The adoption was confirmed," I speak loudly so he can hear me over the weather.

"So it's all sorted? The little guy's yours?"

"Yep."

"Congratulations! I'm so pleased for you." I know he means it.

"I'm going to get him, okay? So you can say hello."

"Oh, great," Richard says, surprised.

I carry the laptop into Elliot's room where he's playing with a Lego set on the carpet.

"Elliot. This is Richard. I told you about him. He's in Singapore. Remember we looked at where that is on the globe?" I crouch so the camera is level with his face.

"Hello." Elliot waves into the screen, not sure exactly where to look.

"It's lovely to meet you," Richard says. "What have you got there?"

"It's my Halloween Lego. It's a witch."

"That's brilliant. Oh yes, Halloween soon."

Elliot's attention goes back to his toy and he swivels slightly, turning his back on the laptop. It's weird for him to meet a strange adult this way. At least he said hello in a friendly manner. Back on my feet, I carry my laptop to the living room.

"He's a bit shy," I say.

"It's lovely to see him. It really is. Hey, your apartment's nice." Richard is leaning closer to the screen, looking over my shoulder.

"It's okay. It's quite big for London. But now the adoption is confirmed we're free to change address so we'll move somewhere much cheaper soon."

"I spoke to the Kiwi solicitor this week—your mother's probate is ongoing but you know if you need money, if I can help you out in any way, I'd really like to."

"No, really, we're fine." I don't want money from my mother's estate and I don't want Richard's either. I should have just told him we were moving to be closer to Elliot's school. "Elliot's school is quite far from here, in Greenwich, on the other side of the river. It's the same school he was attending with his previous foster family. What I mean is—we're not moving only because of money. So don't worry." That's true, but Elliot doesn't love his present school, and we're probably not moving to Greenwich to be closer to it. I think he's happy to change schools one last time.

"I'd still like to help," Richard says.

"Thank you, we're fine." He knows not to pursue it further. "What have you been doing lately?" I set the laptop on one end of the sofa and perch on the other.

"This and that. Pottering around the apartment." I suppose he's getting used to being single again, and doing things without my mother. "I might take a trip next year."

"Oh yeah?"

"Europe, somewhere. I might fit London in too." He smiles and there is a subtle raise to his eyebrows. He's waiting for a reaction from me. "It'd be good to see you and the little guy properly." The smile gets bigger.

Suddenly this all feels too much. I need time to think about how much I want Richard in my life. I cannot introduce people to Elliot, have him get to know them, and then they disappear.

"I need to go," I say.

"Right, okay. I guess it's late for me anyway. I hope we can talk again soon. Enjoy the rest of your Sunday."

I say goodbye and end the call.

In the morning I have a few hours to spare while I wait to receive materials for a translation job. I scan two property websites and compare the average cost of two-bedroom flats in various areas. I make a list of a few postal codes that I think we can afford. There are two flats available now with potential, both in Ealing. I decide to catch the subway to inspect them from the outside before I contact the agent. It will also give me an opportunity to walk past the local primary school to get a feel for it.

The moment I arrive at the first street, I know this is a waste of time. The flat is two doors down from a small bar which is newly opened and not on Google Maps. I want us to live in a proper residential street, somewhere reliably quiet, without people coming and going at all hours. I don't know exactly what Elliot's home life was like before he was taken into care, but my guess is it didn't have those qualities.

The second flat is below ground floor and I could tell online that it would be dark, but in reality it is a total dungeon. It's just too grim for a six-year-old. I walk back to the station and resign myself to looking for flats further out of London, zone 5 or 6.

I jump on the train and as we approach Knightsbridge, think back to the Polish witness and the alibi interview. Where was it that he said both he and Sandra's killer lived? *The tunnel. Undercover walkway on Brompton Road.*

There is still an hour until I'm expecting my work for this afternoon to be emailed through, and so I make a snap decision to alight the train. I exit the station. It is lunchtime and people in elegant suits weave along the footpath carrying takeaways. Out of curiosity I want to see if that man is still living there, where he described. Mariusz Dorobek, the lying witness.

When I turn down Sloane Street, I realize the covered walkway is temporary, a shelter erected while redevelopment work is carried out. The tunnel is wide enough for several people to walk side-by-side and the roof is coated with fluorescent lights, flashing in orange, changing to red, then lavender and sky blue. The ground is the typical concrete path, and I think of how cold it will be to sleep on here later this month and for the coming winter.

I see him. Will he recognize me? I keep walking at a steady pace and look straight ahead.

"*Hej!*" a voice calls out the Polish "hi." "*Hej. HEJ!*" Now that he has seen me, I am annoyed at myself for coming. What does it matter if he still lives here or if he's moved on? An ugly thought plays that I have come here to gloat. I changed his alibi statement, I caught his lie, and Sandra's killer will be convicted, and on some level I want him to know that I won.

He gets to his feet. I nod, reluctant, and try my best to look surprised. A coincidence, to run into a former client on the street. In Polish, he tells me his friend was arrested and he doesn't know what to do.

"I need to go," I say in Polish. I hold up my palm and keep walking.

"Wait," he calls out. "Please. One thing."

I stop, sigh, and turn around. The man is holding something out toward me. I step backward, keep a safe distance away.

"This belongs to Adam," the client says. He unfurls his palm to reveal a key ring with a plastic photo frame. "The girl is his daughter, I think it's the only photo he has. Can you get this to him? Take it to the prison?"

"No!" I spray the word. "I don't work with the police in that way—I'm a freelance interpreter. I only go in when I'm called."

"Even if I could get past Belmarsh security, there's the trouble of paying for the transport . . ." He wants money. That's what this is. People stream past us and avert their eyes.

"I don't have any cash," my voice cold.

"Please, get it to him? I don't know who else to ask. It would mean a lot." He takes two steps closer to me and thrusts the key ring to my chest. I put my hands up to defend myself and somehow the key ring ends up in my fingers. I'll take it and toss it away. "The police don't believe me when I say Adam was with me the night that woman was murdered. Just because he did a robbery once before. Twenty-five years ago! He was nineteen. He's changed. He never did anything like that again. You know, he told me that one mistake determined the whole rest of his life. Limited the work he could get. He could only get garbage jobs so when he became ill, no sick leave—he couldn't pay his rent. That's how he became homeless. One mistake and he was punished forever. The world would not let him forget it."

I can't listen to any more. I start to walk faster this time, turning it into a jog. I run to the end of the walkway and continue my pace until I'm back in Knightsbridge station. Inside, I lean against the wall and massage the stitch forming in my side. What was that? Coming here was a rash and stupid thing to do. But Mariusz Dorobek did not behave as I expected. He seemed sincere. He was genuinely concerned for his friend. Does he think Adam Birch is innocent? Is that why he lied for him? I replay the interview in my mind. He gave his lies away by repeating the detective's questions and overexplaining his answers. It's possible he did those things because he speaks limited English. Repeating the questions could have been a natural response to needing more thinking time, because he was trying his best to follow along the conversation in both languages. The overexplaining might have been nerves—the additional stress of taking part in a police interview in a foreign country, speaking through an interpreter. No. I'm being too generous. My fingers knead roughly at my side. I saw through him in that room, and now, out here, I'm letting him manipulate me. I won't fall for it.

The key ring is still in my hand. The girl in the picture is about five years old with pink-framed glasses on her nose and an Arsenal football scarf laced around her neck. Her father is a murderer. I hope she's with her mother somewhere, living a much better life. I bury it deep into my handbag and board the train.

That one mistake determined the whole rest of his life. One mistake and he was punished forever. The world would not let him forget it.

I've let myself be rattled by those words. Mariusz Dorobek doesn't know what that sentence could possibly mean to me. But I am not the same as Adam Birch, and we are talking about two very different wrongdoings. He went twenty-five years without committing another crime, and then he commits a senseless killing? I don't believe it. I bet he just got better after that first robbery and didn't get caught again until now. Just like me, a voice inside says, I don't get caught. I shut my eyes and push my fists against my forehead. Stop that line of thinking, I tell myself, I can't let that man get to me. I will feel better when I tell Doreen everything.

On my phone, I open Facebook. She hasn't yet replied to my message. It's okay, I wasn't expecting to hear back from her immediately, she needs time. I told her I wanted to talk and I'm confident that eventually we will.

At home I check my email and see that my Russian translation job has come through, and I sit down to work. When I get up to make a cup of tea, I remember the key ring. With one swoop I fish it out of my handbag and throw it into my kitchen trash can where it belongs.

18.

I complete the Russian translation job the following afternoon, in time to collect Elliot from school. When I arrive, I see he has a balloon tied around his wrist. It's made of foil, taut with helium, and it towers over his head. The front of it has a full-color rainbow reaching across, interrupted by black and white lettering that simply reads *Congratulations!*

"Who gave this to you?" I ask Elliot.

"I don't know." I look around and see that none of the other children have one.

"Where did it come from?"

"There," he points to the school receptionist. I grab Elliot's hand and we approach the desk.

"Excuse me. Hi, I'm Elliot's mother. I'm wondering where this balloon came from?"

"Someone dropped it off," the woman says.

"Who?"

"A courier. They said it was for Elliot Lee but there's no card or anything."

"Odd."

"Thoughtful though!"

I suppose. Do they mean congratulations on the adoption?

"Okay, thank you," I say, and turn to Elliot. "Let's go."

As we walk to the street: "Did anyone at school say something to you today about me being your forever mum?"

"Nope," he says as he jumps up to tap the balloon.

At home, we untie it from his wrist and it bobs against the

ceiling, following us around the flat like a silent drone. It's a harmless little gift, but I would like to know who sent it. It is strange to have not included a card, and why send it to his school instead of to our home? I told Exia almost a year ago that I was applying to adopt and needed their professional reference, but gave them no other details and nor did they care to ask. I strongly doubt it was them, but just in case, I send an email to one of the account managers. Who knows we had the court hearing? I send both Lydia and Elliot's previous foster family in Greenwich a text asking if it was them. The judge? The courts wouldn't do something like this, surely. To be certain, I send Lydia a follow-up message asking if it could have been them or someone at the local authority. Richard is the only other possibility. It is getting late where he is so I text him quickly, even though I don't see how he would possibly know the name and address of Elliot's school all the way from Singapore.

Elliot wants me to cut the balloon's ribbon shorter, so that it's more fun for him to have to jump higher to reach it. I snip a length of about a dozen inches, and when I go to throw the excess ribbon in the trash, I see the key ring from the Polish-speaking alibi witness. The photo of Adam Birch's small daughter looks up at me. I cover it with a chip bag and shut the lid.

Sandra's daughter is who I am concerned about, not the offspring of her killer. What did Sandra say her girl's name was? Tala. Presumably she's been living with her father or other relatives since Sandra left for the UK—maybe a grandparent. I hope whatever situation she's in can be made permanent. Otherwise, will she be taken into care in the Philippines? The system is bad enough for children in this country, I hate to think what it must be like in one that is still developing.

It occurs to me that someone may have set up a fundraiser for Sandra's family. I search online and land on her Facebook profile, now made a memorial page. There are dozens of recent comments in Tagalog. Not a language I can read, so I hit the translate button. One person has posted a link to a British newspaper article published the day after the murder. The headline: MAID OF BABY-KILLING HIT-AND-RUN HEIRESS, DEAD, paired with an interior shot of the Knightsbridge home, all lush wallpaper, sculptures and bronze busts, blood-spattered but still aspirational. Another person writes a farewell message to Sandra. The translation isn't great but it's obvious this woman was a close friend. I scroll down and see she has also posted a link to an article from several years ago about a domestic worker in Hong Kong murdered by her employer. A number of other people have replied to this story. I use an online Tagalog dictionary to better translate the comments.

They always get away with it.

I warned Sandra not to work for that woman.

She would still be alive xxxxxxxxx

Another woman has written that in the days before her murder, Sandra resigned from her job and the heiress did not take the news well. She delayed her weekly pay, increased her household tasks, and changed the Wi-Fi password, causing her to miss a birthday call with her daughter. These people all think the heiress killed Sandra. I can tell from their profiles that some of these online friends are writing from the Philippines. They aren't aware of the full facts of the case and that's why they think the heiress is responsible. I don't doubt that the heiress is a bad person and an appalling boss, but she didn't kill Sandra. Adam Birch did.

Then a text message arrives from Lydia: *No, balloon wasn't me. Also would not have been the agency or the court.* Someone at Exia has replied, also denying it was them. I still can't see how it could have been Richard—the sender must be the Greenwich foster family. It's a nice thought. Perhaps they didn't want to put their name to the card out of discretion, so as not to maintain their relationship with Elliot now that he has moved on with me.

Shortly, Richard writes. His message is as expected: *Hi Revelle, no it wasn't me. Have a good evening and hope to speak soon, R.*

I bring my attention back to Sandra's Facebook page. I read through the comments once more, double-checking the translation of some of the trickier words. The crux of the messages remains the same—these people think the heiress is responsible for her death. English is widely spoken in the Philippines. It seems likely these friends of Sandra's would have sought out some of the British news stories about the murder. They must have read that Adam Birch's DNA was found on her body. I start to type a comment on the page but quickly delete it. I can't have any public connection to Sandra, just in case when Adam Birch goes to trial and the alibi is discussed, someone notices that I was the interpreter. It will go to trial and he will be found guilty because Adam Birch killed Sandra and the case is closed.

Heat rises to the surface of my face. I open the kitchen window to cool things down. After only a couple of minutes I close it shut again, not wanting to make the flat too cold for Elliot. There is a bite to the air this afternoon and it will be quite a chilly evening. An image of the Polish witness, Mariusz Dorobek, comes to mind. The flattened strip of cardboard I saw in the tunnel yesterday with his belongings, his lack of properly warm clothes.

The police don't believe me when I say Adam was with me the night that woman was murdered.

The police don't believe him, and now the jury won't either, because I changed his statement. I tell myself that I need to stop this; it's misplaced guilt. Once I can speak to Doreen, everything will feel clearer. I did the right thing mistranslating that alibi statement, I remind myself. "I got justice for Sandra," I say, under my breath. I repeat the affirmation even as I dig through the kitchen trash and retrieve the key ring. After I rinse it under the tap, I return it to my handbag. *Please, get it to him? It would mean a lot.* It can stay in my bag for now, just in case.

I check that Doreen hasn't written back to me and then I resolve to stay away from Facebook and Sandra's memorial page. The harder I try not to think about the alibi statement, and my conversation with Mariusz Dorobek yesterday, the more my mind drags me back to Doreen. I call up memories of the newspaper headlines at the time. BRITAIN'S WORST SOCIAL WORKER screamed one, KICK HER OUT! That day we met, filling time in the café, talking so much that we almost arrived late for the supervised contact session across the road, the reason we were there in the first place. We walked up the stairs and went into the room and now I remember exactly how it felt, folded into that plastic chair, jittery and not sure what to do with my hands. I focused on the lumpy red ball in the corner and the ancient snakes and ladders board game that passed for the local authority's toy provision. The little boy entered the room and went straight for the ball. His mother made a play for his attention. I didn't catch her name but I didn't need to know it. I was grateful Doreen was there because the mother didn't look like someone who I'd want to be alone in a room with. Wobbly chair pushed back behind her, she crouched on the carpet, with long limbs pointing every which way and her face a misshapen bundle of blotchy skin. Her nails were filed at sharp angles and as she scratched her arm, which she did regularly, they drew blood. I will stop thinking about this now, I instruct myself. But I can already hear Doreen's voice as she clapped her hands together. "Let's get started," she said.

No more.

Happily my phone pings, bringing me back to the present. There's a new message. It's from Elliot's Greenwich foster family.

No sorry, we didn't send you anything. They were the last people I was waiting to hear from. I look across the living room where the balloon now hovers above the TV. A chill tickles the back of my neck. I go to the kitchen window, expecting to see that I've left it ajar, but it is closed tight.

I return to find my sister sat cross-legged on the rug in the living room as though she is thirteen again. An open bottle of white sherry, our father's favorite, rests on her knee.

"What are you doing?" I ask, although it is entirely obvious.

She giggles. "Going through some family photos." Her unwashed fingers turn over the page. She has evidently gone into the library while I was out and excavated the old family albums. "Look!" She points to a picture on Kodak paper. There we are aged ten and twelve on our uncle's farm. A time before I knew rage, when I could look at her and feel cheer rather than contempt. She takes a swig of sherry straight from the bottle.

"You could have come and visited." Her face is buried in the photo album, too timid to meet my eye. "In jail, I mean."

"I know what you mean," I snap. Then she shoves a chocolate-covered almond into her mouth, one of my almonds, from Fortnum's, chews it twice, then pushes in a second one. "Did you make any friends in prison?" My otherwise useless sibling may have some helpful criminal connections. Someone she can introduce me to. "Anyone you're going to stay in touch with?"

She ignores my question and lies back on the rug, spreading her feet wide. "Did you meet anyone in there for murder?" Isn't prison said to be university for criminals? The incarcerated come out better educated and equipped to commit crimes than when they went in?

"Yeah," she says, draining the last of the sherry. "One girl was in a knife fight where the other girl bled out."

"Anything more sophisticated than street fighting?" Stabbing you to death is not what I have in mind. She must have met someone in there whose services I can utilize, who could at least refer me on to a professional.

"Umm . . ." While she thinks, she absent-mindedly grinds a chocolate almond into the rug with her heel.

"Jesus Christ!" I rush out to find a bottle of soda water to lift the stain. In the kitchen, I see where the sherry came from. In my haste to lock up the alcohol supply, I completely forgot about the two untouched bottles in the display cabinet by the fridge.

When I return to the living room, the atmosphere has altered. My sister has been into the library and found my other photo album. The album I made of me and him. We should be living our lives together as mother and son; these are wasted years. So I made an album to reflect the kind of life we should presently be enjoying.

"You . . . you've cut up photos of you and him and pasted the heads onto—what is this—bodies of random people you've ripped out of magazines? Boarding school catalogues?" She lies back and cackles, her hideous face made even uglier with amusement.

"Give that to me!" I rush to her and rescue the album from her grasp.

"Oh my Lord!" she says, scrambling to her feet. "Is that whole album faked photos of you and . . ." Say his name. Say his name. "That must have taken days to put together. That's sick." Say. His. Name.

"You're drunk." I walk to the library where I lock myself inside.

I don't want her assistance, and I don't need her criminal contacts. I will not involve my sister in my plans in any way. From behind the oak door, I listen to her clomp about the house, colliding with the furniture. The photo album goes back onto the shelf, the row dedicated to my son and me. There's an album for his last day of primary school; in the next one he begins secondary school; one book shows us celebrating his A-level results; another documents our vacations in Tuscany and New York and Tokyo, just the two of us; then him starting university, I move to the same city to be near; his graduation, me there in the front row; his wedding; the birth of my grandchildren. One album charts my deteriorating health and old age—he *refuses to admit me to a care home; my son steps away from all of it, his wife, children, his executive job, to attend to me, all the way through palliative care to my last breath. My boy wants nothing more from life than to be next to me. It's all there in the photographs. My sister isn't capable of understanding.*

Her footsteps fade and it sounds as though she has gone upstairs to her room. I check the lock on the door once again to satisfy myself that I will not be interrupted. Then I take a seat at the mahogany desk, use the key to open the drawer, and take out my favorite photo album of them all: yours.

19.

I lie awake until after one o'clock in the morning, my eyes insisting on staring at the ceiling. It's the balloon. It's absurd to be unsettled by something so trivial, but I know I won't be able to sleep until it's gone from the flat. Out of bed, I take the kitchen scissors and stab the foil, slowly letting the helium escape. I scrunch it all into a ball and take it outside to the garbage. Away from our home and not in the kitchen trash can where Elliot might see it.

In the morning, he notices immediately. "Mum, where's the balloon?"

"It bumped into the light fixture during the night," I try to sound disappointed. "It got a hole in it and all the helium leaked out. I'm sorry. I'll get you a better one for your birthday, okay?"

Something else to feel guilty about—depriving my son of a fun toy because I'm freaked out and had to throw it away. But I am glad I did because later this afternoon, Elliot's school receptionist calls me again. We've been sent another gift.

"Sometimes, I don't know if I'm running a school or an Amazon parcel locker," laughs the receptionist.

"I don't know who would have sent this," I say. "I still haven't worked out who sent the balloon."

"Unless Elliot is enjoying a spot of online shopping during his lunch break?" Her back is turned as she takes a bright red gift box from a shelf. "All these others are for Miss Parker in the library. I'm up to my absolute neck in ASOS parcels." She pushes the box across the counter. The label says *Elliot Lee*, but there are no details for the sender. I examine the sides, and peer under the base.

"You said this was also dropped off by a courier?" I ask.

"I have a degree you know. *Two* degrees. And I'm accepting packages for six-year-olds." She rolls her eyes. "London!"

"Speedtrack?" At least this time there's a label. "Is this the name of the courier company?"

"I suppose so. I quickly squiggled on their electronic signing thing and they left."

I open the package, but there is no delivery receipt inside. No note.

"Okay, I'll call them," I say, pulling the box toward me. "Thank you."

Inside is a plush toy. I'm startled to see that it's a dragon. Compact, only around six inches tall with a swollen belly, shrunken wings and a disproportionately small tail. It is eerily similar to Elliot's toy.

I go outside and wait for the school bell to signal the end of the day. Meanwhile, I take a closer look at the toy. The fabric has been sliced in places. Long, deep cuts have been made to the surface where white stuffing now leaks. On reflex it drops from my hands. Another parent walks past, looks down at it on the ground and wrinkles his nose. Reluctantly, I pick it up. An arm is missing. Someone has ripped off a limb, taken a knife or something very sharp and stabbed repeatedly at the chest. I drop it again as my blood runs cold. I look down and see the dragon has landed face-first into the dirt. On the base the label says "Kyoshi." There's also a serial number—just like Elliot's dragon. I jump backward as though the toy is alive.

The bell sounds. Clots of children and parents spread across the road. A feeling rises that something has happened to Elliot. I forget about the toy and push my way into the school grounds, moving against the flow of human traffic. "Elliot!" I call over the din of excited children. "Elliot Lee!" I am transported back to that day at the Old Bailey.

There are students everywhere. How can I find him in this crowd? I shove two mothers out of my path and they scowl at me.

"Mum!" I see his backpack first and then his face. Elliot is fine. I pull him to me and ruffle his hair.

"Let's go home."

We walk to the road and I see from the corner of my eye that the toy is still there on the ground where I left it. I don't want Elliot to see it, but I should keep it in case it's needed as evidence, if I have to go to the police. I am nauseous at the thought. I take Elliot's hand and swerve us to the left. I pretend to drop something and scoop the toy into my handbag when he's not looking.

Where's the red box it came in? I must have also left it on the ground. I can't see it. But if I need proof of harassment, the toy should do it. Bile swells in my gut. My hand wraps tighter around my son's and we catch the wrong bus. We hop off, and jump on another. It takes us twice as long to get home, but it means we aren't followed because I have a feeling that someone was in the crowd of school parents, waiting, watching us.

We enter the flat and I hear the deadlock click. Although I usually don't bother, today I also pull the gold chain across the latch.

"Elliot," I attempt to level off the panic in my voice. "Did anyone behave a little weird today at school? Did any adults other than your teachers talk to you?"

He thinks about the question for a moment. "No."

"No strangers approached you?"

"Nope."

"Or anyone—any of your old parents? Anyone you used to live with?"

176

"I haven't seen any of them for a long long long time."

"Okay, just checking. You can tell me though, if you do. I won't be upset. I just want to know."

He works his way through a cranberry muesli bar as he starts on his Lego project. He's building a Halloween pumpkin to accompany the witch he's already built.

I leave the room, and when I'm certain Elliot isn't listening, I phone Speedtrack. The phone call does not last long. They are a courier company, but they have no further information about the sender. They don't even seem to have a record of the delivery.

I need to think through logically who this could be and why they're sending these things. First the drug dealer comes to our flat during Lydia's visit. Local criminals, apparently, assessing my suitability for robbery. But my first thought that day, my instinct, was that Elliot's birth family were attempting to sabotage the adoption. They did object to the adoption order after all—his birth mother appealed and tried to stop it. Then the faked letter from the family court telling me to go to Swindon—sent to me and then later stolen from my flat. I text Lydia, my fingers typing at a furious pace, telling her everything. She replies almost instantly, claiming it's impossible his birth family would know where he lives or goes to school. She's no longer his social worker, she reminds me. If I have any further inquires I'll need to direct them to the adoption agency. I'm on my own.

If his birth relatives know what school he attends and where we live, they've had opportunities to take him. Why send the threatening gifts and not try to kidnap Elliot? They're drug addicts, maybe this is what they do. Send poison pen letters and childish threats with no intention of actual follow-up. The knife wound on the toy—why send such a disturbing thing to your own child, which is bound to scare them? Two ostensibly expensive toys. This is a message, a warning. Elliot's name is on the box but clearly this toy is for me. How did the birth family find our address to send the drug dealer and the letter? Elliot's school? Could it have been leaked? Accidentally included in some of the legal documents during the adoption court process, made available to his birth parents' solicitors? That seems plausible. Then what other details might they have seen?

I take my handbag into my bedroom and shut the door. I pour the toy out onto the floor. It's definitely the same as Elliot's Draggie. And there's no way the knife wounds could be dismissed as accidental. It sniffs of hatred. We can't live like this. We need to get out of this flat. We have to move now and Elliot has to change schools.

In the kitchen I stash the knife-wounded dragon in the high cupboard above the fridge where Elliot can't reach. Then I squat beside him and his Lego.

"Elliot. Your dragon toy. Who got him for you?"

He is concentrating on the model pumpkin and doesn't respond apart from a distracted "Hmmmm."

"Can you remember?"

He's thinking about it. "I'm missing a piece!" Then he starts crawling around the carpet, groping for a lost brick.

"Elliot, stop for a moment." He's not listening. I grab his wrists. "Elliot! This is important!" My hands clamp around his forearms. "Who gave you the dragon toy?" I don't know when I started shouting, but now I am roaring so loud that I make myself flinch. The carpet burns my knees. Elliot's eyes blur then erupt with tears. "Oh love, I'm sorry." I try to pull him to me but he refuses, distraught. This is the first time I've ever shouted at him. "I'm really sorry. It's okay. I was just wondering where your toy came from. I didn't mean to yell." His chest heaves as tears travel down his cheeks and finally he lets me hug him. Once he is settled, I make him a hot chocolate and leave him to play.

After Elliot goes to bed, I stay up until two o'clock in the morning working my way through property websites, making a list of available rentals and firing off requests for an inspection.

In the morning, an agent accepts my booking for a video tour of a two-bedroom maisonette in Streatham. A few seconds in, I see why it's in my price range. Even on the screen it's visibly rundown and dark and I am mildly despondent as my eyes dance over a crack in the bathroom wall. By the end of the tour, I convince myself this place is decent enough for the short term. The local school is well regarded, at least; I already checked. On my phone I submit an application. If we're accepted, I'll go and see it in person before I sign. Looking for a place to live is a full-time job, but I need to keep working if I'm going to be able to pay for movers and put down a deposit. I accept a translation booking at the National Crime Agency for the afternoon.

The train trip to Vauxhall is relatively quick, but getting through security at the NCA building is an ordeal. Eventually I am sat at a bare desk in the world's most uncomfortable chair where the tips of my toes skim the floor. I get to work. I'm not told the context of the situation but my job is to translate a Spanish document that appears to have come from that country's coroner's office. It seems a Briton living in Malaga was convicted of murder, but has since been released following a review of the evidence. The document is short but dense with complex scientific information. On a laptop, I write my English version against the background sounds of a person at a nearby desk snacking on something very crunchy, marring the otherwise quiet space. As I work my way deeper into the report, I gather from the material that the British man was initially convicted of murdering a tourist with one of the key pieces of evidence being his DNA at the scene of the crime, a hotel room. The conviction was overturned on appeal when an expert forensic witness testified that the presence of the DNA could be explained in myriad ways. It is not proof, the report states, that the accused was at the scene of the crime or indeed had even met the victim.

Primary DNA transfer is when a person handles an object, such as a weapon, and they deposit their DNA on that object. Secondary transfer concerns an intermediary. For example, if before touching a gun the perpetrator buys something in a shop, they are likely to deposit the shop worker's DNA on the gun, as well as their own. Tertiary transfer involves two intermediaries. This chain can continue.

I read through this section again and double, triple check my translation of the Spanish. In the scientist's example, the shop worker never touched the gun, and yet their DNA was found on the weapon, as clear as day. I think back to Mariusz Dorobek's alibi interview, and what the detective said to me in the kitchen.

We have his DNA on the body of the deceased. All over it. He did it.

I can't be expected to understand the intricacies of this document without a scientific background. I tell myself to translate the words and not to think about the wider context. Just get the words right. There is no similarity between this wrongful conviction in Spain and Sandra's murder. But as I keep working, I replay my conversation with Mariusz Dorobek in Knightsbridge; his sincerity, his vulnerability and honesty. No, not honesty, I correct myself. I will check over my work one more time and then I will go and collect Elliot from school.

Elliot. Is he safe? I make a quick call to his school receptionist. No, there have not been any other mysterious gifts sent to the school, and nor has there been any kind of incident to report. I thank the receptionist for her reassurance and get back to work.

The crunching from the nearby desk continues and I don't know how anyone is expected to concentrate in here. The British man in Spain was simply unlucky to have been in that hotel at the time of the murder. Anyone who was occupying his room then would have found themselves connected to the crime. That isn't the same as Adam Birch, who is known to the Knightsbridge area. An eyewitness saw him loitering by the heiress's house on the day of Sandra's murder. He's there walking down the heiress's street on the CCTV. He was seen in the area on numerous other occasions being aggressive with the neighbors. He pleaded guilty years ago to another breaking-and-entering robbery only a few minutes' walk from the house. I've heard police say, multiple times over the years, that criminals tend to commit crimes on their home turf, in areas known to them where they feel most comfortable. Adam Birch wasn't only arrested because his DNA was on Sandra's body.

The endless crunching from someone in this office is like nails driving into my brain and I need to know, I cannot go home from here without knowing if Adam Birch's DNA could also have been transferred to Sandra's body.

I get up from my desk and walk through the open-plan area. "Excuse me," I say to the nearest person. "Do you know where Officer McKay is?"

"Down the hall." The man points.

I find my supervisor seated behind two large computer monitors. "All done?" she asks.

"Yes, almost. There are a couple of difficult words, phrases actually. I'd like to check the intention from the report writer. Is there any chance I can call someone in Spain from the coroner and have a quick conversation?"

"No," McKay says, without looking away from her screens.

"I pride myself on my accuracy. If I could have five minutes on the phone with the person who wrote the report then I could make sure the translation is exactly right."

Now she looks at me. "We can have another translator check the work if you're saying your skills are lacking. Perhaps you shouldn't have accepted this job."

"Any qualified person would have the same issue. Words can be translated in different ways, and some words don't have a direct equivalent at all. I want to speak to the Spanish report writer to make sure I haven't deviated from their intention. Five minutes is all I need."

McKay says nothing but lurches from her desk and I gather that I am to follow. She walks into an empty office with a landline phone and after consulting her mobile, scribbles a Spanish phone number on a piece of paper. "Ask for Gili," she says, and leaves.

My call is picked up on the second ring. Gili is out for lunch. I rub my eyelids with my thumbs. "Do you know when he'll be back?" I need to leave in an hour to get to Elliot's school.

"I've no idea," the Spanish receptionist says. I leave my name and number and beg for a swift return call.

There is a computer in this office and I move the mouse to see if it is awake. I log in using my guest credentials and navigate to the search engine. I type "DNA transfer" and land on a website about the Rotherham case, all those girls abused up north.

DNA was found not only on the clothing of the perpetrators but on the clothing of other *people in their households, their wives, their children, months after the crimes had been committed. DNA can be transferred in millions of ways, including in washing machines—dozens of washes later and you can still detect traces.*

A killer could wash their clothes—clothes they were wearing at the time of the murder—at a laundromat. DNA from the victim travels from their clothes to the washing machine. The next customer to use that machine, DNA from the victim is there, all over their jeans. You can imagine a situation where this innocent person is picked up for murder.

This is a blog run by a university research student, so I don't know if it is credible. Twenty-five years after his first crime, Adam Birch attempts another breaking-and-entering robbery and it goes wrong, and he murders Sandra, then flees without taking anything. That's what happened.

The phone rings and I answer in English and in Spanish. It's Gili.

"I'm working for the British National Crime Agency. I'm translating your report about DNA transfer in the case of . . . a British man—I don't seem to have the name."

He rescues me. "Yes. In Malaga. I know the one you mean."

"Um, I wanted to double check my interpretation of your report in a couple of areas."

"Yes?"

"You say that the presence of someone's DNA on the body or at the scene of the crime doesn't mean they were there or have ever even had contact with that person before?"

"Correct. You need to determine if the DNA was deposited directly by someone involved in the crime, or if it was carried to the scene by someone else."

"How can you tell?"

"It's difficult. At first, DNA transference was only noted in lab experiments. It took a while for investigators to accept that it could apply to real-life crimes. Are you having trouble understanding my report?"

"No," I say. "That clarifies things, thank you." I don't want him to flag with the NCA that I'm incompetent and not equipped to translate Spanish. NCA jobs sometimes pay well and I can't afford to lose the work. "I suppose I'm also interested in learning more, for myself," I say. "Curiosity."

"Ah." I can hear him smile. "DNA profiling itself is new, yes? It's only been around since the 1980s. A lot of investigators don't want to acknowledge its problems—because now they rely on it so heavily. Yes, our technology is getting better and better, and we can detect more DNA from small samples, samples which become smaller each year. But this actually means things are becoming worse. Sensitive lab tools can detect a match now from a tiny number of cells. And a tiny number of cells can easily travel. That's how DNA can have the wrong person sent to jail. That's my report." As I listen, I finger a pen in my left hand. The cap like a noose around my thumb, cutting off all circulation. "DNA is science, it cannot be challenged," Gili says. "That's what people think." How much of Adam Birch's DNA was on Sandra's body? *All over it*. That's what the detective said. Too much to travel, yes, that's what the detective must have meant. Although he's not a scientist.

"What trumps DNA evidence?" I ask Gili. "How did you prove this British man's innocence?"

"The key is to explain how the DNA got there, the chain of transference."

There is no obvious connection between Adam Birch and Sandra. But they lived in the same area. With Adam Birch there in the public thoroughfare, they may have passed each other on the street hundreds of times. Impossible to pinpoint. "What if you can't do that?" I ask.

"Alibi. An ironclad alibi is the best defense against DNA evidence. I understand that is how the British man was granted his appeal."

I mumble my thanks and hang up. An alibi. The very thing Adam Birch had, and I destroyed.

"I'm finished," I say to McKay, standing at the door of her office. "Everything's signed off. I need to go." I collect my bag and dash through security. This Spanish case is a completely different situation to Sandra's murder. I will not think about Adam Birch any longer. When I exit the building, I visualize all thoughts of him remaining upstairs, solidified and left there on the desk, and not coming home with me. I board the bus to Greenwich to collect my son. When I sit down, I see the fingerprints of my own DNA on the ticket machine, the pole I touched, and the back of the seat in front.

20.

After Elliot goes to bed, I revisit Sandra's memorial Facebook page. Some new comments have been posted, mostly tributes from family and people in the Philippines. One claims that Sandra told friends in London that she was afraid of her employer. The police must have investigated the heiress in the days after the murder. Initially, at least, the heiress would have been the prime suspect. She was home at the time of the killing. It was only the heiress and Sandra in the house, and so she had no alibi. Detectives must have their reasons for discounting her involvement. I close out of Sandra's page. Then I check my Facebook messages even though I know there is nothing there. Doreen has not written back. It's possible she hasn't seen my message request. I'll make contact once more and then if she doesn't want to speak to me, I have to respect her decision.

I know you don't want to hear from me, but there's something I need to tell you. I think you'd like to know. Please get in touch. I don't want to bother you and I'm not interested in causing you any trouble. I hope you are well, I really do.

After I press send to Doreen, I type the heiress's name into Google. She's not mentioned in any recent news stories, aside from a photo in the social pages taken last weekend at an opening night of a theater. I add "Sandra Ramos murder" to my search terms and land on an online forum. This whole channel is devoted to people discussing the crime. It has over two hundred members. I scroll down to the bottom of the page and scan through the posts chronologically. A great deal of the discussion concerns the heiress. Some people claim to be ex-employees, others say they know her from charity boards and mutual social contacts.

I work at a labor hire company, which I won't name. Several times we supplied catering services and waitstaff for functions at her house. She was always unpleasant and difficult to deal with, but to be honest, many of our clients are. One day there was an administrative mix-up and my chef did not receive the note that one of the heiress's guests was allergic to peanuts. He went ahead and prepared a Malaysian dish with satay sauce. When the heiress discovered what had happened, she flipped out. She verbally abused my staff and threw a silver tray at the head of one of the girls. She also smashed two glasses in the vicinity of one of my waiters. I know we made a mistake. My business takes errors seriously and I am aware that people can die when allergy information is not communicated correctly—but there is no excuse for violence. That woman is volatile and you can't help but think that the maid did something to upset her and she simply pushed her down the stairs.

Mistakes can kill, I know that. I untangle my fingers which have knotted together. The heiress running over the pregnant woman in the parking lot and now this story—she certainly seems capable of killing Sandra. She should never have been in a position to be able to hurt her. She should have been jailed for what she did to the pregnant woman. I think back to the Old Bailey, and the Italian witness I interpreted for, supporting the defense. Errors might kill, but if I had mistranslated on that trial, if I had helped to get the heiress convicted, then maybe I could have saved Sandra's life.

I read the rest of the webpage, hungry for more information. Another person says the heiress lied about not hearing the intruder downstairs.

The heiress told police she was in her bedroom on the top floor of the house where she was listening to Spotify, loudly through headphones. I don't know exactly what time the maid was killed on September 16. But I'm a white-hat hacker, and I can tell you that the heiress's account was not used the day or night of the murder; in fact she hadn't logged in for a full week. She was NOT listening to Spotify while Sandra Ramos was on the ground floor being pushed down the stairs.

I close the laptop because the words are now swimming across the screen.

The room begins to spin. I leave the computer on the coffee table and lower myself to the floor. Is the heiress going to get away with Sandra's murder because I changed the Polish man's alibi? I have to contact police and tell them what I've done. The room starts turning in the other direction. Both of my hands morph into a claw trying to grip hold of the carpet. If I confess to having interfered with an alibi statement, I could be opening up the possibility of every police interview, every trial I've ever interpreted being challenged and overturned; countless violent, dangerous people going free. I could claim that day I was ill. I could tell police that I've since realized I made another error that day while poorly, and I'd like the opportunity to double check my translation, just in case. It won't work. It would only take one defense team to hear about it, seize these grounds for appeal, and some rapist, some violent gang leader or killer from one of my past assignments could be released. Free to abuse, to kill again, and then how many other shattered lives would I be responsible for? Besides, police may not believe me. If I come forward and say I've realized my mistake, they might connect me with Sandra, see on the Silver Balloon app that I used her as a babysitter, discover that I interpreted on a trial involving her boss—and then they'd charge me with perverting the course of justice. I'd never be able to interpret again. Who'd hire me? No one, because I'd be in jail and Elliot would be back in the care system. I can't have that. I climb back up onto the sofa and force myself to endure the dizziness. There must be a way to get Adam Birch out of prison without causing further destruction.

Adam Birch's key ring—the photo of his daughter. Where did I put it? I stagger toward the fridge, remembering that I left it in the high cupboard. I open the door and see that I have it wrong. This is where I put the toy dragon with the knife wounds. The dragon peers at me. Its single eye glares angrily, unhappy about being banished out of sight. A smell hits the air, a reek that wasn't here before. I cleared out this cupboard recently so it can't be from expired food. I use a tea towel to carry the dragon toy to the floor. The smell intensifies. My hand flies up to cover my nose and it's there on the cotton. The stench is definitely coming from the toy. Black bubbles from the socket where the dragon's arm is missing. Fur on the creature's face clumps together, the fabric crusted by something thick and viscous. The aroma is overpowering and I cover my nose and mouth with one hand while the other, protected by the tea towel, flips the toy onto its base. Liquid oozes. I make a double-glove with the tea towel—it's going straight in the trash after this—and poke at the seam. The toy's stuffing squishes between my fingers, rubbery and soft. I take it outside to where the garbage cans are kept—my senses can't take any more of the smell—and stab a finger at the seam. Inside I see an object.

No, not an object. It's *alive*.

Or, *was*. It's a small organ of some sort. A heart? No, wait—is it *two*? I can hardly look. Organs cut from a mouse or a rat or a bird. Before my mind catches up, my arm has lobbed the toy into the open garbage can and I close the lid shut. Back inside my bathroom, I smother my hands in soap, scrubbing all the way up to my elbows until the skin goes tight and sore. A surge of nausea has me grip the basin. I breathe through my nose until I can stand upright. I nudge open Elliot's bedroom door and check to see if he's still asleep. He's tucked under the duvet. I can hear him breathing steadily, he's okay.

Everything in that cupboard I take out to the garbage. I want it all out of our flat. I open our living-room windows and let the cold air charge through, blow away every trace of the meaty smell and animal blood and Elliot's birth parents. Someone in his birth family found out where we live. The mother? She somehow worked out when Lydia had made an appointment to visit. She sent a drug dealer here, faked a court document, broke into our flat and then the balloon and now this—letting me know that they can reach Elliot at his school. Does the family want him back, or do they want to hurt him? Punish him? In their minds, did he betray them to the social worker, tell their secrets when he was interviewed and taken into care? I call Lydia but she doesn't answer. I send her a text and an hour later, she replies:

Revelle, I don't know what's going on with you but as I said before, it's impossible that Elliot's birth parents would know where you live and where he goes to school. Look, they are not wealthy. His father is in prison in Manchester, and his mother is currently in hospital. She's over eight months pregnant and there's been some complications. It's physically impossible that they've been harassing you. I was intending to tell you when the baby was born.

Eight months pregnant. A brother or sister for Elliot. A half-sibling? I can't think about that now. How long has his father been in jail? Could he orchestrate all this from there? That seems more likely than a hospitalized pregnant woman, although it was her name on the court appeal documents. I want to ask Lydia who from Elliot's birth family, if anyone, turned up at the court hearing, but I'm worried about antagonizing her further. I check the bolt on our front door, shut the windows, and jiggle the latches on every possible opening in the flat. We have to get out of here.

Online I view my application for the maisonette in Streatham. There's no update, but I can't wait any longer. Anything with two bedrooms, in my price range within Greater London, is now a candidate. I start submitting tenancy applications for dozens of properties, sight unseen. This toy was delivered to Elliot's school, I remind myself; moving house alone doesn't solve the problem. He can't go back there. Tomorrow we'll call in sick. I'll contact the local authority and find out what we need to do to change schools. Our new address will be the perfect excuse—there'll be a school nearby that can take him. Until we're safe in a new home and a different school, I can't let him out of my sight.

In the morning Elliot is thrilled to learn that he can stay home from school, but by lunchtime he is bored and irritable.

"I hate Lego!" he says, as he flicks an orange tile across the rug.

"Since when? You made a witch, a pumpkin. You're all set for Halloween! Let's make something else."

"It's stupid."

"You're tired of it. Okay, we'll do something different." I called the local authority this morning about changing schools. If I'm overreacting, I've pulled my son out of class for no reason, disrupted the already patchy education of a disadvantaged six-year-old. "We're going on an excursion, all right? Let's go."

On a Saturday, the line to enter the Natural History Museum is lose-your-child-in-the-crowd busy, but on a Friday afternoon, you can walk straight in. We join the tail-end of a volcano demonstration and when the museum staffer asks Elliot his name, he replies, "I'm not at school today, Mum says to tell people that I'm poorly!" and I wish to be swallowed by the hot, red lava.

From the museum, we catch the subway to Northwest London to inspect two potential flats. Elliot is not impressed with the first. The second is near the ground for Wembley Football Club, which is probably the reason Elliot says that he likes it. It's available immediately and pending a credit check, the estate agent says that the landlord should be happy to accept my application. It's drab and they've obviously not had much interest. Wembley is about fifteen miles from Elliot's current school in Greenwich and five miles from our flat on Finchley Road—a reasonable distance away for me to feel that we'd be starting again from a place of anonymity.

"It'd be better if we were going to be living near Arsenal Football Club. We should try to move there next time," Elliot says as I tuck him into bed. "They're the best team."

"Let's see if we can make it happen when you're a bit older, okay?" He's already drifted off.

Arsenal.

I find my handbag and see Adam Birch's key ring is still there in the bottom. I hear Mariusz Dorobek's voice. *Please, get it to him? It would mean a lot.* In the photo, the football club's red and white scarf hugs his daughter's neck. I recall Adam Birch's mug shot from the news and see in the little girl's face the same mellow brown eyes.

21.

Adam Birch is in Belmarsh prison, often referred to as the British version of Guantánamo Bay. On YouTube I play a short documentary filmed by a journalist who was granted permission to stay there overnight, but ten minutes in, I need to run to the bathroom to be sick. If Adam Birch is convicted, I could be responsible for banishing a man to that hellhole for the rest of his life. An innocent man. Adam Birch's DNA could have been transferred to Sandra. A neighbor placed him on the heiress's street on the day of the crime, and he was also recognized from the CCTV. But that street footage isn't very clear, and even if that was him near the heiress's house that day, it doesn't mean that he's also the shadowy figure on the other CCTV clip, the one taken from the heiress's back garden. As for the neighbor recognizing him on the street, eyewitnesses make mistakes; I've heard detectives say that firsthand accounts can derail the early days of an investigation because even when we're trying really hard, humans are so unreliable. Often we're simply not capable of accessing the truth. So much points to the heiress—she's the one with the motive to kill Sandra and she had the opportunity. During a trial, the alibi could have made all the difference. Oh God, what have I done? The floor rushes up at me in a wave of vertigo. I am disgusted with myself, and I know my guilt won't help Adam Birch. I need to do something. I have to get this key ring to him and then I have to get him out of prison. I look down at the face of his daughter, the spectacles, the Arsenal scarf. A key ring but no key; a token of another life when he had a family or simply somewhere at the end of the day he ought to be.

Online I search for the name of his solicitor or barrister—they're usually referenced in one media report or another. I find it. A news story on the BBC website quotes him as a man named Roger Lipman, with an office on Wood Green high street. It is after ten o'clock at night; there's nothing I can do about it now. I'll mail the key ring first thing Monday morning. I think Adam is more likely to receive it if I send it to his solicitor rather than directly to the jail.

In the morning, I'm groggy and it takes me a few minutes after waking to remember that after this weekend is half-term. I'll need to come up with ideas to keep Elliot entertained and figure out how I'm going to balance work with him not being at school. We have toast with bananas and honey for breakfast. I try to rub the sticky spread from his arm but somehow only smear it further. We dress and walk to the park nearest to our flat, and spend half an hour passing a football to one another. The sky today is a determined gray, and even though it's Saturday, the park is deserted. My skills only extend to kicking the ball a dozen yards away and so Elliot is quickly bored and ready to go back indoors. I tuck the ball under my arm and we wander to the local library to browse the children's section. We borrow one book about space and another about dogs and I realize this is something else Elliot doesn't have: a pet.

In the afternoon I remember that the estate agent yesterday said that he worked on Saturdays, and so I call him. I ask if there has been any update to my Wembley application even though it has only been twenty-four hours. If there's ever an occasion where I need to be pushy, this is it. Estate agents aren't allowed to charge application fees anymore, but I offer him £150 for an extra-speedy credit check. I don't think it's actually possible to rush through the paperwork so quickly, but he agrees to pocket my money, and on Monday first thing, I receive a formal acceptance, and I don't ask any questions.

I phone my current landlord and explain that a family emergency means we need to vacate within the next week. We are moving abroad, I say, and I cannot provide a forwarding address, in case mail isn't the only thing he sends to our new home. He agrees to let me out of the contract with another two months' rent. I'll be going into my overdraft again. I call the local authority with our new address and begin the process of enrolling Elliot in a new school. Thank goodness this week is half-term so I have a bit of time to organize his new uniform and what else he might need. The estate agent says I can collect the keys tomorrow, so I book movers for Wednesday morning.

In the meantime, I need to pack, try and earn some money, and somehow keep Elliot amused. I also need to see Mariusz Dorobek. I'll have one more conversation with him and if I still think he's genuine and Adam Birch is innocent, then I have no choice but to do something about it.

Elliot and I catch the train to Knightsbridge. We step into the covered walkway and I take his hand as we approach the Polish man. Will my son be scared or upset to see Mariusz's possessions on the ground, to realize that some people are forced to live this way? "Batman," I say. "I need to have a little conversation with this man, okay? I met him at work. He's really nice."

"Okay."

"We'll talk to him and then we'll have lunch somewhere. This afternoon, we'll go home, I'll do some packing for our new flat, and you've still got your library books to read." I search his face for approval. "Sound all right?"

He shrugs. "No school!"

"It's just a holiday. Don't get used to it." I give his arm a playful nudge.

We walk the rest of the way to Mariusz who stands to greet us. He looks drained. How could anyone live here, sleep here, ever snatch a moment of peace among the roar of the traffic, both vehicle and human?

"Hi again," I say in Polish. "This is my son, Elliot." I repeat it in English so that my boy understands.

"Hello there," Mariusz says in English, extending his hand for Elliot to shake, which he does with enthusiasm. Elliot is always delighted when people treat him like an adult.

"I'm going to speak to Mariusz in Polish for a bit," I tell him. He nods and accepts my phone to keep him occupied.

"This time I'm not just walking past coincidentally—I came here to see you," I say to Mariusz.

"All right."

"I still have your friend's key ring with the photograph of his daughter," I tell him, extracting it from my handbag. "I wanted to let you know that I'm mailing it today. I'm sending it to Adam Birch's solicitor. I'm sure the solicitor will get it to him."

"Okay, thank you." All I see is a smile.

"Well. That's it. Sorry I didn't send it on sooner." Mariusz grins at Elliot. What am I looking for? Any sign that this man could possibly be a liar? One last chance to convince myself that I've done nothing wrong? But I'm not going to get it. "Okay. Say bye, Elliot."

Before my son can speak: "You know where Adam's solicitor is?" Mariusz says.

"Wood Green. I looked it up."

"Could we go there?"

"It's an office. I think anyone can walk in." Then I realize what Mariusz is really asking me.

"I'd like to speak to them," he says.

"I'd be happy to help you get there," I say. "Pay for transport."

"I'd need an interpreter." I cannot be seen with Mariusz Dorobek, especially not in front of Adam Birch's solicitor. It's too risky.

"I need to go. I'm moving and . . ." Inside, I cringe. Of all the excuses to employ, why would I say that I was moving in front of a homeless person? "My son is changing schools. I can find you an interpreter." I take out my phone and open the Exia app. "I'll pay for it, of course."

"No, no, don't worry. I wanted to make sure the solicitor knows that Adam is innocent." This man is telling me the truth.

"It's no problem." My finger veers wildly across the phone screen. "I'll find you one." I owe him. I have to help.

"It's okay." He brushes my arm, giving me permission to stop swiping. "The solicitor probably won't pay attention to what I say, anyway."

"But it's worth a try." If I take Mariusz to meet the solicitor, it might become apparent how I can help Adam. If I don't meet his solicitor, how else am I going to make amends? "Let's go. I'll come with you."

We move to the main road and the three of us climb into an Uber.

The office windows of Roger Lipman & Associates are crusted with decades of filth, the door peeling and shaky, with stairs leading up and over the gloomy betting shop below. Barristers complain about the savage cuts to legal aid that came in the wake of the 2008 financial crisis and have kept coming. It's a favored topic of conversation in courthouse corridors, the stuff of safe small talk between warring counsel waiting for their cases to be called. Then there's the barrister strikes. Legal aid is hemorrhaging competent solicitors for the financial security of private practice, especially in London. If the cuts are as bad as they make it sound, you have to wonder about the caliber of those who stayed behind. How much active investigating and evidence gathering can Roger Lipman & Associates possibly be doing on Adam Birch's behalf?

Elliot is beside me as we take the stairs, Mariusz following behind.

"Do you have an appointment?" asks a woman on the front desk. I show her the key ring.

"This photograph belongs to Adam Birch, a client of Roger Lipman," I say. "It's a possession which is really important to him and we'd appreciate it if he could get it to Adam, when they next meet." The woman looks at the key ring but doesn't take it. I rest it behind her computer monitor, next to a mug of pens. She looks to me and then at Elliot. "Do you think you could do that for us?"

"Adam Birch, you said?"

"Yes."

"I'll give it to Mr. Lipman." She has lost interest and resumes tapping away on her keyboard. She still hasn't touched the key ring. She'll probably do what I did when Mariusz asked me the same favor—throw it in the trash. I was deluding myself thinking this trip would make me feel better, as if delivering this small token would relieve me of my guilt. Adam Birch may have been arrested without me, but I've sealed his fate. I cannot ignore this and do nothing, like last time. I cannot let the wrong person take the blame.

"Could we also have a moment to speak to Roger Lipman?" I ask. "Is he in?"

"You need an appointment," the woman says, eyes on her keyboard. She didn't say he wasn't here. "Five minutes, please."

A sigh. "Because I'm in a good mood, you can have three." She shouts toward the back of the office and waves us through. I tell Mariusz what's going on and whisper to Elliot that this will only take a few minutes.

We find Lipman at a desk, smothering an armless office chair. A loose blue tie circles his neck. "Excuse me," I say. "Sorry to bother you. I dropped off a small possession at the receptionist; we were hoping you could deliver it to your client Adam Birch. It means a lot to him. It's a photo of his daughter."

"What's going on?" Lipman pushes back from his desk. I can't come right out and ask him what I can do to assist the defense. He'll question my personal connection to his client and I can hardly say that I was the interpreter for his alibi interview.

"I'm an interpreter and this is my client. His name is Mariusz Dorobek. He asked me to accompany him here today because he'd like to speak to you about the case." I can feel my cheeks flush. Is Lipman looking at Mariusz and wondering how it is he can afford to pay me?

"How are you today?" Lipman says to Elliot. My boy ducks his head down and wraps himself around my middle.

"Sometimes he's shy," I say.

The solicitor nods and collects four chairs from unattended desks and wheels them to the far corner of the room. We sit in a rough circle. I think it's safe to assume that Lipman doesn't speak any Polish, so I whisper to Mariusz in his language: "Go ahead. What do you want me to tell him?"

"Say I want to help," Mariusz says. "Police obviously didn't believe me when I said Adam was with me that night. So what else can I do? He's my friend. There must be something." I repeat it in English for Lipman and explain that Mariusz was Adam's alibi.

Lipman blows a cloud of air from his nose. "Look, it happens. Alibis without hard evidence don't always hold up." He pauses for me to repeat it into Polish for Mariusz. As Adam Birch's defense solicitor, Lipman would have received from police a copy of Mariusz's alibi statement. If he's read it, he would know that Mariusz contradicted some of the details in his client's statement. My eyes go toward a pile of papers on Lipman's desk, to the bloated and ancient filing cabinets against the wall and the desktop computers that needed replacing in 2010. He's swamped with cases, that much is clear. I bet he hasn't read it yet.

"So what can he do?" I say. "To help his friend?"

"I don't think there's anything he *can* do. If I need something I'll get in touch."

"What would constitute an alibi *with* hard evidence?" I ask. Elliot is spinning on his chair and I reach out a hand to steady it.

"CCTV that shows his whereabouts, GPS data, mobile phone records ..."

"Is there any CCTV near your spot in the tunnel? Would there be a chance Adam was recorded on the night of the murder?" I ask Mariusz in Polish.

Lipman interrupts: "But we're not going to pull up any CCTV at this point. Anyone can do a freedom of information request but footage is typically only kept for thirty days. The murder was five weeks ago. Alibi-wise, it's no help now."

"Can he be re-interviewed by police? He's concerned that he didn't come across as reliable during the interview because he was speaking through me. Interviews are difficult with an interpreter."

"Look, alibis are never very strong when they come from a friend or family member, anyway. Ideally they are someone without an existing relationship to the accused. Now, I need to prepare for a court appearance, but thank him for coming in." Lipman wobbles his chair back toward his desk.

"Wait," I say. "He *really* wants to help. There must be something he can do to assist. Aren't you supposed to be doing your own investigation, challenging the evidence the police have against Adam?"

The solicitor kicks the brake on his chair and turns to face me. His eyes rake my skin. "Did he really just say all of that to you in Polish?"

Acid ravages the back of my throat. I'm just the interpreter, I remind myself. I must appear personally unconcerned about Adam and the case. At the very least Lipman could pull me up for continuing with the interpreting job even when I realized that it concerned Sandra, somebody known to me. I move Elliot's chair closer to mine. "Mariusz said that to me in the car on the way here," I say. "I'm just doing my job."

"And me too. Thank him for coming in to see me, won't you." Lipman's hands go to his hips.

Mariusz mumbles complaint that he knew the solicitor wouldn't take him seriously and I seize the opportunity to pretend to translate his words. I can't leave here today without at least one idea as to how I can help Adam. "He wants me to stress again that he feels to blame for his friend's situation," I say to Lipman. "Because he was the alibi police didn't believe." Adam Birch is in Belmarsh prison. Alongside convicted serial murderers and terrorist bombers and Julian Assange. I need to undo what I did, or else he'll never get out.

"Like I said, an alibi defense can be weak at the best of times. Sure, it would have helped if Adam was sighted by a reliable witness, a stranger . . . Tell him this isn't his fault." Lipman gestures for me to relinquish our chairs. "Thanks again for coming," he says, with no attempt to hide his insincerity.

"There must be *something* we can do." *We.* This is dangerous, very dangerous. But the words are out now, and I can't reel them back in. Lipman must be sensing I'm personally interested in Adam's case. "What I mean is: Mariusz wants to know what evidence the police have against his friend. If he knows the extent of what they have, then maybe he can identify a way to help."

"They have his DNA," Lipman says. Yes, I know, but what else? Lipman must be aware of details that haven't been made public. "Adam was arrested for begging earlier in the year. It's a recordable offense. An offense where police can force you to provide DNA, to add to their database. That's what happened to Adam. And they matched it to what was collected at the scene." So that's how police had Adam's DNA on their database: because being homeless is practically a crime. "Because of the facts of the case—the alleged victim was pushed down the stairs after a struggle—we might get the charge down to manslaughter. And if he's found guilty, we have strong mitigating factors for sentencing. He has fairly severe asthma, he's been in and out of hospital a lot." I repeat it in Polish for Mariusz.

"Adam's ill," he agrees. "That's why he's homeless. Because of his health, he couldn't work, his marriage broke down, then he's living on the streets . . ." If he's convicted, because of me, Adam Birch will almost certainly die in prison. Lipman has a resigned look on his face. He thinks Adam is innocent. But he doesn't seem confident that he can win the case. I cast my eyes around the decrepit office again—I doubt this solicitor is capable of winning any case.

I go to translate Mariusz's words for Lipman but he cuts me off. "As I said, I need to go. Look—something might come up in our favor. A few days ago police located the bag—the bag that Adam Birch is allegedly carrying in the CCTV taken from the Knightsbridge street. His DNA was not detected on the bag. Adam Birch's DNA is on the alleged victim's body, but not on the bag he's seen carrying."

"So what does that mean—that isn't Adam Birch on the CCTV?"

Lipman stays coy. "That's what I'll be arguing." He passes us back over to the receptionist who shows us out.

Police don't have CCTV placing Adam on the heiress's street on the day of the murder. They have a neighbor eyewitness who says she saw him hanging around—but she probably saw a different homeless man, whoever it is on the CCTV footage. It seems as though Sandra's murder is an excuse for the heiress's neighbors to launch a vendetta against the local homeless population. The prosecution will have Adam's DNA on the body, his past conviction, and his known connection to the area. They have his broken alibi, thanks to me. I still have a bad feeling about the heiress. But I don't know what I can do about it.

Back on the high street: "Thank you for being patient," I tell Elliot. "You were so good in there. We're just going to take this man home and then you and I will go to lunch." I rub Elliot's back and he nods. Home. I said we were going to take Mariusz home. I scrape the nails of my right hand over my scalp. How can I just dump him back on the street and go back to our flat and pack for our move and get on with my life? Not after everything I've done.

Everything I know about the dark web I took from a BBC Two documen-
tary. I learned that you can use it to buy credit card numbers, drugs, guns,
counterfeit money, stolen subscription credentials, criminals-for-hire, forged
documents, software to break into computers, and even human beings. I saw
that you could navigate your cursor to Heaven & Hell Market and pay
someone to do just about anything you want. I arranged a VPN and down-
loaded the Tor browser. Money isn't a problem for me; the rest of it was
really quite easy. I used a credit card in the name of one of the family shell
companies registered in the Cayman Islands. It probably wasn't necessary. I
realize as I say this now: I don't actually mind if I'm caught.

I'm checking my phone as I walk and on my phone is your email ac-
count. Apparently the installed malware raises your phone's core temper-
ature and you might realize that even when idle it's much warmer than
usual. If you have noticed you don't seem to recognize it as a symptom of
being hacked. I swipe through your phone messages, WhatsApp, emails—
everything is in order. I've seen enough for today, I decide, and close it down.

I went into his room this morning while my sister was out. Then I went
next door to the playroom and switched on the train set and watched the
carriage pull into the miniature Paddington station. He'll be too old for
it soon. He'll be wanting to play violent computer games and he'll think
he's too big for anything wholesome and soft. You've robbed me of time, and
theft is the one crime I never imagined would affect me. I can't get back
what I've lost, but I can take everything away from you.

I access your calendar and scroll through your appointments once more.
It's almost time.

22.

I order an Uber and insist Mariusz let me take him for a meal. "Mariusz is going to come with us to lunch," I tell Elliot. My son seems comfortable enough around him, and a decent meal is the absolute least I can do. Mariusz has most of his possessions with him—on the streets people must live like turtles, he explains: they carry their homes, everything they own, stored on their person at all times, or else expect to find it stolen. We go to a Polish restaurant in Belsize Park, somewhere nice. Our Uber passes chain pasta joints and greasy spoons that Mariusz says are fine, but I don't want him to feel that I think *any* food is good enough for him, that he should be grateful to have any kind of meal at all. I came to this restaurant once several years ago with some clients while interpreting for a Polish trade conference. Now that we're here I fear I may have taken things too far the other way. The entrées average thirty pounds. The menu is Polish fusion with hyphenated ingredients I can't pronounce. Is Elliot going to like any of this food? And how am I going to pay for it? I picture my next credit card bill, the balance maxed out. But I can't back out of this now. The maître d' directs us to an opulent round table by the side window, eyeing Mariusz with suspicion. Am I embarrassing him? There is a whiff of leprosy about the gulf between our table and the nearest neighbor. I really can't afford this, but now we've sat down, I feel like there's nothing I can do. I glance around the room and feel swollen and obvious.

"Miso in Zurek soup?" Mariusz says, eyeing the menu. "It's not traditional, but I'll give it a go."

"Do you cook?" I ask. What a stupid thing to say—he doesn't have a home at the moment, let alone access to a kitchen.

"I trained as a pastry chef in Warsaw. Doing construction in London for a year was supposed to raise money for me to open my own restaurant." I try not to appear surprised then silently chastise myself. Of course he is a person with plans and ambitions for his life.

We place our order and for the next hour we talk about food. Mariusz tells me about the pierniki cookies from his hometown, delicate and spicy. The cookies are traditionally shaped as moons and stars but at his local bakery, their signature shape is Copernicus' silhouette. He shares his own recipe for Polish honey cake with plum butter, sugared orange-peel ice cream, and poppyseed pancakes. I enjoy the conversation so much that I forget why we're here. I think about Doreen, the first seeds of our friendship, the day of the social services interpreting job, us in the café across the road. Mariusz asks about my life and I answer as me because I am not the interpreter right now. I remind myself not to get too comfortable. This is not a lovely long lunch with a colleague or friend. This is for Mariusz, not for me. I don't deserve his company.

I steer the conversation back to why we're here. "So Lipman is going to argue that it's not Adam on the CCTV taken from the street, as his DNA wasn't on the bag," I say.

"That's *not* him on the CCTV," Mariusz says.

"I believe you. I think the only other thing that can be done to help your friend is for another alibi to come forward. A stranger, as Lipman says, someone credible because they have no relationship with Adam." I must be careful with how I phrase things. This man needs to think I'm a Good Samaritan and nothing more. He cannot start to question why a virtual stranger would be so concerned with his friend's case. "Are there any other homeless people based in the area who we could approach?"

He shakes his head. "It was only Adam and me in the tunnel.

Now it's only me. Sure, there are others who live close by, but no one who could vouch for Adam that day."

"All right—so passersby then. Thousands of people must go through that walkway each day on their way to and from the train station."

Mariusz takes a mouthful of rosehip tea. "People don't look at people living on the street. They can't look away fast enough. Who's going to remember whether they saw two men sitting on the ground that night, or one? Or three?"

"We can get data from Transport for London. They can tell us who exited and entered the subway at that time and we can contact them. Someone must have seen, will have really looked and noticed you as they passed."

"They'd give us that information?" His question is hopeful and sincere but my plan is desperate and unfeasible and we both know it. I stuff my mouth with a piece of fatty meat.

"You're right—Transport for London won't hand over data about who went in and out of the train that night, but we can do our own public appeal. Those signs calling for witnesses that police put out in front of subway stations after a crime has been committed? We'll do one of those, place it near your spot in the walkway. *Someone* will remember seeing you both. We can put my cell phone number on there. It can't hurt to try—see if anyone comes forward."

I can see that Mariusz is skeptical about my idea, but he's trying to show enthusiasm.

"All it would take is one person," I say. "A stranger walking past, and there'd be another, independent alibi." If I can produce another alibi for Adam Birch, then surely along with the revelation about the CCTV and the man with the bag, police will be forced to re-open the case.

We finish lunch and I grit my teeth as the waiter takes my credit card to pay. I find us another Uber. Mariusz goes back to the walkway and Elliot and I go home. I print out a sign calling for witnesses and attach it to the sturdiest cardboard I have. Tomorrow I'll go back to the tunnel and pin it up and I don't know what else I'm going to do about Adam Birch. Perhaps the prosecution's case against Adam will grow weaker and weaker and he'll be found innocent despite what I've done. But how long is that likely to take? I've interpreted on murder trials where the crime took place as much as two years prior to the court date. That could be two years of Adam's life in jail. I need to somehow get him out, now.

Online, I look for updates on The Lad's sexual assault case. Has the Crown Prosecution Service charged him yet for assaulting the other three women who came forward? No, it looks like the investigation is still ongoing. I need to know that I've had a positive impact on *one* case, that my misinterpreting helped to get justice for one person who deserved it. All of this has to be for something.

I have to get ready for our move on Wednesday. I place Elliot's things into boxes and when he goes to bed, I start packing up the rest of our flat. Long before minimalism became fashionable, I learned to travel light, and for years, with my mother, ensured that I could carry everything I owned in only two suitcases. Over the last few years I've allowed myself to accumulate and now, really for the first time in my life, I have excess. Shoes and items of clothing I rarely wear, shoulder bags that still have the tags on. When I get to the end of my closet, I find that I've filled two large boxes with my clothes alone. I'm not going to take all of this with me, I decide. I sit cross-legged on the floor of my bedroom and dig through the first box. There's a bottle-green carryall I really like, red boots in my size I couldn't believe my luck finding last year in a charity shop. Nice clothes and accessories that aren't appropriate for court. Why did I ever think that I deserved these things? That I should have anything nice at all? Adam Birch is in prison wearing whatever it is they make inmates wear and I have a pile of clothes and hats and scarfs I can't even remember using last. I empty both boxes, tip it all into a mound on the carpet. I rifle through the pile, my hands in a frenzy, sorting out my work clothes from everything else. The everything else is the majority. I fold it all neatly and manage to get it into one box. In thick black pen I write CHARITY SHOP and seal it up. Black ink has leaked onto my fingers, branding me.

"Elliot," I say the next morning. "I'm sorry that today is going to be quite busy. We need to collect the keys for our new flat, and I also have to make a trip into central London. I have to quickly see that man, Mariusz, who we met yesterday."

"What about school?" he asks.

"It's school holidays, remember? We'll do some fun things this week too, I promise." I want him to enjoy this week, and I need to tell him that he's not going back to his old school.

We take the train to the estate agent's office where I sign the paperwork and collect our keys. On our way to central London, Elliot plays a game on my phone while I hold the cardboard sign, rolled up tight. We alight at Knightsbridge and I'm relieved to see that Mariusz isn't there in the walkway. Some of me is eaten away each time I see him, and every time I think about Adam Birch. I worry that soon there might be nothing left. I pin the sign to the wall near to his possessions and make a mental note to check by in a few days to make sure no one has removed it.

The rest of the day is a flurry of packing and I manage a few hours' sleep before the movers arrive the next morning at 8 a.m. I've always lived in furnished flats in London so the job is done swiftly, Elliot's bed being the only large item that belongs to me. We take an Uber and follow the van ferrying our boxes. As we drive, I keep my eyes peeled to the street, looking for things that could form part of our new life. We pass clay tennis courts, a library, a supermarket that I think will be walking distance. Inside our new flat, I have the movers stack our boxes against the wall of the living room and I give the place a vacuum before I start to un-pack. Here we are, living in Wembley. I've not changed my address on the electoral roll, informed the NHS, my bank, Exia, or anyone. Only Elliot's new school has our details. It feels simultaneously safe and terribly lonely that no one really knows we're here.

Our new building is an ex-council tower with upward of a hun-dred flats. It has a secure external door with a buzzer. Our flat has a balcony but we are on the eleventh floor so only Spider-Man would have the ability to break in this way. There is a double dead-lock on our front door. We're going to be okay here.

"Did you see the park down the end of our street?" I ask Elliot. "When we drove past?"

"I wasn't looking. Can we play football there?"

"I'd say it's big enough for us to kick the ball around." It looked to be a bare and depressed little park but it's better than nothing. I open up the balcony door and walk out to peer over the edge. A ginger cat is patrolling the ground and after Elliot sees it, we go downstairs to say hello.

"I seem to remember you wanting pizza earlier?" I say to Elliot.

"Yes please!"

"We passed a Domino's in the car." After the rush of the last couple of days, I can't face cooking.

At some point in the evening, I fall asleep in front of the tele-vision on our new brown faux-leather sofa. A notification on my phone wakes me.

It's Facebook Messenger.

Hi. Yes, it's me.

Doreen has written back. I lean on my elbows and push myself up to sitting. I read the message again. Those four short words are enough for a dopamine spike. This doesn't mean she's back in your life, I tell myself. We are not friends again, because I'm not worthy. It's time to tell Doreen Sanderson what I did to her.

23.

"Every woman should have a younger friend," Doreen had said, two fingers pinching the stem, wine glass held almost horizontal. "You know how some women say you should at least once in your life sleep with an older man? That's bullshit. That's a man telling them to say that. What they *should* have is one friend who's twenty, thirty years younger." She pointed her glass at me, then refilled mine from the bottle of Shiraz on our table. "Cheers! To in. Intah. Aaahh. Inter . . ." She'd evidently had a few drinks before I'd arrived.

"Intergenerational?" I offered.

"Yes!" Her goblet held high above her head. "Intergenerational friendship!"

"Cheers!"

"Do you know," Doreen's words were sticking together. "Why it was *you* who I wanted to come out with tonight?" The sleeve of her blue cardigan was perilously close to the tip of a candle flame. Before ignition, I caught her wrist and dragged the candle closer to me.

"Because I was twice nominated fire marshal in my university halls of residence?"

"Because you're *young.* I hate that 'authenticity' is such a buzz-word now, but it's *true* that younger people react authentically to shitty situations. You have no experience of them yet, they haven't happened to you. So you're not performing, you're not acting according to the rules, just copying what you did the last time one of your uncles died or when this or that happened to your father. This is all new to you. So you *feel* it. And you're *listening.* You're not sitting there nodding along but actually thinking about your pending divorce or how you're not going to meet your next mortgage payment."

"I am a bit worried about my next rent payment actually."

"Cheeky sod. Drink your wine."

"I really like this place." Gordon's Wine Bar is essentially an underground cellar by the Thames. A cave that's cozy in winter but ferociously stuffy in summer, its Dickensian décor survived the turn of the twentieth century and the Blitz. My favorite drink is the delicate pink port.

"It really is the best bar in London for when something shitty has happened."

"Are you going to tell me now what that is?" Doreen had called me yesterday, upset. I knew it was work-related but she didn't want to talk about it over the phone. Now she raised one finger while she threw her head back and chugged the rest of her wine.

"A child died on my watch this week. I was his social worker. His mother, he was in care and we ... I ..." Her voice gave out, she exhaled and rallied. "*I* made the decision to return him to his birth mother six months ago. He's from a good family, they aren't underprivileged in any way. The mother had him in the car on Monday when it was ninety degrees Fahrenheit, with all the windows closed up. Tinted, so nobody could see inside. She went off to score drugs and by the time she went back to the car hours later, he was dead."

"That's terrible. I'm so sorry." I'd read something in the newspaper about a little boy dying and wondered if it was the work-related incident Doreen had obliquely referenced on the phone.

"The child was my client, but it's not my fault."

"Of course it isn't."

"What could I do? She was a junkie, sure. That's why she forgot him in the car. But I followed guidelines. There were no grounds for going down the adoption road. Foster care is supposed to be temporary. The best result is a child returned to birth parents. That's what we're supposed to aim for."

I subtly moved the remaining bread and hummus from my plate over to her side of the table and encouraged her to eat. I'd had enough nights out with Doreen to know that the articulate phase of her drunkenness was when I should really be worried.

"I'm sure you didn't do anything wrong." I'd only known Doreen for a little over six months but we had become fast friends.

"Let me show you this." Doreen fumbled in her bag. A droplet of wine escaped my glass and soaked into the wood. She extracted her phone, then shoved it toward me. A news article from a tabloid with the headline: WORST SOCIAL WORKER IN BRITAIN.

And under that, a picture of Doreen. I gasped.

"The mother had a history of drug abuse. I returned the boy to her. I was responsible for him. I may as well have killed him myself." I darkened Doreen's phone screen and swatted away her hand when she went to open the article again. "I've been told to expect more. In the tabloids. I'm going to be famous."

"I'm sorry. I don't want you to read them but I know that's a stupid thing to ask you not to do."

"Of course I'm going to bloody read them."

"I know."

We were silent for a moment while I adjusted Doreen's necklace which had twisted around her throat. There might be half a dozen of the same crimes in the UK each month. Women murdered, children neglected, violent home invasions. For some reason only one of these ever eats up the media coverage. The cutest child, the whitest woman, the most beautiful home, as though readers only have capacity to empathize with one victim in each category. Unfortunately for Doreen, her dead child-in-care would become the one that rose to the surface. And people love to hate civil servants.

"What is work doing for you? To help, I mean? It's their responsibility to fix this, right?" I asked. "Make these articles go away."

She shrugged. "I went to the doctor today for some sleeping pills. He asked me what was going on, I ended up telling him everything. That I was basically accused of being a child killer."

"No one's calling you that."

"They *are*, Revelle. I'm being recognized on the street. Anyway, he refused to prescribe them, the bastard."

"I think you'll sleep well tonight." I nodded toward our second bottle of wine.

"It feels worse today. Tuesday was when I heard what'd happened. Now the shock's rubbed off, underneath is all the guilt. It's really latched on, like a leech. Feasting off me."

"Do you want to keep being a social worker? You're not trapped, you know. You can do something else. If this is how they treat you ..."

"They've given me two weeks' leave from work to 'get over it.' So. I can drink as much as I want tonight. I'm going to go out every night for the next two weeks except for Saturday. Gotta leave one night a week for the amateurs."

"I can take the day off work tomorrow," I offered. "We could have brunch—lunch if you're sleeping off what will be your epic hangover. See a film. Wander around a gallery. Yeah?"

She puckered her mouth and shook her head. "Don't worry 'bout me. Work's just covering their arse in case I'm suicidal like Jenny in HR over her Shetland pony."

"You can tell me if you are," I said. "Having ... thoughts."

"I know." We paused as chatter from surrounding tables rose to crescendo. Then Doreen started speaking again. "When I was fifteen I bought two packets of stuff from Superdrug, a pale green and red label, the strongest painkillers you could get over the counter. I was planning to take them all very early on a Sunday morning. I got up at five o'clock while everyone in the house was still asleep. I used the family power-cut flashlight and sat on the floor in the dark, looking up the drug in my father's medicine dictionary. It said that death was rare so I started to worry that two packets would only put me in a coma. I went back to bed. Got up again at six, filled the bath with cool water and threw in my mother's hairdryer. When it was time for me to jump in—I just stood there; I didn't want to die anymore. Now I can't remember why I wanted to do it in the first place. But that was it—I only had to try it once. I've never thought about it since. Even now. The experience of doing it, of physically going through with it, of knowing I could plan it and take it through to the end if I wanted to, seemed to shock me back into life."

"No pun intended."

"What's that?"

"You said it 'shocked' you back into life." That sent Doreen into such a fit of laughter her cardigan was almost lit by the candle once again and our empty wine bottle rolled and bounced along the floor. After the laughter came a deep lull.

"I never went to religious schools and my mother didn't have any kind of faith," I said. "But sometimes my international schools would cover world religions in class. I always remember this thing in the Jewish Bible, called Cities of Refuge, do you know it?" She shook her head, hummus clogging her teeth. "I might not be recounting this exactly right but basically God told Moses that he had to reserve a certain number of his cities to serve as places of asylum for those accused of manslaughter, for anyone whose actions accidentally led to the death of someone else." Immediately I regretted my use of the word "manslaughter." I was trying to be a supportive friend but worried I was only making things worse.

"I didn't mean to suggest this is your fault. It isn't. I *know* it isn't." I was leaning forward, both hands splayed on the table for emphasis.

"I know what you mean." She smiled. "It's a nice thought."

"The idea is that the accidental perpetrator would be looked after inside the city walls. Protected from acts of vengeance or undue punishment. They'd live within the walls until the current reigning high priest died. Then there'd be a kind of reset. While everyone else was busy mourning the death of the priest, the accidental killer would quietly return to their home, everything forgotten."

Doreen considered this for a moment, then her phone began to ring, and she pushed it to my face. "It's this journalist who's been trying to call me all afternoon."

"Ignore it. Let's get some more food. Those fries from Five Guys. You love them. The ones that soak up booze like cheap bathroom rolls."

"He'll keep calling. Answer it for me. Please," her voice a cross between a slur and a whine.

"What do you want me to say?"

"Something stupid. Talk bollocks so they'll stop calling. Tell them you're my publicist."

I swallowed and pressed accept. Doreen crouched by me, her ear next to mine. I told the journalist I was Doreen's friend and they asked me what she was like.

"She's a volunteer netball coach," I said. "And on Wednesdays, after training, she takes the girls to her husband's hairdressing salon for a free haircut."

Doreen mouthed "What the? More bollocks!" as I stumbled over "ahs" and "umms," wondering what else to say.

"She also does it for the elderly. Doreen will bring a carload of senior citizens in from the nearest care home every Friday and let the new color technicians have a go at doing highlights or tints or scalp bleaches for the very first time—you know, trying things out on someone who doesn't know what's going on. Isn't that lovely? She's very community-minded."

Mission somewhat accomplished: the journalist realized he was being punked and hung up.

"That was brilliant!" Doreen held her side as she laughed. "Wow, you're dark. I didn't know where you were going at first. I thought: bloody hell she's actually going to talk about the time I was coaching Lauren's netball team!"

"How is Lauren?" Doreen's eighteen-year-old daughter was up in Durham for her first year of university.

"She's joined Extinction Rebellion. You know the environmental activist group who shut down roads and train stations and stop people from getting to their jobs?"

"Right." It was obvious that, underneath, Doreen was proud.

"I keep telling her that human extinction is probably a good thing, the *best* thing if you want to save the planet, and the animals. I mean, what's their number-one problem? People!"

"I know you won't leave without a whiskey for the road," I said.

"I won't leave without a whiskey for the road."

"You sit. I'll get them. And mind that freaking candle." She put her hands up all innocent. "By the way, your outfit is ridiculous," I called from my way to the bar. Her individual pieces of clothing were perfectly fine, but the combined effect was one of a scrambled rainbow.

"I wanted to look as though I was deranged in case one of those journalists snapped another pic of me for their paper. Make *them* look ridiculous for harassing a clearly unstable menopausal woman."

"If they're going to your house, why don't you come and stay at mine tonight?"

"Didn't you move last month to a studio in Deptford with rats?"

"You remember," I said, hand to heart in mock flattery.

"Okay. Yeah, staying with you is a good idea. Just for tonight."

When I brought our whiskies back, Doreen's phone chirped and she whipped it out of her bag. "It's another news story."

"Stop reading them. It will drive you mad."

She was quiet for a minute as her eyes raced across her phone screen. Then she passed it to me to read.

"They've been calling him 'Child X' for privacy reasons, but now they've finally released his name and photo."

I stopped blinking. My body ceased to breathe and pump blood and fire neurons and whatever else is required to stay alive. Doreen saw the frozen look on my face.

"Oh, yes, you recognize him," she said. "In all the craziness I forgot—you saw that little boy once. Max. That was how you and I met, wasn't it? The mother's native language is German. It was your first interpreting job for the local authority." I looked up from Doreen's phone. I couldn't meet her eye so I focused on a picture of the queen on the wall behind her head. How could I look her in the eye ever again?

"He . . . seemed like a nice kid." My words came from some dark, hollow place inside me.

Doreen nodded then rested her head on the table. I excused myself for the bathroom, pushed my way into a stall and fell to the floor, sobbing.

24.

For the rest of the week, Elliot and I settle in to the flat and explore our new area. I complete the enrollment of my boy in the local school and sort out his uniform, and on Sunday we have a final outing to a cheap Thai restaurant and a mini-golf course. We both go to bed earlier than usual, exhausted. When I wake, it is daylight. I scramble for my phone. It's ten past seven in the morning. Elliot's first day at his new school. I tumble to my feet. "Elliot! Wake up. Breakfast now, come on." I'm thankful to myself for at least sorting his schoolbag last night. I get him fed and dressed and we are out the door by eight. On the footpath, Elliot walks slowly by my side, scuffing his feet.

"Are you nervous, Batman? It's natural to be scared about starting a new school. But it'll be fine. You'll make friends. The children will be friendly." I hope that's true.

He lifts his head. "I'm not scared."

"Okay. Good, just checking."

This school is a little bigger than his previous. There is more concrete and fewer plants, but the play equipment looks new and the classrooms more spacious. We arrive with five minutes to spare before the bell and I introduce myself to his teacher. He seems nice, twenty-two years old at the most, with all the zeal of someone newly qualified. I leave the school grounds feeling that I've left Elliot in good hands.

Back home, I unpack the last of our boxes, which I've been putting off. I haven't had a chance to find a suitable interpreting assignment for today. I'll have to do some extra overnight shifts on

LanguageLine to compensate for the income I missed last week, and the fact I'm paying two rents. While I'm adding new cushions to our cracked, faux-leather sofa, I see that there's a handle on the side. It's not just a chair but a pull-out sofa bed. I think of Mariusz Dorobek sleeping outside last night, and every other night. Before, he had Adam Birch for company and for safety, but now he doesn't even have that. He could stay in here, on this sofa bed. No—I dismiss the idea as quickly as it arrives. Elliot is my priority. Mariusz seems very nice, but he's still a stranger and I can't invite just anyone into our home. If I didn't have Elliot, then I could help him. If my circumstances were different, I would do something, which is probably what everyone tells themselves as they walk by him in the tunnel, eyes trained on the dirty walkway, on the concrete, never on the human.

Later that morning, a text shows on my phone:

Hi, I'm Alicia. I saw your sign in the tunnel @ Knightsbridge. It was me who called the paramedic for the homeless man that evening. He was struggling to breathe. I'm sorry that I didn't stay. I've been thinking about him . . .

The sign has been up in the Knightsbridge walkway for a week and this is the first proper response. Here we go—this is something, maybe exactly what we need. I type a message back to Alicia as fast as my fingers can manage. What paramedic is she referring to? I remember what Lipman said in his office about Adam having severe asthma, and being frequently in and out of hospitals.

This woman called an ambulance for Adam? This could be it, I tell myself. A rock-solid alibi. I fly around my living room, looking for my handbag. Where is it? I need to go, go! I find it and yank the nearest pair of shoes onto my feet and head to the train station.

Mariusz is dozing when I arrive. I gently shake him awake and translate the text message.

"The paramedic came at around noon," Mariusz says in Polish. "Adam has these breathing episodes sometimes—they look like asthma attacks. Someone walking past at lunchtime must have called an ambulance. When they turned up, Adam refused their help. He hates hospitals. He says he never wants to go back into one again, unless he's bleeding to death."

"Adam told this to the police?"

He nods. "The ambulance was gone by twelve-thirty. The murder didn't happen until between six and eight o'clock that night. Many hours later. So it was not relevant."

"Right," I sigh.

"A while after the ambulance left, Adam was feeling a bit better and said he wanted to sleep, so I left. I went to get food and drinks, and I came back to the walkway at five o'clock and was with him all night. Like I said in the alibi interview."

"So this Alicia person," I gesture to my phone.

"Can't help us with an alibi." Our cardboard sign is dirty and struggling to adhere to the wall. Mariusz unpins it and slowly rolls it into a subway. "It was worth trying," he says. "It was a good idea."

But not good enough. "Right," I say. "This woman isn't a witness. But what about the paramedic? If Adam was so unwell he needed medical attention, he's unlikely to have broken into a house that same day and killed someone."

"Adam said that to the police. He was still weak for the next twenty-four hours. He couldn't have fought anyone, killed them. But because he refused help from the paramedic and didn't show his ID, police said there was no patient that day with his name. No medical record, no proof."

"If he had gone to the hospital, he probably would have been in accident and emergency all evening, or on the ward. An inarguable alibi."

"I should have tried harder to convince him to go."

"No, I didn't mean that." I can't have Mariusz think any of this is his fault. We stand there, both looking into the distance, out through the exit of the tunnel into the dull autumn day. We come to unspoken agreement that we've reached a dead end. Neither of us knows what to do for Adam.

In the silence my mind wanders to the supposed pits of the dead close to here; bodies from a leper colony buried near Knightsbridge subway station. I rub into the dirt underfoot and ice goes up my spine. I lead Mariusz into a nearby sandwich shop and insist he let me buy him whatever he wants. I don't think I can spend any more time with Mariusz after today. I don't trust myself in his company. The urge to reveal, to tell him everything, is becoming irrepressible. Sometimes I think confessing is all I ever really wanted: about the German job, about Doreen, everything. I wonder if I adopted for insurance. Because I'd never want to expose them to the consequences of me confessing, I'd never go through with it for as long as I had a child. Plenty of criminals give themselves up in police interviews, even before they're presented with the mounting evidence against them. I've seen suspects in interview rooms blurt out details of their crimes before we've even properly sat down. Why are humans incapable of carrying around a secret? We'll risk everything for the promise of forgiveness, so hard to resist. But I cannot confess. I cannot risk other criminals from my past assignments going free, and most of all, a jail sentence for perverting the course of justice, and Elliot thrown back into the care system. I'm so sorry for Adam. But this is what being a parent is: I have to choose my boy over everything, even my own morality. I say goodbye to Mariusz and tell him that I'll be in touch, but I think we both know that I don't really mean it.

On the way home, I call the communications department of the London Ambulance Service NHS Trust. That woman Alicia walked past Adam for thirty seconds and called an ambulance as she continued on her way. No use to us at all. But maybe the paramedic recorded something in his notes about attending a man that day who refused treatment? Even if he doesn't know the person's name.

The call picks up. "This is the Patient Experience team. Are you wanting to send a thank-you card to a member of staff?" a man asks. I decide to go along with this.

"Yes, my friend refused treatment," I say. Perhaps my best strategy is flattery. "But your colleague was so kind to him. I want to buy him a gift, but I'd like to speak to him first. If you could kindly find out the name of the paramedic who attended and have him call me back. My friend didn't give his name but it was outside, in Knightsbridge, in the pedestrian walkway, at around noon on Saturday, September sixteenth." I give a physical description of Adam and his age and we hang up.

If I can't get Adam out of prison now, I must at least ensure he has the best possible defense team and is acquitted at trial. I need to find out how much a good legal defense costs. When I'm back inside my flat, an internet search tells me £400 per hour is a typical fee for top solicitors in London. Hundreds of hours of work would be needed for a murder trial, probably thousands. And that isn't including the barrister's fee and other court costs. I think of Lipman's dirty office in Wood Green and what kind of representation Adam will get if he's left to legal aid. He is going to need hundreds of thousands of pounds. I could work two hundred hours a week all year and I'd never raise enough to cover even half of it. I am soon short of breath, trying to slow my palpitating heart. I'm not anxious about the money, because it's actually already here, available to me. But I would rather work a million hours; I'd prefer to work a single shift which never ends—anything instead of taking that money. But I have to think of Adam and what I've done, and I know that I no longer have a choice.

Hi Richard, I type on my phone. *Can we speak? I've had a change of heart about my mother's estate.*

I send the text, and in my mind's eye see my mother calmly walk to her closet, turning to ensure I'm trailing behind. She extends the step ladder and pulls her wheelie suitcase down from the high shelf. And she packs. Slowly but methodically, she makes me watch and I am hooked, I can't look away; it's like the climactic scene of one of my favorite films. She's leaving, she says. She has had enough of me and is going to live somewhere else, but she won't tell me where. She says that I can beg, that's the only option available to me. I can drop to the floor and plead for her to stay. I am five years old.

The chime of my phone brings me back to the present. Richard has replied. *I'm glad. I'll call you later tonight your time. I want you to have it all. Actually, I wrote my own will this week. I've been meaning to ask you if I could make you executor. Could I leave it all to you and the little guy, when my time's up? Think about it. I would like that a lot. Talk later.*

I put the phone down and go into Elliot's bedroom. Until it is time to pick him up from school, I lie on the bed, face-down, breathing through his pillow.

I have become a gasper. Just like Michael Hutchence and that MI5 agent they found in a trash bag. This is not auto-erotic for me, but how else am I supposed to practice if not on myself? There are dirty corners on the internet where one can take instruction in the fine art of self-asphyxiation. What materials to use (I prefer stockings), which precise spot on the neck to apply pressure (I've marked mine with a fabric pen), and which immobile object to assist you with the knot (I quite like a simple door handle). Accidental suicide is obviously the greatest risk, but I am being very careful. I have a great deal to live for, after all: my son. A couple of times during my rehearsal sessions I've seen sparkly stars and almost lost consciousness but I am always able to bring myself back from the brink.

Some doctors say it takes seven minutes for a human to die of a complete loss of oxygen. Others claim even four minutes is enough to render the average person brain dead. There is a formula—it isn't foolproof, but there's a way you can calculate the approximate time it will take to kill a particular person this way based on their size and your own weight and strength, assuming you're the one who is going to apply the pressure. Do you want to know what your number is? Oh, I've no doubt you do.

Not yet, I'm not ready. First, I need to train on someone. It has to be a person of roughly similar size and strength to you.

"Where's the flippin' vodka gone?!" My sister's voice charges up the stairs and destroys my quiet. "It was HERE!" she's shouting as I hear her open and slam the cupboard door. I've ceased trying to hide my pills and keep her away from alcohol. Let her self-destruct is my approach now—if she breaches the terms of her parole then that would be ideal, she can go back to prison and be out of my life. It's best she is not here when my boy

returns—in fact it is imperative. I will not have him influenced by such a person, not after everything he has already been through.

"Vodka!" she shouts again, and my nails spear into my palm.

"Coming!" My voice is dripping in honey. I need to practice on a neck that isn't mine. "I have some damson liqueur I've not opened yet," I tell her when I reach the kitchen, eyes glinting up at hers, my smile wide. "It's a new batch. Would you like to be the guinea pig?"

25.

I left the ladies' restrooms in Gordon's and shuffled back to Doreen. I noticed she was looking brighter.

"Did you have to swim out of the bowl or something?" she said.

"Sorry." I fixed my gaze on a dribble of wine on the table that looked like blood. "Long line." There was a crushing sensation across the length of my breast bone. A fist was squeezing my heart like a stress ball. I wondered if this was what a heart attack felt like. A catastrophic stroke at twenty-five.

"Is the offer still open to hang out tomorrow?" Doreen asked.

My last chance to tell her. If I left it any later to confess, it would be unforgivable. It probably already was. That German word, *Torschlusspanik*, "gate-shut panic." German. The language the little boy and his mother spoke that day.

"Because I have ten more days off work and I haven't done anything spontaneous in about thirty years, I'm thinking I could go to Greece. To Mykonos. Get a last-minute flight tomorrow. Leave all this behind for a week. And you could come."

My lips parted but no words came out. I could not go with Doreen to Greece. The more time I spent with her, the more likely she was to look right through me and see the truth on my face, moving through my veins. All I had to do was claim to be busy, explain that I had forgotten about an interpreting job which could not be canceled; I couldn't take the day off. My voice deserted me and I said nothing.

"What do you think? We can drink ouzo and choke on feta."

We'd only known each other for such a short time. The

friendship wasn't old enough to weather something of this magnitude. I was still establishing myself as a freelance interpreter and the few clients I did have would quickly vanish if everything came out. I could never tell her. If I did, I'd have nothing left. I couldn't bring him back. The little boy was already dead. In that moment I vowed to never speak German again. I would never work on child protection assignments or for the family courts but I would keep my interpreting career and the only proper friend I'd ever had.

"I . . . well, I guess I could," I said. Doreen's face really lit up then.

"Screw it," she said. "Let's go!"

I gave a weak smile and hoped for the stirrings of cardiac arrest in my chest to follow through and end it all.

The only available flight was six thirty-five in the morning. We confirmed our tickets in the back of a black cab, threw some clothes into a bag at Doreen's and stopped by my place on the way to the airport, where we slept while our phones charged, leaning against a pole. We found a cheap hotel in Athens and went for a coffee to perk us up. The Psiri neighborhood felt like Camden Town. Late-night bars, tavernas, artistic graffiti, and scruffy-but-cool market clothes. Our rickety hotel did have Wi-Fi but we weren't given the code and didn't ask. Doreen's phone would ring a few times a day, but unless it was her daughter, ex-husband, or her brother, she didn't answer it.

Here was a week without the internet or British tabloids where no one recognized Doreen's face or asked her on the supermarket line why she didn't just go and kill herself. A former colleague from Doreen's child protection team had been doing a series of media interviews, claiming he'd quit his job because he foresaw that under Doreen's chaotic leadership, something tragic would eventually happen. Another ex-colleague had turned on her and given a similar quote to the BBC. In reality, Doreen had fired them both for underperforming. But she was being painted as a serial incompetent, the social worker linked to a number of child protection cases with appalling outcomes over her thirty-year career. The deceased child's mother had been arrested, which was a relief at first, but only served to highlight to the public that Doreen was getting away with her role in this, the press coverage reasonable as it was her only punishment.

So she ignored the phone calls and the internet, and made me pose for selfies under the boulders of the Arkadiko Bridge, the oldest functioning bridge in Europe. She dragged me to the Acropolis with the crowds and then the lane where all the houses are painted hot pink and we watched the changing of the guard at the Athens Parliament. For the first couple of days, she kept asking me what was wrong. Didn't I like Greece? Wasn't I having a nice time? She must have thought me a bore, the world's worst, most sullen travel companion, swearing to herself that she'd never vacation with me again.

While we were away, Doreen never mentioned the case or what she was going to do when we got back to London. As the week drew to a close, her spirit dimmed. Normal life and reality an infection, slowly taking hold. She didn't want to go back and wasn't ready for the nightmare waiting for her. I couldn't wait to get out of there, but then I realized things were going to be so much worse at home. If the case was still going to be present in the news, how could I do anything else with my days other than read the stories over and over, and stay up all night replaying that day in my mind? So I booked our onward travel and an Airbnb on Mykonos for an extra week and told her once it was done.

"Oh, thank goodness!" she said, when I showed her my phone. "Thank you, *really*. I thought you were hating this and couldn't wait to get home. I'm so happy to stay. You're saving my life here." Then we went for ice cream.

Every extra day we were in Greece was a day we both avoided

the screeching headlines and cruel op-eds about Doreen. The click-bait journalists who used this situation to excavate every tragic case of her social work career, every unhappy family resolution she oversaw, despite the outcomes being largely beyond her control. How could I endure another radiant photo of the dead little boy? All that scorching air that smothered me when I thought of him suffocating in his mother's car.

Mykonos was all about Paradise Beach, Agrari Beach, sunset views and windmills in Little Venice. We bought too-big swimsuits from tourist traps and thin towels the colors of the Greek flag. We drank and ate and guzzled endless shots of ouzo. There were moments where I forgot what I'd done and for a few hours allowed myself to unwind and laugh. On nights when this happened, I'd wake the next morning with a hangover, head throbbing with alcohol, but mostly with shame. One night Doreen went back to the hotel of a retired Israeli soldier she met in a nightclub where the floor was coated in artificial grass.

We decided to spend a day apart. After breakfast one morning, Doreen headed to a museum while I sat around the hotel scouring eBay and Amazon on my phone. I had this idea of finding a book on German etymology, of discovering a long-lost link between the two German words I had confused, some perfectly reasonable explanation for why I could have mixed them up. The hotel cleaner charged into the room and pointing to the orange sunshine spilling in between the curtains, shooed me outside. I didn't want to be out enjoying the hum of the city. I wanted to prevent myself from enjoying anything ever again. I found a soulless shopping mall full of French tourists and colorless window displays; white was evidently in season, but to me the dresses and trousers only looked watery. I would roam this mall, that was my plan for the day, doing laps and riding the escalators until it was time to go and meet Doreen for dinner.

I could not stop dreaming in German. I couldn't remember the details when I woke but each morning I was convinced she could hear my thoughts from her bed on the other side of the room. As I walked past Greek swimwear shops and hairdressers and nail salons, some for the second and third time, I visualized draining the German language out of me, one word at a time, letting it leak and wash away.

On the escalator I noticed a girl, about three, trailing after a young woman, possibly still a teenager; her mother. The woman was talking on a phone, hands free, gesticulating to herself, pausing every few steps to admire a window display. The little girl trotted after her, hurrying to catch up. At one point, she tripped over her own feet and fell flat on her nose, but she immediately got back up and kept running. I thought this was the strangest thing—wouldn't most children of that age have stayed on the ground, howled and cried, demanding their parent pick them up and soothe them? Something was wrong with this little girl. The dynamic between her and the mother was off. Was her blank expression a symptom of neglect? Abuse? I abandoned my route around the shopping mall and started following them. Minutes went by and still the mother was babbling away on her phone, not even turning to see if her daughter was keeping up. "Hello," I said to the girl, in English and in Greek. "Is that your mum, are you okay?" That was the extent of my Greek vocabulary. The girl stopped running after the woman and turned to me. "I don't know what you're saying," I said. "Do you speak English?" She was chatting away and I didn't understand a word. This is unusual, I thought, this has to be a cry for help, a child of this age talking so enthusiastically to a complete stranger. She's asking me to intervene. She's begging me to rescue her.

I didn't know the phone number for the Greek emergency services. "Hello, excuse me," I said, grabbing the arm of the nearest person, an elderly man, white plastic bags in each hand. "Do you speak English?" I said in Greek. He shook his head and kept walking. "Hello, I need some help. Help!" I shouted in English and in Greek. Shoppers darted away to avoid me. I knew some of them could understand me. They behaved as though I couldn't see them murmuring to one another, taking hold of their partner's arm and steering them out of my way. I was wasting time. The woman on the phone had walked far enough ahead that she was almost out of view, her daughter in the yellow dress, too small now to properly see. "CAN ANYONE HELP ME!" I yelled in English, tipping my head back, letting the sound be carried by the high ceilings and the over-polished shopping center floor. I had to do something.

I pressed the emergency call button on my phone and after a few unfamiliar beeps it seemed to reroute to a local ringtone. I spoke in English. When a voice responded in Greek, I kept talking over them until the phone was passed to someone else. "Yes, hello," a woman said. "You may proceed." In English, I told her where I was and what was happening with the little girl. I didn't know how to call child protection and thought it was probably a police matter, anyway. As it turned out, there was a police station a few doors down from the shopping center. She gave me directions and I ran there. A young constable greeted me at the door with the English "Hello," apparently warned that I was coming. I was ushered into a room and given a cup of lukewarm coffee.

After half an hour or so, I emerged to find the bathroom and down the corridor I saw them, the young woman and the little girl. The woman had her hands draped casually around her daughter's shoulders, her phone was gone; now the child was given her full attention. She stood with a policeman, speaking calmly in Greek and laughing. The two of them sharing joke after joke. She wasn't young, I could see that now; definitely not a teenager, probably closer to forty. The girl came up to her mother's chest, so I supposed that she was older than three after all. I had gotten a number of the details wrong. But that wasn't the point. That girl should be taken away and given a better life. She can't go home with that woman today, I said to myself, she must be protected. Then the police officer waved the woman and the girl goodbye and they both left. She put on a display for him. The most abusive parents know exactly what to do. That's how they get away with it for so long: they turn on the charm as soon as social services gets wind of what they're up to. I would still make my report. I wanted what I saw today in the shopping center on record. All it would take is someone else to contact Greek child protection and then they might have enough to step in.

I walked back to the room where my now stone-cold coffee was and heard two voices from inside. I paused at the door and listened. They spoke in a mixture of Greek and English and I wondered if one of them was an interpreter sent to speak for me. There was a flurry of Greek words and then a female voice in English "mentally ill . . . she may have lost a baby . . ." They were talking about me. I ran out of the police station and kept going all the way back to the hotel. The cleaner had finished in my room. The soaps and shampoos were rearranged, the towels folded and put back in their original positions. The room looked vacant, the only sign of life a used glass with the faintest imprint of a mouth along the rim. I sat on the floor until Doreen returned.

The final day of our trip was equally horrible. It poured with rain, our real lives reaching across the sea and pulling us back to Britain. Before we'd even disembarked the plane, Doreen must have picked up the Gatwick Wi-Fi and her phone flooded with texts and notifications. New articles had been published. More newspapers calling for her to be sacked or charged with manslaughter, as ridiculous as that was. She seemed to represent everything the public loathed about child protection. The lone punching bag, forced to absorb every blow. We got a giant Toblerone in the airport and passed it between us on the train. The melty chocolate comforting, clinging to our skin.

Now, eight years later, Doreen has written back to me and I need to tell her everything. Doreen, Adam Birch. One by one, I must undo my mistakes. I start to pace around the flat, hoping the rhythm will help me to get the words exactly right. Even after all this time, I don't know what to say to her. What if I can't do it?

My phone sounds and I jump. A message blinks on the screen. It is from a familiar number. Mine.

You changed a word. That was a mistake. Tomorrow, do it again. Wood Green Crown Court, Court 6, 10 a.m. Replace the French interpreter Paul Beaupert. Change NOT GUILTY to GUILTY.

I read it through twice, three times. SMS received 8:42 p.m. I cross-check each digit with my own phone number. It matches. I've heard of spammers using this tactic—they can block their own number and have the message appear as though you sent it to yourself.

You changed a word.

Someone knows.

I lunge for the balcony door. It's really far too cold to go outside but I need oxygen in order to think. I lean over the railing and cast my eyes down to the concrete below. Someone has realized what I did during Adam Birch's alibi interview? Or the witness testimony during The Lad's sexual assault trial? The police interview with the Hungarian care nurse? No, I didn't change a word with the nurse—I thought about it, but I didn't go through with it.

Back inside the flat, I read the message again. I go over each word, hoping I've misunderstood and the sentences will transform on the phone screen in front of me, morph into a nonsense scam text or a message clearly sent to the wrong person. Somebody knows what I've done. A police officer? A solicitor? A clerk who types up the transcriptions? They want me to say "Guilty" when the client says

"Not Guilty." This is some kind of blackmail, but it makes no sense. I don't have control over which cases I'm assigned to, and I haven't misinterpreted on any French assignment. Changing "Not Guilty" to "Guilty" is impossible. Tomorrow must be a Plea and Trial Preparation Hearing, and everyone in the room will realize if I change the plea. Is this some kind of test? If an interpreter changed a plea in any hearing the judge would simply throw them out, assume they're having a breakdown or are completely incompetent. Even if I could change the word, the message says "replace the French interpreter Paul Beaupert" as though removing another interpreter who is already booked is something I can possibly do. If the person who sent the text is savvy enough to realize I changed a word somewhere, they must know that what they're asking is absurd.

I type a reply. *Who is this?* The message goes nowhere—I've simply sent it to myself. This is only a text message, I tell myself. One anonymous SMS from someone too cowardly to confront me. They haven't threatened me with harm, they haven't approached me in person—they're obviously not going to report me to the police and have me arrested. They're a blackmailer. I can ignore them. Maybe this really is a test—someone suspects I changed a word somewhere but they have no proof; they'd certainly have no proof that the mistake was deliberate.

I put my ear to Elliot's bedroom door—he's breathing softly, he's asleep. The whole building is quiet. I've passed a few people in the elevator and on the stairs, but I haven't had the opportunity to formally introduce myself to any of our new neighbors. Now it's after nine at night—too late to knock on a stranger's door. So I spend the next half an hour writing friendly notes and push them under the doors of the two flats either side of me. I need to befriend these people. I might need their ears and eyes looking out for us, and it would be good to feel less alone here.

When I come back through my front door, my phone buzzes

with a new message. This one also appears as sent from my own number. *YOU SHOULD BE HERE*. And an image. A photograph of a large gray building complex. What is that? I do recognize it, but am struggling to place exactly where it is. Then my hand falls, and the phone plummets to the floor. I know that building. I've been inside there once before for a job. It's a women's prison just outside of London. Whoever this is knows that I've committed contempt of court or perverting the course of justice. I do this job for them tomorrow or this is where I end up.

I go out to the balcony again and brace myself against the railing. I need fresh air. I try to keep breathing. What evidence would they possibly have on me? I'd lose my work, I couldn't interpret again, but I could live with that now. I could start a new career translating Indian marketing material or French children's books—something. The maximum sentence if I was convicted of either offense is extremely unlikely. I'd pay a fine perhaps. I could do that, with the money from my mother's estate, the part that isn't going to Adam Birch. But there was that judge in London a few years ago who lied to police about who was driving during a traffic incident, and she was sentenced to sixteen months in prison. And what I've done is much worse than that. How long would I get? It wouldn't matter because Elliot would be taken from me and fostered, back in the care system, shunted from one family to another. If he was lucky, he'd be adopted by someone else, someone better than me. But I told him we were each other's family and would be forever. I promised he would never be homeless, that I was his mother and nothing would ever change that. I won't tell him that was a lie. I will not go to prison and lose him.

Now I'm shivering and wasting energy that I should be using to figure this out. I lug my body back inside the flat. If I can somehow take the place of Paul Beaupert on the trial tomorrow, the moment I "accidentally" plead Guilty instead of Not Guilty the judge will have me dismissed anyway. If that's what these people want, I can do it. The judge will submit a complaint about me but I can say I had a medical episode—that one single error won't destroy me. But how do I actually get on that trial? Convince an interpreter I've never met to step down without raising suspicion? What possible reason would I have for wanting to be assigned to his trial, other than to interfere in the proceedings?

You'll have to ask me very nicely, my mother would say. *Beg and I might stay.*

The pounding in my head intensifies. I close my eyes and feel my way to the bathroom. There is a shoebox on the bathmat not yet unpacked. Soaps and toothbrushes and various ointments and bits of medication. I haul myself to my knees and dig through, looking for something to kill my headache. My fingers wrap around a bottle of pills I'd forgotten about. A sedative; a prescription from a previous bout of insomnia after I worked on a murder trial. It's heavy, almost full. I swallow one and lurch upright. It's almost ten o'clock now. Twelve hours until I need to be at court.

26.

The washing basket suffocates with dirty clothes, which makes dressing fast. In the morning I select my only remaining pair of clean trousers, my last bleached white shirt. Sensible shoes I polish with a splash of hand sanitizer and I am out the door. I look professional. Playing the part of trustworthy language aide. I tell myself that everything will be all right.

After dropping Elliot at school, I stand on a cramped train platform and am bundled onto the subway. Nerves about today jangle the length of my body, and I can't stop myself from chattering. Earbuds into my ears, pretend I'm listening to music; for anyone watching, I'm dancing, that's the reason my limbs are moving; I am in control.

Woodall House on Lordship Lane: a Masonic school for the moral education of boys, college for schoolmistresses, later headquarters for the gas board and now home to around a dozen courts; prison cells showcasing the full spectrum of criminal cases. Wood Green Crown Court remains a Victorian Gothic mansion on the outside. Walking through the grounds, past the hibernating cherry tree and clipped green lawn, you expect a National Trust volunteer at the entrance to check your ticket, not security poised to rifle through your pockets.

I take a seat in the waiting area and scan the crowd for Paul Beaupert. Mercifully, he's on the register of public service interpreters and so last night I was able to see a headshot of him on the website. I'm looking for someone in their fifties with a light beard, cropped blond hair, and freckles sprinkled across his nose. A man perched on the end of a row meets the description. I breathe out and let my shoulders drop before I approach.

"Excuse me, hi. Are you an interpreter?"

He glances up from his book. "Yes, are you . . ." Then he shuffles through papers in his bag.

"I'm not with your client. I'm an interpreter too. I've just joined the interpreters' association and I'm looking at forming a new local committee. Do you live in North London?" I need to get him talking and somehow steer the conversation to me taking his assignment this morning.

"I'm not interested in joining the association," he says. "Sorry."

"Totally understandable." Should I pretend there's been a double booking? If I look desperate and unreasonably upset, he might graciously back out and let me take it. No, that won't work. The court won't have any record of me and they'll insist Paul needs to do the job.

Paul Beaupert is looking at me properly now. "Are you new?"

"Yes, as I say, I just joined the association."

"I mean, is today your first court job? You seem nervous."

I try to laugh. "Is it that obvious?"

He lifts his coat from the vacant chair next to him. "I've been doing this for twenty-five years. I'm trying to get out. I do some casual French tutoring at a university. The minute I can make it full-time, I'm gone."

"Oh yeah?" I say.

"A piece of advice from a veteran: the key is to not get emotionally involved."

"Right." Too late for that. If only I'd just said the words and gone home. None of this would have happened.

"In your client. In the cases, any of the material you witness. You've got to treat it the same as if you're standing up in court reciting fairy tales."

"I don't actually have a booking for today."

"Oh?"

"I'm really keen for work so I thought I'd just turn up at the court closest to me and hope that something comes up. Maybe an interpreter doesn't show and I can step in," I say.

"You should sign up to one of the agencies. You won't get much work just hanging around." Now he thinks I'm an idiot.

I look to the clock on the wall. There is about twenty minutes until his case is likely to be called: I need to hurry up.

"You'll be happy to quit court interpreting, you said?"

"I sure will." His eyes go back to his papers, this conversation only continuing now because he is too polite to tell me to go away.

"If you'd like to quit today, I'd be happy to take your booking." My tone is assertive, insistent. He looks up at me, perplexed, wondering whether I'm socially inept or just mad. "I mean it. I want the work. I need the experience and I'd appreciate you, as a veteran, letting me have this turn." I am hissing at him, I realize. I'm keeping my voice down, not drawing attention, but it is spiked with venom.

"You need to speak to the Court Listing Officer," he says, sharply. "I can't help you."

Then he raises his papers to his face, a way of blocking me out. Now what am I going to do?

"I'm sorry. I was being weird. Can I get you a drink? I'm getting a coffee from the machine. A thank-you for the advice and an apology."

"No thanks. I don't drink coffee."

My smile feels more like a grimace. I need a moment away from him to think and come up with a strategy. I head to the vending machine. I must maintain conversation with Paul Beaupert. Maybe he'll feel worn down and think it's easier to relinquish his job than to sit there and listen to me. I feel my neck, my shoulders, the muscles down my arms, all droop. This is probably a stupid game and

I should just go home. Last night's messages were meant to scare me, that's all. I scan the room, looking from face to face. Is one of these people my blackmailer? Did they come here to watch my ridiculous misinterpretation? "Guilty?" the judge will say. "Your client said *non coupable*. What are you playing at, interpreter?" I wish I knew why they want me to do this.

I press my credit card to the machine. When the button releases for hot chocolate, a thick, claggy gloop pours out. I sip it: it's pretty tasteless. I press the button to add hazelnut and butterscotch syrups. Then, when I think that no one is watching, I take a sedative from my bag and attempt to swallow. My throat is too tight and the tablet won't go down. I drop it into my cup and stir; it dissolves easily. I need to relax. I drop in another pill and swirl.

"I went with hot chocolate," I say, as I retake my seat. "Machine gave me two. Can you help me out?" Paul looks at me, wary. His hand extends.

"Sure, thanks." His fingers bend around the paper cup in front of him and it goes to his mouth.

"It's not bad for a vending machine," I say. "Better than nothing. It's cold in here today." My voice is cheery and I will charm this man as best I can.

"This place is a shambles. Did you hear that?" He's focused on a trio of people gathered at the side of the room, one of them in a wig and gown. "Chinese terp is running late. There's a job for you. Don't speak Mandarin, do you?" He laughs. He probably thinks I'm not qualified to interpret any language.

"No. I tried to learn. I think I've conceded defeat at this point." I take a greedy gulp of my drink and visualize the sedatives stroking my nerves.

Then it hits me. I stirred the pills into the cup in my right hand, and when I sat down, that's the one I handed to Paul. *He* has the hot chocolate with the drugs. I need to get it back.

"These drinks need more syrup," I announce. "Let me top you up." I wrap my hand around his cup and pull it to me, brown liquid sloshing over the sides.

"Jeez," Paul says, irritated. I walk back to the machine. This is crazy, I accidentally drugged this man. What if he'd drunk the whole cup before I realized? He might be on other medications that could be adversely affected. This whole thing is ridiculous. I'm leaving, I decide. I put the paper cups down and as I do, feel my phone vibrate. A new message. It's from the same person or people as last night, again the message appearing as though I've sent it to myself. There's no text this time, only an image. A photograph of Elliot's new school. My mouth fills with vinegar. The blackmailer knows I have a child and they know where he goes to school. A school he only started attending yesterday. They're following me. They probably also know where we live. It must be a barrister, or a corrupt police officer who's discovered what I've done. Someone with the resources and means to track me. I have to get Paul Beaupert off the hearing. The bottle of sedatives presses against the seam of my pocket.

I find my credit card again and hit the button for two hot chocolates. Discreetly, I start to grind a handful of pills inside my coat pocket. After I interpreted for a defendant on a murder trial a few years back, I stopped sleeping entirely. Eventually a doctor prescribed me these pills which would tug me to sleep so forcefully that I'd struggle to wake in the morning, my leaden head unable to lift from the pillow even as my alarm grew more and more shrill. Eventually most of my symptoms abated on their own. Or I learned to ignore them, squirrel them somewhere inside. The medication takes up to thirty minutes to work at full strength but if I can get him to drink a cup's worth, it'll start to have some effect, possibly enough for him to want to go home ill. At first he'll feel a pleasant giddy sensation behind his eyes, a gentle suggestion that he might like to close them and rest for a while. Then his head will begin to feel very heavy, as if he doesn't lean back against the wall, his neck will buckle and snap under the weight. He will see black and white dots in front of his eyes and his breathing will slow and he'll feel calm and peaceful and decide he quite likes this feeling, might like to feel like this all of the time. His speech will slur but that's all right because he won't want to talk anyway, he'd rather have a little nap right here on the floor.

Am I really going to drug an innocent stranger? I don't know what my blackmailer is capable of, and they might already be at Elliot's school. An usher appears and announces a case is ready to go through.

"Forget my drink," Paul raises his voice so that I can hear him across the room. "That's me." His chin points toward the usher.

No, no, no. Stop him. Tackle him. He cannot go into that courtroom. That hearing is mine. I watch Paul Beaupert say something to the usher, then he snorts, laughing perhaps at his own joke. The snort collapses into a cough. A rasping sound. Paul's hand covers his mouth, as his head tucks into his shoulder. "Excuse me." His chest rattles, his breathing so loud each inhale sounds as though it's sawing against his throat.

I walk closer and hear the usher say: "Are you all right, sir?"

Paul waves, knocking a fist against his throat; he can't speak. I drop the drinks and catch his bag just as it falls from his shoulder. This isn't the tablets. They have the opposite effect—Paul seems to be *more* agitated by the second. A small circle forms around us. Paul's fingers claw at his neck and his lips turn red and blistered.

"I think he's having an allergic reaction," a woman says. Oh, God.

On the floor now, Paul's head is between his knees. But on the woman's words it moves up and down. A nod. "Is that his bag?" she asks me. Once again, I am struck dumb with inaction. Mouth gaping like a fish, mind too timid, I am too slow to work out what's going on. "Give it to me." She has seized Paul's bag and tips its contents on the floor. "Epipen!"

I am elbowed aside as the woman stabs the Epipen into his lower leg. Immediately Paul's throat muscles relax, his mouth opens wide and his chest fills with air.

"Call an ambulance!" the woman shouts at the security guard.

"Nuts." A croak from where Paul's voice should be.

The hazelnut syrup did this. It was me. I didn't know that he can't eat nuts, how could I? He's a grown man, with a serious allergy; he should ask before he consumes anything. But I did try to drug him. I would have gone through with it had the usher not called him away. I was going to poison a man with sedatives. I've already destroyed an innocent person's hope for a fair trial and freedom, and now I could have killed someone.

When the ambulance arrives, I gather Paul's possessions from the floor and put his bag into the back. "Which hospital are you going to?" I ask the medic.

"Whittington." Will he be all right? I won't be able to live with myself if he isn't.

I watch the vehicle depart then approach the Court Listing Officer with my interpreter's ID. There's nothing I can do for Paul now. I need to go ahead with what I'm here to do, for Elliot. "I'm a French interpreter. I was with Paul, Paul Beaupert. I can cover his assignment."

His eyes dance around the papers on his desk. "Ah yes, court six," he says. "Plea and Trial Preparation Hearing—ineffective. Defendant's absent. You—Paul, are free to go." The defendant didn't turn up. I came here for nothing. Paul was hospitalized for nothing.

I feel the crushed pills in my pocket, like gritty sand between my fingers. A yellow *Danger: Floor slippery* sign is propped in the center of the room. A cleaner sweeps a mop in a figure eight, water in the bucket turning a darker shade of clay with each squeeze. The two paper cups now empty, I watch them rock back and forth along the rim.

I take the rear stairs to the basement. I haven't been inside this second cellar room for many years and I've forgotten what it looks like. The slate floor is ice cold against my bare feet and the ceiling forces me to duck. There is a heavy wooden door with an iron bolt. Yes, this will do quite nicely.

In the afternoon, I prepare two paintbrushes and tins of paint and meet my sister in the utility room. "Come on," I say, smiling. "You need a project, you need to keep busy. So we're going to repaint the second cellar downstairs. You said you painted in prison, so you can show me what you learned."

On the stairs I carry both containers of the dark gray lacquer.

"There are dead spiders in here," she says when we arrive. "And my arm's sore," she complains almost immediately. "I told you I didn't like having to paint the prison wing."

"Give it a chance. Five minutes. You might find it meditative."

She slaps some paint onto the wall, putting in a mediocre effort.

"It's so cold down here," she says, and I know this is my moment.

"I'll get you a coat."

I exit the room and shut the door firmly behind me. With one confident push I close the bolt.

Through the wood: "What was that? Have you locked me in?"

I fired the last of my staff this week, canceled my regular deliveries and weekly gardener. I cannot have anyone around me now, to witness, to overhear something they shouldn't. I don't have the courage to kill my own kin, and at least down here she is out of the way. If she looks inside herself, if she is honest with her soul—she'll accept that this is her place and she should never have been let out of prison. A life sentence, no possibility for parole.

In the morning I nudge her breakfast under the door. Even death row prisoners are fed.

"What is this—rye?" she asks. She'll be rationing the water that's already in there and having toast and pizza every day, unless I can think of what other foods are flat enough to fit underneath. I will not risk opening the door. "Come on, you've had your fun. Let me out now!"

I don't respond, but she can surely hear that I haven't walked away.

"HELLO? You can't do this!" She's pounding on the door now. "Let me out!"

If she wants to talk, we can talk.

"Do you even remember his birthday?" I will say his name. "Johann's?"

"He doesn't answer to that name."

"That's a no then."

"I hate that name! He hates that name." She's growling now. "I never wanted to call him that!"

"It means gracious and merciful. Johann's birthday was eight months ago."

"This isn't enough food!" she shouts.

"If you're hungry you can eat the dead spiders."

There's a species of spider native to South Africa where less than half of the females reproduce. The ones that don't instead care for and protect their sister's babies. After they hatch, the velvet spider will feed her niece or nephew by mouth until her own body begins to liquify, and then she will allow them to feast on her, encouraging them to slowly eat her alive. She did not give birth to the baby spiders, but her love for them is incomprehensible. Forget fierce maternal love. It's the aunt you should really be afraid of.

Upstairs, my sister's cries are silenced by the concrete floor. All windows and doors are secured. I am alone, I will be undisturbed. I open my laptop and watch the blinking red dot, your phone's GPS location, tease across the screen.

27.

I burst through the courthouse doors and land back on the high street with relief. The defendant not turning up today saved me. But Elliot is not with me. I unlock my phone and open the last message received—the photograph of a building. It isn't my imagination—I recognize the gate and the color of the stone—this image is unquestionably taken from out the front of his new school.

A pleasant voice answers on the second ring. "Hello, I'm Revelle Lee, Elliot's mother, in Year One, Leopards and Panthers class. I need to know that he's okay right now, can you check please? Thank you." My words are running together, and I reach the end of the sentence without a breath.

"Good morning, sorry, Elliot did you say? Is he poorly today?" the woman asks.

"No, he's not ill but I need you to check on him. See if he is safe in his classroom right now, please."

"Are you expecting him to be somewhere else—was he brought to school this morning?"

"I dropped him there, yes. No—he should be in his classroom but I want you to look please, Year One, Leopards and Panthers class." I'm teetering on the edge of hysterical but this woman won't help me if I explode at her.

There is a pause. I can hear a printer whir in the background and paper being scrunched. "You want to know if he's here?"

"*Please* can you go there now and ask the teacher to identify him. I'll wait on the line for as long as it takes." There is a tear in my voice, a rip right through the center.

"Year One was it?"

"Leopards and Panthers!" I am shouting now, I can't help it. A taxi driver stopped at traffic lights peers at me through his open window, and a woman passing on the footpath gives me a sidelong glance.

A few minutes later, the woman comes back on the line. "Hello, are you there?"

"Yes, yes! I'm here."

"Elliot Lee is in class."

"Oh thank you."

"He's fine. He's helping to make a model solar system at the moment. He's painting Venus."

"Thank you. Thank you very much for checking." I hang up and can practically hear the receptionist recounting this anecdote to her office colleague about their newest pupil's crazy mother. I don't care. He's okay, and that's all that matters.

Whoever is blackmailing me—surely they're not really interested in Elliot. They know that I've misinterpreted on a case and they're using him as leverage to threaten me, that's all. They would be aware by now that today's hearing didn't proceed; through no fault of mine, I couldn't do what they demanded. Unease creeps up behind me. So what happens now?

I head home and when I exit the stairwell, see paper protruding from under my door. It's a reply to one of the notes I wrote to the neighbors. I stand there and read it to the end, and as I do, I hear the door to my right opening. A woman emerges.

"I'm Gurmeet." She smiles. I place her as sixty-something. "Can you read my handwriting? I'm glad to catch you. Welcome to the building."

"I'm Revelle. Thank you. Have you lived here for long?"

"Almost thirty years."

"You must like it then?"

"It's changed a lot. But yes, it's home for me and Monday. That's my Pomeranian."

"I was wondering if the estate agent allowed pets. I want to get something for my son, Elliot; he's six."

"Well, he's welcome to come and play with Monday anytime."

"He'd like that," I say. Gurmeet seems nice. I feel better about having her next door.

"Don't let me keep you. You're probably busy."

We say goodbye and I go inside, locking the door behind me.

It's just past noon. I should log in to the Exia app and see what work I can pick up for this afternoon. I need the money. But how can I continue interpreting with this blackmail threat hanging over me? I can hardly take a booking and pretend this isn't happening, not when it isn't clear what they want. It could even be someone at the agency who's doing this. But why?

I spend the next two hours thinking through my past assignments where I misinterpreted, drawing up a list of who could be behind this. It's the same as before: The Lad's sexual assault trial and Adam Birch's alibi interview. The Hindi-speaking witness in the former may have realized I changed his words during cross-examination, but blackmailing me in this way doesn't make sense. Why not demand money? He's an Uber-driving student—why would he want me to now change words in someone else's trial? Maybe it is a police officer, a detective. Not someone corrupt necessarily. They might believe they're doing the right thing, that changing a key word could make a difference and ensure a guilty person goes to jail—someone just like me. Let's see how they feel when they put the wrong person away.

At two o'clock I begin the walk to Elliot's school. I arrive far too early to collect him, so I sit in the bus shelter across the road. Whenever someone approaches the school, the muscles in my legs fire up, ready to run in there to Elliot. He dawdles out after the bell rings. I grab his hand and we walk home. "Alfie says strikers are the best position," Elliot says. "Alfie says because they have to do everything and they have to score goals." I just want to listen to him chatter away after school for one day, one single afternoon, without having to worry about his safety or whether or not I'm going to keep him.

"Alfie's your new friend? In your class?"

"Yeah. He's on the football team. Can I join?"

"Of course, that sounds great. We'll look it up later when we get home." As we turn into our street, my phone starts ringing. It's a blocked number. Oh no. I won't answer it. It stops and rings again. It could be Exia or a court official who knows what I've done. There's no use avoiding it.

"Hello?"

"You've been trying to contact me," the voice is loud and urgent. "I'm the medic who attended a homeless man in Knightsbridge on September sixteenth. At least I tried to."

"Oh, yes." Adam. I've scarcely thought about him all day. "His name is Adam Birch." So wrapped up in my own problems I haven't had time to think about the innocent man I've probably imprisoned for life. Please let this be good news. I give Elliot's hand a gentle squeeze.

"Sorry 'bout the noise, I'm outside the pub. I've been working night shift. The only free time I've had to call you back has been three a.m. Assume you didn't want that. Hence the delay."

"It's fine, thanks for calling." I explain a version of events to the paramedic. I say we are looking for evidence to support the fact that Adam was so ill the day of September 16 that he would not have been physically capable of breaking and entering, much less of following it up with murder. I am aware he didn't have a chance to properly examine Adam and so I'm not sure how much he can say. But anything would help.

"Arrested?" he says. "For a murder?"

248

"That same day."

"Right, wow, okay." He sounds shocked. Could he have really not come across it on the news? Not recognized Adam's face as someone he's seen before? Maybe he avoids those kind of stories in the media; he might get enough blood and guts at work.

"Look. What I can tell you is that at 11:53 a.m. I arrived attending to a homeless gentleman," he says. "On that shift, my partner was driver and I was talking to patients and doing attend. Your friend—you say his name is Adam Birch? My notes say he refused attention, refused to show ID or come to A&E," his voice slipping into formal mode. Then, almost whispering: "You're saying that man then killed someone?"

"No, he didn't. It's what the police believe but I'm certain he didn't do it. What time did you leave him?"

"Notes say 12:12 p.m."

"Would he have had the strength to overpower someone and push them down the stairs six or seven hours later?"

"Blimey," he says, whispering again.

"He's been wrongly accused."

"Did he kill his friend? The Polish chap who was with him?" he asks, titillated, as though this is harmless gossip.

"No, *listen*." My exasperation is clear to Elliot, who drops my hand and slows his walking pace. "He didn't kill anyone." I am whispering now, realizing that I've been freely talking about murder and my son is standing right here. "A woman was killed. Nearby in Knightsbridge. Adam Birch is taking the blame."

"In Knightsbridge? Huh." The paramedic's voice climbs on the final word as though he is thinking of something curious.

"You know which murder I'm talking about? You must have seen it in the media."

"Yeah," his voice is noncommittal over the din of after-work drinkers but I can hear something there, a thought he's holding back.

"I know legally . . . I realize that officially you probably aren't allowed to—"

He interrupts me. "Holy—wow."

"What? Tell me," I hiss, putting my hand on Elliot's shoulder so that he knows my frustration isn't directed at him.

"I saw it." There's a pause. "I was . . . *there*," the paramedic says.

"What do you mean?"

"Reading my notes now I'm putting two and two together. After I left your friend, I went back to base for a while. I was called out to Hyde Park, then, right before the end of my shift, back to Knightsbridge to attend to a woman. Someone else in the house with her called 999. I couldn't pronounce her dead but she was obviously . . . look, my notes say 'purple +++.' 'Purple +' means presumed deceased. Basically the more plus signs the more presumed, if you get my drift."

Sandra and Adam shared a paramedic. "Are you saying you attended Adam that day *and* Sandra Ramos? The murdered woman?"

"It looks like it. Right. Wow." He went from Adam, and then to Sandra.

You need to determine if the DNA was carried to the scene by someone else. The Spanish forensic scientist from the National Crime Agency job. The paramedic tried to treat Adam during his difficult breathing episode, then he attempted to revive Sandra—he touched them both. *He* transferred the DNA.

The paramedic's voice reverts back into formal mode: "Look, there's a legal department. Your solicitor can make a request in relation to witness statements and police inquires—there's information on the website."

With an explanation for the DNA, Adam doesn't need an alternative alibi. Police don't have his DNA on the bag and now without the DNA on Sandra's body, police have little else.

"Patient Liaison said you wanted to send me a gift, a bottle of wine?"

I need to get this information to Adam's solicitor. I take down the paramedic's full name and contact number and promise to call him back. "About the wine?" he asks.

"Sure, yes. I'll call you back about the wine." I hang up and turn to Elliot. "I'm sorry. That was a man from work. I'm not angry with him. I'm happy actually, because he gave me some good news." We are standing out the front of our flat now and I unlock the door. Could this really be it? The key that all but forces police to drop their case against Adam Birch? Aside from going to Knightsbridge and hoping to run into him, I don't have a way of contacting Mariusz to update him. I still need to get this information to Adam's solicitor so he can present it to the police, and I have to do it without incriminating myself.

I sit down and phone Adam's solicitor in Wood Green. I leave a voice message saying I work for the ambulance trust, and I give the name and contact of the paramedic I spoke to. I explain that he has just realized that he attended both Adam Birch and Sandra Ramos on the day of her murder and that the solicitor might like to investigate the possibility of DNA transference. Then I call back the ambulance trust and say I work for a solicitor who needs to speak to the paramedic about the possibility he inadvertently transferred DNA from one patient to another. One will call the other back, and surely between them they'll work it out and no one needs to know I was involved. This is the breakthrough I've been looking for. I stretch out along the sofa and let my head hang over the side. I can't relax too much, I remind myself—Adam isn't out of jail yet.

Doreen. I still haven't written back to her. I open Facebook Messenger and type. I don't allow myself to dwell on my sentences or choice of words. I just need to type, get everything down, raw and honest. I press send and bite my lip.

Our two weeks in Greece didn't change things. Five minutes back in the UK and it was obvious the media stories had kept up in our absence, the hounding of Doreen set to continue. The tabloids had decided to wage a full-scale war against social services, calling for a complete departmental overhaul and national reform. Doreen was its scapegoat. As she lived alone, we made a plan that I'd text her twice a day, once in the morning and once in the evening, as a kind of welfare check. Overnight, she was famous, abruptly thrust into the public spotlight. No riches or perks, just misplaced hatred from strangers. How much could a person take?

The evening we got back to London, I messaged Doreen as planned and she replied:

Argh, I can't face unpacking. Feel rough as guts from all that Toblerone.

I sent her another text in the morning and she wrote back again. But in the evening, nothing. When I dialed her number, the call rang out. I left it overnight. I thought perhaps she was feeling better and I didn't want to crowd her, especially since we'd been together almost twenty-four hours a day for the last two weeks. Another day passed without a response, so I went to her house.

"How much?" Doreen opened the front door only enough for her head to fit. "How much did they pay you?"

"Who?"

"For the photos. Or do you mean *who* because you sold them to more than one newspaper? So many that you've lost track."

"Doreen, what's happened?"

"You gave them to the *Mail*."

"Gave what? I don't even read the *Mail*. Is there an article? A new one, about you?" My mind raced to catch up—was she talking about photos of the dead little boy? Did she think I took photos the day I interpreted for his supervised contact session?

"Now the whole of England gets to enjoy your happy snaps of me at the beach in Athens, the Arkadiko Bridge, the Acropolis . . . The headline in the *Sun* is my favorite: 'Callous social worker parties after toddler dies,'" Doreen said.

No. No. No. "You're talking about Greece," I said. She knew I was taking those pictures. She posed in them; most of them were her idea. But it was me who put them on Facebook. "Oh no." I rubbed my temples with both hands. I initially put two up. That's it. But they were only visible to my friends, the people I knew from university and former classmates from my dozens of schools from around the world; none of them truly my friends at all. I wanted to show Doreen off. Prove to them, and to myself, that there was someone who chose to spend time in my company. Not a fellow student at university who needed to accumulate friends and grabbed me as the nearest available— Doreen was the first person whose life I seemed to improve simply by being in it. I'd visited dozens of countries in my childhood, but never on vacation—it was always about my mother's work. Doreen was almost my mother's age, and when someone from university asked if that was her in the photo, I said yes and posted more.

"I didn't sell them. I didn't give them to anyone. I had no intention of sharing them beyond a couple of friends," I said. "I don't know how the newspapers got them."

"*I thought* we were friends," Doreen said. Then she mimicked herself, a nasty sarcastic laugh. "God, 'I thought we were friends.' Listen to me, *pathetic*. I sound like a teenager. I sound like my daughter."

"I did not send those photos on to the media, Doreen. Listen. That makes no sense. Why would I do that? I don't even remember which ones I put on Facebook. Which photos exactly do they have?" I took my phone from my pocket and searched for the article. I was concerned for Doreen, of course I was, and I was equally worried about my own image being in the press. I could not afford to be connected to that little boy. As the interpreter, my name was there somewhere in the authorities' files, certifying the report; but this was front and center, publicly linking me to his case, to Doreen.

"I don't know why you did this," she said. "But I suppose I haven't known you that long. I don't know what you're capable of."

"Can we sit down, *please*?" Later I would check and the photos were definitely only visible to people I knew. I never found out who took them to the media. "Let me in and I can explain." Then she slammed the door in my face. This was eight years ago.

If she had let me inside her house that day, would I have confessed? Told her everything? I doubt it. Because it was obvious by then that I was going to get away with it. And that's what we humans do, don't we? Avoid pain, shirk punishment. Psychologists call it "the cheater's high." Getting away with things makes us feel good. It's evolutionary. Guilt might come into it later, but the thrill of doing something wrong and going undetected, of evading justice, is addictive to us. The guilt did come, it flattened me, and I don't expect Doreen to forgive me. It's difficult to accept that if none of this had happened, I probably wouldn't have adopted, and right now Elliot would be in Croydon or Wimbledon or Liverpool with a different surname. And me? I don't know where I'd be, but it would likely be alone.

Now, kneeling on a chair at the dining table, Elliot is unpacking his school bag. I can't face homework today. "Elliot, there's a little dog next door who would like to meet you."

His school things are abandoned and Elliot is at Gurmeet's door. He is nuzzling Monday when my phone vibrates with a text message.

Tomorrow. Old Bailey, Court 4, 10 a.m. Replace the interpreter Steffi Neumann. Change word "plates" for "doors." Language is German.

My phone hits the floor. I step out of Gurmeet's flat to the corridor; I don't want to scare her or Elliot with the look on my face. German. I can't do it. I can't do what they're demanding in any language, but especially not German. I lean against the wall and slide to the carpet. I pick up my phone and see that underneath the text is another image. A photograph of this building.

28.

WHO ARE YOU? I type and press send. Once again the message goes nowhere. I hurl the phone across the corridor. It bounces from wall to carpet but thankfully doesn't break. I read the text again. Are they demanding I change these words tomorrow because today's trial was canceled? Or is their intention to keep blackmailing me indefinitely? That's what blackmail is: they have one thing over you and then another—once you're in their grip there's no escape. I squat on the floor. From down here, the ceiling feels very high, the space inside this building cavernous. Twelve floors, upward of one hundred flats. We could vanish here, Elliot and I, disappear into the walls, and I'm not sure that anyone would even miss us.

The person on the other end of these messages knows where Elliot goes to school, and they have our address. Our address that I've not given to anyone except to the local authority. Is it the detective from Mariusz Dorobek's alibi interview who's behind this? It can't be Mariusz. The detective would have access to the council's data and could easily find my tenancy agreement for this flat and Elliot's school enrollment. When the detective saw the times were different on the signed alibi statement, perhaps he didn't assume it was the fault of the witness. Because he and I talked about whether or not Mariusz was telling the truth, and he told me about the DNA on Sandra's body, he might have concluded that I was playing vigilante, because maybe it's something that he's done too. I helped him close that case, and now he wants me to do it again? If it is him who's behind this, I wonder what he'll do when the new evidence is presented about Adam's DNA. I hope he doesn't try to stop his release.

Whoever it is, this person knows where we live. They're making it clear that they can get to us, to Elliot. But the direct threats to my son have stopped. There have been no further balloons, no organ-stuffed toys sent to his school. The drug dealer never came to our door again and I've safely received papers from the family court that weren't intercepted. Have Elliot's birth parents given up on harassing us just as these other threats have started? It seems too much of a coincidence. It has to be the same person, or people, behind all of this. But how could Elliot's pregnant mother, or father from jail, possibly know that I've misinterpreted? It doesn't make sense that they would want me to change words in a trial. And what am I going to do tomorrow? We're not safe here, and Elliot is not safe at school. I have to do it. There's no choice but to go to court and try to give them what they want. I step back inside our neighbor's flat. Gurmeet and Elliot sit on the floor, laughing as Monday the Pomeranian wags her tail and trots between them. I cast my eyes around her flat: it looks homely, completely normal and comfortable.

"Okay, Elliot," I say. "We better make a start on dinner. Say goodbye to Monday and Gurmeet and maybe you'll get an invitation to come back tomorrow."

"Oh anytime," Gurmeet smiles. Elliot walks ahead of me into our flat. Once he's out of earshot I speak to our neighbor.

"I know this is weird. But I'm a single parent so my options are pretty limited. I was wondering if you could look after Elliot tomorrow for about half a day? I need to work. In court—I'm an interpreter. Is there any chance you could help me out?"

"Oh," she says, surprised. "Well, sure. Why not."

"I'd pay you, of course."

"No, don't be silly. That's not necessary. But is he not at school?"

"The truth is, he's being bullied. I'm waiting to hear back from the local authority about an alternative school." I can't tell Gurmeet the truth. I don't want her to think that I'm putting her in any danger.

"Oh I'm sorry to hear that. He's such a lovely boy."

This can't go on. I can't keep withdrawing him from schools and moving us around. I think about my mother's apartment sitting empty in Singapore. Moving us there could be something to consider. Richard messaged me this morning, trying to send me money, but I don't think cash is enough to get us out of this situation, at least not yet. I thank Gurmeet and we agree to check in with one another first thing in the morning.

Then what happens after tomorrow? Elliot was removed from an unsafe birth family for a better life and this is what I've got him into. He doesn't have a passport yet, so we can't get to Singapore. Whoever is behind this, they won't harm him, surely. That wouldn't achieve anything. But how can I take the chance? I sprint to my bedroom and throw clothes into a bag. I think through what else we need: Elliot's adoption paperwork, our identity documents, some clothes for him. Then I go into his room and open a drawer, stuffing socks and underwear and T-shirts into my bag.

"What are you doing?" Elliot looks up from the bed where he's reading a book.

"We're going to take a trip, okay? A little impromptu holiday."

"What are you doing with my clothes?"

"Well, you're going to need them, aren't you. Bring your book. Put some shoes on. We'll go out for dinner on the way," I say, adding a comb and two school books—he'll need something to do, wherever it is we go.

"We're going *now*?" He makes no effort to move from the bed. "*Where?*"

I don't know. I have no idea where we could go where they

wouldn't find us. I don't even know who they are, or why I'm so important to them. Elliot looks at me over his book, confused, maybe even a little afraid. He's unsettled, and I can see fear in the shape of his mouth. Because my behavior is erratic and I'm making his life chaos, and that is what he was supposed to have left behind.

"We're not going anywhere." I place the bag on the floor. "I was just joking. Not a joke—practicing in case we needed to run—a fire drill. Have you done one of those at school?"

"Yeah, at Greenwich. But you're doing it wrong. The teacher said in a fire we're not allowed to take our bags, we have to leave everything in the classroom, even our favorite stuff."

"That's right. That's absolutely true. See—that's why I need to train for it."

"I should do the next fire drill."

I unpack the bag and return his clothes and things to their place. "Agreed."

In my room, I read through the text once more. *Language is German.*

How does this person even know I speak German? I was only listed on the public service register with that language for a few months until I had it expunged.

Replace the interpreter Steffi Neumann.

Who are you, Steffi Neumann? I check to see that Elliot is still happily reading in his bedroom and then start to search online. Some interpreters are enterprising freelancers and have their own websites. They pursue corporate clients, aren't signed up to any agency, preferring to set their own rates and hours without a middleman. Steffi is one such interpreter. Thank goodness. But what am I looking for? I sift through the pages, read about her translation work and fees. There is no link to Exia or mention of another interpreting agency on her website, and the "contact me" page lists a personal email address and mobile phone number.

Okay, I can work with that. Steffi Neumann's assignment at the Old Bailey tomorrow is likely to be a booking made with her directly. That makes things easier, but still it won't be simple for me to try to replace her. She appears to be in her fifties and looks absolutely nothing like me. She has shampoo-ad caramel-blond curls, a sturdy nose, and arched, razor-sharp eyebrows. Her record is searchable in the directory of public service interpreters and I take down her registration number. The interpreter has a Home Office Counter Terrorist Check, a Ministry of Defense Security Check, and a police check high enough to grant her unsupervised, unrestricted access to police premises and systems. It's obvious why she doesn't bother with Exia—she has decades of experience and is probably offered more assignments than she can humanly accept. The thought of crossing someone so highly accomplished gives me added cause to worry about what it is I'm supposed to do. I can't just ask her to hand over this assignment; it didn't work with Paul Beaupert and it definitely won't work on a bigger trial at the Old Bailey. *Replace her.* I'll need to *be* her. Oh no. I'm going to have to impersonate this woman.

I take a screenshot of Steffi's ID from the online register and open it in Photoshop. I bought the software during my brief career translating marketing collateral for advertising companies. It makes it easier when working on booklets and signage if I can edit the text directly into the design file. But I have no training in this program and use it so rarely that, each time I open it, I'm forced to relearn everything from scratch. The cursor flickers around the screen and I cannot remember how to do this.

On YouTube I jump from one tutorial to the next until I figure something out. Eventually I go back into Photoshop, play around with the tools until I find the right shape, create a black box where Steffi's image is and insert over the top the photo from my own ID card. Then I lower the resolution so the whole identity card is slightly fuzzy, and save it as a jpeg to my phone. This is completely crazy. Anyone who looks at this is going to know that it's a home job.

Next I fish my physical interpreter's ID card from my purse. I need to somehow fade my own photo, make it blurry enough so that I'm not recognizable. During my first year at university, most of us living in the halls of residence, away from home for the very first time, were useless at cleaning and washing our clothes. The best of us put our jeans through the machine once a term. Inevitably forgetting to sift through wads of tissues and nightclub ticket stubs from our pockets, which would disintegrate and render the wash almost entirely pointless. We'd also forget to take out our student ID cards. It was a joke on campus that every first-year student who lived away from their family had a ghost ID card, their plastic photograph faded beyond recognition, their name and student number bleached from unplanned rides in the washing machine. When you presented it to a librarian or security guard they'd sigh and recommend you pay for a new one. It seemed so innocent: we hadn't deliberately tampered with our ID cards, we were just helpless. But as identity documents, they were almost interchangeable. If I left my ID card at home, I could simply use someone else's. Yes, that's what I'll do. I drop my real ID card into the washing machine and turn it on. Let's see how it looks after a thirty-minute cycle with plenty of suds.

While I wait for the machine to finish, I look up the Old Bailey court listings for tomorrow. Most of the cases are murders. Two with knives, one with a machete. One trial for death by dangerous driving; one of corporate blackmail, the company name suppressed for legal reasons; one for supply of a Class A drug.

Court four: Trial of Christopher Ball accused of attempting to murder former business associate, Boris Behrens.

From the names I can probably assume that the victim is the

German party, and so I'm likely interpreting for a prosecution witness of some kind. My blackmailer could be offering up my services as a corrupt interpreter for money, telling the defense I can be bribed into helping them secure an acquittal. That would make sense: Steffi Neumann is interpreting for a prosecution witness, my blackmailer wants me to undermine their testimony to aid the defense. But how does that connect to Elliot's adoption, to his birth family? A look through the trial listings for the past week shows two previous mentions of the Ball case. Tomorrow is day three of the trial. Even if I can somehow pretend to be Steffi Neumann, I can't just go in there and speak German. I'm not sure my body would obey. When the grandmother and child went missing at Thorpe Park, I wanted to help, but I couldn't go through with it.

Although I haven't spoken it for a long time, I've inevitably been exposed to the German language. Smatterings of sentences caught on TV, residue of strangers' conversations while walking around central London. I've read the headlines in *Der Spiegel* in the newsstand in Canary Wharf that used to sell international newspapers. But eight years ago I promised myself I'd never speak it again and I've stuck to that commitment.

"*Ich verspreche,*" I say under my breath, "I promise." Then I say it again, and again, again, raising the volume a little each time. My cheeks pull taut to make the proper sounds, muscle memory gradually returning. German comes from the back of the throat. It's a language that requires confidence. It *gives* you confidence because it is commanding and authoritative; no nonsense. I love how orderly it is, rules-based and tidy. Learn the correct format and off you go, you know what to do. English is the cruel language. The one that tries to trip you up with endless exceptions to the rule and random variations that are illogical. Bully-boy, dominant English, you think you rule the world.

Out of the washing machine, my interpreter ID card is scuffed and the details of my photograph rubbed away, but my registration number and REVELLE LEE remains quite clear. My signature is also still visible. I toss it to the floor in frustration. There's no way I can pull this off. I suppose I can try the washing machine one more time. My ID card goes back in for the heavy-duty cycle. The next wash seems to do the trick. A butter knife scratches away the final tell-tale letters; it slips a few times and nicks the surface of my skin. This will have to do. The ID card looks terrible but I can't think of any other way.

A scraping at the front door triggers all of my senses. Through the peephole, a woman is there manipulating the bolt. My breath catches as she takes something from her hand and jams it against the handle. I keep my eyes tight on the woman as I lean toward the kitchen worktop and reach for a heavy pan drying on the rack. It's a woman who's doing this. My blackmailer. A relative of Elliot's? Is this his mother? I have to call the police, and I'll have to tell them everything. I might go to jail but at least Elliot will be safe. My fingers lock around the handle of the pan.

"It's the wrong flat, you stupid cow." Then a man appears in the peephole, pulling the woman back.

"Ah, shit!" she says. Slowly she turns and lets him maneuver her away. One boot on her foot, the other in her hand, which jerks across her body as she sways down the corridor. My pulse cools. They're drunk, they're both drunk. They live in one of these flats and they got the wrong door. They're not after us. I hold the pan to my temple and let the chill of the metal soothe me.

29.

Over breakfast I explain to Elliot that he can't go to school today because there is a teachers' planning day.

"No one said yesterday," he says.

"I know. I think everyone forgot." I turn away from him and put my head into the fridge while I speak. Here I am, lying to him again. How long until he realizes that something is obviously wrong? My aborted plans for us to flee yesterday, the fake fire drill excuse that I'm not sure he fully bought. The skin on both eyelids starts to quiver. I haven't slept properly for weeks and I am an appalling mother; maybe Elliot would be better off if he was taken back into care. "And I need to go to work for a couple of hours, I'm really sorry, Batman. I'll be away for maybe half the day. But Gurmeet says she'd like to have you next door. To help her look after Monday. Would you like that?"

"I can walk her."

I have images of Elliot leaving the building, then being bundled into a dark car with the barking dog left on the footpath.

"As long as Gurmeet goes with you, yes, but not too far."

I pass him a second slice of toast and on my phone check for news about Adam Birch. Nothing—it's too soon for the police to have released him and issued a statement. Will the DNA explanation be adequate to get him out? Please let it be enough.

The idea of food makes me retch, but I force myself to chew a dry piece of toast. I'm going to need energy and the ability to think if I have a chance of pulling off this crazy stunt today. I gnaw slowly at the crust, and the toasted crumbs cut into the back of my throat. I clean up and take Elliot in to Gurmeet, then I book a cab for 9:15. Timing will be tight this morning but frazzled always-running-late mum is exactly the look I'm going for. When the clock hits 9:01, I block my number in the phone settings and ring the mobile on Steffi Neumann's website. Here goes. My heart rattles in my chest.

It rings. Rings.

Voicemail.

"This is a message for Steffi Neumann," I say, willing my voice to come across as professional, and this message routine. "I'm the Court Listing Officer calling from the Old Bailey." I sound like a petrified child. "You were booked for the trial this morning in court number four—your services are no longer required. You'll still be paid for the half-day. If an interpreter is needed at a later point in the hearing, I'll call you again. Thank you and apologies for the inconvenience."

End call. My blood pressure soars. That sounded okay in the end, I think. Steffi will be annoyed as she's going to be on her way to court by now; she's probably in a subway tunnel without phone reception. Last-minute cancellations happen all the time in court interpreting and there's no reason for her to think this one is unusual.

Shit. A voicemail. I didn't even put on an accent. If something goes wrong today, I've left recorded evidence in my own voice. The top half of me sags onto the kitchen worktop. It's too late to worry about that now. I just hope that Steffi gets the message in time and doesn't show up. What if she doesn't check her messages? I should send her a text and an email—she might be more likely to see those come through as notifications. I should have thought of this last night and set up a fake email and phone number, somehow. Too late. I squeeze my hands into fists. There's no way I can figure out how to do either of those things in the next five minutes. My eyelids are still quivering, faster than before, as though there is a tiny heart under each one, pumping to stay alive. Visions of the real interpreter turning up to court play in front of my eyes. I can't freeze—if that happens, I must not let myself panic. So, then what? I'll stick to my story: my name is Steffi Neumann—Steffi is a very common name in Germany, as is Neumann. I'll insist that I'm Steffi Neumann too and that this is all a bizarre coincidence and then I'll quickly get the hell out of there.

My taxi is here. The journey is interminable. When the car comes to a stop, I don't want the doors to open. I can't go through with this. My legs are refusing to work properly. At the curb in front of the Old Bailey, the driver is staring at me and asking what's wrong. I pay and push myself out. I untuck my shirt and ruffle my hair. Court four is in the older building and I barge through the entrance.

"Morning," I say to a security guard, thankfully not one I've seen before. "Ohmygod—I'm an interpreter. Court four. I'm running late." I show my bag and flash my laundered ID card in one swift motion. "Went in the washing machine with my son's things," I say. "I've ordered a new one. Ohmygod I *am* late, aren't I?" I am a tornado the security guard doesn't want to stop. I keep moving and head straight to the Court Listing Officer, display my real ID card on the desk. My hands tuck behind me because they are visibly shaking.

"I know it's hard to read. I forgot it was in my coat and it went through the wash. I'm *still* waiting for my replacement." I give an eyeroll for good measure. "Here's my digital version." I present Steffi Neumann's doctored ID on my phone. Steffi's registration details with my photograph. If the Listing Officer decides to cross-check it against the online registry, I'm finished. He turns to his computer screen. No, no, no. Don't check my details, please not today. "I'm so sorry I'm late. This morning my son was ill and

I suppose I should hurry and find my client, they'll be looking for me, won't they? I am sorry to rush you."

His eyes run from the computer, to me, then back to the screen. "You're in court four." Then he passes me a claim form.

Inside my trouser pockets, my fingers unwind. "Yes, thank you." I don't know Steffi Neumann's bank details obviously, so I write down bogus account numbers. The payment will bounce and eventually someone from finance will phone her to check the information. The real interpreter will still get paid.

"Hi there, we've met before, haven't we?" A friendly voice steals my attention.

"Yes, I—" I say, meeting their eyes. I've forgotten his name but I recognize his face. He's a terp I met on a course, four or five years ago. I'd be happy to chat with him but today he could destroy me. Don't say my name, I think to myself. Please don't remember my name and say it in front of the Court Officer! I throw my claim form back to the man and leap away from the desk. When I'm certain we're out of earshot: "Hi," I say quietly. "Long time no see."

"How've you been?" Good, he hasn't used my name. Maybe he can't recall it either.

"Look, I'm—it's good to run into you but I'm late."

"Which court are you in?"

I ignore his question and ask my own. "Where are you?" I need to know which courtroom he's in without giving any of my own information away. It's possible for there to be two or even multiple interpreters on the one hearing. If we're working on the same assignment that makes things even more difficult. He may not recall my name exactly but he might be dubious that it's something as German as Steffi Neumann.

"Blackmail trial in court two," he says, and I breathe out.

Okay. I can keep this going. Now it's time to move. "Sorry, I've got to go," I say. "It's good to see you." I follow the corridor to the witness room.

"Steffi, is it?" There's a pause before I remember that's my name today. I turn around. "Yes, I'm Steffi," I tell the barrister. She offers me a brisk this-is-all-you're-getting smile. I'm just glad she obviously hasn't worked before with the real Steffi Neumann. "Sorry I'm late."

"Are you up to speed?" She's referring to the court papers.

"No."

Her mouth becomes an instant frown. She shoves paperwork toward me and I read it hungrily. The defendant in this trial is a British man called Christopher Ball who works for a German car company in their London office. He is charged with attempting to murder a German business associate. The prosecution witness I'm interpreting for is a Munich-based colleague. Now use of the words "plates" and "doors" makes some sense. Does my blackmailer want the accused acquitted? Presumably that's why I'm supposed to change the word "plates" for "doors." Although it isn't clear from this quick scan of the witness statement where those terms will be spoken. The blackmailer must know. They're privy to these details because they work for the courts, is that it? Or they know someone involved in the trial. But what's the connection between this case and the plea hearing at Wood Green? And to my adoption of Elliot?

The barrister leaves me alone with the witness and I need to estimate how much English he understands. It's incredibly risky misinterpreting a witness statement in open court. It's difficult to see how I'm going to manage this without being discovered. If I change the words and someone picks up the error, no one will jump to the conclusion that it was deliberate—they'll put it down to incompetence and dismiss me. But when an inevitable check is made into the qualifications of Steffi Neumann and a complaint submitted, it will come to light that someone stole her identity. And that someone has committed fraud, and possibly conspiracy to pervert the course of justice. Crimes worth charging. There I'll be, on the CCTV. And the real Steffi has my voicemail to prove it.

"I might try to find the bathroom," I say to the client in German.

"Sure," he says, straightening his tie for the fifth time—he's nervous too.

"Through those doors?" I say in English, pointing to the exit.

"Pardon?" he replies in German. I switch back.

"Oh sorry, wrong language!" All jokey bluster. I leave the room and pretend to find the bathroom. All right, so not a conclusive test. He could still very well know the English word for "car door" or at least know the difference between it and "license plate." This is complete madness—he's going to hear it. If I change those words, even that one word, someone is going to spot it.

I recall classes during my master's degree when the teacher played audio clips of famous examples of interpreting errors. Some of those mistakes were astounding, simple, incredible errors in high-stakes rooms full of politicians, world leaders, and diplomats. And yet no one noticed.

Court hearings are boring. Even juicy murder trials are tedious and slow. Boris Behrens could be bilingual but between his emotional state and all the jargon, I doubt even he'll be listening with unwavering attention. Save for the legal teams, most people in the room are never listening intently to everything that is said. For the majority, the words drift in and out of focus, their concentration perking up when they detect a slam-dunk cross-examination question; a thrill in the air. If I switch around the word "plates" for "doors," one word, one quick change, there's a chance I can slip it through. My client is a prosecution witness. He'll have rehearsed and possibly even memorized his answers for today. He's an actor trying to remember his lines. He won't be listening to me; he'll be focused on what he's saying, and while I'm speaking he'll be busy anticipating the next question, my voice swimming out of view. It'll probably become obvious with any follow-up question that some kind of mix-up has happened, but maybe that's precisely what my blackmailers want. To cause a moment of confusion, and discredit the witness in the eyes of the jury. Then, hopefully, my job is done. But are they really going to leave Elliot and me alone? We'll have to move again, and this time much further. I'll worry about that later.

Christopher Ball is brought up from the cells. From the back of the court he looks toward me. Does he know what I'm supposed to do today? Has he been prepped, or did he arrange this himself? Pay my blackmailer in order to help have him acquitted? If this is about money, if someone is taking bribes on my behalf, who would have paid for me to change the plea in Paul Beaupert's hearing in Wood Green? That makes no sense. Christopher Ball can't be a relative of Elliot's—can he?

A redheaded woman in the front row of the public gallery unbuttons her blue coat. Leather gloves in her lap, she glances at the man sitting next to me in the witness box and inhales him in one shallow breath. My body breaks out into an uncomfortable sweat. Is Elliot all right with my neighbor? Will my blackmailer realize that I haven't sent him to school? My eyes track along each row of the public gallery. They could be watching Elliot, or they could be here. They could be any one of these people.

I do my swearing in and translate the judge's remarks into German, hushing the words into my client's ear. He answers the first question and my voice splits as I repeat his response into English.

"Usher, please give the interpreter some water." I'm so dizzy, I can't tell where the voice is coming from. A glass is pressed into my hand and miraculously, it finds my mouth.

Then the second question. I interpret accurately, my full German vocabulary flooding back.

The third question. No mention of plates or doors.

"Your Honor," a barrister says. "A matter of law has arisen."

The wigs approach the bench and speak in a tight huddle. A minute passes, and then another. This is purgatory. I'd rather get this over with and be sent straight to hell.

"Court adjourns," the judge booms across the room. Lunch. Thank goodness. I can't wait to get out of the courtroom. On my feet I move quickly to the exit, but I don't want to go right outside onto the street. I feel suffocated and can't be around people right now; the urge to be alone is irrepressible. I look for the restrooms. When I reach the front of the line, I rush into a stall.

On the floor my body coils. I don't care if anyone can see under the door, I'm not thinking about how disgusting it is to be lying on these tiles. I can't go to jail. I can't lose Elliot.

But I can't do this either.

No new phone messages from my blackmailer. But another flashes, unopened: it's from Gurmeet, a photo of Elliot playfully rolling on the floor with her dog. He's fine. He looks happy. I could almost kiss this grungy floor. I yank myself up onto my elbows. I'm all right, I can survive this, I tell myself, one more day. This afternoon. I'll change those words, and I'll stay safe, I won't be caught. I'll be clever and choose my words carefully and by tomorrow, my blackmailers will be satisfied and this will all be over. It has to be.

I exit the bathroom stall and rinse my hands in the sink. A long line snakes out of the ladies, not helped by me occupying one of the stalls for the last ten minutes. I hear a German accent. The redheaded woman from the public gallery.

"The timetable for the legal ethics seminar is ridiculous," she says. Her accent is German, but she speaks English plain and clear.

"Have you finished the essay yet?" her friend asks.

"I started yesterday," she shrugs her shoulders. "I'll do an all-nighter." A law student. She's bilingual.

Alarm flares in my stomach. I insert my palms into the dryer. There's every chance after the break she will go home or into the public gallery of a different courtroom. Law students frequently come to observe but most come specifically to admire the performance of barristers. Even if she does return to my courtroom, it's possible she won't listen closely enough to detect my word change. But she's a student—she's here to study and to learn from other people's mistakes. My hands are overheating in the dryer; I whip them out. I lean close to the mirror. Breath from my nose fogs the glass as I look myself deep in the eyes.

30.

I've come this far. I need to finish the job and get back to Elliot. I'll have to ensure that German student is refused entry to court. What causes people to be ejected from the gallery? If they're found eating, taking photos—none of which I can make her do. A phone going off—mobile devices are forbidden for members of the public. Yes, that might be something I could arrange.

I push my way out of the restrooms and head toward the high street. Cash machine. I need to get some money out. There. I spot a black cashpoint on the other side of the road and dart across between two cars. Notes in hand, now I need a phone shop. I start to jog toward Holborn. I see a Tesco Express. Supermarkets usually sell cheap phones and SIM cards, but this shop is teeming with people scouting for a cheap lunch; it will take too long. I check my watch—twenty-five minutes until I'm due back in court. I cross the road again and keep running along the other side. There is a Carphone Warehouse down near Embankment, but even in a taxi I doubt I would get there and back in time, and they might ask me for ID. I open Maps on my phone and search. Reception is weak. "Come on," I will my 4G signal to grow stronger. There is a Three Mobile shop within a five-minute walk, but they're also likely to ask for ID. I need a kiosk, one of those small mobile phone accessories shops. My map shows there is one in the other direction but within five minutes on foot if I'm fast. I know from interpreting police interviews with suspected drug dealers that there's no requirement for those shops to ask for documentation. I put my phone away and start to run.

Other pedestrians see my stricken face and dodge out of my way. "Sorry," I mouth, after almost crashing into a woman with a stroller. Then I see it. I rush into the shop and go straight up to the counter. "Hello. My phone was stolen. I've been mugged. I need a replacement. Really quickly. Can you get me up and running with a burner phone? No need for data." My words reach him in a single breathless stream. He listens then silently turns and selects a box from the shelf behind him. I lean on the counter and let myself rest for a moment.

I spell it out to myself: I'm buying an untraceable phone with cash, which I'm going to somehow force upon a stranger. I can hardly comprehend this is really happening. When I was a child, I'd often get this sense, not quite déjà vu but a similar uncanny feeling. I'd be at school or at home not doing anything remarkable, and I'd glance down at my arm holding my schoolbag or the TV remote control and it would look foreign, as though it wasn't part of me. My eyes would move from my limb to the rest of my body and I couldn't quite believe that it was all under my control; its every action my own doing. The man in front of me is opening the cardboard box. Some of me is untethered and is now drifting away, not having any part of this lunacy.

"This one will work straight away, will it?" I ask him.

He nods, but doesn't look at me. I've scared him I think, with my urgency. He takes the phone from the plastic casing and expertly removes the back with one assured motion. I watch the man push a SIM into the slot and switch on the phone. "You'll activate it for me? So I can make a call now?"

"Yes," he finally speaks. "The battery is only sixty percent though. There's a charger in the box."

"That's okay. That will do."

"Forty-nine pounds."

"Okay, yes, money, I have that." I reach into my bag—I withdrew

£100 from the machine. I hand him the cash and watch him manipulate buttons on the phone. "Is it working?" I check my watch.
Twelve minutes to go.

"It's searching for the network," he says, looking at the screen.
What's my plan here—I'm going to sneak this phone into the German student's bag and then call her? I can't do that. It will be impossible for me to make a call in court without anyone noticing
what I'm doing. I need the phone to make a noise, enough for the
judge to hear and for the ushers to toss her out. An alarm.

"It won't make calls yet but what about the alarm, will that
work?"

"Alarm? Yes, you don't even need a SIM for that."

"Perfect," I say, snatching the phone from his hand. I should
have thought of that already, I've been wasting precious minutes.
"Thank you, I'm in a rush!" I dart out of the shop.

My fingers work all of the buttons on the phone until I figure
out how to set an alarm, then I turn the volume up to maximum. I
run all the way back to the Old Bailey. I stop dead a few yards from
the entrance to catch my breath and smooth down my disheveled
hair. I can't go in like this and attract attention. When I'm satisfied
that I look reasonable, I walk inside.

Now to find her. I do a lap of the waiting areas and the ladies' restroom. If the German law student doesn't show, all the better—I'll
turn the phone to silent and dump it in a garbage can after court.
Five minutes until I'm due in the witness room. I hover within view
of the public entrance, and lean against the wall. I can't just stand
here staring at everybody, so I find an old paperback in my handbag
and crack the spine.

Her friend appears. Then red hair. My book pushes up to hide
my face. Her bag is a slim satchel, flap jiggling as she walks. She
joins the end of the bathroom line and this is my chance. I breeze
past and when I reach her, my fingers nudge the flap and drop the

phone inside. Oh God, I've never gone through someone's bag before or stolen anything. The woman didn't feel it, she didn't see. But someone else did. An elderly woman lurking in the corridor scowls at me. She's on the move; she's going straight to the German student and she'll point to me.

"Dropped her purse," I say. "I didn't want to draw attention to it." I whisper because I am polite and discreet. The woman stops in her tracks. I'm not a thief, I'm a good Samaritan. She sees my empty hands and her face sweetens.

After today, no more lies.

It's time to look for my witness.

My shoes stick to the floor, slowing down my walk back to court. No part of me wants to be here. I'm powerless, and let my body be gathered by the flow of human traffic. I locate the witness and we are summoned back inside. In the witness box, I suck a mouthful of water and wonder how much I'd need to drink in order to drown. The noise of the room intensifies as the public gallery refills. The friend of the redheaded woman enters and settles in the front row. Sweat from the witness next to me infects my skin. Then a swish of scarlet hair. No, no, no. The German law student drops onto the bench. Is the phone still in her bag? From here at least, she looks relaxed, and surely if she'd found mysterious contraband in her bag she'd be freaked out. I finish all of the water in my glass; I do not drown. I hold on to the seat underneath me as though I might fall off.

Proceedings in court four recommence with questions from the prosecution. My face feels hot. I look around for a heat source, a light bearing down from the ceiling, but there's nothing. I wiggle out of a layer of clothing, a navy cardigan, as discreetly as I can. It doesn't help. The witness sits tall and confident, speaking into the microphone. I repeat his statements into English and wait for the word "plate" to come up. I need that bilingual law student out of the room. From the

275

corner of my eye I check my watch. The alarm should have gone off a minute ago. It's not going to sound. The man in the phone shop was wrong, or I didn't set it correctly, or maybe the volume is off. I should have known this wasn't going to work, and now I can't go through with it because this woman will notice my words. She'll get the judge's attention or wait until the end of the day to approach someone and either way, I'll be exposed.

"There was some disagreement with Boris over the plates on the test cars." The German words bite through my thoughts. There it is. "A petty argument, really," the witness continues in German, speaking into the microphone. He leans back in his chair and now it's my turn to interpret. "There was some disagreement with Boris," I repeat in English. Here is where I should say "over the doors." Will the law student notice?

Then a bland chirping sound pierces the room. Court ushers bolt down the aisle.

"Mobile phones are not permitted in the public gallery!" the judge bellows. "Ushers, please remove the person responsible!"

The phone continues to buzz. The German student looks along her row—the offending device is obviously close by, but she can't work out where the sound is coming from. An usher takes hold of her shoulder bag and something vibrates from within. She is guided from the room and her friend trails behind. My eyes follow her gratefully. There is no guarantee they're the only bilingual speakers in the room, but at least my known threat has been neutralized.

While the judge speaks to the gallery, I sneak a look at Christopher Ball in the dock and now I cannot wrench my eyes away. Attempted murder is simply a murderer who couldn't get the job done. Am I really going to do this? Changing words in the testimony of a prosecution witness is only going to help the defense, improving the chances of this would-be killer going free.

What about the victim? Apparently I don't care about justice anymore. All I've been thinking about is protecting myself and Elliot, but that victim has a family. If I change a word today and undermine this prosecution witness, I am standing in the way of justice. I should be caught and charged; I should go to prison. I continue looking at Christopher Ball.

If my purpose today is to have Ball acquitted, why hasn't my blackmailer said that's what I need to do? Why force me to change only one word? Changing the word "plates" into "doors" may not achieve their aims—and then what happens? If this attempted murderer, Ball, has been promised a not-guilty verdict and he doesn't get it—he might come after me too. My arms drop to my sides and grip hold of the seat again. Elliot falls ill at school one morning, he's sent home, I bring him here, to this very court, and less than two months later, here I am, on the brink of losing everything. I don't know who would wish this on me; who would care enough about me, one way or the other.

People seated in the public gallery fidget after the disturbance of the cell phone.

"Quiet please," the judge says.

Whoever is blackmailing me has access to court information—they know which interpreters are assigned to which trial. Someone with that knowledge would surely have an understanding of the court proceedings. They must know that me blindly changing "plates" into "doors" isn't going to achieve anything except see me caught. The German word for "license plate" even sounds like the English "number." The English speakers in the room will likely realize what I've done, let alone anyone bilingual. No interpreter could get away with this. If it's a court official or a police officer or even a sophisticated criminal behind this, they'd understand that the best strategy would be for me to change the questions coming from the prosecution, the words whispered into the witness's ear.

None of this makes sense. It's as if they don't want me to do a good job of misinterpreting.

A dark speck floats in front of me. My eyes trace it as it glides through the air and settles on my knee. I don't think my black-mailer *is* trying to have Ball acquitted, and they never cared about the French defendant at Wood Green. I touch my fingers to my knee to catch the speck: there's nothing there. Now it all seems so obvious—I've been searching for a connection that doesn't exist. The point was never to help free Christopher Ball, or interfere with the hearing at Wood Green. They're incidental. Misinterpret in open court, on audio recording, for everyone to hear. Steal another interpreter's identity. Leave a trail of evidence.

The goal is me.

They want me to be caught.

Now there are hundreds of black specks in the air, twinkling like midnight stars, and I have to fight to stay conscious. Unless that's my way out of here.

My shoulder hits the floor first.

I am concentrating on keeping still and press my eyes closed. Every bone in my upper body thrums with pain. I've lost track of time but I better move now or else they'll think I'm dead. I open my eyes to a ring of people gathered around me. "I'm okay," I gurgle.

I hear the judge say court is adjourned for the day. Someone calls an ambulance.

"I can stand," I say.

I look around the room: the public gallery is emptying out. My blackmailer could be here, having sat among the onlookers this whole time.

"I need to go home," I say to my circle of helpers. A barrister leans over me, releasing a puff of sweaty horsehair wig.

A court usher flies into the room. "The paramedics are here!"

I can't become trapped here. My blackmailer might be waiting to pounce, or they could have gone straight to Elliot.

"I don't need medical attention," I say, "I'm fine." I hear protests as I sprint from the court building, turning down Old Bailey before hailing a cab on Newgate Street.

I give the driver my address. When we pass Shepherd's Bush, I ask her to take a detour and get off the Westway just in case I'm being followed.

"No problem." I appreciate that she doesn't ask me why I want to take the slow route home. "How's your morning been?"

"Okay," I croak. "How about you?"

"Oh, uneventful," she says. She switches on the radio and upbeat pop music begins to play. I rest my head against the seat and silently count to ten. I can do that; I can get to the end. Nine. Ten. Then I start again.

I wonder when the safety feature became mandatory, the one which stipulates doors must automatically lock whenever a black cab is in motion? What happened for authorities to decide that passengers needed to be locked inside the car for their own safety, to prevent them from leaping to their deaths when the vehicle sped up or turned a corner? Could a car ride truly be so bad that one is driven to suicide? Click. Click. There the lock goes again. I like having you trapped in here with me. But this isn't about me, I remind myself. It doesn't matter how I feel at the end of this. The important thing, the only thing, is that you feel as though the surface of the world is breaking apart, and then feel nothing at all.

It takes three to four years' worth of study to pass the Knowledge exam and become a black-cab driver in London. If you offer to match a driver's annual salary in cash, and call it a reward for passing the test, your own Tesla given as collateral, they will lend you their car for a couple of hours.

I am usually a conscientious driver but my eyes are on you in the rearview mirror rather than the road and I have come close to hitting a street sign, twice. You didn't notice.

"Do you mind the radio?" I ask in my best cockney accent.

"Go ahead." Aren't you delightful?

It is not the radio I switch on but my special playlist.

The first song starts. "INXS. My mum loved this band," you say softly and I am not sure I was supposed to hear. I increase the volume. You lean back against the leather seat and close your eyes to the music. I'll wake you when we get there.

31.

I open my eyes and look through the car window. We are still fifteen minutes from home. I shouldn't have asked the driver to go the long way; I need to get back to Elliot, now. The taxi passes a cluster of shops, a bank, a brightly lit convenience store. A woman sits on the ground out the front of a busy pharmacy, red sleeping bag and a shopping trolley spilling over with possessions, the bottom half of a suitcase without a lid. Adam. On my phone I look for updates on his case. There. A news article released an hour ago. Adam is free, all charges dropped. I let my forehead knock against the glass, and my neck muscles release. He is out. But released to where? I turn and look through the cab's rear window, the woman by the pharmacy now a blur of red and silver, retreating from view. Adam has his life back, that's the main thing, but I need to do more for him, somehow. I speed-read an article in the *Independent* which says police don't know who killed Sandra. There is no mention of the heiress. I can't think about that now. Adam is free and I need to focus on keeping Elliot safe from whoever is blackmailing me.

My phone shows no new messages. They could be at our flat already. I close my eyes against the image of what they might do when they get there. I need to work out who they are. Elliot's birth mother? Or someone else connected to Elliot's birth family? A person who wants my misinterpreting exposed because I've changed a word of theirs, or of someone they care about? They do all this instead of going to the police. Why? Because they are the police, or they have a criminal background. I've been a police and court interpreter for a long time and they think that they won't be believed. They know I made an error somewhere but they can't prove that it was deliberate. That's the missing piece. This person was never interested in extorting me or getting me to influence the outcome of a trial. They want justice. They want to see me punished. I changed an alibi statement that could have seen Adam convicted and imprisoned for life, and he is innocent. Did my actions help to convict someone else innocent, too? The Lad in the sexual assault case is guilty—there are now five women who've come forward. He is clearly from a privileged family—during the trial he had the finest counsel money can buy. If he suspected me he would have sued me, used me as grounds for appeal—not gone about things this way. His case and Adam's are the only times I've misinterpreted, twice in eight years. Two deliberate, calculated mistakes.

Suddenly the taxi careens around the corner and I cover my ears to a blast of horns coming from both sides of the car. "Sorry about that," the driver says. "Utter maniac in the BMW in front, did you see that?"

"No." I didn't see.

I am the best interpreter they have—how many times have I heard that from Exia and from the courts? I never cancel on a booking. When they need the best, they call me. A perfect, unimpeachable translation depends on Revelle Lee. They trust me. Only because they're not aware of what happened.

My eyes follow the road outside the car window. We're still about five minutes from the flat. I think of the medical appointment I interpreted a few years ago, a Portuguese patient diagnosed with an autoimmune disease. As I repeated the consultant's words, it struck me that the experience of this illness is similar to what it's like to have made a catastrophic error. After an autoimmune attack, you assess what's happened, you learn what triggered it, you know what to avoid, what to never do again; you move past it even, and some days you will forget that it was ever part of you. But every so often it will remind you of its presence. You have learned to live with it but it remains dormant inside, threatening to return. In some patients, the doctor explained, in certain types of disease, it's this fear, the anxiety of it coming back that is the worst part of the illness, and that possibly even causes it to recur. Because what happened once can happen again.

What was the name of that patient's illness? I can't recall. How can I not remember it? I sit up straight and run my hand over my scalp. I can't summon the English or the Portuguese word. But how did I interpret it for the patient that day? Think, I tell myself, but it's blank, my memory completely dry. Did I know the correct term during the appointment? My breath becomes solid, too dense to move through my chest. I press three fingers to the place where it's stuck. I can't recall the word now, but did I ever know it? Portuguese patient. Consultant. Autoimmune illness. Think. I've forgotten. The mass under my clavicle expands and I may have got the term wrong that day. I could have mistranslated the doctor or the patient's words, during that appointment and so many others.

"Are you all right there?" The driver is eyeing me in her mirror.

I move my head up and down in a nod, because I cannot speak.

How many errors have I made? I don't know. I can't count them. Count to ten instead. Nine. What comes next? I don't know, I can't think. I speak eleven languages, but I don't know the word for anything.

My phone makes a noise which bores into me. My fingers like butter, the device slides and falls to the car floor. I reach for it and see the sound is a fresh notification from Facebook. It's from Doreen. She's written back a second time.

Revelle, for years now I've thought I'm being followed. Watched. Not every day but every few weeks something will happen to remind me that there's someone out there. They found me, somehow. One of the nutters who became obsessed with the case in the news, I assume. For a while I wondered if it was you.

I type:

It's not me. Where are you? What exactly has been happening to make you think that someone's watching you?

I press send.

Finally, the taxi pulls up at our building. I pay and take the stairs, two at a time. Inside our neighbor's flat, Elliot is standing on a booster step at the kitchen worktop. He's okay. I pull him toward me and flour from his arms sticks to mine.

"Did you have a good day?" Gurmeet says, wrestling with an egg beater in a bowl. There are cookies cooling on a rack.

"Yes." I can't involve Gurmeet in this. In ten minutes' time, Elliot and I will be gone.

"We're not finished," Elliot says to me. "I don't want to go home yet."

I'll leave Elliot here for another few minutes. I can pack faster without him. I should have asked the taxi to wait. I hurry to Gurmeet's balcony window and look down—the car's already left.

"Is everything okay?" Gurmeet asks.

I smile instead of answering.

"Five more minutes," I tell Elliot. "If that's okay with you, Gurmeet?"

"Sure. And you'll have to take some of these cookies home with you." We don't have a home and I don't know where we're going.

I put the key to my door. Here goes. It pushes open to reveal an empty flat. Everything appears as I left it this morning; no one has broken in. I find my bag from the other day and begin stuffing clothes and essentials inside. I place three balls of Elliot's socks in the corner and see there's a soap dish of all things. I picked that up a moment ago and put it in the bag. I pull it out and fling it to the floor. I can't be trusted to do this task properly, I can't think clearly.

Stop, I tell myself, come up with a list of what we need. We're not coming back so I have to get this right. Then there is a quiet knock at the door. Gurmeet has brought Elliot back, but I'm not finished packing yet. I rush through the living room and open the door to a woman who is not our neighbor.

"You left this in my car." It's my black-cab driver. "People do it all the time. I collect about three phones a week." She laughs. "I should open a stall."

She is holding a mobile in her hand. I turn to see if my phone is in its usual place on the coffee table. No. It's in the bag in my hand, I'm sure I just saw it. "I don't think that's mine," I tell her. How did the cab driver know which flat I'm in? She dropped me out the front but this building is twelve stories high. "I have my phone," I feel for it through the fabric of my bag. "Yours must belong to another passenger." I look up and see the phone come toward me, but she's holding something else too. It is swinging upward toward my face and I'm still wondering how she found me when everything goes dark.

32.

In a council building across the road, I'm about to undertake my first ever interpreting assignment with a local authority. I am sitting in a café with a social worker I've just met, Doreen. "Holy cow, it's ten fifty-nine!" she says, throwing a tenner onto the table, and we run across the road, laughing as her shoe catches the edge of a pot-hole and she limps the final stretch.

I've been a freelance interpreter for three months and so far I've had few bookings. I've signed up with three different agencies and I know there's plenty of work going around, but it isn't being offered to me. Mostly I've been doing police work. I need to take every job I can get, make connections and build up my CV.

Today's assignment is called a supervised contact session, and it's between a mother and child. Doreen leads me to the top of the stairs and I see that the council building is an absolute wreck. I had one job last week—in a legal chambers in central London. The chairs in their boardroom were actual antiques and in the kitchen they had a coffee machine with those capsules—you can make a flat white as good as any East London café—and they have a tap for chilled sparkling water, and each morning someone slices thin lemon wedges and arranges them on a plate.

Doreen stalks the room and checks her watch. "None of them are here yet," she says, shifting her gaze to me. "You look nervous."

"Do I?"

"Or is this just how you look?"

I laugh. "Yes, I think it is."

"I'm joking. You'll be great. This should be straightforward. I appreciate you being here." I like that she is motherly without being patronizing. I suppose some people might say she verges on being unprofessional, but it's nice that she isn't cold.

I am also joking, because I *am* feeling very jumpy.

"So you translate for me everything that's said in German, everything the boy and the mother say. You shouldn't need to speak to them directly, so don't worry." She checks her watch again. "Where are they?!"

"Will the mother and the child just be sitting in here talking?" I ask.

"Yes, they'll try and pretend we're not here, that's the idea. The boy, Max, is four—they'll play with the toys and basically we'll just sit and watch."

I look at the council's toy provision on the carpet: a lumpy red ball that I doubt would even roll, and a snakes and ladders board game more museum relic than functional play equipment. Doreen catches me staring at it. "I know. It's what we have."

I try to shake the excess electricity from my arms and legs without Doreen noticing. It's all right, because she's at the window again, her attention on the parking lot below. "I think the mother's here."

"The child is coming separately?"

She nods. "He's in care. And she's in *recovery*," the last word a whisper. Doreen steps closer to me and speaks quietly into my ear. "I'm trying not to be biased. They're from a really good family. The risk of harm is probably low."

"He might go back with her?"

She nods. "Unless she gives me a reason today why he shouldn't." Doreen's eyes are still fixed on the window. "The child is here too. Good, we need to get started." She adjusts the position of the plastic chairs in the room, claps her hands together and looks right at me: "Are you ready?"

I need the bathroom again even though I went in the café ten minutes ago. I'm too embarrassed to ask Doreen if there is time, so I hold it. I hear people climbing the stairs and adjust the sleeves of my new cheap suit, feeling like a child in dress-up.

I get another booking with Doreen's local authority. I have two assignments at police stations in South and Southeast London and I travel to Luton for a court hearing, and that is the sum total of my week. Doreen is not directly involved in the translation assignment at her local authority, but she sends a text and asks if I'd like to join her afterward for lunch. The job is simple—I work through a short stack of documents from a Hungarian child protection agency pertaining to a family who is now living in the UK. I finish the papers earlier than expected and spend a moment on Exia's website, looking through available jobs for this afternoon.

It comes to me so quickly. There's no telling where it was hiding or why now it decided to make itself known. Like the title of a book or a film you've been trying to recall for weeks and it suddenly drops into view.

Tickle.

Last week's assignment with Doreen: *Mummy, please don't tickle me again!* That's what I'd heard four-year-old Max say in German to his mother; how I interpreted it for the social worker.

Tickle. Tickle. Tickle.

That's how she recorded it in her notes.

But the word was *Schlagen*. Meaning: to hit, beat, strike.

I'd interpreted it as *tickle. Kitzeln.*

Not even close—the German or the English words sound nothing alike.

Schlagen is what Max said to his mother. *Mummy, please don't hit me again!*

How is it possible that I mixed up those two words? A total, catastrophic brain snap.

I botched it. My first interpreting assignment for a local authority and I've made a simple, embarrassingly basic mistake. How could I be such an idiot? I feel myself shrink to three feet tall. I love German. It's one of my strongest languages. Already I'm struggling to get enough work to amount to a full-time income and then I go and do something like this.

I return to my pile of Hungarian pages and my English translation. I'll go over everything once more, twice, to make sure I haven't done anything like that again. I read through my work, slowly and methodically, and do not find any mistakes. Okay, I tell myself, today's job looks fine. I did well; I'm not losing my mind. Last week was just a bad day. The local authority wanted me back today, they specifically asked for me to be assigned to this Hungarian job. They didn't catch the mistake last week, I realize. How could they? The only documentation for that session is the notes in Doreen's folder. She wrote down my English interpretation—there's no record of what the mother and child said in German. The only way my mistake would be discovered is if Max's mother looks at the report and says that she recalls her son asking her to not *hit* him again, and she's hardly going to do that.

Doreen appears at my desk. "Ready for lunch?"

"Sure." I log out of my computer.

"There's an epic Thai place around the corner. I eat there about three times a week, I'm totally out of control."

We walk to the restaurant and I think about explaining it to her when we sit down. I'll apologize and Doreen can correct her files. I guess it will mean she won't recommend me for further jobs and after today, I'll probably never work with this local authority again. Will she be angry? I shouldn't have accepted this lunch invitation. It's going to be awkward after I tell her.

In the Thai place, we are seated by the kitchen, close enough to watch the chefs flip heavy woks over a flame. We both order coconut juice and they arrive quickly.

"After I met you last Thursday," Doreen says, "my week went ballistic. My dog had to have an emergency operation after eating one of my socks. Two thousand pounds. Can you believe it?"

"What do people do if they can't afford it?"

She shrugs. "Surrender them at shelters, I guess."

"Thanks for putting me forward for this Hungarian job this morning," I say. "I appreciate the work."

"Thanks for hanging around last week. I know that contact session went massively over time."

I can't believe I have to raise this in conversation, and confess to such a rudimentary mistake. There are meaty chunks of coconut in my juice and I use the tip of the straw to spear them. I was nervous the morning of that assignment, but even so, such basic words. "Hit" and "tickle." What's wrong with me? Then, I remember something about my mother. When we were living in Vienna, she befriended a retired geography professor who agreed to lend her his collection of rare historical maps. It was a Saturday and all day she had been poring over the precious objects, sprawled on the rug in our living room, making notes by leaning on a footstool. I was bored. I had no friends in Austria and didn't speak enough German to be able to do anything to entertain myself. The day stretched on and on. I employed strategy after strategy to try to divert my mother's attention from her work. I told her some jokes I'd heard at my international school, I performed a few funny cartwheels—nothing succeeded. I was so jealous of those maps, envious that scraps of two-hundred-year-old paper could hold her attention in a way that I never could. I crouched behind her on the rug, lined up my hands under her arms and tickled. My mother bucked involuntarily and yelled for me to stop but I only tickled her harder. Trying to shake me off, her foot kicked and swung, knocking over a nearby glass of juice. A glass which should have been well out of range of those priceless artifacts. The drink soaked through the paper of two of the maps. My mother screamed. She scooped them up, clutched them to her chest and ran to the dining table where she spread them out and dabbed them with absorbent paper for hours, paying them a tenderness she'd never shown to me. Later, when she accepted that one of the maps could not be salvaged, she hit me, one firm slap across the cheek. It wasn't the slap which bothered me, it was the look in her eye. When she surveyed the full extent of damage done to the artifacts, I saw in her face realization of exactly what her life had become. This was the moment when my mother fully understood the irrevocable situation in which she found herself: me.

"See how big the scar is?" Doreen is showing me a picture of her dog on her phone. The creature splayed on his back, a long vertical line down his stomach.

"Poor thing," I say. "Hey, what happened to that little boy, by the way, from the contact session last week? Max?"

"I can't really say." She looks down and puts her phone away.

"Of course, I'm sorry, I know that. It's confidential. I don't tell anyone about the work I do, I promise." I shouldn't have asked her so directly.

"It's fine, relax." She casts her eyes around the restaurant, presumably looking for anyone from her office. "He's back with the mother. I'm not sure about her, but you can't take someone's child based on gut feeling." Doreen reaches the end of her coconut juice and makes a gurgling sound. It's too late. I've really messed this up. The "hit" from the little boy was a red flag, maybe all that Doreen needed to hear in order to keep him in care. But they're not going to take him back a second time.

"If you have room, they do a terrific fried ice cream here," Doreen says. What if I hadn't realized today? Most people who make translation errors aren't ever made aware of what they've done. I would never have asked Doreen about what happened to Max, and wouldn't have known that he was back with his mother. If for some reason Doreen had mentioned it, I wouldn't have thought it had anything to do with me. The moment's passed. If I tell Doreen, she'll be upset but she probably can't do anything about it now. It's best for everyone if I pretend to be blissfully ignorant. I can do that. And besides, shouldn't a child be with their mother? Even if they hit you, you still love them.

"What are you doing next Saturday?" Doreen asks. "I'm having birthday drinks."

"I'm free. I'd love to come." I am trying to build a career for myself, a life, and maybe, finally, make a real friend.

33.

Fibers scratch my eyelids awake. Tiny loops with crumbs and dust—carpet. I see the legs of the coffee table, and Elliot's stray sock lies directly in my eyeline, though I can't reach it. I'm in my living room. But the room is the top deck of an ocean liner, tossing me to one side, then to the other; I'm at the mercy of a choppy sea. I must have slipped and hit my head. All of that pretend fainting has really taken effect. The black-cab driver. My cell phone. How did she know which flat I was in?

My arms do all of the work getting me to my feet. The front door is closed. The balcony too. The flat is silent except for my racing heart. The cabbie gone. I take it one piece of furniture at a time. I let go of the coffee table only when I can reach the sofa, transfer my weight to the bookcase, and then seize the wood of the bedroom door. Where is Elliot?

An idea plays that you are not supposed to sleep when you've had a head injury. A concussion can take hold if you give it the chance; tempt it and it will pull you under. I strain to keep my eyes open but the lids are like opposing magnets. Made for each other.

A presence in the doorframe. There he is. My head goes slack with relief: my boy is all right. No, it's too tall for him—not Elliot, a woman is standing there.

"Who are you?" I say. She is long and slender. "How'd you get in here?" Do I know her? She looks familiar, but my brain is thick with fog. Elliot, I think, as I look down at the carpet. Elliot, as my eyes roll up toward the ceiling. I think of my son as I try to decipher the stranger in front of me. He's next door. He's with our neighbor. I need to call Gurmeet, warn them to stay away. But my phone is not here. There is a candle in a heavy glass jar and I think it is a good idea to have this in my hand. It's the cab driver, I realize. She came up to return the cell phone that isn't mine and she's still here. I fall back onto the bed and the candle drops and rolls, my weapon out of reach. Her hands take hold of my ankles next and she yanks me to the floor.

"Where is he?" she says.

"I don't know what's going on."

"Where is he?" She's shouting now. "You probably don't even know, do you? Anything could be happening to him." A heavy heel of one shoe is pinning down my ankle. "The world is full of beastly mothers."

Everything inside me is syrup, thick and stuck together. I cannot move, I cannot do anything, but I have to get to Elliot. I try to roll toward the door. There are only a few inches of plaster wall between me and the inside of Gurmeet's flat. I strain my ears and listen for my son.

"Some mothers would cut the heart out of our chest for our child. But not you."

I didn't leave my phone in her car. She isn't a real black-cab driver. She knew which flat I was in because she's been tracking and harassing me all this time.

"Elliot's mother." My words bleed out. Blood. From my skull, it rains into my eye. My head is either in terrible pain or completely numb.

"You brought this on yourself, you know," she says, as I concede to the darkness again. "Adopting. *You!* Rubbing my face in it." Her words invade my sleep. I want to scream, shout for help. But if Gurmeet comes out, Elliot might follow, and I'll be leading his mother right to him. I can't shout, anyway. Because she is pushing a needle into my arm, containing invisible straps that hold me down.

"I'm his mother now," I say, but it comes out as a gurgle and I fear that I may never see him again. "I promise you, I love him with everything I have. I would do anything for him." My eyes sting. Behind each one, hundreds of tiny blades. I stop trying to speak because one of her hands is under my jaw, the other pinching my nose. She is strong enough to close my airways and there are only a few seconds of oxygen left.

She's going to kill me and then she's going to take Elliot.

I summon everything I have; I must fight her off. I open my eyes, one lid at a time, and grit my teeth. Her stomach is level with my eyeline. Isn't she supposed to be pregnant? I look at her flat belly. It's almost concave. Lydia said she was heavily pregnant. She must have lost her baby. Perhaps that was the final straw for her grip on sanity and why she's back to claim Elliot. I see the wrinkles by her eyes, the shadows under her jaw. I think she's in her early fifties, at least—she wasn't pregnant recently. There is a relentless ringing in my ears and I cannot think; I cannot get purchase on her words but in her voice I can hear an accent. Subtle, but it's there. German.

Oh God.

It can't be. Max Graf's mother is in prison. She was convicted of involuntary manslaughter.

"What does it feel like?" Now the woman's mouth is practically inside my ear. "To suffocate?" I swivel my head left to right but can't loosen her grip. "Is it the lack of air that's the worst part?" Her tone is genuinely curious. "Or is it the panic? When you realize that there's nothing you can do? I've asked doctors. I've got second and third and fourth opinions. I had to find out. I had to know if at that age, he would have realized what was happening." Keep resisting, I tell myself, stay alive. She will tire out. I need to hang on. "His small fists against the glass. Pushing against the locked doors. The relentless sun in the sky that day. Would he have understood that death was close? That the heat in the car was about to consume him?" Her fingers drop away and my chest heaves for breath. "You're not going that quickly. That's just a little taste."

"Max."

"He is called *Johann*. He was supposed to have a new life with me. A safe, beautiful life." She killed her own son.

"Prison," I say, because I cannot seem to form a full sentence.

"You're the one who should be in prison." She crouches down, her face right by mine, our cheeks touching, and she sniffs me, like an animal. "I'm his aunt, you stupid fool." I see her younger face in my mind's eye, from the news around the time that Max died. Mellie Graf. Apart from his mother, she is the boy's only known relative. A journalist took a photograph of her leaving coroner's court, I remember now. So thin she'd snap if you breathed on her. She wore the thickest coat I've ever seen, a metallic weave through the fabric, like a knight's shield stretched across her back. You could tell she was wealthy. She would have given Max a great life. He'd be living in her mansion right now, wearing luxury children's clothes, enjoying the finest education, endless overseas vacations, afforded every opportunity. If not for me.

Now Mellie Graf goes to my balcony, the click of her heels absorbed into the carpet. She unlocks the door. Fresh air slaps my cheeks. What is going on next door? I told Gurmeet I'd be back to collect Elliot in five minutes. I've lost track of time but that has to have been at least twenty minutes ago.

"My sister had only just come out of drug rehabilitation, for the *third* time. It was only a matter of *when* she'd start using again. And social services simply hand her son back to her, just like that." Mellie clicks her fingers and I jump. "There's been some kind of administrative error, I assumed; they'd confused Max's file with someone else's. I argued with them. I contested my sister's custody, I hired three lawyers. It didn't work—the local authority refused to listen to me and it only served to antagonize my sister, who

296

then stopped me from contacting Max at all." She is pacing back and forth between me on the floor and the balcony. She's going to throw me off, that's how she wants to kill me. Push me so I'll fall eleven stories below.

"Then, one day, a phone call. I *knew*. Somehow I could tell from the second that phone began to ring, what the news would be." She's going to get me out of the way and then she's going to take Elliot. "After she was arrested for murder, *then* my sister wanted to be in contact. She wanted money, of course. I refused, told her to use legal aid. Her solicitor apparently advised her to plead guilty, so that she'd get a reduced sentence. So that's what she did, and after the conviction, she called me from prison. I didn't want to speak to her except for this one time. I wanted to let her know how happy I was that she was locked away." I hear Gurmeet's dog bark next door. Don't come in, I send a silent message to my neighbor. Don't bring Elliot here.

"My sister said she pleaded guilty because the lawyer told her to, but that Max's death wasn't her fault. She claimed social services was negligent. They should never have returned Max to her. While she was on remand, she looked at all the reports, all the paperwork from social services and saw something that stood out. A transcript of a supervised contact session where Max said, 'Mummy, please don't tickle me again.' That was wrong, my sister said. He said 'hit' that day. And I know my sister is telling the truth because she never tickled him in her life, but she is a monster and she did hit him." Mellie Graf is still pacing. The ringing in my ears is beginning to subside. Through the wall shared with Gurmeet's flat, I think I can hear Elliot laugh.

"My sister pointed this all out to the lawyer but I don't think he believed her. He convinced her that it was best to take full responsibility in front of the judge, to be remorseful and get the minimum sentence." She is now waving a stack of documents in her hand, the knife edge of the paper slicing clean through the air. *You changed a word.* The text messages. This has always been about my mistake. "Either *you* got the word wrong, or the social worker did. So which one of you should I kill?" The wind is blowing inside, lashing my loose hair against my face. I'm going to hit the concrete and die. And I won't be there to protect Elliot.

Mellie Graf is walking back toward me, thrusting out her phone screen where a woman appears in black and white. The room is a kitchen somewhere, and the woman is standing at an island, with a bowl and spoon in her hand. There is what looks like a plastic bag of grocery shopping on the table. It's Doreen. Where is she? The screen flicks between two images—one face-on and the other is taken from behind her. There's no sound. Doreen doesn't look up. She doesn't know the cameras are there.

Doreen's message from earlier:

Revelle, for years now I've thought I'm being followed. Watched. Not every day but every few weeks something will happen to remind me that there's someone out there. They found me, somehow. One of the nutters who became obsessed with the case in the news, I assume. For a while I wondered if it was you.

"Don't hurt Doreen, please," I say.

"Who got the word wrong? You or her? One of you has to die," she says, grinding the side of her phone into my forehead. I'll do my best for Doreen, but I need to keep this woman away from my son. "Or both. Killing you both is also an option. If a task is worth doing, my father always said, then it's worth doing thoroughly."

On the phone screen, Doreen is rinsing a bowl in the sink. Her mouth is moving. She turns around. Is there someone there in the room with her? The bowl drops from her hand and shatters against the floor.

"Please don't do this."

Mellie Graf laughs and spins toward my balcony again.

Must. Run.

While her back is turned, I get to my knees and then shift my body weight to my feet, one at a time. Three large steps and I'm at the front door. Hand outstretched, the handle in my fingers now, I pull it back as a fierce blow lands on my head. The world is not completely black but clouds of white and gray fill my eyes. The carpet grazes against my skin and my bones form a puddle. She's dragging me again, heaving and pushing me along the floor; my head bounces, prone. Now Mellie is leaning over me. I watch her fiddle with the needle again, or is it a second one? She wants to punish me for what I did to her, to her nephew. She thinks I got away with it. And really, I did. More blood falls into my eye, my thumb smears it away. Color returns to my vision, allowing me to see her more clearly. Mellie is taking the syringe apart, testing it, holding it up to the light. I wait until the last second, and channel everything I have into my right foot. I kick the syringe and it breaks. "Shit!" she shouts. "You stupid little bitch." She mumbles to herself while she works to fix the needle. I almost feel sorry for her.

My strength is coming back. I could get to my feet again. I think I could make it to the front door. Now. Go, I tell myself. Must move faster. I cannot close my eyes. I need to get to Elliot. The black nothing is so delicious, it is so tempting to let it erase me and everything I've done. I know that's what I want, deep down, and what I deserve. I should yield to it. No. My son. I would cut my heart out for him, I would, just like Mellie said. I imagine toothpicks propping open my eyes. I have Elliot to go to.

My legs skate from under me. But I'm up and on my feet. Now, move.

I turn to the doorway and see Gurmeet. Elliot is there too.

"What is . . ." Gurmeet sees my wounded face, Mellie, and clocks the needle in her hand.

"Stay back!" Mellie points the partially disassembled instrument at my neighbor.

But Gurmeet lunges at her, pushing Mellie to the floor. I'm not going to freeze. Not this time. Mellie is on her knees, straightening up, now rising to her feet. I reach for the heaviest object within range: the floor lamp. I hug it to my chest with both arms and lift. I'm fast, but not fast enough. Mellie sees what I'm doing and kicks at my ankles. I wobble as my legs buckle. Before I hit the ground I manage to spin, the stone lamp still clutched to my middle. I collapse onto her, there's an incredible sharp pain in my left forearm, but the lamp is weighing me down, helping me to pin her to the ground. The candle. The candle in the glass jar has rolled under the coffee table. I look toward it and Gurmeet reads my gesture. She picks it up in her right hand, squeezes her eyes and slams it against Mellie's skull. Then Gurmeet drops it as though it's electrified. "Oh my," she says. "What have I just done?" Mellie is okay, she's semiconscious but alive. I push the lamp off me and stumble to my feet.

"The balcony," I say. I take one of Mellie's legs and indicate for Gurmeet to take the other. We use all of our strength to pull the woman outside. I close the balcony door and turn the bolt, locking Mellie Graf out. Soon enough she wakes, snarls, and bangs on the glass.

"Who is that?" Gurmeet is asking, but I'm not listening as I spin from the balcony and lock eyes with Elliot. He is outside our flat, through the open door in the corridor, curled into a ball of shock. I drop to the floor next to him.

"It's fine, love," I say. Behind me, I can hear Gurmeet calling the police. I hold Elliot to me, pulling him tight. I close my eyes and can imagine him slipping right inside my rib cage, safe. "That lady's ill." I am trying to block Elliot's view of Mellie. "We're getting her some help." He looks terrified at the state of my face. "It's nothing, it'll come off—see?" I rub the worst of it with my shirtsleeve to demonstrate.

"Police are two minutes away," Gurmeet says. "They're bringing an ambulance."

I nod and stand, Elliot still clinging to me. The three of us go back inside Gurmeet's flat and Elliot hugs Monday. I stand guard at the door. A few minutes later, there are sirens in the air. Gurmeet understands I won't leave Elliot now, so she volunteers to meet the police in my flat while I stay, tensed, until I hear the snap of handcuffs.

"You haven't tried my cookies yet," Elliot says. I follow his gaze to Gurmeet's kitchen. The squares dusted with icing sugar, resting on a metal rack.

"I'd love one." I find us a plate.

After his football game, Elliot says goodbye to Alfie and we walk home via the market. "Decide what you want for lunch," I tell him. "They have pies and pasties here." We are standing in front of a pastry stall and the air tastes of warm cinnamon and burned sugar. I think of Mariusz and his interrupted career.

"Can I help you?" a woman says, after I've been staring at the Danishes for quite some time. That day I took Mariusz for lunch, he gave me a recipe, from memory, for a Polish honey cake with plum butter. I should have written it down.

"I'll take one of everything," I say.

At home, I get Elliot cleaned up, wiping away the streaks of mud from his legs and the bits of grass that have nestled in his hair. We eat our pies and Elliot puts aside a donut for later. "Let's go out for a bit," I tell him. "And see a friend of mine."

Elliot and I exit the subway at Knightsbridge, but Mariusz is not in the walkway. "Who are you looking for?" a woman asks from beneath a blanket. This week, the days have hovered around forty-five degrees Fahrenheit. I hope this woman has somewhere to go at night.

"Mariusz Dorobek. He's usually right here."

"He's gone to the shelter on Fulham Road."

"Thank you." I tuck a ten-pound note into Elliot's hand. He places it in her upturned woolen hat.

Elliot and I walk there, following the map on my phone. When we arrive, I explain to the man on the desk that I'm here to drop off a gift for one of the residents. Mariusz is close by and he notices us. I wave and walk toward him, into a large common room where football plays on a TV.

"You remember my son, Elliot," I say.

"Hello there," Mariusz says in English. As before, he extends his hand for Elliot to shake.

"You're speaking your other language again," Elliot says to me. He knows what I do for work, but I suppose he hasn't heard me speak another language at length, except for Polish the day we took Mariusz to lunch.

"He thinks I only speak English and Polish," I tell Mariusz.

"Polish is your favorite, right?" Mariusz winks.

"I want to learn, too," Elliot says. Mariusz gets the gist of what my son means and, using his hands to bridge the language gap, tries to teach Elliot to say "My name is Elliot."

I pass Mariusz the box of pastries from the market. "This is amazing, thank you," he says, accepting them. Then I see him. On a blue sofa in front of the screen: Adam Birch. I recognize him from the newspapers. I need to leave.

"Let's go, Elliot." I start to guide him back the way we came.

"Wait, wait," Mariusz says in Polish. "Let me introduce you to . . ." Now he's calling out to his friend. "Adam! Come here!"

I cannot smile and say hello and pretend that I did not wrong this man.

"He's watching the football. Don't let me disturb you, I just wanted to drop the pastries off—we should go." I am walking toward the exit but Elliot is no longer in front of me. He has squirmed away and is sitting on the floor inches from the screen.

"You won't get him back now until halftime," Mariusz laughs. I can't stay here. I can't speak to this man. But Adam is looking at me and offering his palm, and I have no choice but to take it.

"Hi, it's good to meet you," he says. I shake the hand of the man I almost imprisoned for life.

"Lovely to meet you."

"I wanted to thank you. Mariusz told me that you tried to help after his police interview."

"Oh, no, I didn't do anything."

"I appreciate it." He takes my dismissal for modesty. I hate that I have him fooled.

"It really is nice to meet you. But I have to go." My cheeks are red, I know they are. He can tell; there's a screaming neon sign on my forehead declaring what I did. "Elliot!" I call, but my son pretends he can't hear.

"Let him watch the game," Mariusz says. "Relax for a minute. Have one of these." He opens the box and holds it out for me to take a pastry.

"No, I brought those for you."

"That's your son?" Adam says, looking toward Elliot.

"Elliot. He's six. Six and three quarters, if you ask him."

"Nice age. My daughter is about to turn ten." The little girl in the key ring, spectacles, and Arsenal football scarf.

"Have you had a chance to see her since you've been released?" Inwardly, I wince at my choice of question; it's obvious he doesn't live with her, but I want to know if she's still in his life.

"Not yet," he says. "But I'll be seeing her next week. She's down in Brighton."

"Oh, that's good. Really good."

"Your little man have any siblings?"

"No, I only had the one."

"Me too." He grins. Earlier this week Lydia emailed me with a brief note to say that Elliot's mother had her baby, a little girl. The child was immediately removed and taken into care, and is now seeking permanent adoption. A sister for Elliot. His father is still in jail. There was a moment where I considered calling Lydia and saying I would take the girl, but I knew it was madness; I can't possibly care for two children on my own. Once the baby is placed with a family and is a little older, I'll get in touch and organize for Elliot to meet his half-sibling. They can write to one another and visit during school holidays. I'll make sure they're given every chance to have the best relationship possible.

"Well, thanks again for everything," Adam says. He heads back to the TV and takes a seat on the floor next to Elliot.

"To tell you the truth," Mariusz says, "I need you to stay so I have someone to talk to while this is going on. I've never watched a football game in my life." I can't be in this room. I can't have a friendly conversation with these men and pretend I'm innocent. On the screen, there is a break in play and Adam takes the opportunity to explain to Mariusz and me the rules and the state of both teams.

"Watch it for five minutes, five minutes!" Adam says. "You'll like it, I promise you."

"Then we've got to go, Elliot," I say.

I wonder if Mariusz and Adam have been here in the shelter all week, and if this television plays the evening news. Sandra's inquest concluded on Thursday and it's been in the news most nights. Police failed to arrest her real killer because there isn't one—the coroner has ruled her death an accident. The finding is that Sandra tripped and fell down the stairs in the heiress's house. She was likely rushing to go down to the basement floor where the staff bathroom is, the only bathroom in the house the heiress allowed her to use. Sandra tripped and knocked over some glassware during her fall—initially believed to have been signs of a struggle. The shadowy figure on the CCTV taken from the heiress's back garden is thought to be the same homeless man with the bag who appears on the CCTV footage taken from the street. Sandra had left the back door open and was making trips out to the garbage because she didn't work on Sundays and Monday was trash day. The homeless man with the bag was walking the neighborhood, as is his habit the nights before the recycling is collected, filling his bag with empty jars and glass bottles tossed into garbage cans. Then he takes them to one of the supermarkets that has a reverse vending machine offering ten pence each. So the neighbors *were* correct that they had seen this man loitering in the area on numerous occasions. They just couldn't tell the difference between him and Adam—to them homeless people all blur into one. The man with the bag was released without charge, police having no appetite to arrest a homeless person for relieving wealthy residents of their garbage.

Silence falls between Mariusz and me. His eyes drift toward the TV screen, and mine follow. I wonder if Adam saw the news and translated for him. As for the heiress, she didn't kill Sandra but she was lying about not hearing what was going on in the kitchen; that story about her being upstairs with headphones listening to music wasn't true. During the inquest, she was forced to admit she had heard glass breaking that day; she heard Sandra scream and fall. She assumed an intruder was in the house and was afraid for her own safety, so instead of going down to help her maid, she hid under the bed. After two hours of silence, she felt safe enough to emerge and walked down to the kitchen, saw Sandra's body and called an ambulance. She told police the story about Spotify and the headphones because she was ashamed. Now there is talk of her being charged with giving police false information.

A cheer goes up among the half a dozen men clustered around the TV. Somebody scored a goal. Elliot leaps to his feet and high-fives Adam. Without thinking I take my phone from my back pocket and snap a picture. I can't have a photograph of my son with the man whose life I almost destroyed. I go to delete it, but it's kind of perfect. Both of Elliot's feet are off the ground, and his expression is entirely unselfconscious, just a little moment of pure joy.

I attach it to an email and send it to Richard with a camera emoji, football emoji, and two different types of smiles.

Richard is still insisting that he doesn't want anything from my mother's estate. He remains keen for me to be the executor of his own will and I made him promise me that it isn't because he's sick or has something which he isn't telling me. The sale of my mother's flat in Singapore went through yesterday. First, I will pay off the credit cards and then I will think about Elliot's future. I'm also going to find a way to get money to Sandra's daughter, somehow. I'll contact one of Sandra's friends online.

"You may as well stay until halftime now," Adam says, turning away from the television to face me. "Only ten minutes to go."

"Yeah!" says Elliot. Somehow half an hour has passed. I've been chatting to Mariusz and lost track of the time.

"Two pastries left," Mariusz says. "Your last chance." He nudges the box toward me. "You deserve it."

My hand hovers for a second before I take one.

When the first payment from Singapore hits my bank account, I leave two gifts at the homeless shelter, anonymously: an Arsenal season ticket for Adam and an M&S gift card for Mariusz. Elliot asks when we can go back to the homeless shelter and watch another football game. "That's their home, love," I tell him. "We can't really invite ourselves over to watch the telly. But I'll tell you what, pick a football game and I'll buy us tickets, yeah?" He chooses a match at Emirates Stadium between Arsenal and a German team, FC Nürnberg.

On our way to Emirates Stadium, Elliot asks me to teach him a few words in German so that he can call out to the Nürnberg football team from our seats. I've never said that I can speak German. I did tell him I spoke more languages other than Polish, and now he assumes I can speak them all and is incredulous when he asks me to say something in one that I don't know. I keep a tight hold of his hand in the crush of the football fans entering the stadium. "*Danke schön*," he says to himself, over and over.

As we file in to the grounds, Elliot wants to stop for a photo every couple of minutes. He pokes out his tongue and I click. Yesterday I sent Doreen a similar photo of Elliot from inside the London Eye after we spoke on the phone. We talked about everything that had happened; I told her about Mellie's arrest and at least now Doreen feels safe. It turns out Mellie had hired a dubious private investigator to follow Doreen for years. Recently, Mellie had him install cameras in Doreen's house. We don't know if he would have hurt her, had Mellie made the order for him to do so. He's been arrested for stalking and a number of other offenses.

I'm not sure if Doreen and I will speak again, not because she's still particularly angry with me, but you can't just pick up an old friendship where you left off after so many years, and I don't expect her complete forgiveness. She has moved on with her life and left social work and England behind. I told her that I wasn't interpreting anymore, and wasn't sure if I'd go back to it. The money from my mother's estate is funding a career break. While Elliot is at school, I spend my days at a community center in North-West London that helps migrants settle into life in the UK. I help to translate the jargon on government websites and fill out forms and applications for people still learning English. There's a social element to it too. Some people have come to the UK alone, without a family or a set community to slot into. I didn't anticipate how nice it would be to step away from crime. Technically it isn't work; I'm a volunteer at the center. I'm a helper now, and I have my own stories and things to say, no longer only the human dictionary. A person with a name, not just the interpreter.

Elliot and I take our seats and the football game starts with a deafening roar from the crowd. He is so excited to be here, and it's a battle to keep him contained on his seat.

"Mum, did you see that?!" I've no idea what he is referring to but I agree that it was amazing. I wonder if Adam is here, using his season ticket. We seem to be in a part of the stadium with a high concentration of German fans. I assumed Elliot was supporting Arsenal, but he seems to like the German side. "*Danke schön!*" he's shouting at the field: "thank you very much." He is the world's most polite football hooligan.

As the game progresses, a friendly German man seated in front of Elliot teaches him a few more words so that he can participate in the chanting coming from the German fans. I grin at the sight of Elliot taken under this man's wing, and laugh at my son's attempts at a German accent. FC Nürnberg scores again. All around us cheering German fans get to their feet chanting their club song. Elliot pulls me up from my seat. It's easy enough to learn the words to this German song. Next to me, Elliot is singing his heart out. Oh, why not. I join in.

Now in Emirates Stadium, it is halftime. I pry Elliot away from his new German friends and head to the upper section of the stand to buy some snacks. In the line, Elliot is telling me all about the game, but my attention wanders to a man in a nearby seat. He's been harassing a young steward for the whole ten minutes we've been standing here, making lewd remarks and inappropriate comments in both English and German. The teenage girl has tried to ignore him with a tight smile, but I can tell she is very uncomfortable. Is he going to sexually harass her for the whole match? I focus on Elliot and try to turn the man's offensive German words to babble.

We get our drinks and sit back down. Until the game restarts, Elliot decides to draw a picture of his favorite German player. I set him up with my notepad and a pencil and he opens to a new page. I glance back up the stand and see the man still harassing the steward. She must have been told by her supervisor that's the spot where she's meant to be for the duration of her shift and so she can't move away from him. The players jog back onto the field. There is a very bulky man seated in front of the harasser, arm draped over his girlfriend or wife. "Stay here," I say to Elliot. "I'll be back in one minute."

I race up the aisle.

"Excuse me," I say to the muscled man.

"Yeah?" His accent is English.

"I'm a German speaker," I talk from the corner of my mouth. "An interpreter, actually. I have to tell you, the gentleman behind you has been making sexually explicit comments about your partner since the beginning of the match. Disgusting, really. I thought you should know."

I am back in my seat as the first punch makes contact. Two male security guards push their way through the gathering crowd. The pervert is escorted out. I look to the steward, still standing in her designated spot. A smile shoots across her face, instantly quashed: the consummate professional. But I saw it; she enjoyed that. She resumes scanning the crowd with her chin higher.

Oblivious to the action, Elliot has drawn his German player with one oversized foot. The Striker.

"That's absolutely lovely, Elliot." I hold out the paper, admiring. "What about his other foot, you've only given him one?"

He hands me the pencil and I sketch it in.

"There," I say. "Now, they're even."

Acknowledgments

First, I'd like to thank the real-life interpreter Lauren Shadi, who shared her story in *The Guardian*'s Experience column all those years ago, without whom I'd never have given thought to this fascinating profession and come up with the idea for this novel.

My thanks to Bloody Scotland for having me as part of the 2020 Pitch Perfect, and for the judging panel that year who gave me the confidence to finally write this book.

Enormous thanks to my agent, Katie Greenstreet, for making developing, pitching, selling, and publishing a book seem extremely easy and calm. That expression about the serene duck with the fierce paddling going on unseen under the water comes to mind. It's been such a pleasure. Thank you for everything. Big thanks also to Catherine Cho at Paper Literary. I'm so grateful I landed with you both. Likewise, Luke Speed did some book-to-screen magic and also makes it all look very easy. Thank you to Luke's whole team.

Thank goodness, I think to myself, repeatedly, daily, that this book landed with Katie Ellis-Brown at Harvill Secker. Katie is the best, most fierce book champion anyone could possibly hope for. Emily Griffin at Harper is the other half of our fabulous transatlantic editing team. Thank you, Emily, for your endless enthusiasm and dedication. The passion for this book from the whole team at Harvill Secker/Vintage has been really humbling and so much more than I would have dared to hope for. Huge thanks to Kate Fogg, Liz Foley, Hannah Telfer, Sophie Painter, Mia Quibell-Smith, and Graeme Hall. My thanks also to Malissa Mistry, Nathaniel

Breakwell, Caitlin Knight, Rohan Hope, Jade Perez, Justin Ward-Turner, Amy Carruthers, Charlotte Owens and Sophie Ramage. Extra special thanks to Sania Riaz for coming up with the brilliant shoutline!

Hayley Shepherd went above and beyond with a superb copy-edit, as did Sarah-Jane Forder with a diligent proofread. Thank you.

Most of my research for this book came from peer-reviewed academic papers and the work of forensic linguists in universities around the globe. I'll single out one for anyone who wishes to read further on the topic: the books and research of Professor Sandra Beatriz Hale from the University of New South Wales were invaluable to me. If you'd like to read something from a real interpreter working in London, Cordelia Novak's *View from the Dock, Diary of a Court Interpreter*, available on Amazon, was very helpful. Thanks for sharing your story, Cordelia. I do hope you write another.

Thanks to Lyndon Smith and colleagues for answering my policing questions with such thoroughness and dedication. Endless thanks to the real-world interpreters who answered my questions anonymously on Twitter, over email, on internet forums where I lurked, and through the Association of Police and Court Interpreters. Like Revelle, I've made some deliberate mistakes for the sake of good drama, so please forgive me for that.

Thanks to Dr. Lili Pâquet and Dr. Sophia Waters at the University of New England, Australia, for their enthusiasm, kindness, and generosity. Varuna, The Writers' House in Australia, and City of Melbourne Libraries both kept me going these last couple of years. Thank you.

Finally, thanks to friends and family for everything, particularly Gabriella Margo for help with the Hungarian language.